Readers love Lord Mouse
by Mason Thomas

"Please just trust me when I say this writing is a joy with which to spend your precious reading hours. The dialogue, the descriptions, the unexpected twists and turns, and revelations. Every story should be so lucky as to be told like this."
—Prism Book Alliance

"*Lord Mouse* was a welcome surprise and I found myself appreciating nearly every minute of the book."
—Joyfully Jay

"It's so much fun when I try a new author, and they blow my socks off with a well written story that is so full of twists and turns that you have trouble putting the book down. Such is the case with *Lord Mouse*."
—The Novel Approach

"The action was exactly as promised, and I loved the relationship between Garron and Mouse as they slowly moved from forced companionship to friendship, and eventually to something more."
—Just Love: Queer Book Reviews

By Mason Thomas

The Witchstone Amulet

LORDS OF DAVENIA
Lord Mouse
The Shadow Mark
Three Tales

MASON THOMAS began his writing journey at the age of thirteen when his personal hero, Isaac Asimov, took the time to respond to a letter he wrote him. He's been writing stories ever since. Today he is ecstatic and grateful that there is a place at the speculative table for stories with strong gay protagonists.

Mason, by all accounts, is still a nerdy teenager, although his hairline and waistline indicate otherwise. When his fingers are not pounding furiously at a keyboard, they can usually be found holding a video-game controller, plucking away at an electric guitar, or shaking a twenty-sided die during a role-playing game. Mason will take any opportunity to play dress-up, whether through cosplay, Halloween, or a visit to a Renaissance Faire. He pays the bills by daring middle school students to actually like school and encouraging them to make a mess in his science classroom. He lives in Chicago with his endlessly patient husband, who has tolerated his geeky nonsense for nearly two decades, and two unruly cats who graciously allow Mason and his husband to share the same space with them.

Website: masonthomasbooks.com

Facebook: www.facebook.com/MasonThomas999
Twitter: @MasonThomas999
E-mail: masonthomas999@gmail.com

THE SHADOW MARK

MASON THOMAS

Chapter 1

THE NIGHT had taken on an ill wind.

It was enough to stir Auraq Greystone from his musings. He looked up from the flames of his small campfire and scanned the tree line. The clearing was still quiet, but Spirit had lifted her head from her feedbag. The young bay's ears perked up, and she stamped her hoof twice. She sensed it too.

Auraq focused his attention on the night sounds in the surrounding forest. The campfire bathed the clearing in warm light but didn't reach far beyond the first circle of trees. If anything was out there, he wouldn't see it. Nothing out of the ordinary reached his ears. He lifted his nose and drew in a few long breaths—the smell of smoke from his fire, the sweet fragrance of the scorched meat on the spit, the lush forest loam beneath him—again, nothing he wouldn't expect.

But a deeper, more primal sense registered something else. There was a trace of malice in the air. Faint, but undeniable. He could feel it brush against his skin like a night mist moving silently through the trees.

He sat very still, waiting.

He wondered if it was just his imagination. After his earlier run-in with brigands, he was understandably jumpy. But the feeling was prickly enough that he was reluctant to ignore it. Perhaps the wiser thing after all would have been to take a room at the inn he passed some ways back, but his purse had grown too light as it was. He didn't need to spend good hard-earned coin on a needless luxury when he could make do perfectly well on his own in the wild.

Besides, a crowded inn could carry more danger for him than a dark forest in the middle of the night. There was no risk of someone recognizing him here.

Nothing happened. The forest remained still.

With a tight frown, he returned his attention to his dinner. The plump rabbit was nearly ready. Fat dripped down to sizzle and hiss on the hot coals. He gave it another quarter turn on the spit and then sat back again to stare at the flames.

Something moved out in the dark wood.

The sound was clear and distinct. A dry twig snapping. He lifted his head and his back straightened as his hand drifted to the hilt of one of the swords on the ground beside him. It could have been an animal out foraging, but something about the sound made Auraq reject that. He waited, straining to pick up anything beyond the crackle of the fire and the sizzle of fat. Then heard it again—the sound a boot makes when snapping a twig on the leafy ground. It came from the direction of the road. Auraq curved his fingers around the grip, ready to slide the blade from the sheath.

Brigands again? Either a new band was thinking he was an easy target or the same ones from before had returned, thinking to retaliate for their bloody failure.

The warm fire and isolation from the road had persuaded him to take off his heavy leather jerkin. He wore only his undertunic. Now, he wondered if he had the time to slip the jerkin on before an ambush. Unprotected, he could be killed by a well-aimed arrow or crossbow bolt. But even with his vest on, there were no guarantees.

More sounds. He could hear breathing now, and the whisper of brush being pushed aside. Someone was approaching his camp. Perhaps two by the close proximity of the sounds. Either they were poorly trained at stealth or no longer cared about being heard. Bandits were at times overconfident in their ability to overwhelm their victims.

He caught movement. The firelight reached out just far enough and at the right angle to catch the white of a tunic sleeve.

"Ho there!" came a warm and friendly call. A leafy branch was lifted aside and a shape emerged from the darkness. "Hail and good eve, friend. You'll not be needing that weapon for us."

An old man stepped into the clearing. His face was a chaos

of white hair, but among the mess, Auraq spotted a gentle smile peeking through. A rustle of foliage behind him announced the arrival of a second visitor. A man much younger than his companion. Twenty maybe. He stood partly in shadow behind the old man's shoulder.

"We saw your fire from the road, good sur."

Auraq didn't respond and held his fingers to the hilt of the sword. He waited, measuring the two of them, wondering if this was an elaborate ruse to get him to lower his defenses.

"We hoped you'd be kind enough to share it with us at this late hour. We have provisions we could share in return for the kindness."

The two hovered at the edge of clearing waiting for an invitation. The old man was dressed simply, but well for travel. Heavy breeches and thick boots for long days on foot, a tunic and jerkin and a thick woolen cloak. He had a small canvas haversack on his shoulder and a line of pouches and purses on his belt. Auraq caught the glint of metal underneath the cloak. A dagger or short sword, still sheathed. The younger man was less adequately attired. His boots were well-worn, and he had on only a thin tunic with no cloak upon his shoulders. A bulkier pack was slung on his shoulder.

The old man maintained his warm smile down at Auraq, but the younger man stared at his boots and shifted awkwardly. Nervously. When the moments lumbered by without a response from Auraq, the younger swore under his breath. "Leave it, Tan," he grumbled. "Let's return to the road. We'll find something."

Auraq felt his mouth turn down. He thought he'd traveled deep enough into the wood to not be seen from the road. He'd been romanced by the clearing he'd found, counted himself lucky at finding it in the gathering dark, and hadn't bothered to check if it was safe. He'd been foolish and sloppy. If they had spotted his fire from the road, others might too.

The old man must have seen the change in Auraq's expression. He nodded in resignation. "Sorry to disturb ya, then." He glanced at his companion over his shoulder and signaled with his head to leave. "We'll leave ya to—"

Auraq broke in with a grunt deep in his throat. "No." He lifted his hand from the hilt of the sword. These two were just as they seemed—travelers like himself, out on the road at too late an hour. "You'll find nothing nearby on the road tonight."

The two stood frozen, the younger one half turned to head back into the trees. They exchanged glances, telling Auraq they weren't sure if it was an invitation. Auraq wasn't sure either, until he found himself gesturing toward the ground on the opposite side of the fire.

"Oh, many thanks, sur. Many thanks," said the old man. He scrambled to join the fire. Dropping his haversack, he lowered himself to the ground and extended his hands toward the flames. "Oh, it's a cold one tonight, sur. It would have been a long night without your generosity."

The younger man approached more slowly, clearly apprehensive of Auraq. No surprise—Auraq tended to have that effect on many. His size alone was enough to cause people to give him a wide berth. But the long days on the road had him likely looking as if he'd been dragged by a horse. The younger man kept his eye on Auraq while he slid the heavy pack from his shoulder at a distance from the fire. He joined the old man only to be slapped on the thigh before he sat down.

"Whatcha doin' leaving the pack way over there, lad? Bring it on closer."

Whatever Auraq sensed earlier, whatever ill forces had passed through the wood around him, these two were not part of it. They settled in across from Auraq, with the pack now positioned between them.

"We will leave you to your thoughts. We've no interest in being a nuisance. Kane, pull out what we can share with this kind man."

Auraq held out his hand. "No need." A part of him was surprised to discover he was happy for the company. A rarity— most of the time, people grated on his patience. But it had been too long since he had spent time with others, and perhaps these other souls might distract him from his own thoughts. He had spent far too much time alone with them lately. And it would certainly be better than spending yet another night staring at a fire until sleep took him.

"Nonsense," the old man replied. There was a genuine warmth to the man and Auraq, despite his own trepidation, felt drawn to him. "We have fresh pears that we found today and a goodly number of hickory nuts. Kindness should be rewarded, sur. I insist."

"Very well. Then share my catch tonight too. It is more than I can eat anyway."

The offer got Kane's attention. He looked up with wide eyes first at Auraq, as if he couldn't believe what he'd heard, and then at the sizzling roast.

Kane pulled from the sack what they'd foraged while Auraq took the rabbit from the spit and, using his dagger, divided it into quarters. The food was passed around, and the three of them sat in silence while they ate. The meat was juicy beneath its crispy charcoaled skin and tore easily from the bone. The pears were ripe and sweet. One by one, bones and cores were tossed into the fire. When the last bone of his quarter was picked clean, Auraq leaned back licking the remnants from his fingers. The old man did the same, while Kane helped himself to the final quarter. He showed no signs of slowing.

"Shall we wash it all down with this?" the old man asked with a grin, pulling a skin from the sack.

Auraq lifted a brow.

"Not the best vintage, I'll admit," the man said as he pulled the stopper from the top. "But much like a woman, it's better than having none at all." He took a swig and passed the wineskin over to Auraq, who raised it to his new companion as a toast, and took a swig from it himself.

"What's your name?" Auraq asked.

"Mentanus from the duchy of Har Purdea, at your service."

"Auraq, at yours," he said with a respectful nod. Out of habit he omitted his surname and his own place of origin.

"Friends call me Old Tan," Mentanus added. "A bit of jest, on account I'm a tanner by trade. This here is my apprentice,

Kanteron Elrus."

The younger man flashed a glare of annoyance at Old Tan. "Kane will do."

Auraq narrowed his eyes at Kane. Apprentice? Seemed old for that title. Auraq would have expected journeyman by now. At the least. He dropped his chin in a single nod in his direction.

Kane tossed the last of the rabbit bones into the flames, then rested his elbows on his raised knees. He stared into the fire without expression.

Auraq had thought perhaps the old man was his father or grandfather. Not his master, certainly. There was something curious about the two. Why would a master and his apprentice be traveling alone down an old road late in the night?

They sat in silence for a time, each seemingly retreating into their own thoughts while passing around the wineskin. The wine was better than Old Tan had intimated. It felt good going down Auraq's throat and left a warm glow in his stomach.

He glanced in Kane's direction again. The younger man still stared at the flames and absently rubbed his thumb over his forearm as if it were sore.

Old Tan pulled a wooden pipe and leather pouch from inside his vest. He pinched out black leaves from the pouch and packed them into the pipe. Gripping the end of the pipe between his teeth, he held a flaming stick from the fire to the open end. He sucked in air and the end flared red like a single demon's eye. While he puffed out pillows of white smoke, he tilted his head to look at the space beside Auraq. His brow tightened in a curious expression. "Two swords, friend?" he asked. "You wield them both?"

Auraq felt his shoulders stiffen. "I do."

"Not sure I've seen that practiced before. Most folk settle for one and use a shield for protection."

"It is a preference of mine."

"They are not the same blade either, I see. One at least is military issue. Were you enlisted in the king's army?"

Auraq tensed further. The questions, though innocent enough, were making him uncomfortable. "I was," he replied.

"Some time ago."

Old Tan must have sensed his discomfort. "Forgive me. I don't mean to pry. It's just that I'm a former military man myself, and it's always nice to share a story or two with another veteran at arms. But alas, I forget I've had more time for my wounds to heal. And seen less than many. I'll not press if you've no wish to speak of it."

"Appreciated," Auraq replied. The man had read his thoughts. He had no desire to speak of that time, brief as it was.

"Ah… but that one is well-made by the look of it. You were of some rank then, I gather. Me, I was just a lowly recruit. Signed on by my father at age sixteen. He dragged me to the noble commander by the ear and left me there. Thought it'd make a man out of me, and make one less mouth to feed at home." His voice dropped an octave. "'Let the king foot the bill for that bottomless stomach of yours,' he used to say to me." He chuckled at the memory, then sighed. "Served six years with the company. Fought in the battles that gained us the Lendera province."

Auraq's stomach cramped at the name. Lendera. Small world indeed. He'd been stationed there to protect what this man had fought hard to earn.

Old Tan shook his head. "Good lads, they were. Never seen their like before or since. Fearless. Wouldn't even blink in the face of those barbarians." He looked up and grinned. "It's where I learned my trade, you know."

"That so?" Auraq responded dryly. The old man had apparently already forgotten his promise to not be a bother.

"Yep. Began by helping with skinning the deer we caught. Didn't take long for them to figure out I had a penchant for forming the leather, so they put me on repairing armor. In a year, they had me making new." He shrugged. "Been doing it ever since. Have my own shop in West Tunniville now."

The Tunniville River ran along the eastern edge of Har Purdea, and close to the wild margins of Davenia itself. These men were far from home indeed.

"Not so much armor these days," Old Tan continued. "Lots

of belts and saddlebags and such." He paused to take a swig from the skin, then passed it on to Auraq. "What direction you heading, lad? If you don't mind my asking, that is."

Auraq bit the inside of his cheek and averted his eyes to the fire, the wineskin forgotten in his hand for the moment. He'd been reckless—allowing his brief feelings of solitude to govern his decision-making. Having these two join him had been foolish. Conversations came equipped with questions. Ones he was not keen on answering. Old Tan's inquiry was innocuous enough, but Auraq had grown wary of these types of prying questions over the years for fear of where the answers might lead.

"Har Diamante," he said.

"As are we," Old Tan replied with a wide grin. "Perhaps tomorrow we can share the road together."

Kane's head jerked up. He threw a sudden worried look in Old Tan's direction. The expression was clear. He wondered if this stranger could be trusted. Sharing his fire and his meal was all very well—almost a necessity. But Kane was certainly uninterested in forming any partnership with him.

Auraq didn't blame him, really. He was brutish-looking, surely. And after months on the road, he doubted he looked the trustworthy sort. His hair was overgrown and hadn't seen a comb in a fortnight, and his ruddy beard was wild and untamed. But Kane's unease seemed to extend beyond the healthy concerns one should have when traveling. He was guarded and suspicious. Auraq couldn't help but wonder what had caused this deep-seated wariness of strangers.

While Kane glared at Old Tan, Auraq took the opportunity to study him further. Since they'd joined him at his fire, Kane had hardly spoken a word. He was comely and well-formed— someone not unaccustomed to physical labor. His dark hair had been recently groomed, and there was only a shadow of growth along the length of his jaw. But he was pensive and withdrawn. Auraq could see the tension he held in his shoulders and the deep furrows in his brow. His dark eyes revealed little of his thoughts, but Auraq recognized the sorrow behind them nonetheless.

Auraq had seen this look on other men, ones he'd served with in his company. The ones who'd experienced too much for their young years. Kane bore deep scars.

He wasn't sure why, but despite his own reservations, he found himself compelled to agree to Old Tan's offer. Less for himself, and more for them. A vision of the two of them alone on the road was unsettling, especially considering the highwaymen he'd encountered earlier. They would be easy targets.

"It is always better to travel with others when you can," Auraq said. "I will join you tomorrow." He looked directly at Kane. "As long as all are in agreement."

Kane held Auraq's gaze for several moments as if trying to gauge his character. "You travel by horse, sur. We will slow you down." His voice had a deep resonance that surprised Auraq.

Auraq shrugged. "I've no appointments at the moment. And I walk more than I ride anyway." Kane's subtle lift of his eyebrows betrayed his skepticism about the truth of that. "You seem decent folk," Auraq added. "I would appreciate the company, I think."

"You know nothing about us."

Auraq felt the corner of his mouth lift a fraction. "I know enough."

"And we know nothing of you."

"But we know enough," Old Tan put in gently.

Kane glanced at Old Tan, then made a barely perceptible shrug of one shoulder. "Very well," he said, attempting an air of nonchalance. "If we'll not be inconveniencing you."

"Not at all," said Auraq.

Old Tan's grin widened. "Well, then, there it is. What a happy meeting this turned out to be, yes?"

The fire was dying down. Flames hugged closer to the wood and burned redder and tamer. The fragile cathedral of spent wood collapsed in on itself with a crackle. Auraq reached over and grabbed another pine log from his meager pile and tossed it onto the flames. Bright sparks leaped into the air riding the eddies of smoke.

"Sleep," Auraq told them. "I'll keep watch for now."

Old Tan's brow furrowed, and he looked as if he was on the verge of protest, but Auraq cut it off before he could voice it.

"I'm not tired," he said.

Old Tan looked like he wanted to argue, but Auraq could see the fatigue winning over. After a long pause, he nodded.

Kane glanced over at his master a moment, then turned his eyes back to Auraq. "Wake me when you're ready. I will tend to the fire next."

Auraq replied with a nod. Old Tan wasted no time curling up on the ground in his cloak. Eyes closed, he fell into a steady rhythm of breathing almost immediately. Kane, on the other hand, spent time clearing away sticks and pebbles from his spot by the fire, smoothing the ground out with his hand. This was not someone accustomed to sleeping out under an open sky. He tried first to lie on his side, grunted, and moved onto his back. Arms folded over his chest, he closed his eyes.

Auraq leaned back, propping his torso up with his arms behind him, and stared into flames eating up the fresh wood.

Then the ambush began.

Chapter 2

"YOU'VE NOT a cloak of your own?" Auraq asked in a low voice.

Kane opened his eyes and rolled his head to face Auraq. "Lost. About a day ago." He paused with a small sigh and lifted his eyes, looking a bit sheepish. "A long tale; I won't bore you with it. I plan to buy a new one when we reach Har Diamante."

"I have a spare blanket." He stood. "You are welcome to it."

Spirit stamped her hooves at his approach. "Easy, girl," Auraq told the bay, with a pat on the neck. "Not getting your saddle. Your work is still done for the day." He bent down to where the packs were arranged on the ground and unknotted the thong securing the spare roll.

But Spirit continued to toss her head and fuss.

Auraq looked up at her—her ears were pinned back.

He froze in place and strained to listen out into the dark beyond the clearing. For a few moments, nothing. Then….

He flung the bedroll aside and leaped to his place by the fire. Squatting, he grasped each hilt of his two swords, and in one fluid pull, unsheathed them.

"Ready yourself," he growled.

Kane stiffened and brought himself up onto one knee. "What's happening?"

Old Tan jolted awake. He sprang up too, gaining his feet with surprising agility for a man his age. The deeply rooted training from his past hadn't abandoned the old soldier yet. He looked up at Auraq, alarm in his eyes.

"Someone approaches," Auraq said. "Two at least. Perhaps more."

The old man threw a worried look over to Kane, and then swung his gaze back to Auraq with regret in his eyes. "I fear we may have put you in danger, friend."

Auraq had assumed it was bandits, but Old Tan had clearly drawn a different conclusion. There was no time to ask questions, although Auraq had several burning his tongue.

The old man had produced a short sword—as old as Auraq was by the look of it. Kane was unarmed. Auraq doubted he had ever wielded a weapon in his life.

Old Tan gripped Kane by the arm. "Listen to me. You stay behind me now."

The noise coming from the trees was clear now. Whoever it was, they'd abandoned their stealth and were approaching fast. Thanks to Spirit, they'd lost their attempt at surprise.

Auraq adjusted his grips and rolled his shoulders one at a time. The cool night air had stiffened his joints. He made a few swipes through the air in front of him with the heavier and longer captain's sword gripped in his right hand. Most would wield it with a two-handed grip, but Auraq had enough strength in his hand and arm to control it deftly with one. The left hand held the shorter blade he was awarded on the day he was commissioned.

The first of the attackers lunged from the shadows, sword high. He was armor-clad—a fine, well-crafted leather, dyed black. Effective to hide his movement in the dark. He wore a black cowl over his head, and a cloth was tied over his face exposing only his eyes. Auraq was ready for him. He deflected the attack with the flat of the longsword, and stepping in with his left foot, thrust with the short sword. Auraq expected to feel the blade run through the abdomen, but the attacker twisted his torso and easily avoided the jab.

Two more attackers sprang into the clearing, identically clad and wielding similar arms. Firelight glinted cleanly off the steel. They were quality blades.

These were no common highwaymen, desperate riff-raff preying on travelers. No, these men were too well trained, too well armed. And they coordinated their assault with practiced efficiency. These were hired men. Mercenaries.

Assassins.

And Old Tan had expected them. Or at least wasn't

surprised by their arrival. He and Kane were on the run.

There was more to these two than Auraq had previously guessed.

His attacker made a powerful backhand slash at him, followed with another quick diagonal chop aimed for his neck. Auraq pivoted beyond the sword's reach. But the man came at him yet again. His style was aggressive—and overconfident. Auraq easily avoided the assault, and the next as well. Then he recognized the strategy. The two others assassins were closing in on Old Tan, who struck a defensive stance in front of Kane. Auraq's opponent was there to keep him occupied and out of the way.

No time to tease out weaknesses. He had to turn this around fast. Auraq took the offensive and lunged.

The assassin's eyes seemed to smile in satisfaction.

Auraq moved in with the short sword, direct and obvious. The assassin deflected aside the attack with an almost contemptuous parry. Then, believing Auraq had opened himself up, he countered with a thrust of his own.

Exactly what Auraq had hoped he would do.

Auraq stepped into the attack. He counted on the assassin not expecting someone of his size being able to move with any speed or agility. Using the long blade, he guided the assassin's thrust over his right shoulder. At the same moment, with a flick of the wrist, he switched his grip on the short sword, pointing it downward like a dagger. He pushed in closer and drove the tip downward. It plunged into the gap in the man's leg armor, just above the knee. A precise strike. It sliced easily through the thin leather trousers beneath the protective gear, pierced through flesh and bone, and escaped out the back side of the knee.

The assassin let out a high-pitched scream that exploded through the clearing. His knee gave out and he collapsed. Auraq twisted the blade as he ripped it out again, rending flesh and tendons. The assassin hit the ground in an inelegant heap, shrieking in agony. But he knew what was coming next. Desperate, he flung himself onto his back and pulled up his sword to ward Auraq off. Auraq batted the blade aside, pinned the man's sword arm to the ground with his boot, and then, with a quick thrust, pierced the man's unprotected neck.

One down.

He sprang directly over the fire, hoping to catch the others off guard. The larger of the remaining two saw the threat coming. He pulled off his attack on Old Tan to face Auraq, while the other continued to press Old Tan hard. The old man knew how to use a sword—that was clear. But it had likely been decades since he'd wielded one. Time had atrophied his ability. Age had robbed him of strength and reflexes. He wouldn't last long.

Kane, hovering directly behind Old Tan, grabbed a branch from the ground. He brandished it clumsily like a boy with a lance and waited anxiously for the chance to swing it.

The larger assassin was nearly equal in height to Auraq, but leaner. He met Auraq's leaping assault with a quick parry, and shuffled backward in case Auraq followed up with another. He was light on his feet, his movements smooth and elegant. He then launched at Auraq with a heavy slash. Auraq deflected it, but the force of the impact made the hilt buzz in his hand. Fuck—the man was strong. When Auraq returned with a quick riposte, his opponent was already nimbly pivoting clear. Auraq drove in again with three quick strikes in succession. Left. Right. Left. His opponent avoided each with ease.

Auraq's jaw clenched. The man knew how to defend against two weapons. This was a seasoned fighter. And a smart one.

Defeating him could take time—time Old Tan and Kane didn't have.

Old Tan's attacker came at him with powerful two-handed swings. The old man brought his blade up in time for each assault, but was losing ground with each parry. They were nearly forced back to the tree line. Old Tan's face was flushed crimson, and the tendons in his neck protruded like tent ropes from the strain. Kane attempted to come around and distract the assassin with wide swings of his branch. Old Tan shouted at him to get back.

Auraq's opponent was holding back, happy to stall and provide defense to his comrade. He understood he didn't have to expel the energy to defeat Auraq. Time was on his side. Old Tan would fail soon, and despite his branch, Kane would be struck down right after.

Auraq had no choice. He had to risk a more aggressive strategy, force the man into engaging him.

"Walk away, friend," the man said behind his black mask. "This isn't your fight."

"It is now, *friend.*"

He vaulted for him, sacrificing a portion of his tight control—a hot and reckless assault he hoped would overwhelm. But the man was ready for it, countering each thrust and jab. His reflexes were remarkable. He guided the weapon with a nuance Auraq would not have thought possible. He seemed to anticipate each of Auraq's moves.

But he remained defensive. He was taking the less perilous approach, waiting for the other one to finish off Old Tan so they could confront Auraq together. Yet, in his maneuvering, he'd positioned himself between Auraq and his comrade. He now had nowhere to go. If he moved, he would give Auraq access to the other man's back.

Old Tan was driven back as far as he could go. The attacks were too powerful and too frequent, and the old man's reflexes just weren't what they might have been long ago.

Auraq had only moments before it was lost.

He unleashed a flurry of attacks born of frantic desperation—risky with so smart an opponent. He'd leave himself vulnerable and open to countermeasures.

One. Two. Three. Four. From left to right, he kept the attacks coming. The assassin fended them off—less cleanly now. Auraq's two blades moved faster than his opponent's single one. He kept them coming. Five. Six.

His arms were tiring. He could feel the burn begin in his shoulders. He would not be able to maintain this speed and force for long. And weakness would provide the opening his opponent needed. He would not hesitate to take it.

Then the assassin miscalculated. Only slightly, but it was enough. Auraq struck. The long captain's sword hit the shoulder but glazed off the thick studded armor. Again, the assassin tried to adjust, catch up, but his rhythm was lost.

Auraq came in again, his opening now clear. He knew it was over before the blade even made contact. The tip of the short sword penetrated under the arm where the man's armor did not reach. Auraq felt the resistance against his hand as the sword shattered the edge of the shoulder blade and exited out the man's back. The assassin cried out as his arm lost function and fell limp. The sword dropped from his grip. Eyes flung open in pain and shock, and he tried to twist away. But in doing so, he exposed his neck.

As Auraq withdrew the blade, he ran the long sword's true edge across the man's throat just beneath the ear.

Before the body even hit the ground, Auraq turned to confront the third and final assassin. But he was too late.

The two were against each other, like old friends embracing. Old Tan gripped the assassin's shoulder with gnarled white fingers and stared up at the sky, unseeing. Color was lost from his face. He made staccato gasps, trying to pull air into his lungs.

Auraq could see the bloodied steel protruding from Old Tan's back. The blade had run him through.

The assassin grunted with disdain and pushed the old man away. Old Tan dropped his own weapon, and as he stumbled backward off the sword, his hands dropped to clench the blade protruding from his gut. Several of his fingers were sliced off cleanly as the sword was ripped out. He looked down at his injury with more sadness than pain. The front of his tunic was awash with crimson.

He sank to the ground.

The assassin laughed behind his mask. He turned to Auraq. "You're too late," he chuckled, the triumph evident in his eyes, then raised his sword again to go after Kane. He was close enough to reach him before Auraq could stop him.

As the assassin turned around, Kane cried out in primal

fury and struck him in the side of the head with the branch. A great crack rang out like the felling of a tree. Auraq didn't know if it came from the branch or the man's skull. The man staggered, but remained standing. He clutched his head and fought to keep on his feet as he swayed like a drunkard.

It was all the opening Auraq needed. He crossed the distance between them in an instant and ran one sword through the man's side and the other through his back. The assassin made a sickly gurgling sound in his throat as his head fell backward. He dropped to his knees.

Auraq kicked him off the two blades and let the man collapse to the ground. "Guess again."

Chapter 3

FOR A time, there was only the silence of the night and the sound of Auraq's own breathing. He looked around, waited. More could leap through the trees. His heart raced, the fury of the battle still raging through him. But none followed. It remained just the two of them.

"Are you injured?" Auraq asked.

Kane stepped backward from the horrors around him. His face was ashen.

"Are you injured?" Auraq said louder.

Kane seemed to become aware of the question slowly. He shook his head and dropped the branch. "No," he said. It was barely a whisper. He staggered and fell on his knees beside Old Tan. Auraq didn't know if he was answering his question or reacting to the sight of the old man, who lay motionless on the ground. His frame was twisted, his face in the dirt.

Kane rolled him over gently and positioned him in his lap. "Tan," he breathed. "No, Tan. Not this."

Auraq squatted down opposite Kane. Old Tan still breathed, but it was shallow, and blood spilled over the top of his thin white lip to gather in his beard.

Kane looked up with sudden fire in his eyes. "Don't just sit there, you clumpish oaf. Do something!"

Auraq shook his head. "There is nothing to be done." It would take a mage—and a powerful one indeed—to alter this man's course now.

"Don't say that. You have bandages or… or something in your packs, certainly."

"He is beyond my help. I'm sorry."

Kane turned his face away, his mouth pressed into a tight line.

Old Tan surprised Auraq by opening his eyes. Kane gasped, and his eyes lit up with hope. "Easy, Tan. Don't try to move. It's all right. You're going to be fine."

But Auraq could see in the old man's eyes he knew the truth of it. Old Tan shook his head slowly. "He's right, lad," he said, then coughed. Red bubbles formed at the corners of his mouth. "My time, it seems."

Kane shook his head. "No. No, we'll fix this. We'll find a way. We always do, right? You know that we do. The wound… it… it isn't so bad…." The last he added with a singsong inflection that carried no truth. Grief was worming its way to the surface through the thick layer of anger and denial. He lifted his hand to touch Tan's bearded face, but the hand was caked in blood like a single red glove. Kane gasped at the sight of it. The hand shook and he made a fist to try to stop the tremors before pulling it back again.

The blood pulsed from the old man's gut in torrents onto the soft loam that accepted it quickly. He had only minutes before he lost consciousness and was gone.

"Lived longer than I had any right to anyway, lad." He was fighting. Fighting for these last few moments he knew he had. "Not so bad, really. No pain." His eyes drooped and threatened to close entirely. Then they widened again with new intensity. He reached out and grabbed Auraq's wrist. "Friend, I know you not, but strangest thing, I can see your soul now."

The way he looked at Auraq at that moment sent duck flesh running the length of his arms. Something in his eyes was unsettling, as if the old man's vision reached down into him somehow. Auraq didn't know what to say, so he said nothing.

"It's a glorious thing to see." Old Tan smiled as if witnessing something beautiful to behold. The old man's hand tightened around his wrist. Auraq was surprised by the strength of it.

"You're a good man. And this lad needs a good man. You must help him."

Kane cut in, leaning closer. "Tan, stop it now." The first signs of tears were beginning to gloss the corners of his eyes.

"We'll fix this. We will." But the conviction was gone from his voice. Auraq could tell he no longer believed it himself.

Old Tan did not appear to even hear Kane. His wide, bright eyes were fixed solely onto Auraq. "Promise me, friend. Promise me you'll see him safely delivered."

Auraq started to shake his head. This was not a promise he could make.

"Promise me!" Old Tan said louder and tried to rise. It spurred an attack of sputtering coughs, spitting blood on Auraq's arm and chest.

"I promise," Auraq said quickly, easing him back down to the ground. The words had spilled from his mouth, surprising even him. "I promise." But to what did he just agree? Deliver him to where?

Auraq's words seemed to satisfy Tan and he settled back into Kane's lap looking content, a calm smile lifting one side of his mouth.

Kane turned away, squeezing his eyes tight, but still the tears leaked from the corners and drifted down his cheeks. He pounded the bloodied fist onto the ground beside him. "It wasn't supposed to be like this," he growled. He shook his head in despair, looking like a lost child. "Not like this."

Old Tan lightened his grip on Auraq's wrist. "Finish what I could not," he said, almost dreamily. "Oh, the Gods, friend. The Gods... they've seen you, the Gods have seen your crimes." His voice faded to a whisper, and his eyes were nearly closed.

Auraq felt his entire body go rigid. His crimes? What could this man know of his crimes? He fought the urge to pull the old man's hand from his wrist and stand away.

"The Gods forgive, friend. You know that, yes? And the Gods have forgiven you. You bear no blame for what happened."

He then rolled his head to look up at Kane and smiled fondly at him. "He will protect you, lad." The old man reached up and rested his hand against the side of Kane's face. Kane put his own hand against it and held it there.

And he was gone. Old Tan released one final breath and

the life left him.

Chapter 4

AURAQ FROWNED and gently pulled Old Tan's hand from his wrist and placed it on his chest. He leaned back away from the man.

The Gods forgave him? He almost wanted to laugh. Horse bollocks. The old man had slipped into some delirium before death took him. What would he know of the will of the Gods? Or his crime for that matter? And it didn't really matter whether the Gods had forgiven him or not. The *living* men searching for him still were not so quick to write up a pardon, and they were a greater concern to him right now.

But the old man's visions in death had managed to pressure him into a promise he should never have made. He was irritated with himself for agreeing so readily. He had no idea why he had. But there it was, and there was no going back on it now. One simply did not renege on a promise made to the dead.

Kane's entire body had gone rigid, as if Tan's death had turned him to stone. His eyes were vacant, his face absent of emotion—he had retreated deep into himself.

Auraq rose to his feet. He would leave Kane alone a moment to mourn while he prepared. He approached Spirit slowly and gave her several long strokes against the side of the neck. The battle and the smell of blood around the camp had unsettled her, but his familiar hand against her and his voice in her ear were quick to calm her. "Sorry, girl. Looks like your night isn't over yet after all."

He lifted Spirit's long flat saddle and blanket from the ground and negotiated them over her back, then strapped it into place. Spirit whinnied her irritation and stomped the ground a few times, but otherwise didn't fight him. She knew as well as he did that it was time to quit this place.

Once Spirit was saddled and ready, he used the side of his boot to kick down the burning pile of logs in the fire pit and spread apart the coals. Immediately, the night closed in around them. The shimmering remains of the fire cast a faint red glow about the small clearing.

Behind him came the soft voice of a man who'd lost everything. "What are you doing?"

"There may be others," he answered flatly. The fire was reduced to shimmering embers and tiny flames clinging to life on the undersides of the charred logs. "Fetch your belongings." He grabbed one of his packs from where it was sitting by the fire and attached it to the back of the saddle.

Kane lifted to his full height. "We aren't going anywhere."

"Retrieve the old man's cloak. You'll need it tonight."

"Did you not hear me?" Kane marched over to him. Even in the near complete darkness, Auraq could see the hard resolve in his face. He stared up at Auraq with bewilderment. "I'll not leave him here like this. Not left for the wolves."

Of course, Auraq wasn't insensitive to Kane's grief—he'd seen enough death among comrades to know what Kane was going through—but he would not allow the man's naïveté to endanger them both. He turned his back to Kane and focused on securing the packs to Spirit's saddle. "What you think of as your master is gone. Nothing remains but… husk."

"He deserves better," Kane replied. Auraq could feel the heat of his anger against his back. "We may not be able to send off his spirit properly, but I will not leave him to be torn to pieces by the wilds. I will remain to bury him."

Auraq turned back around. "I made a promise to—"

"I heard it." Kane cut him off sharply. "But I've no need of your aid. Leave if you wish. I'll not hold you to the words you spoke to him."

It was grief speaking, not reason. Auraq knew he would not last long on his own. If his pursuers did not catch up to him first, bandits or starvation and exposure would. He did not have the skills or sense to survive in these lands.

"Look," Kane continued. Auraq could tell he was trying to

soften his delivery. "I appreciate your kindness. And your help in the fight. I do. But this is not your concern." He returned to Old Tan's body and sat cross-legged on the ground next to him. In the soft glow of the dying fire, Auraq saw Kane put a hand on the thin arm as if trying to gently wake him.

Auraq sighed. He realized then how tired he was. It had grown late, and the fight had left him surly and more than a little sore at himself. He could feel his patience thinning like spring ice. He loosened one side of the pack and pulled out a long, flat digging tool and a small hatchet, then he carried them over to where Kane sat on the ground. He dropped the tools next to him.

"Be quick about it," he said. "I leave with my tools in an hour."

ONCE THE horse was saddled, the remaining supplies collected, and all the packs secured over Spirit's rump, Auraq made a thorough search of the bodies. Each had a purse tied to their belt that jingled promisingly. He cut the strings to remove them, and spilled some of the coin into his palm. No foreign currency. Not one coin. Auraq wasn't sure why that surprised him. For some reason, he half expected these villains to be from somewhere else—perhaps even the barbarian lands to the south and west. Their combat technique was unique, like nothing he'd encountered before. It would require training certainly, but it wasn't military training. At least not the type of military training he had experienced. These men were trained for a different purpose.

He didn't take the time to count out the coin, but it was clear by weight alone each purse contained more than he'd seen for some time. A bit of an unexpected windfall, that. He consolidated the coin into one purse and tied it to an iron ring on his saddle instead of adding the coin to his own belt pouch. Not knowing from where the coin had come, Auraq felt there was something black and unsavory about mixing his hard-earned coin with theirs.

He gathered all their weapons and cataloged what they

had. They were of surprising quality. All in all, he found a crossbow, three swords, and a number of daggers and throwing knives. The crossbow he'd likely keep, but he had no interest in the other weapons. They'd bring a decent price in the city, but carting them along with Kane was more than he was willing to burden Spirit with.

The search yielded little that would help determine who the men were or who they worked for, except for a strange insignia one of them had embroidered onto the breast of his tunic. Auraq didn't recognize it. A circle with a profile of an odd type of canine. Not a dog or wolf—something else. He cut out the emblem with a dagger and stored it in his belt pouch. Satisfied he'd discovered everything he could about the three would-be assassins, he dragged the bodies into the woods. There wasn't much point in the exercise—he was just tired of looking at them.

Kane hadn't made much progress. A hand's breadth down, the soil was heavily bound with roots from the surrounding trees. He dissolved into wild chopping more than digging. And the anger that had fueled him earlier was waning, leaving behind fatigue and grief.

They would be there all night at this rate.

Auraq grabbed the spade from him and took over for a while. Kane sat heavily on the ground and watched Auraq, who focused his energy and strength on a smaller circle instead of the long rectangle Kane had started. In less than an hour, the hole had grown to knee deep. Auraq climbed out and tossed the tools on the ground.

"That isn't finished," Kane said with alarm as he stood.

"It'll do."

"No." Kane was at his side as Auraq moved toward Old Tan's body. "No, it's hardly dignified."

Auraq scooped the old man into his arms. The body seemed to weigh nothing. He carried him to the small grave, while Kane followed him, making quiet little noises. Auraq stepped inside and gently placed Old Tan on his side at the bottom of the hole, curled in a small ball. He stepped out, picked up the spade again, and held it out for Kane.

"Do you want the honors?"

He expected more protests, but Kane only stared back at him with a tight jaw and his hands tucked under his arms. He made a quick wipe of his cheeks with the heel of his hand and shook his head.

"Last words?"

"I said them already," Kane replied. "While I was digging."

Auraq nodded and proceeded to return the excavated soil to the hole.

Chapter 5

AT THE apex of a hill, Auraq glimpsed a small cluster of buildings along the river's edge through the break in the trees, the source of the chimney smoke he'd spied earlier against the predawn sky. He pulled the reins left, guiding Spirit down the road that led to the settlement, then wiggled and jostled his shoulder about until the soft weight against his back shifted and lessened. Kane made a few grunts as he came awake and sat up straight in the saddle.

"Guess I fell asleep," Kane grumbled groggily. He shifted around behind Auraq, stretching.

Auraq didn't reply. Spirit's gentle rocking gate lulled Kane asleep an hour into their journey. Propped against Auraq's back, he hardly moved the rest of the night.

"Where are we?" Kane asked. His voice was low, barely audible, like a man crushed beneath the weight of the world.

"Not far from an inn." The road ahead listed downward toward the quiet hamlet that hugged a lazy curve of the river. Another road converged in from the south.

"An inn?" Kane's voice lifted. His body stiffened behind Auraq. "We aren't stopping, are we?"

Auraq could feel the surge of unease radiating off him. "We'll need to eat. And talk."

Kane fell quiet a moment. "We should keep moving. It could be dangerous." Old Tan must have had them avoiding places that were public and open. "Plus, my purse is nearly depleted, and I need what I have left to last."

Auraq reached down and jingled the assassin's purse tied to the saddle. "Courtesy of our visitors last night."

He guided Spirit along at a steady, unhurried pace. He had no desire to push the beast, considering the night she'd had with the added burden of Kane. The road descended into a swath of young forest for a time, and they broke from the trees just outside the perimeter of the tiny hamlet. Most of the buildings were small mud-brick homes, arranged in a haphazard jumble like toy blocks dropped in the dirt. At the center of them, standing proudly at the convergence of the roads, was a two-story structure of wattle and daub. White smoke twisted up into the sky from a stone chimney, a beacon of welcome. As they drew closer, Auraq could see the wooden placard in the shape of outstretched wings hanging from an iron rod above the door.

Spirit lumbered across the central yard of the inn. A stableboy sprinted out to meet them, a small stool tucked under his arm. Auraq pulled back gently on the reins, and the lad skidded to stop at Spirit's flank. He positioned the stool on the ground under Auraq's right foot.

"Good morn, good surs," he said brightly. He took hold of the bridle and waited for the two men to dismount.

Auraq looked over his shoulder.

Kane gazed off at nothing in particular, his eyes unfocused, his attention elsewhere. Auraq could guess where.

"You first," Auraq said.

Kane snapped back into the present. "Oh. Right." He swung his left leg over the back of the horse and slid down. Once on the ground, he put his hands low on his hips and arched backward with a groan.

Auraq dropped beside him, landing on the hard, graveled earth with barely a sound. He removed the assassin's purse from the saddle and uncinched the pack tied on one side of Spirit's rump and slung it over his shoulder. From his belt pouch, he pulled out two copper coins and handed them over to the lad.

He stared at the coins in his palm as if they were something magical. "Thank you indeed, good sur. Staying long?"

"Not sure yet," Auraq told him, "but she could use a break from that saddle and a thorough brushing."

"Very well, sur," the lad replied cheerily and clicked his tongue to coax Spirit into following him. She resisted at first, but a gentle pat on the rump from Auraq was all the reassurance she needed, and she went along with the lad willingly toward the small stable.

Auraq headed toward the inn door, not waiting to see if Kane followed. After a moment, he heard the crunch of the gravel a few paces behind him. He looked up at the weathered placard as he passed under it, shading his eyes from the stark morning sun. The inn's name was carved and painted across the length of the outstretched wings.

"The Harpies' Fury," he read aloud. "Not the most welcoming of names." He glanced over his shoulder at Kane, who looked at him directly with a knitted brow. "Surprised I know my letters?"

Kane shook his head vigorously. "No. No, of course not."

The assumption that those in the military were unschooled was largely true. One didn't need to know their letters to fight well. But unschooled and stupid weren't at all the same. Auraq always chafed at the implication that those who swung a sword for a living were idiots. "Don't believe everything you hear." He grabbed the latch and pulled the door open.

He stood at the threshold of the inn a moment to scan the environment before delving in deeper. The place was small and dark, and his eyes were slow to adjust. The sudden invasion of stark sunlight made the patrons sitting about the tables look up like startled ghouls in a crypt.

"Old Tan would say this is a foolhardy risk," Kane griped behind him.

Auraq bit back an impulse to respond.

"We cannot trust it is safe here," Kane added.

"It's daytime," Auraq replied flatly as he stepped inside. "And it's public."

The assassins wouldn't have expected Old Tan and Kane alone to be any trouble. They hadn't accounted for Auraq being there. It would take time for the failure to be discovered, first of all. Then, once this mysterious organization realized their assassins were dead, they would need to track what direction Auraq and Kane had traveled. And having badly underestimated their quarry, they would proceed with caution until they learned more.

All of which gave Auraq a sufficient window of time to deliver Kane to a safe location.

Kane stood at the threshold peering in with squinted eyes. Auraq pulled him forward, then closed the door behind them. He pointed to an empty table near the wall.

The Harpies' Fury's tavern room was unremarkable in every way. The two windows along the outside wall were shuttered tight, allowing in none of the bright morning sun except through the seam between them. Oil lanterns hanging from beams provided the only light, which was a weak amber glow. The room was small compared to most city taverns. On its busiest night, there'd be perhaps room for twenty patrons, if many were willing to stand and drink their ale. It had six wood-plank tables, a stone fireplace in the back, and a stubby little bar counter in the far corner. The ceiling was low and lined with heavy hand-hewed beams that tall drunks undoubtedly concussed themselves on regularly.

Its only redeeming quality was the welcome smell of food wafting out from beyond a narrow door lined with a ratty old curtain.

The sole serving wench leaned against the back of a chair and chatted casually with an older man. She watched Auraq and Kane take their seats—not with suspicion or distrust, just an idle curiosity. The two of them must look quite the unlikely pair.

She excused herself from the man and glided over.

"Good morning, lads," she purred. Though dressed in a revealing shift and bodice normally worn by far fresher maidens, she had obviously been at this vocation for some years. Her wavy dark hair was graying at the temples and her face was lined around the eyes and mouth. She was a comely woman, by all measures, and Auraq reckoned she would have been striking in her youth. She smiled down at them, revealing a tooth that stuck out at an unfortunate angle. "Get ya somethin'?"

"Two meals," Auraq told her. "Whatever you have."

The serving wench pinched her mouth and looked up at the ceiling in thought. "That'd be boiled eggs, sausages, some cooked beans, and warm cooktop bread. Wager there's a few roasted turnips around yet too. I've got some hot brew in the kettle if you'd like."

"That'll do," Auraq answered.

Kane lifted his head and gave her a single nod, then looked back down at his hands. He retreated into himself again. Recounting the events from the night before, Auraq reckoned. Wondering if there was a way things might have turned out differently.

Auraq waited for the wench to amble off toward the kitchen. "Where would you like to begin?" he asked.

Kane kept his head low, eyes on his lap. "With what?"

Auraq raised a single eyebrow.

Kane leaned back against the chair. His eyes shifted to survey the thin crowd in the tavern. Auraq could tell it was in part a way to stall his answer, in part to evaluate the threat around them. The three other patrons in the tavern didn't look remotely dangerous. Even at this early hour, they didn't look sober. Kane rubbed the heel of his hand into the corner of his eye. "I don't know," he said after a time. His hand dropped back into his lap as if he lost the strength to hold it up. "I don't know why they were after us."

Auraq could tell he was lying. Tired and short-tempered, he was in no mood to chase the truth out of him. "Professional assassins don't target random people," he said.

Kane looked up and glared at Auraq with some fire behind his eyes. "If there's a reason, I don't know it." He held Auraq's heavy gaze a moment but then dropped his eyes to his hands again. "At least not entirely."

Auraq bit the inside of his cheek as he lightly tapped his thumb on the table. It hadn't taken much to loosen the first strands of that knot.

The serving wench arrived with two wide platters of food, interrupting Auraq's further prodding. The plates were unceremoniously deposited in front of each of them. "Appears Ardy found a few apples back there that weren't worm-eaten or rotten," she said with her wide crooked smile as she stood up straight with her hands on her hips. "Must be your birthday. Be right back with the mugs of brew." She disappeared behind the curtain for a moment or two and returned with the drinks. "Anything else, good surs?"

Auraq shook his head and waved her off. She made a sad attempt at a curtsey before slinking off to rejoin the older patron she'd been flirting with earlier.

Kane mechanically picked up the spoon, but only moved the food around the plate.

Auraq picked up a sausage and bit off the end. "Eat," he told Kane flatly while he chewed.

Kane scooped up soft beans onto his spoon. "I meant what I said."

"And what is it you said?"

"You are not obligated to stay around and play my nursemaid, or whatever it is you agreed to. Go if you wish."

Auraq took another bite from the sausage. "Well, I'm not going anywhere until I've finished with my breakfast." He took a swig from the hot brew to wash it down. It was bitter and lukewarm, clearly having sat in the kettle all morning. "In the meantime, you might as well talk." He looked up at Kane and met his eyes. "So, talk."

Kane sighed. He took a bite of the beans and chewed for a bit. "I don't even know where to begin."

"The beginning is generally the accepted place."

Kane seemed to debate with himself for a time. Eventually, he set the spoon down, pushed the platter of food to the center of the table, and rested his forearms on the space in front of him. He pulled in a long breath and let it out slowly, filling his cheeks. "I wasn't lying to you. I really don't know why they were after us… well, after me. Not specifically. That was why we were heading to the city. For some answers."

Auraq bit his boiled egg in half, chewed, and let the man talk.

"Old Tan feels—" Kane stopped, eyes shifting upward. "Felt," he adjusted softly. "He felt it was our best option."

He looked back down at his plate. Auraq sensed him

slipping into a fresh wave of grief at the mention of Old Tan. He needed to nudge him along to keep him talking. "Tell me about Old Tan. How long was he your master?"

"Seven years. My entire family died in a fire. I was the only survivor. He took pity on me and took me on as his apprentice. I had no skills then. It was always assumed I'd be a farmer like my pa. It was a kindness I could never hope to repay."

Which explained why he was not yet a journeyman. "A late start at the trade," Auraq put in.

"He was hinting that he was going to raise my status soon, but never got around to it. Not going to happen now, I suppose."

Auraq kept his face neutral. Kane likely had a bleak future ahead of him. No one would hire him for work in his trade without his journeyman papers. If he was lucky, he'd land work as a farmhand somewhere or perhaps get work in a city transporting garbage or shoveling shit in a stable. But he'd probably end up in the mines.

"I liked working in Tan's shop," Kane added, pushing food around on his plate. "Stayed in back. It was quiet there. People left me alone. Never had to worry about anyone pretending to not stare at me and think of me as that orphan that Old Tan took pity on."

"How does any of this get you marked by assassins?"

"Some weeks ago, a peddler came through town and called on the shop. He'd acquired some equipment—armor pieces and such—and was hoping to turn a fast coin for them, but some were in need of repair. The man wanted to be gone in the morning, so Old Tan put me to work on some of the pieces straightaway. One of the items was a pair of heavy leather bracers. Quality ones, sturdy and well-made, but they had lost some of their studs and several of the buckle straps had torn. I put them right, and to make sure they were fitted properly, I attached one to my own arm."

Kane self-consciously rubbed his hand over his left forearm. "As soon as I had it buckled, I felt a burning. Here, on my skin, as if the inside of the bracer was lined with hot coals. I took it off as quickly as I was able and looked at my arm, expecting to see the skin blistering." He made a small lift of his shoulders. "But there was nothing. Not even a blemish or a flushing of the skin. The skin was sensitive to the touch, nothing more. So, I put it out of my mind and finished the work. Old Tan gave the equipment back to the peddler, and he was on his way."

Auraq frowned. The description was enough to assure him magecraft or witchery was involved.

Kane glanced around to see if anyone was looking their way or was within earshot of their conversation. "The next morning, I found this…." He pulled up his tunic sleeve to reveal his forearm, turning his wrist to expose the fleshier hairless underside.

Auraq grabbed Kane's wrist, pulled the arm closer, and leaned in. There on the skin was what looked at first glance to be a tattoo, but something about it wasn't right. It was unlike any ink he'd seen. It was an inflamed red that seemed to glow on its own like weak embers in a fire, and the coverage on the skin was too complete, too pure. The shape of it was long and scrolling like the tendril of a thick ivy branch. They were letters certainly, of some unknown language, strung together in a flowing script.

Holding Kane's wrist, Auraq could feel the power weave into his own hand. His fingertips began to tingle and prick where they were in contact with Kane's skin. Auraq's heart rate increased. He broke contact, and Kane pulled his arm back and held it against his body.

"A mark of augury," he whispered. He could hear the awe in his own voice and was annoyed by it.

Kane slid the sleeve back over his forearm to hide the mark once again. "That is what Old Tan believed."

Such a mark was the subject of myth. It was common for charlatans to claim to have been marked, but most knew it to be rubbish. A village prelate told him once it had been ten generations since a true mark had appeared. Auraq wouldn't have believed it himself if he hadn't just witnessed it with his own eyes—and felt the power in his hand.

"Tan took me first to see an old woman who lives deep in

the woods outside of our village," Kane continued. "A bone reader. When she examined it, she wasn't convinced it was prophetic. Or even divine. Said there are different kinds of marks."

That was news to Auraq. But then he was a man of the blade and stayed well clear of such things. "She couldn't read it?"

Kane shook his head. "By her own admission, her knowledge with such matters was elementary. She suggested we find a mage with more training."

"Which was why the two of you were traveling to Har Diamante."

Kane nodded. "It is the closest city likely to have a mage of any distinction. Hopefully, I still have enough coin to purchase their aid."

"And our visitors last night? How do they fit into this?"

"I honestly don't know. The old woman is the only one we've told, and it was on her insistence that we've kept silent. You are the first I've shown since."

"Old Tan knew the ambush last night was connected to you."

"We'd been attacked once already. We were lucky and managed to escape." Kane shrugged, looking chagrined. "It's how I lost my good cloak."

Auraq agreed with him. The mark and the attacks were obviously connected.

He unlatched the pouch at his belt and pulled out the scrap of linen he cut from the assassin's tunic. He laid it out on the table in front of Kane. "Recognize this emblem?"

Kane picked it up and inspected it, then shook his head. "Never seen it before," he said as he handed it back.

Auraq didn't think Kane had, but wanted to make sure. He put the scrap back in his pouch.

So either someone traced the bewitched bracers to the old man and Kane, or there were methods of detecting and tracking the mark. The latter gave him pause. If they could track Kane, it would put them in constant danger. But one thing was clear:

whatever the mark was, somebody was going through a great deal of effort to eliminate it.

He needed time to think, to take all of this in. Thankfully, their uninvited guests from last night had provided him with enough coin to splurge on a few comforts while he considered what to do next.

"Eat up," he ordered. "I want a bath."

Chapter 6

THE INNKEEPER pushed open the door and stepped aside so Auraq could see into the room. "The only one we provide with a bathing tub, sur. The noble suite." The man was like every other innkeeper in the world—short, bald, and a belly that protruded out well beyond his toes.

Auraq leaned across the threshold and inspected the chamber. Despite the name the proud innkeeper had given it, there was nothing particularly noble about it, nor was it a suite. But it was clean and comfortable, and located at the far end of the corridor.

"It is our finest room," the innkeeper added. He held a polite smile, but his inflection betrayed his annoyance. Auraq sensed the innkeeper was mistaking silence for dissatisfaction and trying to figure out why this man who wore no finery and smelled like he'd been through the privy scrutinized the accommodations like some highborn fop. In truth, Auraq was gauging the security of room—defensibility, potential access through windows and whatnot—but he let the man believe otherwise.

The innkeeper stole a surreptitious glance at Kane. "For about the same amount, I could provide you with two separate rooms if you'd prefer. But you'd have to use the public facilities behind the inn in that case."

"This'll do," Auraq said, and he handed over the coin. The innkeeper lowered his eyes a moment to study the coins in his palm, clearly adding them up mentally to ensure he wasn't being cheated.

Auraq guided him gently by the elbow into the center of the corridor, clearing the doorway so Kane could pass inside. He then plucked the iron key from the innkeeper's other hand. "Hot water," he said.

The innkeeper looked up, confused. He was just becoming aware that he'd lost possession of the key. "I beg your pardon?"

"For the bath."

"Oh. Yes, of course. I'll have Helegus start a kettle on the fire straightaway."

Auraq backed into the chamber, hand on the latch. The innkeeper turned to leave but then twisted back with a finger raised. He opened his mouth to add some other detail he'd forgotten to mention, but Auraq pulled the door closed on him before he could form the words.

Auraq sighed and tossed his pack onto a side chair by the small fireplace.

For a small country inn, the chamber was spacious, but not grand or opulent. The ceiling was higher on one side, and it sloped toward a short wall that had two recessed alcoves with square windows tucked inside. The furnishings were simple. A large bed was positioned against the wall opposite the hearth, and a heavy wardrobe and writing desk were placed between the window alcoves. In the corner nearest the fireplace was a wooden tub that resembled a barrel sliced longways in half.

"This seems unnecessarily extravagant," Kane said as he looked around the chamber.

Auraq wondered if he had ever spent the night in an inn before. The room was serviceable, but hardly extravagant. A true noble would lift his nose at the space and march straight back out again, demanding better.

Kane went to the alcove, squatted down, and peered out the window.

"Stay away from the window," Auraq told him flatly.

"I am only looking," Kane replied.

"Until I know more, I'll not permit any unnecessary risks."

"Permit?" Kane straightened his back and raised his eyebrows, but Auraq noted he did step away from the alcove. "I'll remind you that—"

"I am unwanted here and free to leave." Auraq finished for him as he unlatched the longsword's frog from his belt. He

38

removed the short sword's baldric over his head and laid the two weapons onto the bed. "You've made that clear enough." He tugged at the laces securing the bracers to his forearm. Once loosened, he slid his arm out and tossed the bracer on the bed. "But I am going to enjoy the comforts of this chamber. You are equally free to leave and seek lodging elsewhere if you wish. I will not stop you." He gave Kane a level stare.

Kane's entire body stiffened. He opened his mouth to speak; it hung open for a few seconds, and then he closed it again. His hands rested on his hips, and he turned to face the wall.

Auraq resumed the task of removing his gear.

A knock came at the door. Kane moved to answer it, but Auraq held him off with his extended hand and did it himself. He opened the door just enough to see into the hall beyond. Two young girls stood in the corridor hoisting wooden buckets in front of them. He swung the door wider to allow them in.

They shuffled to the tub with their burdens, breathing heavily, and dumped the steaming contents inside. "We will return with more, m'lord," one said with a curtsey as the second girl scurried out.

"I'm not nobleborn," Auraq said. "I require no such title."

"Apologies, sur," she said with another curtsey. She quickly ducked out of the room with her bucket. Auraq left the door open as he returned to the bed and sat on the edge of the lumpy mattress.

Kane stepped closer to Auraq once the girls were gone and out of earshot. "If we are in danger," he said in a harsh whisper, "why are we here? Explain to me how you taking a bath serves my *protection*?"

Kane was attempting to goad him into anger. Auraq didn't let him. Instead, he loosened the laces of his boots at a deliberate pace and tugged them off. He heard footfalls on the steps at the end of the corridor, so he waited to answer. The girls paraded in with their buckets, dumped the water into the tub, and disappeared once again.

"We have a window of time while those behind the attack

discover what has happened to their men and investigate," he said once they were out of earshot. "I recommend we use it for rest, considering we did not get much last night." He'd learned the hard way that fatigue was more likely to cause a mistake than heavy drink.

Kane puffed out air through his lips in aggravation. "We should be putting distance between us and that campsite," he grumbled.

When Auraq didn't respond but continued to disrobe, Kane took a seat at the writing desk and said nothing else.

It took two more trips for the bath to be filled adequately. "There is soap in a tin box beside the tub," one girl told him as she moved to the door. "And heavy cloth for drying in the wardrobe."

Auraq handed over a half noble as the girls left. They both stared at the coin as if they didn't believe it was real. "Come back in a half an hour," he said. "We'll need the water changed." He closed the door behind them, locked it, and doffed the last of his garments, leaving them in a heap on the floor. Naked, he leaned over the side of the tub to feel the water. It was hot, but not scalding. Good… he wouldn't have to wait to climb in. As he walked to the wardrobe to fetch a drying cloth, he felt eyes on him. He turned to find Kane watching him.

"What?" Auraq asked.

Kane turned away. "Nothing." He sounded annoyed, but his cheeks were flushed a bright crimson.

AURAQ SUBMERGED his body up to the neck, closed his eyes, and allowed the heat to penetrate into his muscles until the tension knotting his shoulders and neck began to ease. He was more tired than he'd wanted to admit. There was no denying that the last full day had taken its toll on him. For a while he forgot that Kane was in the room with him still.

When the water in the tub eventually tempered, he sat up again and scrubbed himself clean with the scented soap. He ducked his head under the water and scrubbed his scalp and beard with his fingernails. Satisfied, he stood up and allowed the water to cascade and drip off him. The water inside the tub was the color of sun-bleached driftwood.

Kane was still seated at the writing desk, thumbing through a leather-bound book he had found somewhere.

"Does it hurt?" Auraq asked him. He pressed his palms over the top of his head to squeeze the water from his hair, and it ran in rivulets down the center of his back and between his cheeks. He then shook the water from his arms and hands. A draft in the room swept cool air against his body. His skin tingled and a shiver raced over his shoulders and down the length of his arms.

Kane looked up from the book, glanced at Auraq, and immediately turned away. "Does what hurt?"

"The mark."

Kane wet his finger on his tongue and turned another page. "It did at first." He lowered his eyes and did not look up from his book as he spoke. "I suppose I've gotten used to it. The sensation is... strange."

Auraq scooped up the cloth from the floor and began to rub himself dry. He remembered the sensation in his own fingers when his hand was close to the mark. "Strange how?"

Kane thought about it a moment. "Hard to explain. The skin feels normal, but I feel a... a presence of something beneath the surface."

Auraq raised his brow. An odd choice of words, that. "A presence?"

"Only way I can think to describe it, really. I feel as if something that is not me occupies the flesh and bone. A kind of warm pressure. And it moves too. I feel it in my hand sometimes, and up beyond my elbow."

"Is the sensation spreading?" That was a disconcerting thought. Were they dealing with some power or entity that was taking over?

Kane clearly hadn't considered that either. He glanced up, brow knitted. "I... I'm not really certain."

His torso dry, Auraq stepped out of the tub and ran the

towel down the length of his extremities. The more he learned about this mark, the more it unsettled him—and he was irritated that he'd allowed himself to be involved with it. Wise men steered clear of such things. The notion that some unknown entity could be attempting to control Kane was disconcerting.

Auraq walked back to the bed where he'd left his garments. Using the now-damp cloth he'd used to dry himself, he wiped down the front of his leather jerkin. Ruddy streaks stained the fabric when he pulled it off again. Once satisfied that most of the visible blood was removed, he pulled on his trousers, tied the laces in the front, and slipped the tunic over his head.

"Are you going somewhere?" asked Kane.

"Heading down to the tavern to see if I can ferret out some information," he said as he wiggled his arms and head through the holes in the tunic, and when his head emerged from the top, Kane was looking at him directly again. The book was closed and pushed aside.

"Is that wise?" Kane asked.

"Whoever is on your trail is unaware of my part in this. At least, so far. I'll be in no danger."

"That was not actually my concern," Kane grumbled quietly. He started to say something else but was interrupted by a timid knock at the door. The girls had returned with buckets in hand. Auraq allowed them in and stood at the open doorway as they paraded in, scooped the soiled water out of the tub, and shuffled out.

"You're safe in here, if that's what you're worried about." Auraq slipped on his jerkin, then cinched his belt around his waist. He affixed the longsword's frog to his left hip, and then slipped the baldric over his head and adjusted it on his shoulder.

"You need both of your swords to poke around a small tavern?" Kane asked.

"They are never separated."

"What can you possibly hope to learn from these people?"

"Residents of these parts will be wagging their tongues about anything unusual they've seen."

The girls bailed out the last of the dirty water from the tub while Auraq pulled on his boots and laced them up. Then they began hauling in fresh buckets of steaming water.

Auraq leaned against the doorframe and waited for them to finish. "Take a bath. Get some sleep."

"I don't want to sleep." Kane returned his attention to the book in his lap. "I don't like my dreams lately."

Once the tub was filled again and the girls were gone, he tossed the key onto the bed. "Lock the door behind me."

Auraq was out of the chamber with the door closed before Kane could think to voice another protest.

Chapter 7

THE TAVERN was still largely quiet. Some new travelers had wandered in since Auraq had gone up to the room, and were taking in an afternoon meal, but other than the innkeeper and his serving wench, the space was thin on locals. It was too early for regional laborers to be there after a long day of toiling in their fields or whatnot. He'd have had better luck if the weather had turned. Nothing brought men into a tavern more predictably than inclemency. It was the perfect excuse to have a pint in the afternoon.

Auraq grabbed a table that was both close to the bar and gave him a clear view of the entire tavern, including the stairs leading up to the rooms.

The serving wench sidled over to him and leaned her hip against the back of his chair. "Back so soon, love? Couldn't keep yourself away?" She reached a hand behind her neck and pulled her long hair out so it hung down in front of her shoulder. She was close enough now that he could smell her clothes—an aroma of sour ale, pork fat, and sweat.

He forced a polite smile, wanting to keep her friendly but not encourage too much overt flirtation. "Dust from the road's still in my throat."

"Ah, I know the likes of that," she replied. "I wager you're lookin' for something more refreshing than that sludge he calls a morning brew, then. Something in particular you've a taste for? He's got three different kegs tapped at the moment."

"Just as long as it's wet," Auraq replied. "And darker than my own piss."

She chuckled and pushed off of his chair. "Know just the thing." She leaned heavily against the bar and signaled the innkeeper over.

Auraq made a casual sweep around him while he waited, and studied each patron one by one. He spotted nothing suspicious or even remarkable about any of the other occupants of the tavern. Three men at one table were clearly a group of merchants of some kind. They were well-dressed, equally well-armed, and having an ardent discussion over something in the open ledger on the table between them. The eldest of them pounded his finger repeatedly on the page. Another table was occupied by a man and a woman of some years. Auraq had seen their kind before. These were simple travelers, likely venturing out from their home for the first time and unaccustomed to the harshness of life on the road. They leaned into their meal and spoke quietly to each other, their faces drawn and weary. Auraq could see the man clutching his purse in his lap as if afraid someone would cut the strings from his belt while they ate.

Auraq hoped they were traveling with a caravan of some kind, perhaps along with the merchants. Their guarded behavior would only signal would-be robbers of their inexperience and vulnerability.

The wench returned with his ale. She set the leather tankard onto the table with care and turned it to position the wooden handle closer to his hand. She leaned on the table opposite him with one arm and arched her shoulder back to accentuate her breasts and the deep cleavage between them.

Auraq took a long draft from the tankard. The ale was rich and full-flavored, with a strong hint of spice. Suds clung to his beard and tickled the skin under his nose.

"Everything you hoped?" she asked with a grin.

"And more," he replied. He set the tankard down and leaned back, letting silence linger between them.

"Name's Zelina," she said. "What happened to your companion?"

"Resting."

She smiled at that for some reason, as if it meant something. "You seem an unlikely pair to be traveling together."

"A favor to his sister," he replied, and took another swig from the tankard. "I'm to get him safely to his destination. Word is this road's grown dangerous."

Zelina's smile broadened. "A personal bodyguard, eh?" She had an impish twinkle in her eye. "How intriguing. Quite a favor to ask of someone, I'd say. This sister of his, someone special?"

He felt his insides tighten and a deep impulse to pull back. This was not the first time a woman had made her intentions clear to him, but such advances always put him ill at ease. He needed her to keep talking, so he played along. "No. Nothing like that."

Her smile widened a fraction. "Wouldn't trouble yourself 'bout any rumors you've heard about these parts. You've a look that you can handle yourself well enough."

"I'd prefer to avoid the highwaymen than handle them, if possible. But I hear there are other dangers as well."

She laughed. "You've been listening to the wild talk of some of the old women round here?" She shook her head. "You didn't strike me as the superstitious type."

From his experience, rumor and gossip always had a thread of truth embedded in it. That meant someone was witness to something unusual. He forced a smile in return and kept his tone light. "Just want to know what I'm in for, is all. What are the rumormongers saying these days?"

She waved him off. "Bunch of silly nonsense, y'ask me. Just keep to the main road and you'll garner no trouble. Especially in the day hours."

One of the merchants at the other table waved to get Zelina's attention and failing that, called her over. The flirtatious twinkle in her eye quickly turned to annoyance. She held up a finger to them, then straightened and adjusted her corset.

"One more question," Auraq said before she turned to leave. He reached into his belt pouch and pulled out the small swath of fabric. He laid it flat on the table in front of her. "Seen this before?"

Her brow tightened as she picked it up to get a better look at it. "Can't say that I have. Not the insignia of any of the nobles that carry manors in these parts. Pretty, though." She dropped

46

the square of linen onto the table. "Why? Where'd it come from?"

"Oh, just found it lying about." He tucked the fabric back into the pouch. "Made me curious." She gave him a level stare but she didn't challenge him. A tavern wench of her experience was certain to spot any shady business without much effort. It was worth a try to ask, but he'd known it was a long shot. The attackers likely didn't come from anywhere local. This whole business smelled too professional, which meant the ones behind the attack came from someplace larger, a place where more illicit types were cultivated. Like one of the larger duchies—Har Tesera or Har Sentoran. But his coin was on Dar Arendia, the capital.

Zelina shuffled off to attend to the other patrons, who were now gesturing with an impatient display of holding their tankards upside-down to make their point.

Auraq leaned in on his elbows and took another drink. He was tempted to talk to the other patrons but wondered if it was worth the effort. The older couple would be unapproachable and too guarded if he went over to their table. Fear would hold their tongues. The merchants by their very nature were creatures of the road and would have a keen eye for things that were amiss. But they also tended toward isolation and keeping out of the affairs of others. They might have seen or noticed something but would be hesitant to pass on any information for fear of getting involved.

He needed locals—small-town folk who had nothing to do but gossip and no sense to keep quiet about it. This inn may be too remote to bring in a crowd, but surely there were farmers and laborers about. They wouldn't be filtering into the tavern until it grew closer to dusk, and he planned to be well on the road by then.

A yawn crept up on him. He tried to stifle it with a fist to his mouth, but it proved stronger than his will. His mouth opened wide and his eyes watered. The lack of sleep was beginning to wear on him. The hot bath and the ale weren't helping either. He would have to try and catch at least a few hours of sleep before they headed out again. Exhaustion was a danger he couldn't allow to take root. Not unlike too much drink, it would affect his thinking and ability to react.

Zelina gathered up the merchants' empty tankards and carried them to the innkeeper for refills. Auraq pushed his chair back to stand. This was his window. He would try his luck with the merchants, see what they were willing to pass on to him, and then he would head back to the room.

But before he could stand, the door to the tavern was pushed open. Auraq squinted and shielded his eyes with his palm as afternoon sunlight blasted into the dim room. He could just make out the silhouette of a large form in the doorway. The figure paused, taking in the surroundings, then moved inside. The door shut behind him again, thrusting the tavern once again back into a drab cave.

The figure wore a heavy black cloak, the hood up to conceal his entire face in shadow. He stood at the entrance and pulled off his gloves, tugging at each finger in a deliberate display before sliding it off his hand.

Not the garb one typically wore on a warm and sunny afternoon, Auraq noted. He rested back against his chair and took renewed interest in the tankard in front of him. While he took a long drink, he kept the man in his sight.

The man tucked the gloves into his belt and crossed the room. He headed directly toward the bar. The innkeeper set the merchants' three refills on the counter, wiped his hands on a rag, and without obvious trepidation, moved down to greet the man. Zelina watched from the end of the bar, the three tankards forgotten.

Everyone in the room felt it. There was something sinister and unnerving about the new visitor.

The man leaned his elbows on the bar. The innkeeper stood across from him with his body rigid. Auraq strained to listen to what the man was saying but couldn't make out any of the words. The exchange between them was brief. The innkeeper nodded a few times, shook his head a few more. He said maybe five words to the man.

But something the man said to him made the innkeeper visibly pale.

The man pushed himself up from the bar and pulled his gloves out from his belt. As he marched back through the tavern, boot heels clapping on the plank floor, he tugged the gloves back on his hands. At the door, he stopped and turned to take one more look around the room. Auraq felt the man's eyes on him from under the shadow of the hood. He stared down at the contents of the tankard for a time, then risked one final glance before the man exited the tavern.

As soon as the man was gone, Auraq made his way to the bar. He had to act before the man recovered his wits from the encounter.

"That fellow sure was an odd one," he said to the innkeeper in a light, casual tone. "Gave me duck skin just laying eyes on him."

"Indeed," the man replied, his voice a little shaky.

Zelina scurried around the end of the bar and put a hand on the innkeeper's forearm. "What in the name of all the Gods was that about, Ardy?" She kept turning to the door as if expecting the man to barge back in with weapons drawn. "You're the color of bone."

"Nothing," the innkeeper said quickly. "It was nothing. He had a few questions, is all."

"Questions? That man had the air of death about him. I could feel it."

"It's all right, Zel. Go and serve those drinks. He… he said he was just on the lookout for some folk."

Auraq shook his head in bewilderment. "Wouldn't want to be those folks, I'm thinking."

"Here, here," chimed in Zelina.

"Did he say who they were?" Auraq asked.

"Nobody I've seen around here, and that's what I told him. Some old man traveling with a younger one. Said they may be accompanied by some mercenaries or perhaps soldiers."

Zelina nodded. "They've not been in here."

"Exactly what I told the man."

"I may have seen them actually," Auraq said, cupping his chin in thought. "Last night on the road. Heading south."

"I'd keep that information quiet, if I were you, friend," Ardy said in low voice.

"A wise recommendation," Auraq replied with a nod. He pushed away from the bar and dropped a few coins in front of the innkeeper.

As he forced himself to make a casual climb up the stairs, the wood creaking beneath his feet, he felt his mood darken with each step. He had to think very carefully about their next move.

Auraq had managed to glean only one detail from the strange visitor before he left the tavern. The man wore no ornamentation or emblem on his person, save for one location—the clasp that secured the cloak around his neck. It was gold, and as the door opened, the sunlight glinted off it perfectly, and although Auraq saw it for a single heartbeat only, he recognized it immediately.

It was round, and inside was the profile of the strange canine creature with teeth bared. The same emblem he cut off the assassin's tunic. The bar wench clearly hadn't noticed it—and Auraq thanked the Gods for that bit of luck. The afternoon might have turned out quite differently if she had.

Chapter 8

AURAQ PRESSED his heel into Spirit's flank, signaling her to move into an ambling gait. He was ready to put some distance between them and the Harpies' Fury, but wanted to preserve her energy should they have sudden need of her speed. Spirit's movement over the old road was smooth, but Auraq could still feel the rhythm of Kane's body pressing against his back as they rode.

"I still don't understand what the point of leaving was," Kane said from behind. "That means they've already searched the area. We could have spent the entire night at the inn."

"I'd rather not be on the road when they expect us to be traveling. And we'd be easily spotted in the daylight."

They'd left the Harpies' Fury at dusk. He caught a few hours of sleep, but his encounter with the dark man in the tavern made his mind restless and uneasy. Kane lay down next to him on the bed for a time, but Auraq suspected he hadn't slept much either, if at all.

Late in the afternoon, he'd forced himself up and dressed again. He filled a lantern with enough oil to burn until after nightfall, lit it, and positioned it near one of the windows. They then made a quiet trip out to the stables and had Spirit saddled and readied. A few extra coins in the stableboy's hand were hopefully enough to ensure the lad would keep their departure quiet. If all went smoothly, no one would know they'd left the area until the next day.

"You learned nothing about him?" Kane asked after a time.

"No," he answered. "His face was concealed."

He'd shared the incident with Kane back in their room, but left out the part about seeing the strange dog-like insignia again on his cloak. No point in telling Kane about it until he knew more about it himself. All it told him for certain was that they were dealing with a professional organization. He'd already presumed that this wasn't a group of thugs hired from some dark corner of a tavern somewhere. The insignia simply confirmed it.

He was even beginning to wonder if he should have kept the entire encounter to himself.

Kane sank back into his own thoughts. The relative safety of the room seemed to have quieted Kane's anxiety. Now that they were out on the road again, the spell was broken. Kane's mood had darkened.

The sun had gone down, but the pale light of twilight still lingered. Bands of clouds swept the breadth overhead, their undersides dusted in vibrant crimson and violet, but the grandeur was fading quickly. All too soon it would be full dark, and no moons yet to light their way—at least for part of the night. Travel would be difficult, and he was loath to light the lantern. It would be worse for them still if the clouds increased.

"Is this the road to Har Diamante?" Kane asked.

Auraq didn't answer.

"Never imagined the world was so big," Kane said in a quiet voice. Auraq felt him withdraw again and go silent for a while.

Kane gripped Auraq's shoulder. His body was tense against his back. "Up ahead. Movement, I think."

Auraq strained his eyes. Sure enough, there were figures approaching.

"Stay calm," he said. It was getting late for travelers to be out on the road, but not unheard of. The gang after Kane seemed to prefer more furtive tactics. Auraq doubted they would be so bold as to travel in a conspicuous group down a main road. Bandits were always a possibility. But that seemed equally unlikely—for the same reason. Their approach typically was to lie in wait and ambush travelers, catching them unawares. The group ahead made no attempt to hide their numbers.

As they neared, Auraq could see two rode on horseback with four or six more following on foot. He caught a glint of armor and recognized the uniformity of the men marching behind the horses. He recognized what he was seeing and his heart thumped harder.

A slight pull on the reins brought Spirit back to a slow gait. He did not want to appear to be in any hurry.

The two mounted on horses were clearly noble commanders. Any rank insignia was hidden beneath their cloaks, but the king's emblem, the lion and eagle, was clearly displayed on their chest plates. Only noble officers were granted such finery. Plus they carried themselves with the stiff-backed haughtiness only the highborn could achieve. Six pikemen marched in two rows behind the horses, weapons resting on their shoulders. Their march was sloppy, out-of-step. Most wouldn't have noticed it, but Auraq spotted it immediately. It was not due to discipline or training—the men were exhausted. They had been at this all day.

This was no simple transfer of troops. Dressed as they were, it was clear they were on official business. Auraq wondered if the bodies of the assassins had been discovered and this small unit had been called in to investigate, but he dismissed the idea almost immediately. He was feeling jumpy and paranoid. The turnaround was far too quick. The nearest outpost was a full day's ride away. More likely it was the increase in highwaymen along this stretch of road—though he'd done his own part to manage that problem yesterday.

As the distance between them shrank, the commanders pulled their horses to a halt in the middle of the road and waited for Auraq and Kane to meet up with them. The pikemen planted the pikes in the ground at their right sides, backs stiff and chins up, all signs of their fatigue vanishing. The message was clear enough—Auraq was to stop. They could proceed when the commander permitted it.

"Good evening, citizens," said the older of the two commanders as they approached. The words were spoken sharply with little warmth. He pulled off his plumed helm and held it under his arm. He looked to be in his fifties, but still possessed a full head of hair that was entirely gray and seemed to glow in the twilight. Wet with sweat, it clung to the sides of his face and forehead like streaks of melting snow. His white beard was cropped short along his square jaw. Dark eyes watched Auraq intently.

"Good evening to you, my lords," Auraq replied with a nod. He forced levity into his tone that he did not feel.

The commander lifted his chin a bit higher and used a single finger of his gloved hand to move a strand of hair that had fallen across his eye. "By chance, did you come across an inn on the road ahead? Or perhaps a farmhouse that would be suitable for a night's lodging and a meal?"

Auraq felt his lips tighten. The king's law decreed that any of his men had free access to anywhere they chose. Be it a place of business or private home, it made no difference. If no room was available, paying citizens at an inn would be dragged out of their beds so the king's men could have them. "An inn, my lord. The Harpies' Fury. We passed it perhaps three leagues ago."

The commander threw an annoyed glance to the other horseman. "Nothing closer? No homestead that looked decent enough?"

Wouldn't tell you if I had seen one, he thought. "My apologies, my lord. Nothing to my knowledge."

The man stared at Auraq a long moment with a pursed mouth, as if trying to figure out if he was lying. "Late for the two of you to be out on the road," he said.

"Two more leagues and we are home. I would invite you fine lords to board with me and my brother, but alas our house is little more than a shack."

The commander studied Auraq's face a moment, as if he was considering something. Perhaps he suspected Auraq was lying. Or worse, was trying to recall where he'd possibly seen his face before.

Auraq kept his face very, very still and took slow, even breaths.

"Very well," the commander said eventually. "Off with you, then. I'd not linger long on these roads. They are not safe this time of night." He pulled on his helmet, gestured to the others, and they were on the move as a single unit. They swerved around Spirit and marched on their way.

Auraq exhaled slowly, then gently nudged Spirit into motion.

"What just happened?" Kane whispered behind him.

Auraq's hand tightened on the reins. He glanced over his shoulder and then back to the road. "Did you not witness it for yourself? I have no knowledge of their purpose here."

"Not what I mean. Your entire body stiffened up when they were speaking to you."

"Did it, now," he said, hoping it would be the end of it. He applied his heel into Spirit's side again to quicken her gait.

"You were military. You feel no kinship toward them?"

Auraq chuckled sourly. "A kinship, eh?"

"You acted like they were your enemy."

Auraq was quiet a moment. "Don't worry about it," he replied. It was little more than a whisper.

HEAVY CLOUDS rolled in after dusk to cloak the entire sky, turning the night black as pitch.

Auraq had no choice but to light a lantern. It was that or hold up until the clouds broke to allow the summer moons to light their way, an option he was loath to even consider. These hours were critical. They had to put as much distance between them and the site of the attack as possible. Every league out forced their pursuers to widen their search radius. But burning a lantern on a dark night wasn't a much better option. It negated the whole purpose of traveling under the cover of darkness.

He climbed down off the horse and made a blind search for the small oil lantern and flint box in his pack. Sitting on his heels, he arranged everything by feel. He struck the flint stone several times before the saturated wick caught fire and a weak sphere of yellow light pushed back the night.

He took Spirit's lead in one hand and carried the lantern low in the other. Riding in the saddle with the lantern would only increase their chances of being spotted. He had no choice but to walk Spirit until there was enough light to guide their way. It drastically slowed their progress, but as long as he kept the lantern below the height of the grass that grew along the road, they should remain invisible at a distance. He started down the road on foot.

He considered leaving the road entirely and heading out cross-country. But that wasn't without its dangers either.

Eventually, he knew, they would come to a road leading north. Their pursuers would likely expect them to head to one of the closer cities, like Har Diamante or Har Sereno. Auraq had a different plan. They would head toward Har Tesera. It was farther than the other provincial cities, but larger, making it a more likely place to find a mage skilled enough to help Kane find answers. Plus, Auraq knew the city well and had contacts there.

But Har Tesera was on the other side of the Southern Spine. To get there, they would have to cross the long range that swooped through the southern region of the kingdom like a dragon's tail. Even though the hills were nothing like the jagged, snow-covered peaks of the northern range, the terrain would still be rough and travel slow.

"What was it like?" Kane asked from behind him. "Your time in the military."

It was the first Kane had spoken in some time. Auraq had assumed—hoped—he had fallen asleep in the saddle like before. On reflex, Auraq's neck and shoulders tensed up. Somehow, he knew running into those soldiers earlier would spark inquiry on the topic. He let the question linger in the darkness, pretending he hadn't heard it.

Kane wasn't put off by Auraq's silence. "Old Tan would never want to talk about his days in the Lendera Province."

"Then what makes you think I do?" Auraq replied dryly.

"Was it as bad as that?"

Again, Auraq didn't respond. He was not interested in having this conversation. Certainly, not now.

"It's a simple question," Kane pressed. Met with more silence, he continued on, undeterred. "We're stuck with each other apparently. I think perhaps I'm entitled to know a little

56

about you."

"My past is in no way related to the oath I made."

"So, I'm to put my life in your hands without question, but I'm not allowed to know anything about you. That sounds reasonable."

Perhaps if Kane could have seen the look on Auraq's face, he might have backed off. But in the darkness, he was oblivious of the dangerous territory he was stumbling into. Auraq forced his breathing to remain level. The army hadn't defined him, he wanted to say, that stories of his time in the Lendera Province would not provide any personal insight. But it was a lie he didn't think he could pull off, so he kept his tongue.

"I'm curious, is all." Kane plowed onward. "You hear stories. I just wonder if the Volfic Nomads are as terrible as it's told."

"There is a reason they are called barbarians," Auraq found himself answering.

"But all of them?"

Auraq sighed. He was being pulled into this in spite of himself. "Some of what you probably heard is exaggerated. Some of it is not." He wasn't about to get into the specifics. Wasn't about to share his personal accounts of what the Volfic barbarians were like. He could predict what questions were on Kane's tongue. Yes, the warriors would eat the hearts of a respected foe for their strength. No, they did not kill children and eat them on a sacrificial altar. That kind of horseshit was created to scare children and keep them in line.

"Old Tan fought there more than fifty years ago," Kane said, more inwardly than for Auraq to hear. "You think the conflict will ever end?"

"They are tribal. Distrusting of each other as much as us. No single treaty will satisfy all the factions. Only one thing will sate their appetite for war, and no, the king will never relinquish Lendera."

Kane fell quiet for a time as he seemed to chew on that. Thankfully. Auraq forced his mind onto other matters to quash the tide of unwelcome images that rose up from the depths and stormed his thinking, like prisoners escaping from their cells.

"Auraq?" Kane said behind him.

Auraq closed his eyes and fought for patience. He waited for the next irritating question to come, but only silence followed. He turned around.

Kane was looking off in the distance. He lifted his hand and pointed toward the south.

He followed Kane's gaze. A shimmering reddish orange came through a line of trees a hundred paces from the road. It was too wide and too intense to be from a simple campsite. The wind shifted and he caught a wave of the acrid scent of smoke on the air. Whatever was aflame beyond the tree line, it was large and out of control.

"Get down," he said.

"Is that what I think it is?" Kane was already complying as he spoke, swinging his leg over Spirit's rump and lowering himself to the ground.

Auraq handed him the lantern and then pulled the captain's longsword from its sheath. "Stay here."

Kane grabbed his sleeve. "Wait. What are you going to do?" His voice had a wild tone that seemed like something close to panic.

"Take Spirit off the road and hide in the grass." Auraq tried to gently pull his arm away, but Kane tugged on it again, harder.

"Are you always this rash and stupid? You have no idea what's out there."

"Someone might need help."

"This could be a trap, you know. Something to lure us out there."

Auraq had considered that—which was one of the reasons why he was going alone. He didn't believe for an instant this was a coincidence, but he needed to be sure. He needed to learn more of what he was up against.

He took Kane by the wrist and pulled him off his sleeve. "Stay out of sight."

AURAQ HAD both blades from their sheaths as he crouched into a low, stealthy walk through the high grass. Wind gusts continued to sweep the smoke in his direction, and it stung his eyes and inside his nostrils. He could hear the distant roar and pop of the fire. The inferno lit his way through the young grove, and at the far edge, still within the cover of the trees, he knelt to the ground and watched.

A farmer's grain field separated him from the burning buildings. Two of them. The barn was fully engulfed, flames leaping and twisting high into the night air like a horrific dance. Hundreds of glowing embers rose up, spiraling with the smoke and drifting off to threaten areas elsewhere. Part of the roof and eastern wall had already collapsed inward. The second structure was once the farmhouse, but the fire had already ravaged it to a blackened husk. Robbed of its fuel, the fire had died down to a smoldering glow somewhere inside. The fire had likely begun there and spread to the barn.

Auraq watched for movement around the buildings. Nothing stirred. Satisfied, he crept across the field to get closer, staying low. Halfway across, he stopped again and studied the scene. Nothing. No movement anywhere except from the fire itself.

He approached the charred remains of the farmhouse. The heat from the barn felt like a blacksmith's furnace against his face. Twenty paces away, he hunkered down yet again and waited. He strained his ears for any noises beyond the thundering wail of the inferno.

Nothing.

He moved into the farmhouse remains, stepping over what was left of a wall. He trod carefully, making sure he stayed on solid ground. He could easily fall through weakened floorboards into a cellar.

Among the rubble, it did not take him long to find the bodies.

There were five in all. Three adults for certain, two smaller ones of childhood age. Auraq lowered himself next to one of the blackened victims. He quickly held his breath when the smell of cooked flesh entered his nose. The victim's frame was larger than the others, the shape more muscular. Clearly male. The hands were still bound behind him—the twine had not entirely burned away. The chair he had been sitting on had collapsed beneath him. Broken fragments of it were scattered around the body.

He told himself the family was dead before the house was set aflame. He couldn't know that for certain, but believing it helped ease the clenching in his gut. He didn't want to imagine them all burned alive. There was no telling why the family had been butchered. The scene suggested the man had been interrogated.

Of course he had no proof that this was the work of the same assassins that pursued Kane. It could have been caused by bandits, or even a jealous husband seeking revenge for the dalliances of his wife. But Auraq wasn't one to wager good coin on coincidence. And the brutality of this scene went far beyond what he'd seen desperate footpads and brigands carry out.

Perhaps the family was suspected of knowing something, or had become unwitting witnesses to something they had the ill fortune to see. Perhaps the assassins did not want word of their presence in the area leaking out. The fire was set to disguise the massacre.

It seemed too wild a gambit to use the fire to intentionally lure them here—unless they somehow knew they'd come this way. No, something else had transpired, and Auraq knew he would never learn what that was. But this did teach him the lengths these men would go to. He'd seen enough now to know that the strange faction behind this was ruthless beyond anything he'd seen.

He circled around the room looking for any other clues but found nothing.

He left the farmhouse ruins and started back across the field, heading for the trees. But something at the edge of the field caught his eye. He lowered into a squat to investigate a patch of ground. The soil there was loose and soft as if it had been recently tilled. In the middle of the patch was a single print embedded deep into the loamy soil.

It had the shape of the wolf print, but was far too large. Auraq set one sword on the ground and put his hand in it to judge its size. With fingers spread wide, his hand fit into the center of the print with room to spare, and digits extended out from there. At the end of each digit was a deep hole. Whatever it was, it had very long claws. And judging by the depth of the impression, it was a heavy beast.

A bear? Auraq pressed his lips together and rejected the idea. The shape of the print was wrong. No, this was something else, and a part of him already knew what it was. But he didn't want to believe it.

As if responding to his thoughts, a great howl erupted out of the night. It came from some distance away, but it was enough to send a chill down the entire length of his spine. A moment later, a second howl ripped through the silence of the night. This one was closer.

Gods! Who in the fuck were they dealing with?

He had to get to Kane.

Chapter 9

AURAQ RUSHED back to the road. The clouds overhead had begun to break, allowing the summer moons to cast a ghostly pallor on the terrain. He emerged from the tall grass to stand on the bone-colored trail, but had no idea where he was in relation to where he first abandoned Kane. Disoriented by the darkness, he had no way to tell how far he was from that spot. Kane had taken his advice and disappeared entirely in the grass. There wasn't even a sign of the lantern.

Auraq whistled.

Spirit whinnied and cantered out of the grass thirty strides from his position. Moments later, warm light filtered out from the grass, and Kane jogged out from his hiding place too, lantern in hand.

"What did you find?" Kane asked as he drew closer. His tone held a sense of apprehension as if expecting the worst.

Auraq wasn't about to get into that now. He blew out the lantern's flame, quickly attached it to a strap on his pack and hoisted himself up into the saddle. He extended his hand down to Kane. "Up. Now."

Kane gave him a startled look but must have recognized the urgency in his voice, for he took Auraq's hand and allowed him to assist him up into the saddle without question.

As soon as Kane dropped onto the back half of the long, flat saddle, Auraq glanced over his shoulder. "Hold on." He gathered the reins and pushed his heel into Spirit's flank.

Spirit launched into motion. Kane's body jolted backward. Auraq felt Kane grab on to his cloak, then quickly bring his arms around Auraq's waist.

Spirit was soon at a gallop. Auraq steered her off the road

and into the high grass, bearing north. The field gleamed silver in the new moonlight, and the wind rolled the surface like ocean waves. Spirit cut through the field like a galleon. The tops of the stalks whipped against his boots and knees. Auraq knew the risks—if Spirit's hoof hit a rut or a rock at this speed, the beast could go down and easily break a leg. But there were greater dangers out in the night.

"Auraq, what's happening?" Kane's torso was pressed up against his back, and Auraq could feel his rapid breaths against his neck.

A screeching howl ripped out of the darkness, loud and shrill. It was behind them, but not far. Then another came from their right—closer still. Two for certain. Likely more.

Auraq hoped he had gotten out of there fast enough, or that the smoke from the fire masked their scent. If not....

"Hang on," Auraq told him.

Kane's arms tightened around his waist.

They careened through the night at terrific speed and the land fell away behind them. Spirit's head bobbed in rhythm with the pounding of her hooves. She made a sudden lurch and sailed over a shallow gully where a stream cut through the field. Spirit had spotted it and she cleared the width of it with ease before Auraq could even react. As she landed on the far side, Kane slammed against Auraq's back and as he bounced back again, he listed perilously on the narrow back of Spirit's flat saddle. Auraq reached behind and flattened a wide palm to Kane's hip to keep him seated.

More shrill howls cut through the darkness. The sound sent duck flesh spreading across Auraq's shoulders and down his arms. They were closer. The odds that they had escaped their notice seemed bleak. And it sounded as if there were three of them.

One was deadly enough.

They cut through a small grove of trees, branches smacking against them, threatening to unhorse them both. Auraq lowered himself in the saddle and allowed Spirit to keep her speed. When they broke free of the trees, Auraq's eyes swept the dark countryside.

Up ahead, the terrain made an abrupt rise. It swooped upward like a gigantic wave. Its crest was a high ridge that ran the length of the horizon. He tracked his eyes down its length, searching.

There.

He found what he was looking for westward, hugging the ridgeline. The structure rose up above the trees, standing out against the dense wood squeezing in around it. He pulled hard on Spirit's rein to guide her left. Spirit's chest and shoulders were wet, but the howling around them drove Auraq to push her onward.

Spirit took the steep rise to the top of the hillside at a canter, encouraged with small kicks of his heel against her flank and clicks of his tongue. They broke over the rocky crown and followed the ridgeline along an old pathway that wended through the old-growth trees. They broke from the wood at the heel of the old watchtower Auraq had spotted from below.

Auraq pulled back hard on Spirit's reins. As she skidded to a halt, Kane dropped off over her rump and Auraq leaped down after. The tower was centuries old. Part of one side had crumbled away, leaving a gaping hole and a massive pile of stone around it—damage taken from some long-forgotten war.

Despite the damage, the majority of the structure seemed solid and secure.

Auraq scurried over the rock pile to enter through the wide opening. The space at the bottom of the tower was vacant except for gathered leaves and the collapsed portions of the outer wall. Whatever had taken out the wall had also destroyed the lower section of the stone staircase that would have climbed the inner wall, leaving the upper part undamaged, like a leg that's been amputated from the knee down. The first stair leading to the second floor of the tower began about an arm's length above Auraq's head.

Perfect.

When he climbed back out of the tower, Kane was holding Spirit's reins. His eyes were wide with concern. The horse was stamping the ground and tossing her head nervously. She could smell them.

They did not have much time.

"Help with her saddle," he told Kane.

Kane nodded without question and immediately started to loosen the straps of her tack. Auraq dug into one of the packs, rummaging through the bottom until his fingers found the leather flask. He pulled it out and shook it. Half-empty. It wouldn't be enough.

More chilling howls ripped through the darkness around them. Not from below in the field, but up on the ridge with them.

"They're closer," Kane said.

Auraq helped him with the last of the straps holding Spirit's tack, then lifted off the saddle and dropped it unceremoniously onto the ground. He gathered up one of the packs, the crossbow, and the quiver of bolts and thrust them into Kane's arms. He slapped Spirit's rump and whistled three high-pitched tweets. Spirit flung her head up, whinnied, and took off at a canter into the trees.

"Where is she going?" Kane asked, alarm in his voice.

"To find somewhere safe." He took everything back from Kane and handed over the leather flask.

"Listen. Go inside the tower and rub the contents of this all over your clothes. Use all of it. Understand?"

Kane held the flask up to the moonlight. "What is it?"

"Hunter's oil. It'll mask your scent."

Kane's eyes widened. "What about you?"

"I'm going to have to improvise. Go."

The main ingredients in hunter's oil were hemlock and cedar, which were common in these parts. At least he hoped so. He plunged into the thick underbrush surrounding the tower. It was too dark to see the types of plants around him. He had to let his nose and his hands guide him. As he pushed through the branches, he pulled any foliage he encountered through his hands and held his fingers to his nose, waiting for the distinctive aroma he'd recognize. He circled the perimeter of the tower, not wanting to delve too deep into the wood—it would mean his death if he strayed too far and could not find his way back.

More howling ripped through the night. They were closing in.

His heart pounded in his ears. There didn't seem to be any of the right types of evergreens in this region. He was quickly running out of time. Heading back and coming up with a new plan was fast becoming a better option than stumbling alone in the dark wood. He was on the verge of heading back when he brought his hand to his face again and the familiar pungent smell reached deep into his nose.

Hemlock.

He sighed in relief as he unsheathed his short sword. With quick chops, he removed a number of the branches, then scooped them into his arms. He doubled back to the tower.

Kane was in the tower rubbing his palms against the thighs of his pants.

"Use all of it?" Auraq asked.

Kane nodded.

Auraq dropped the branches where the old base of the staircase once stood and signaled Kane over. He wove his fingers together, palms up, and held them waist high.

"Step here first, then onto my shoulder, then climb onto the stairs above. Got it?"

Kane nodded again. He put his hands on Auraq's shoulders and for several moments stood in front of him as if he forgot what to do. Then he took in a long breath and stepped up into his hands. In a single heartbeat, he was up and over the edge of the lowest, undamaged stair.

One by one, Auraq threw the supplies up to Kane: the pack, the crossbow, quiver, and finally the collection of branches. "Stand back," he told Kane.

He made a standing jump toward the lowest stair. His fingers caught the ledge, and his body slammed against the rough broken wall of stone beneath it.

Another howl. This time it was right outside the tower.

Auraq used every bit of strength in his arms and shoulders to hoist himself up. Kane grabbed his jerkin behind his neck and pulled too. Auraq's boots slid down the rock face until the toe found purchase on a lip of stone. He held his breath, fearful of making a grunt or growl that would be heard outside the tower. He rose up, arms and shoulders burning, until his torso flopped over the edge of the stair like a fish throwing itself onto a dock. He brought his right leg up and over. Kane strained and tugged on him until Auraq rolled over awkwardly onto his back.

Auraq scooted up a few more steps from the drop-off, panting. He grabbed branches and started rubbing the foliage over his leather armor. He figured the freshly cut branches themselves would be enough to disguise his scent, but spreading some directly on the source wouldn't hurt. Kane opened his mouth to say something, but Auraq thrust his hand over his mouth and made a quick shake of his head, then pointed below.

A dark shape moved over the rock pile and into the tower below.

It slunk in low like a black fog rolling in, and seemed to be made of the night itself. In the darkness, Auraq couldn't fully make out its shape, but it was unquestionably larger than a wolf or a bear. It had an elongated head and four limbs, but it skulked more than walked, with its belly close to the ground. The weak moonlight that filtered in gave mere glimpses of detail. The teeth and claws were yellow, the fur on its hide looked more like iron nails, and the eyes that scanned the inside of the tower were a deep, glowing red.

Its paws made no sound as it circled below, but Auraq could hear a growl deep in its throat each time it exhaled.

It circled twice and sniffed the air, then snarled and snapped as if it knew something was amiss.

Auraq gently lifted the crossbow and positioned his hand under it. He kept the air locked in his chest, though his lungs burned. He slid a bolt from the quiver and placed it in the track. He wouldn't risk cocking it—the sound would get the beast's attention for sure. But he would be ready to fire the bolt between its eyes if the beast looked up and discovered them.

A last resort. If it wasn't an instant kill, any sound it made would signal the others to come. At that point, the hemlock wouldn't matter anymore.

The beast scanned one last time, then bounded out of the tower with a single leap and was absorbed by the night.

Auraq lowered the arm holding the crossbow. He made eye contact with Kane and gestured "up" with a lift of his chin. They tiptoed up the old stairs, still unwilling to make a sound, and climbed until the stairwell broke through to the first level. It was a single room, vacant and dark, spanning the full width of the tower. There were no windows, only vertical arrow slits that encircled the space at regular intervals. Moonlight pressed in through the narrow spaces and splashed onto the stone floor in blue rectangles.

Kane crossed to the opposite side of the room, as far from the staircase as possible. He hugged himself as if cold and stared at his feet.

Auraq went to the arrow slits, one by one, and scanned the dark countryside. He knew there was little chance of him catching sight of one, but he felt better doing it all the same. He heard one more howl break the silence of the night, but it was off in the distance now.

He dug around in his pack and until he found a silver flask. He crossed the chamber, and from behind, he tapped Kane on the upper arm with the flask. "Here."

Kane looked over his shoulder at the flask. "I'm fine."

"Drink it," Auraq told him with some force to his voice.

Kane threw him an irritated look but took the flask. He pulled the cork from the top and tilted it back against his lips. His face puckered and his eyes squeezed shut as he swallowed the liquid down. He made a few sputtering coughs and looked at the flask as if he'd just drank poison.

"This is terrible."

"Doesn't matter. It does what it needs to."

"What was that, Auraq?"

"You wouldn't believe me if I told you."

Kane turned to him and shot him a hard glare.

"A wolvren," Auraq said. "That was a wolvren."

Kane held his eyes on him a long moment, then brought

the flask up again. The chain attached to the cork rattled against the side of the flask as Kane's hand shook.

"Yes, they are in fact real," Auraq said, anticipating the next obvious question. "Not just stories to scare children." He reached for the flask and brought it to his own lips. The liquor burned the back of his throat, and his eyes watered. Gods, it *was* terrible. He'd forgotten just how bad. It had been all he could afford when he purchased it, and at the time, it was better than going without. He handed it back to Kane and leaned against the wall.

"You've seen one before?" Kane asked.

"No, but I've seen what they do." He took a deep breath, remembering. He forced a softer tone. "Finish the rest of that. For now, we're safe. They appear to have moved on."

"For now," Kane repeated dourly.

"We'll leave in the morning. Get some sleep." Auraq lowered himself down, sliding his back down the wall. He propped his forearms onto his raised knees and let his head droop forward.

"I thought traveling by day was a bad idea."

"We'll have to take our chances. Wolvren don't care for sunlight." He didn't know much about them, but he knew they were mainly nocturnal hunters. That didn't mean they wouldn't be out in the day—just unlikely.

The bigger concern was who held their leash. Wolvren did not run free in these lands. If they were here, they were under someone's control. Someone powerful. And their presence signaled a new level of pursuit. After their failure at the campsite, the organization behind this was no longer taking chances. It raised a sobering question. What other dark and vile resources were they going to throw their way?

He dropped his head back against the wall and closed his eyes. Exhaustion was setting in deep. Despite the recent excitement, sleep would come easily.

Sometime later, he was distantly aware of Kane sitting down on the floor near him.

"Woke up," Kane said. "Expected I'd find you gone."

Auraq glanced his way. "Why would you think that?"

"Most would have scampered off, you know. Given up. Not you. Why *are* you still here, Auraq?"

"I told you. I made a promise."

"You take all your promises this seriously?"

Auraq didn't know how to answer that. Duty was a part of it, certainly. Promises should never be made lightly, especially to the dying. And he wasn't ever one to walk away from his commitments. But strangely, Kane was right. Something else kept him around. This oath seemed to leverage him somehow in a way he didn't understand. Was it Old Tan's dying words? Talk of his soul, and the Gods seeing him and his crimes?

Did he feel the weight of their eyes on him?

"I take it back," Kane said.

"Take what back?" he replied groggily, not bothering to open his eyes. He had been drifting off, he realized, his consciousness melting away. Kane's voice hooked him back.

"That I didn't need you to help me." Kane was looking down at his hands. "I'd be dead right now."

"Probably."

"No one would ever believe me if I told them wolvren were after me," Kane said. "Auraq? What does all this mean?"

Auraq opened his eyes a fraction and glanced over at Kane, who sat one stride away from him, hugging his knees. "It means that whatever that mark is on your arm, it has made you a very powerful enemy." Even more powerful than he initially thought. And for the first time, he started to question if he would be enough to keep Kane alive.

Chapter 10

THEY ARRIVED in Har Tesera an hour before dawn.

The sky was easing from black to indigo when Spirit lumbered up the road to the first buildings at the edges of the outer city. A sash of gold streaked across the horizon to the east—the first hint of the coming day.

Auraq dropped down from the saddle. Reaching his arms up high over his head in a full stretch, he lifted his chin up to one side until his neck made a satisfying crack. Another long night on the cold, rocky ground of the Southern Spine's foothills left him stiff in his lower back, legs, and shoulders. Before the sky had even begun to lighten, he had roused Kane from sleep to make an early start of it. And though they'd been on the road for some time already, the night air that had seeped deep into his muscles was slow to surrender its grip.

He took Spirit's reins in his hand. Hoping to loosen his joints, he decided to proceed the rest of the way on foot.

Crossing the Spine had been harrowing, and he'd pushed both Kane and Spirit to their limit. The terrain was rugged and desolate, the little-used trail often treacherous. But after two full days of travel, Auraq was confident they had slipped through the assassins' net. At least for now. He wasn't about to underestimate this organization again. A city like Har Tesera was an easy place for someone to vanish if they wanted to, but he wasn't about to presume they were safe. The organization after Kane was strangely powerful—the wolvren were proof enough of that. And if they were as formidable as he imagined, they would have a presence here in the city—he was certain of it.

Seeing the city walls in the distance made his insides twist. Strange how the fates could manipulate—he vowed he'd never return. But here he was, once again. He had no intention of being here long. If all went according to plan, he could pass Kane on to someone better qualified to help and protect him before the assassins discovered their presence.

Kane groggily clutched the horn in front of him to keep his body rooted in the saddle. But as Spirit clopped along, Kane's head and shoulders swayed and bobbed like an ocean buoy.

The outer city of Har Tesera was already beginning to pulse with life, even at this early hour. Most were women getting an early start to their chores before crowds and the heat of the day commandeered the streets. They toiled through the dirt streets with their heads low, woven baskets or yokes with dangling water buckets on their shoulders. Some were laborers shuffling off to their job sites. Some were men stumbling home from the tavern stools they'd occupied all night. Enterprising vendors had set up carts along the roadway, selling bowls of hot broth or small, warm bread rolls.

Har Tesera was small compared to some of the cities to the north, but it was by no means a country village. It was one of the largest seats in the region and was growing. Too quickly for the city to manage, in fact. It had outgrown the confines of its ancient walls and spilled over the flat plains like a spreading patch of mold on old bread. Some years ago, a new temporary gate had been constructed where the main road skewered into the expansion, but that too had outlived its efficacy, for the new boundary had reached even beyond that.

Auraq approached the outer gate with Spirit and a dozing Kane in tow. The structure was wooden and roughly built. It looked more like something the army would have constructed at the border than what a thriving city with ample access to stonemasons and laborers would build. The years had been unkind to it. The wood was warped and bleached a sickly gray, and it leaned precariously to the side.

The guards flanking the opening didn't even raise a curious eyebrow at them as they approached. Auraq expected at least a question or a scrutinizing look, but they were flagged onward with impatience.

Fighting within the Lendera Provence had spiked once again, sending a fresh resurgence of refugees eastward. The rumor of work brought them to Har Tesera. Auraq and Kane must have blended in well with the unhappy dregs that flooded into the city daily. The city didn't care who occupied the outer perimeter. The inner city, within the ancient stone wall, would be another matter entirely.

Auraq clicked his tongue to keep Spirit moving and passed under the gate, hoping it wouldn't choose that moment to collapse.

The buildings of the outer city were built in clusters rather than in any planned arrangement—a symptom of rapid expansion. All were wooden and hastily constructed. The streets were unpaved, and the rain from the night before had turned the heaviest trafficked sections into a smelly river of mud.

Behind him, Kane began to show more life as they forged deeper into the outer city. Auraq watched him as he scanned the unhappy mass of dwellings around him. He had never seen a city. His whole life had been spent in a village that probably had no more than one hundred people living there.

"How can all these people live in one place?" Kane said, his face showing his confusion.

Auraq shook his boot to fling off a clump of mud that had caked onto the sole. "Not even in the city proper yet."

"How do they live like this?"

"They scrape by. Somehow." In truth, it was worse than he remembered. Dirtier. More depressed. The flow of refugees was taking a greater toll on Har Tesera than Auraq realized. The barbarian attacks must have really ramped up to cause such an influx of people fleeing their homes.

"Back home, I'd cross paths with maybe ten others during a whole day," Kane said. He swatted at a fly that buzzed around his head. "Some days that was eight too many."

Few businesses had established themselves out here beyond the wall, few tradesmen setting up shop. The vast majority of buildings were residential—shacks and hovels likely owned by the richer folk in town who had the means for a quick construction and the vision to recognize an opportunity for income. Rents were likely far too high for what people were getting. But what choice did they have? Move on to the next city? Return home and risk a Volfic raid?

Shielded by the Southern Spine, the duchies to the south didn't see this problem. Those regions had a reputation of being less charitable to outsiders, anyway.

The main road inclined toward the old outer wall, which had once been the city's first line of defense. Some of it had fallen into noticeable disrepair. Today, it would have trouble warding off an army of angry farmhands bearing sticks and pickaxes. The guard presence at the old gate was more conspicuous than at the makeshift gate behind them. Auraq counted at least ten guardsmen as they drew closer, some on the wall overhead, some on the ground. As he suspected, the city was more intent on keeping the riffraff out of the better neighborhoods.

One of the guards flanking the opening yawned and peeled himself from the wall as they approached. He planted his long pike in the ground and attempted to look official.

"State your business here," he said.

"I live here," Auraq replied. He could feel Kane's eyes on him as Kane tried to figure out whether he was lying to the guards.

The guard held Auraq's gaze for a moment, lips pursed a little. Apparently he didn't care enough to question Auraq further. "Go along, then," he told them with a flick of the head toward the open portcullis. Then he stared back over the road as if they were already gone.

They passed through the arched opening of the Outer South Gate and then crossed over the stone bridge that spanned the dry moat—the city had not maintained it for at least a century. At the far end of the bridge was the Inner South Gate set into the larger interior wall.

The grandeur of the South Gate was renowned throughout the kingdom. Two stone giants stood on either side of the passage, facing each other as if gripped in battle. Their massive hands bore the staves of great axes that rose up and crossed over the center of the arch. Both blades were made of solid gold and reflected the low morning sun in dazzling brilliance. They flared out like enormous wings.

In generations past, this was a great symbol of power and wealth.

They passed beneath the statues and into the heavy darkness of the gateway taking them through the thick wall. Auraq glanced up at Kane. "Prepare yourself."

"For what?"

"The city."

And in moments, as they exited the ancient wall, Har Tesera crashed in around them.

Dawn had broken now, so the city's industry and commerce was at full-sail to take advantage of the coming day. The small plaza beyond the gate was a tangle of oxcarts and carriages preparing to leave the city. The guards sporadically ran searches for contraband, but that didn't seem to be the case today. A loaded bullock cart had lost its wheel and blocked access to the gate. Merchants behind the upset cart shouted and cursed, but the owner was more concerned about losing his cargo than moving out of the way. The guards didn't seem to notice any of it.

The congested plaza funneled into a narrow shop-lined street, filled from curb to curb with swirling throngs of people. People were shouting everywhere. Shop owners called out to lure in customers or hurled insults at neighboring competitors.

Kane climbed down from Spirit to join Auraq. "I can barely hear myself think here. And how does anyone tolerate the smell?"

The smell of shit and decay was nearly enough to overpower even Auraq. Either the city had grown worse over the years, or he'd forgotten how bad it was. "You should remain on the horse."

"Legs are sore. And I would think you wouldn't want me so conspicuous."

He had a point. "There is a risk of us getting separated."

"You are, by far, the largest man on this street. I think I could find you easily enough should that happen."

Kane walked a little behind Auraq as he shouldered his way through the churning throng. "I could hold on to your hand if it'll make you feel better."

Auraq didn't bother responding. He was focused on the people around him.

"Is it true what you told the guard?" Kane asked. "You live here?" Auraq would have expected him to be intimidated by the crowd and the congestion, but the opposite seemed true. He seemed oddly invigorated.

"Do you ever answer a question directly when asked?"

"When it's necessary."

"Let's pretend that it is."

Auraq bit the inside of his lip. This was not a conversation he'd wanted broached. "Yes. At one time."

A group of prelates shuffled past. Kane was momentarily distracted by them. His eyes tracked the holy assemblage as they glided through the street as if they were the only ones occupying it. Their colored sashes caught the wind and fluttered like banners, shimmering in the bright morning sun. Living in eastern Har Purdea, it was unlikely that Kane had ever seen more than one prelate at a time. He certainly had never seen anything other than an acolyte with only a white sash about his shoulder. Prelates that ascended higher in the order would not bother with such remote places as West Tunniville.

Beyond the gate district, the streets were still brimming with an ambling populace, people strolling about to peer into shop windows and squeeze the fruit on display, but the crowd's temperament was less frenzied. Auraq abandoned the main thoroughfare and guided Spirit deeper into the city by way of the less trodden streets. The course was familiar to him—more indirect perhaps, but less congested. Spirit seemed to remember the route and needed little urging along the way.

"I hope you know where we're going," Kane said.

They entered the fenced grounds of a small stable. Auraq waited a few moments. When no one came out, he put two fingers to his lips and whistled. A pudgy lad lumbered out at an unhurried pace to meet them, rubbing his eyes with the heel of his hand.

"Yeah?" the lad said, scratching his ass.

"Brushed, watered, and fed," Auraq replied gruffly. He raked his eyes over the lad from foot to head. He worried that the insides of the stable would be as unkempt as he was.

"How long?" the youth asked, sounding bored, taking the reins in his hand.

"Overnight. Maybe longer." He unlatched one of the packs from the back of the saddle, the one that contained his personal effects, and slung it over his shoulder. "I will be back to check on her care."

The veiled threat didn't seem to have any impact. The lad nodded with a yawn and led Spirit off across the yard toward the stable.

Auraq watched him with a tight brow until both Spirit and the lad disappeared through the stable door.

"Doesn't exactly inspire confidence, that one," Kane said. "Surprised you trust him with your horse."

Auraq glanced at Kane. "I don't." But he did trust the stable's owner. He would make a point to call on him later. "Follow me."

"Where are we going?"

"Not far."

Kane sighed but nodded and a fell in step behind Auraq as he took to the street again.

A short distance along an uphill street, they turned into a smaller dead-end alley lined with workshops. The symphony of construction—pounding, hammering, sawing—filtered out to the street from the buildings around them. Auraq crossed the alley's length to where it ended. A wooden placard of a barrel hung over the finely carved door—the most beautiful of all the doors that faced the alley. Perhaps the most beautiful door in the entire district.

Hand on the latch, Auraq filled his lungs, then pulled open the door. He held it open for Kane, who gave him a strange look as he passed through the threshold of the barrel-maker's shop. Auraq released the air in a slow exhale and braced himself for what was to come. He entered after Kane and pulled the door shut behind him.

After the bright sunlight outside, the inside of the shop seemed grim and dark. There was one small window, which did little to dispel the gloom. The morning light that streaked in lit the pallid fog of tallow smoke and dust that churned thick through the air. Auraq's heart skipped. The smell of the place triggered something long forgotten in his brain, but he shoved it down before his body could respond to it further.

The shopkeeper was behind a small counter and had his back to them when they entered. Hunched over, he rhythmically moved back and forth as he planed a strip of oak. He dusted off his hands on his apron and turned around. When he saw who stood at his door, his face hardened.

"You've a set of balls on you coming here," the man grumbled.

He looked older than Auraq remembered. He was still fit and muscular, but his beard had turned whiter at the end, and he had let it grow to a grizzled length.

Auraq was not surprised by the reception—only surprised it wasn't more outright hostile. He wasn't being chased out the door by a madman with an ax. Already this was going better than he expected. "I need your help."

"What a surprise," the man said. "In hot water again, are you?"

Auraq ignored that. "Need the use of your room in back for a few nights."

"That so? As I recall, there are plenty of inns here in Har Tesera. I will even grant you the coin."

Auraq could feel Kane's eyes on him. "Not for me." He gestured with a tilt of his head. "For him."

The man took notice of Kane for the first time. He set the plane down absently. "Who is this?" he asked with suspicion.

Auraq turned to Kane, who was staring back at him with narrow eyes. "Kane, meet Malgar Greystone, master barrel maker and the most cantankerous bastard you will ever meet. He has a small room in the back with a cot. You'll be sleeping here."

"I beg your pardon?" Malgar protested. "I get no say here?"

Kane looked him hard in the eyes, annoyed. "Nor I? We passed plenty of inns on our way here."

"Inns can be searched, and watched. You'll be safer here."

"Safe from what?" asked Malgar. His cheeks were turning red.

Auraq slowly turned to face him again. "Kane is in danger. By no fault of his own. I have been charged with his safety."

Malgar made a low grunt, which might have been a laugh. "Oh, playing at being a hero now, are we?"

Auraq ignored that jab too. "Stay put," he told Kane. "Don't go out without me. Get some sleep."

"And where are you going?" Kane's irritation was mounting.

"To find out something of what we're dealing with."

"Oh no." Kane grabbed the sleeve of his tunic and tugged hard. He leaned in closer. "You're not stranding me here alone with a man who clearly wants you dead," he said through gritted teeth.

Auraq shifted his eyes to meet the old man's, who glowered back at him, his arms folded over his chest. Yes, it was true. The man may not wish him dead but wouldn't mourn him if he was. "He is a good man," he said, "and will do the right thing."

"I'd feel safer with you," Kane said. "And more welcome."

"Too risky if I'm going to be asking questions." Auraq readjusted the pack on his shoulder and pushed the door open, allowing in the morning sun. "You'll feed him something?" he called to Malgar from the doorway, not really looking his direction.

Malgar threw up his arms. "Oh, of course, Your Worship. I'll put out the finest spread I can manage. I've got nothing else to do today."

Kane stepped closer and dropped his voice further. "This

is a terrible idea."

"You can trust him."

"I don't trust anybody. Except maybe you."

"You can trust *him*. Fully," Auraq replied. "He's my father."

One final time, he glanced at Malgar, who was already returning to his work, grumbling to himself. All things considered, it had gone better than he could have hoped. Satisfied, he left the shop.

Chapter 11

AURAQ FELT some guilt needle him as he took to the streets. Kane would likely be forced to take the brunt of his father's annoyance. He could be gruff and irascible, but his rancor had little teeth. He'd complain the entire time, but in the end, he would take care of Kane and make certain he was safe. Other than himself, there was no one Auraq trusted more to do that.

The city felt oddly comfortable. He hadn't expected the warmth of nostalgia to accompany him as his legs took him almost by their own memory through the labyrinthine streets. He'd decided to come here in part because he knew the city. Knew equally well the crowded plazas and the darkened alleys. Despite the years since his boots marched these cobbles, nothing had changed. Not really. A city a thousand years old wasn't going notice his absence. There lay the comfort in it—the stability, the timelessness. Unlike himself, returning as someone he never expected to be.

He forced himself back to the present. Yes, he knew this city, but that too was a danger he had to account for. People knew him here.

In short order he saw the familiar placard hanging from an iron rod over a door. It was in the shape of a small pointy-eared devil holding a foaming tankard. The Saucy Imp.

More memories of an old life swirled around him as he pushed his way into the tavern. The smell that greeted him, the squeak of the hinges as the door swung away from him, even the feel of the door against his hand triggered something mournful in the back of his brain.

The room had an unnatural hush as if it were waiting for bad news. Even at this early hour, a few people occupied tables, and a few more were hunched over the counter. No one spoke.

Most patrons leaned in over their tankards of ale, protecting them with two hands, and stared off at nothing. Auraq's entrance didn't stir enough interest for anyone to look at the door.

The barkeep was behind the counter, sleeves of his tunic rolled up to the elbow as he rinsed out tankards in a bucket and stacked them on a shelf over the tapped barrels. Like the rest of Har Tesera, he was much as Auraq remembered him. Perhaps a bit more gray was in the long hair he had tied off into a tail, and the lines across his brow and around his mouth were deeper. He was tall and lean, yet Auraq could tell by the shape of his shoulders that he had maintained his strength. He could still, no doubt, toss a drunkard out onto the street with little effort. Auraq had learned that lesson himself a time or two. The man didn't look up until Auraq was almost at the counter. His brow tightened with curiosity, then a moment later, his eyes up lit with recognition.

"Ho! Look here. I daresay a specter has wandered into my tavern."

"This was my old haunt, after all," Auraq replied dryly. "How are you, Ruck?"

The barkeep shrugged with his hands in the water. "Still breathing. Never thought to see your mug brighten up my establishment again. Heard you'd gone off to some far-flung part of the kingdom to kill barbarians and steal their gold."

"For a while," Auraq said.

"They finally get tired of your cheery disposition and kick you out?"

"Something like that."

Ruck shook the water from his hands and dried them on his apron. He looked Auraq up and down and his expression shifted to something more serious. "Surprised to see you're still among us, if you'll forgive my frankness. You had a penchant for finding trouble."

"Still do."

Ruck made a low chuckle and reached for a tankard. "You preferred my red, if I remember rightly." He turned toward the barrel behind him, but Auraq held out his palm.

"Not today, Ruck."

Ruck raised a puzzled brow at him, but returned the tankard to the shelf without a challenge. He leaned back and crossed his arms. "So what then brings you around?"

"Left my horse at your stable this morning."

Ruck's eyes rounded. "That's your mare? Fine beast, that one."

"That she is. Your stablehand up for the task of caring for her?"

The barkeep shook his head. "Lazy fucker. He's my nephew, a promise to my sister, but I'm damn near ready to ship him back to her. I'll see to it that the beauty is well cared for. How long?"

"A day or two." He reached into the pouch at his belt and pulled out a few coins and handed them over. "That cover it?"

Ruck bounced them in his palm so they jingled happily. He pressed his lips together and nodded. "You've a look about you that there's something else on your mind."

Auraq shrugged. "Looking for Bendo. He still frequent the place?"

"Bendo? Gods! Not seen him in ages. We're too lowly and ill-bred for his perfumed ass nowadays."

Auraq lifted his brow.

"Not heard? He's *Lord* Bennidar now. He's a gate captain of the fucking city guard, if you can believe it."

Auraq couldn't help but show his surprise. He never thought he'd hear of Bendo falling in with a respectable crowd and making a legitimate name for himself. There was a story in that transformation, surely. "Know what bar counter he leans against now?"

"No idea. Some place you or I wouldn't be welcome, for sure. But I hear he lords over the north gate. That's a place to start, I guess. Don't expect no happy reunion, though. What you in need of him for, anyway?"

"Information." Auraq turned to leave. "Good to see you."

"Leaving my tavern without a drop," Ruck replied, shaking his head. "Never thought I'd see that. What the fuck happened to you out there?"

"See you around, Ruck." He pulled the door open and pushed back into the stark afternoon sunlight.

AURAQ RETURNED to the network of streets and steered himself east. He skirted past the warehouse district and river district, then cut through the adjacent market district, avoiding the square, which would be packed with throngs of shoppers this time of day. Beyond that, familiarity dropped off around him— in small amounts at first, but when he passed through a wide stone gate, the city morphed into something foreign.

It was the one region of Har Tesera he didn't know at all. He never had any real cause to go there. It had nothing for him. And as soon as he crossed over into it, he fought the urge to turn about and head back again.

The streets widened and were void of debris, horse shit, and even loose stones. No filth in the gutters. The buildings that lined the streets no longer crowded into each other. They reached higher and their balconies were adorned with brightly colored banners, as if each were competing for attention. These were no wooden structures faced with white plaster or made of the same ubiquitous gray stone found in the quarries near the mountain. These were built of a beautiful deep-red stone. They had elaborate turrets at their tops, gargoyles peering down to the street, and masterfully carved doors that made his father's shop door seem simple and plain.

This was the Academy District.

The region wasn't consumed by the campus alone, but it did cater almost exclusively to its attendants, scholars, and alum. The academy itself was perched on the crest of a hill and was surrounded by dormitory, tenements, and various shops that supplied students with whatever strange requirements aspiring mages might need for their studies. It was peculiar and unsettling in a way—a city within a city, with its own wall further emphasizing its isolation and elitism. Self-sufficient and largely autonomous.

He didn't care for mages, as a rule. He didn't understand anything of their power and those few he'd met in his lifetime wielded a particular arrogance that grated him. Knowing he was now surrounded by their kind was unnerving. Especially ones just learning their craft. He knew the danger a young soldier could cause as he learned to wield a sword properly. Gods only knew what kind of devastation a young mage might cause when mistakes were made.

He felt unwelcome, like an infiltrator or spy. He couldn't help but scowl as he marched up the hill toward the academy buildings.

The grandiose stone structure at the top of the hill was the main hall for the academy and the only place that nonattendees like himself were welcome. He made his way up the hundred or so steps to the entrance. A broad stone archway overhead was formed by two reclining male nudes reaching over the opening and holding some celestial object at the apex of the arch. At first Auraq thought it reflected the bright morning sunlight, but then realized the side of the building was in shade. The strange orb, held at the tips of the stone fingers, glowed of its own power.

Ten paces within the building was a round reception desk occupied by a young man in a novice's robes. When Auraq approached, the man was hunched over a weighty tome splayed open on the counter. He held up his head with fist propped under his chin, his eyes scanning blurrily across the tiny handwritten script.

Auraq leaned both hands on the counter and waited. Engaged in the book, the man did not realize Auraq was there, or at least pretended not to notice him. Auraq cleared his throat.

"Yes," the man said, not bothering to look up.

"I would like to know how I go about speaking with a mage."

"One in particular?"

"Not necessarily."

The man pushed himself away from the book, stifling a yawn. He turned and grabbed a sheet of parchment from behind him, and his quill and inkwell. He set them all up in front of him and for the first time looked up directly at Auraq.

The man appeared to be about to say something but then, for a moment, seemed stunned into silence. For several heartbeats he just stared back at Auraq with slightly wider eyes and his mouth open a bit. "Uh...." he stammered a moment longer. The man's eyes were crystalline blue, sharp and striking. His sand-colored hair was pulled back into a tail, but many of the strands had come loose and dangled onto his face. His fair skin was turning red at the cheeks. "I'll... uh... need to know the nature of your inquiry."

"Why?"

The man seemed unprepared for such a question. "So... we can best match with your needs of course." He glanced up at Auraq but then shifted his eyes away as if it stung to look directly at him. But in that brief moment, Auraq could feel the intensity of his gaze. It made his insides quiver for some reason.

"Isn't one mage much like another?"

"Hardly," the man said with a smile, clearly amused at Auraq's naïveté in such matters. Again, he looked up into Auraq's eyes and immediately looked away. "Our masters specialize in a variety of disciplines. I assume your interest isn't purely academic."

Auraq frowned. "It is a private matter."

"I see," said the novice. Something shifted in his face. Auraq felt compelled to explain more—he didn't want him thinking it was something torrid or unseemly, like sores he picked up from a dockside whore. "Can you provide me with anything?" he asked Auraq. "I would want to direct you to someone who could assist you properly,"

"It is not for me, actually. And it's not in regard to any malady." He didn't know why it was important to say that. "If that helps."

The man smiled warmly back at him. "Not really. But I will do what I can to find someone... well-rounded in their training." He reached across his counter and put a hand on Auraq's forearm. "Whatever your concern, you needn't worry. We adhere to a strict policy of discretion here."

Auraq fought the urge to pull his arm away. Not out of revulsion or offense, but from something else. Embarrassment perhaps. The attention made him want to shy away.

He was not so thick as to not recognize the man's attraction toward him. Various women had been forward with him before, but this was a first. He didn't know how to respond, so he just kept very still.

"Thank you," he said.

The man lifted his hand from Auraq's arm and reached for his quill. Auraq found himself exhaling. He wasn't even aware he'd been holding his breath.

"I can pen you in for late in the afternoon, if that will do."

Auraq tried to hide his surprise. He didn't know what to expect, but that was far sooner than he anticipated. Had the novice cut him to the front of the line? "This afternoon is fine," he replied.

"At the sixth bell, then. Come back then and one of our masters will see to you. What name should I record?" He dipped the quill in the well and waited with the tip over the parchment.

Auraq told him.

The man repeated the name as if it possessed something wondrous about it as he scribed it onto the ledger. He looked up and smiled again. "My name is Hargan, should you have need of it later."

"Many thanks, Hargan." Auraq bowed and returned a polite smile. As he left the building, he could feel Hargan's eyes on him. He wondered what Hargan would think when later he returned for their appointment with Kane. He wondered why it mattered.

HE LEFT the Academy District and veered north.

The district that spooned up against the North Gate stirred more memories for him. Late-night mischief had brought him once to the guard office there. The incident landed him in a dark cell for a night and sparked a mighty row between him and his father the next day. It was, in part, what first led him down the path of joining up with the king's army.

The memory of that night itched like an old scar as he approached the compound entrance. The army was supposed to redirect the path he'd been on in his youth. And for a while it had, he supposed. Structure and discipline had tamped down his youthful restlessness, and hard training had shelved the skills he used for skulking about the city and replaced them with ones more useful in war. But he could not help but wonder what his life would have been like had he not taken up the legion sword. Would he have found his way on his own? Or was he simply fated for a tarnished life?

He skirted around a group of young cadets in the yard running through drills with practice swords. The trainer circulated through them, cursing and slapping the backs of heads for their poor stance and sloppy grip. "Boar's tooth, you idiot!" he shouted. "Step in to bury the blade or end up with his edge in your throat."

Auraq pushed through the ironclad door and entered the dark cavern of the guard offices. Before his eyes could adjust, he was struck by a hot wave of sweat, stale mead, and pipe smoke. The hum of chatter dimmed as he closed the door behind him and waited for his vision to acclimate. He could feel their eyes on him, questioning what he was doing there. This was the guardsmen's sanctum. Strangers did not wander in uninvited.

Fifteen or so guardsmen were standing about holding up the wall of the main chamber. Only a few looked to actually be involved in anything official. Most looked off-duty. A man in a tattered tunic and no trousers was passed out on the stone floor, his hands shackled behind him and chained to the wall.

Auraq walked up to the one man who appeared to carry some authority. He was seated at a table, hunched over a journal and scrawling away with a quill.

"You're in my light," the man grumbled, not looking up.

"Know where I can find Ben—?" Auraq caught himself, "Captain Bennidar."

The man lifted his eyes to take in Auraq. He assessed him a moment without expression, then lowered his eyes again to the page.

"Next room."

Auraq moved on without another word. He ducked his head through the low doorway.

Bendo stood behind a desk, leaning on his knuckles. Sprawled onto the surface was a map of some part of the city. A younger guardsman stood at his elbow and nodded while Bendo spoke quietly and reached out to tap his finger on a location on the map. Like Ruck, he too looked older: his hairline had receded to form a sharp point on his forehead, and his once plump and boyish face was now pale and drawn. The biggest change, though, was in the distinct air of seriousness and authority he wore like a mantle on his shoulders. It made him nearly unrecognizable.

The two men sensed his presence and looked up. Bendo had a tight brow, clearly irritated at the interruption. Just like Ruck back at the Imp, there was a heartbeat of time while Bendo worked out what was familiar about the man standing in front of him. Then recognition sparked in Bendo's eyes.

"You've got quite the pair of low hangers, and no mistake."

Auraq shrugged but didn't say anything.

Bendo looked over his shoulder at the younger guardsman. "Five minutes," he told him. "Close the door." The guardsman made a quick nod and shuffled off. He circled around the desk and gave Auraq a wide berth, skirting along the wall.

When the door was closed, Bendo pushed off from the desk and crossed his arms. "Any reason why I shouldn't arrest you here and now?"

"That would be your prerogative, of course," Auraq replied flatly.

"But you're thinking I won't. I can't wait to hear your reasoning. Friendly favor? For old time's sake?"

"Those work. But also you know things are not ever what they seem."

Bendo arched his brow. "You're claiming innocence?"

"Extenuating circumstances," Auraq replied.

Bendo bit the inside of his cheek in thought. As he'd hoped, Auraq saw his expression start to soften. Gate captain or no, there was too much history between them for Bendo to take him into custody out of hand. Auraq had counted on that. "Someone out there could recognize you. Your picture is nailed up on the board right in this station. If someone does, I'll have no choice but to put you in irons."

Auraq shrugged. "Seen the picture. Looks nothing like me."

"Close enough. Why you here, Muz?" Short for muscles, his nickname since his youth.

"Need information."

That surprised him. "You're taking quite the risk. Must be fucking important."

"It is." He reached into the pouch at his belt and pulled out the scrap of cloth with the strange emblem on it. He set it on the desk in the center of the map. "Ever seen this before?"

Bendo's eyes widened. He uncrossed his arms and picked up the cloth from the table. He dropped down almost absently into a chair behind him. "Gods, Muz," he whispered. He shook his head.

Auraq's hunch had been right. Bendo had always had an ear to the ground like no one he'd ever known. He knew all of the key players operating in the city. Which meant this position as a gate captain probably caused some wringing of hands among the underground elements. "Tell me what you know."

"Where the fuck did you get this?" Bendo tossed it back on the table.

Auraq picked it back up and put it back inside the pouch. "Someone I had a disagreement with was wearing it."

Bendo couldn't hide his surprise. "You killed one of these men?"

"Three actually."

Bendo raked fingers through his hair. "Fuck, Muz, this is bad news. How did you get mixed up with them? What do you mean 'a disagreement'?"

"They wanted someone dead. I disagreed."

"That was mighty stupid, friend. These are not folks you want to cross."

"Who are they?"

Bendo hesitated. He seemed almost nervous talking of them or even speaking their name. "The Order of the Jackal. Extremists. Real nasty folk. They are possibly a religious order of sorts—no one knows for certain—but can be hired out for jobs. Assassinations mostly, but word is they are very choosey about what tasks they take on, and they require a very heavy purse."

Auraq was tempted to ask if this was knowledge he'd gained from his current position, or from before. He decided it didn't matter. "They have a presence here, in Har Tesera?"

"From what I'm told, they have a presence everywhere. Who were they attempting to kill?"

"No one you know."

"If the target is still alive, I'd stay well clear of him. He's marked and will not survive. No one ever escapes the Jackal. Word is they have never failed."

Of course this order would want everyone to think that. They probably did much to propagate that view, but no organization was infallible.

"Base of operations?" Auraq asked "Their leader?"

"And, here we go," Bendo grumbled shaking his head. "Gods, you haven't changed, I see. You're off to do something really stupid now, aren't you? You're going to save the King's Guard the trouble of hanging you."

"Just tell me what you know."

"Nothin'. And that's the truth of it. Don't want to know any else, either."

Auraq nodded.

"You need to bugger off," Bendo said. "The longer you're here, the more I'm tempted to arrest you. If only to save you from whatever fool plan you have."

"I'll be at our old haunt tonight if you're interested," Auraq said, easing toward the door. "I'll buy you a tankard of Ruck's best, and you can fill me in how you got on this particular path."

He lifted his chin to indicate the guard office.

"Long story. And I don't think it would do great things for my future here if I'm seen sharing a tankard and a table with the likes of you. But," he added with a shrug, "if I catch wind of anything interesting, I'll send word."

Auraq knew that was the best he was going to get from Bendo. He left the station and went back into the city.

Chapter 12

AURAQ TOOK a circuitous route back to his father's shop. He was being overly cautious, he knew, but he wanted to ensure he wasn't being followed. He had no reason to believe this strange order had any knowledge of him yet, but Bendo's report had unnerved him. Auraq had seen firsthand what the organization was capable of, but even Bendo was noticeably uneasy about them. They were even more ubiquitous than Auraq had originally feared, and he grew more apprehensive about the length of their reach. He'd left the guard office with knots constricting the muscles between his shoulders and the base of his skull.

The worry that they had means of tracking the mark somehow gnawed at him. The Order had magecraft at its disposal, certainly. The wolvren were proof enough of that. They could already be closing in on Malgar's shop. Unwittingly, Auraq could have brought the danger right to his father's doorstep.

He quickened his pace.

He arrived back at the old neighborhood around midafternoon. He was nearly at a jog as he came up the alley. At the shop door, he put his hand on the latch but then stopped. Muffled sounds of voices filtered through from the other side. Then banging. Auraq held still as he listened, hand near the hilt of the longsword. At the first clear sign of a struggle, he would kick in the door. The words were indistinguishable, but he could tell it was Kane and his father speaking—not in anger or alarm, but calm and relaxed.

He allowed himself a long slow exhale. They were safe— he'd half convinced himself to discover otherwise. He closed his eyes, aware only then of his rapid heart rate.

Damn. *This* was why he traveled alone.

He no longer wanted to bear the responsibility for the well-being of others. That was in his past now. He'd turned his back once and for all on ideals like *duty* and *obligation*. All they'd ever done was consume him, and his life was better without them. They may have once made him a gifted lieutenant, but they had also played a role in his downfall.

Thumb still on the latch, he realized that this whole unplanned deviation could be over soon anyway. The appointment was set. Kane would learn the cause of his mark and—should luck be with him—the mages of the academy would take over from there. Kane would safely be in their hands, and the oath he made to Old Tan would be fulfilled. And then….

Well, then he would figure out what was next for him. But he would be alone. Unfettered. As it should be. He'd likely head south again, crawl back under some rock and disappear.

If they departed soon, he and Kane had just enough time to walk back to the Academy District and catch their appointment.

Someone inside made a small laugh. Kane. He'd recognize his father's laugh. For some unknown reason, the sound of it made him bristle with irritation.

Malgar the barrel maker could be disarming when he felt the need. It was part of his businessman repertoire. He knew how to charm and keep the gears of conversation moving—the reason merchants somehow always paid a premium for his barrels.

Auraq depressed the latch and pushed his way in.

The conversation between the two stalled as soon as Auraq entered the shop, the casual mood extinguished. Auraq felt the shift in the air immediately. They both looked to the door, like two lads caught throwing stones at a shop window. Kane was sitting on the counter with a steaming mug in his hand, apparently keeping Malgar company while he arranged and clamped the wood staves into place.

"Don't let me interrupt," Auraq said.

His father's face hardened, and he turned back to his task.

Kane set the mug down next to him. "You didn't. He was explaining to me how this all works. Always wondered, really."

Auraq knew more about making barrels than he ever wanted to know. "Grab the pack."

Kane's back straightened. "Is something wrong?" He put his hands on the edge of the counter and slid himself down.

"We have an appointment."

Kane looked confused, but he picked up the pack from the floor. "Tonight? With who?"

But Auraq was staring at Malgar, who kept his back to him. He waited to see if his father acknowledged his return. But Malgar worked with renewed focus on the barrel as if he were alone in his shop.

"May not need the cot after all, Pa. I'll send a message if plans change."

"Don't bother. Can't promise I'll be here anyway. If you still need the place, I'm sure you remember how to get in."

Auraq pressed his lips together and nodded to no one in particular. He marched out of the shop without waiting to see if Kane followed.

KANE JOGGED to catch up with Auraq and joined him at his side. Auraq kept a hard pace. He told himself he was walking fast because he didn't want to be late for their appointment, but there was fire in his veins pushing him. Both of them were quiet for a time, for different reasons, certainly. Auraq wasn't really interested in hearing what Kane had to say at the moment anyway.

"Where are we going?" Kane asked.

"I've arranged for you to speak with someone."

"Gathered that. Care to tell me who?"

Auraq didn't feel like getting into that here on the street. He was focused on the people around him, keeping an eye out for anyone who appeared to be watching them. Bendo's description of the Order had burrowed deep into his head and made a home there.

"Was that one of those questions you deem unnecessary?" Kane added when he didn't respond. "One not worth the bother of answering?"

Auraq's jaw tightened. "I don't know who precisely. But someone who can hopefully provide you with answers."

"Someone we can trust?"

Auraq made a half grunt. His eyes were on a group of thugs huddled under a shaded awning, whispering to each other. They were a conspicuous bunch—not the caliber he would expect from the Order, but he watched them nonetheless. They seemed to be surveying the crowd, but not looking for anyone in particular. Their attention never swung toward Auraq and Kane as they passed by them.

Kane sighed and fell quiet again.

They crossed the Merchant District, Auraq's second time that day. The streets were congested again. A spike in afternoon heat had driven people from their homes—a convenient excuse to wander the district in search of bargains. Merchants had dragged their wares from inside onto tables in the street to lure potential spenders, and food vendors materialized at street corners with steaming kettles on portable fire pits. A narrow channel down the middle of the street was the only passage through it, forcing them to slow their pace.

The volume of people made it harder for Auraq to keep his eyes on everything going on around them. If they were being followed, it would be difficult for him to spot it. He had to stay vigilant.

On instinct, Auraq kept his hand low near the drawstring purse at his belt. The place would be ripe with cutpurses looking for unsuspecting victims. He would not be one of them—the coin there was going into the hands of the mages.

"So," Kane began after a time. It was spoken like a hammer hits an anvil. Sharp and direct. Auraq could already sense where this was going and felt his ire fume. "You're a defector, then."

Auraq teeth clenched. "Told you that, did he?"

"He did." Kane let that sit for a moment before he

continued. "He didn't elaborate. I think he wanted to see my reaction, tease out how much I knew about you. See if you told me yourself."

Sounded like his father.

The implication was clear in Kane's tone. Auraq *should* have told him about it himself. But defecting from the king's army is not the sort of topic one brings up casually in conversation. Auraq had learned early to keep his mouth closed on the subject. People in general had a high tolerance for a multitude of sins, willing to overlook, if not forgive, almost anything—oddly, defection wasn't on the list. People took the safety of the realm seriously.

He forced himself to return his attention to the crowd, scanning for anything that might mean danger. He would not get goaded into this conversation right now. But he found his focus splintered by his father's loose tongue.

"And what did you tell him?" Auraq prodded, if only out of some dark curiosity.

"That your past was no concern of mine."

A noble reply, but Auraq wondered if he actually meant that. Otherwise, why would he be bringing it up at all?

"Your father was somehow testing me, I think," Kane added.

Someone up ahead rushed toward them, cutting through the crowd like ax wedge. Auraq couldn't make out much of him other than the simple brown flat cap on his head, but he was heading directly for them. Auraq's hand drifted to the hilt of the longsword as the man wove through the people, arm out in front and turned sideways to minimize the space he needed to move at such a pace.

Auraq pulled on the hilt a little, exposing the blade within, and was ready to pull it out farther—but ten paces ahead of him, the man veered and approached a nearby merchant's table. Panting, he handed a small drawstring sack over to a woman waiting there. Her forgotten coin needed for a purchase, apparently.

Auraq dropped his hand again. "He would find it difficult

to understand how someone like you is connected to me."

"Someone like me?"

"A good and upstanding citizen," he said. It came out far more sardonic than he intended, but he was growing impatient. The conversation was distraction, one he couldn't allow, but to his rising irritation, he found he couldn't disengage from it.

"Ah," Kane said, nodding. "Strange that he would come to that conclusion so quickly."

"He is a savvy man of business, with a keen eye for the disreputable."

"Then all the more strange that he cannot see past this offense of yours and see that you are in fact an honorable man."

Auraq chuckled low in his throat. "Honorable," he repeated tonelessly. They rounded a corner onto another street, and he swept his gaze over the new crowd milling about the wares on display.

Kane forged onward. "I am curious, though. Why does this affect him so?"

Auraq looked over to him again, this time with his brow raised in astonishment that he would even ask such a thing.

"Don't give me that look," Kane replied. "I'm serious. You are not the first man to fall out with his father. But this animosity between the two of you runs deep. He takes your defection personally somehow."

Auraq quickly looked around them to see if any nearby passersby had overheard Kane. No one seemed to have noticed, but that did little to alleviate his unease, the slow twisting in his gut. He was not accustomed to speaking so openly about these events. Kane simply did not understand. For some reason, he seemed to view Auraq's crime as some mild transgression, not fully grasping its true weight and impact. Auraq forced himself to keep the same pace, eyes forward. "He was an officer. Like myself. Also serving in the Lendera Provence. My disgrace tarnishes his own legacy of service."

Kane's lips tightened. "His deeds are independent of yours, I would think."

"Not in the eyes of the king's army."

They passed under the grand arch leading into the Academy District. The sudden change in scenery was enough to distract Kane from his current line of questioning. He spun about with renewed fascination at the architecture.

"Gods! Who knew they could make buildings so tall?"

The streets here were near vacant—none of the loiterers circulating through the Merchant Distinct wandered past the Academy's threshold. There was nothing for them here. Only small packs of young men and women dressed in novice robes drifted through the district. They hugged close to the buildings, whispering with each other—probably heading home to their dormitories after a long day of studying their mysterious craft. The empty streets suited Auraq fine. It was quiet and nothing was preventing them from making their appointment at the public building of the academy campus.

The afternoon sun was low enough now to submerge the region in shadow, but the lamplighters had not yet made their rounds. The district had an eerie, abandoned feel.

Auraq's eye instinctively followed the line of crenulated tops of the buildings around them, searching for signs of archers positioned up there. A perfect ambush spot, he realized too late. He had no idea how much security the mages provided in their compound. How easily would it be for an assassin to get up to the roof of one of these and lie in wait for them to arrive?

"What is this place?" Kane asked.

"The Academy District."

Comprehension lit up his eyes. "Mages."

"Yes."

Kane's expression tightened into anxiety. Precisely the reaction Auraq expected. It was the reason he'd kept their destination quiet. Everyone was tense the first time they encountered a mage. Auraq himself had never fully gotten past the deep feeling of unease whenever he was in their presence.

They climbed the long marble staircase toward the Academy Building. Halfway to the top, Auraq could hear Kane's breathing. He had retreated again into himself—the upside to his sudden influx of anxiety. He was no longer pushing

Auraq to talk about the past.

But near the top, Kane stopped and grabbed the back of his arm.

"One moment," he said.

Auraq turned, thinking that perhaps Kane needed a break from the climb, but Kane was standing with hands on his hips looking off to the side. He did not look winded, but instead deep in thought.

Auraq frowned. He suspected he knew where this was going. He was only surprised it took the entire walk here for it to surface.

Kane looked up, and then his eyes shifted left as he looked past Auraq. Someone was heading down the steps—Auraq could hear the footfalls on the marble. Kane waited until the stranger passed by before he turned his gaze toward Auraq.

"I know I said it was none of my affair. But will you tell me?"

"Tell you what?" he replied on reflex. He knew what Kane wanted to know.

"It seems plain to me that you loved your service in the army. And I have seen for myself that you do not shirk from a promise you've made. So, yes, I want to know. I want to know what would drive a man like you to defect."

"A man like me." Auraq felt a surge of anger flush his face. "You feel you've grasped my measure?"

"Enough to know it was no sheer whim that drove you to it."

Auraq nodded but fell silent for a time. "Come," he said finally. "I've no wish to miss our appointed time." He climbed the remaining steps and heard Kane fall in beside him. He wondered if the same young mage would be behind the desk.

At the top of the stairs, beneath the massive figures reaching over the threshold of the building, he stopped again. He looked up at the great orb suspended between the figures' hands. It glowed with a radiant golden light and bathed the landing at the top of the stairs in its warm luster. Auraq sighed and turned about.

He forced himself to look directly into Kane's eyes.

"Murder," he said. He spoke with force behind it, but his throat constricted involuntarily at the end of it all the same. Forming the words brought on an unexpected wave of physical pain that coursed throughout his whole body. "The murder of two people led me to defect from my position and title. I defected to avoid the ax. Still view me as honorable?"

Chapter 13

A DIFFERENT novice occupied the stool behind the wide desk—a woman this time. Her back was to Auraq, so he could not see her face, but her hair was pulled back into a severe but flawlessly constructed bun on the top of her head. She was bent over a large parchment scroll held open on the counter with books strategically positioned at corners. Her head rested against her knuckles, while the forefinger of her other hand tracked a line of text across the page.

Hargan was nowhere to be seen, his shift at the desk presumably over. Auraq was somewhat surprised that the young mage didn't make a point to stick around for their return—or perhaps he had misread Hargan's intentions in the first place. For some complicated, inexplicable reason, he was simultaneously disappointed and relieved not to find him there.

He stood a moment, waiting, fingers drumming lightly on the counter. Kane stood behind him a step, but Auraq could feel his eyes burning into his back. He could feel his judgment. This would change things, he realized. He regretted telling him now—he wasn't even sure why he did. Some part of him had wanted to shock him, perhaps to push him away, stop him from prying and asking so many damn questions. But he needed Kane to trust him. Surely, that would be affected now.

But then… did that even matter?

He hoped that after their visit with the mage, Kane would no longer be in need of his protection anyway. The academy would see to it. What did it matter if Kane lost trust in him?

The woman made no effort to acknowledge them. Auraq cleared his throat.

"A moment!" she answered sharply. She picked up her quill and scribbled notes onto a separate page.

Auraq didn't recognize the strange fluid script on the scroll. It could have been arcane mage-writing of some sort, or just a language he didn't know, but he could tell by the deep color of the scroll and the small tears along its brittle edge that it was extraordinarily old.

She thrust the quill into the inkwell and leaned back as if spent.

"Can I help you?" Her tone still had a thread of impatience. She looked up at Auraq with dark eyes. She attempted a smile, perhaps in greeting, but it was largely a failure. Auraq could tell her mind was still on the parchment.

He recognized her as the academic sort that had little time or tolerance for people. She was more comfortable in the company of books and scrolls. He had had dealings with their type when in the king's army—scholars of war, those studying the mind of the barbarian hordes and such. She was not being intentionally rude or dismissive. She wanted to deal with this interruption quickly so she could return to her work.

"We have an appointment."

"With whom?" she asked. She moved the paper she was scribbling on aside and grabbed the ledger Hargan had used earlier.

"We were not given a name."

"Well, that's certainly helpful," she replied dryly.

"My name is Auraq Greystone and this is our appointed time," Auraq said. "I'm certain that someone as learned as yourself can ferret out the rest."

She looked up at him again, her eyes tightened into narrow slits. She smiled slightly more authentically.

"I'm certain you're correct," she replied. She leaned her head to the side and looked past Auraq. "And this is?"

"The concern of the mage we are scheduled to speak with," Auraq replied flatly.

A flash of something—curiosity perhaps—crossed the woman's features. Still eyeing Auraq with a tight brow, she repositioned the ledger in front of her. She pulled her gaze from him to scan down the page, dragging her forefinger down the center. She flipped to the next page and dragged her finger down again. Then she stopped, raising her head a fraction in surprise.

"Chenigal," she muttered with a noticeable lift in her voice.

"I'm sorry?" Auraq asked.

Her lips pressed into a line and her brow formed a sharp point over the bridge of her nose as if this was some puzzle to unravel. "You are scheduled to visit with Master Chenigal." She scrutinized Auraq anew. The look made him feel he had somehow cheated at a game he was not aware he was playing. Hargan *had* apparently pulled some strings for him.

"You have the full amount with you, surrah? Master Chenigal will not receive installments. It's full payment up front for services or nothing."

"Payment?" asked Kane, suddenly alarmed.

"Understood," Auraq put in quickly. The amount to pay would certainly empty out his purse, exhausting all the coin he'd taken from the Jackal assassins. Mages did not come cheap, even if it was only a consultation. He reached down to his belt.

"No money is exchanged here," she said. "He will take the payment when he receives you." She raised her arm into the air and snapped her fingers. A guardsman appeared at the desk, but the livery he wore was not that of Har Tesera. The academy employed their own private guardsmen.

"He will direct you to his office. Do not stray from him. The Academy has a strict policy for visitors. There are areas here in which you are not permitted." She turned to the guard. "East. Second floor. Master Chenigal."

The guard evaluated Auraq with a sweep of his eyes. "Your weaponry, surrah. You are not permitted within the academy compound armed."

He nodded. He removed both swords and laid the sheathed weapons on the surface of the desk. He didn't like the idea of leaving them behind, but he wasn't going to let Kane speak to the mage without him either.

Without comment she lifted the weapons from her desk one at a time and stored them underneath. Auraq was tempted to ask for some assurance that they'd be secure, but he doubted the desk was ever unattended, so he held his tongue. As the guardsman took them deeper into the building, she was already turning back to her scroll, the two of them forgotten.

The guard led them through the open hall. Their boots echoed conspicuously on the elaborate mosaic floor. Two rows of massive twisting pillars lined the hall's entire length and reached up to the far ceiling. Kane lingered several paces behind them, his neck craned back as he stared at the frescos that covered every fraction of the distant ceiling. Was he taking it all in, Auraq wondered, or using it as an excuse to intentionally keep his distance?

Tucked into the spaces between the pillars were small gatherings of mage folk, talking in quiet voices as if afraid of being overheard. Their conference would cease when Auraq and Kane drew near, and then gently begin again once they had moved past.

Their guide cut between two pillars at the halfway point of the hall and led them into a passageway. In place of torches, the way was lit with glowing orbs set into iron sconces spaced evenly along the wall. Absent was the sharp smell of pitch or tallow, and the ceiling wasn't covered in black soot. Instead, the corridor was clean, comfortable, and warm.

They traversed a wide stone staircase to the second floor and passed through a few more corridors before the guard spun about on his heels and gestured to a door.

"I shall await you here until your meeting with Master Chenigal is concluded," he said.

Auraq nodded and knocked on the appointed door. There was no immediate answer, so he knocked again.

"Yes, yes" came a muffled reply. "Give me a minute, will you?"

On the other side of the door, there was the metallic scrape of a latch being slid back, and the door swung open on protesting hinges. A bearded face filled the gap. Master Chenigal wasn't particularly old, but there was enough gray in his beard and lines around his eyes to grant him an air of experience. "What is it?

I'm busy."

"Master Chenigal, we have an appointment."

"At this hour? Nonsense. Are you certain?"

Auraq was not about to be turned away. "Quite."

The mage took notice of the guard standing to the side. "Going to have to chat with that boy about my availability," he grumbled as he stepped back from the opening. Hargan, Auraq presumed. "Very well. Come in, then." The door was opened wider, allowing the two of them passage into the room. Auraq gestured for Kane to enter first; then he followed him inside, closing the door behind him.

The three of them stood in a small antechamber. To the right, three stairs descended into Chenigal's study.

He didn't know what to expect from a mage's private chambers, but he was surprised nonetheless. The room was neat and organized to an excessive degree. Nothing seemed the slightest bit out of place or askew. Every book and scroll was meticulously arranged on the tall shelves that encircled the chamber. Vials and jars were stacked on shelves and categorized with parchment labels pegged beneath them. There was an inviting sitting area around a large stone fireplace and a round wooden table by a window. A small wine service and a vase of small red flowers had been placed on a tray in the center of the table.

An acrid smell lingered about the room, the scent of some unknown substance that had been burned. It was the only hint as to what business Chenigal was involved in before they knocked.

"Come, come, then," Chenigal repeated as he stepped down into the room. He picked up a scroll that was placed on a small side table—the only item that seemed the slightest bit out of its particular place. He tightened the roll, slipped it into its bone case, and placed it gently on a shelf among others. "Take a seat."

Auraq forced himself to move deeper into the mage's domain. He passed through the seating area, strangely aware of how thick the carpet was beneath his boots, and worried that the remnants of the street on his heel might soil it. He sat down on the end of a plush settee with his hands on his thighs. Kane followed along the wall but remained on his feet with his back to a bookshelf. "If it's all the same to you," he said, "I prefer to stand."

Auraq glanced over at him. Kane chose to stand in a place that put him at equal distance between both the mage and Auraq. Kane watched Chenigal's movements closely, like a mouse watching the path of a cat, but never once glanced Auraq's way. His shoulders were pushed back in a show of confidence, but his face was pale.

Chenigal's expression did not change. "Whatever you prefer." He positioned himself at the fringe of the seating area, resting one hand against the back of another chair as if posing for a painting. He was dressed in simple black robes, not unlike the robes worn by the woman at the desk. The hem had embroidered runes stitched in black thread. The scrolling symbols were nearly invisible, but they caught the candlelight differently enough to be noticed. "So, how can I be of service at this late hour?"

A subtle reminder that they were past accepted meeting hours and were taking up his valuable time.

"A consultation," Auraq said. He reached for the purse at his belt, but Chenigal produced a stiff smile and showed Auraq his palm.

"Allow to me hear why you've come first."

"Do you require our names?" Auraq asked. His own name he knew was documented in the ledger, but he was hesitant to reveal Kane's yet.

"If you wish it. But it is not necessary." Again, his expression remained unchanged. If he was surprised by the question, he showed no sign of it. "If discretion is your concern, the details of our conversation will not leave this room. Who would come to us mages for aid if people believed we betrayed the trust of our clients?"

He turned his cool gaze toward Kane. "I presume you have something you wish to show me?"

Kane straightened, alarm registering in his eyes.

The corner of Chenigal's mouth lifted a fraction more. "Your hand is paying much attention to that forearm."

Kane looked down with surprise and quickly pulled his hand away. Chenigal was right. He had been unconsciously massaging his forearm with a thumb.

The mage stood and glided over to the round table by the window. He moved aside the wine service and pulled out a chair. He gestured with a sweep of his hand that Kane should take the seat, as he strolled around to the other side. "Might as well show me, then, yes. It is why you came." Chenigal's eyes shifted over to Auraq's with a raised brow, challenging him to deny it.

"It is," Auraq confirmed. He tried to give a nod of assurance to Kane, but Kane held his eyes on the mage and didn't see it.

Kane hesitated. Then, with pressed lips, he crossed the chamber and took a seat on the chair. He sat for several moments with his hands in his lap as if debating whether to proceed. With a snap of commitment, he pulled the sleeve of his tunic up to the elbow and extended his arm across the table.

The room fell silent as a tomb. Chenigal stood very still. His face remained firm and unreadable, but Auraq could sense a change in him.

The mark on Kane's arm glowed red like a blister.

"My, my," Chenigal said in a very soft voice.

He slid out the chair opposite Kane and seated himself. Gently, he took Kane's wrist between his forefinger and thumb and turned the forearm until the mark was facing upward. He leaned in but seemed hesitant to get too close.

Auraq found he was standing again and had stepped closer. He could tell Chenigal had already forgotten he was in the room.

Still holding Kane's wrist, Chenigal glided his other hand over the mark without touching the skin. His fingers rose and dropped in waves as if pulled by strings. The rune shapes surged brighter, angrier, as the mage's fingers crossed over them. Kane sucked in air through his teeth.

"You're hurting him," Auraq said in a low voice.

Chenigal ignored him and spoke only to Kane. "When did

this appear?"

Kane told him a brief version of the story. He seemed intentionally vague.

"And these runes?" the mage asked. "Ever seen them before then?"

Kane shook his head. "I'm no mage. I know nothing of runes."

Chenigal sighed, let go of Kane, and leaned back in the chair. His gaze swung to Auraq. "Who knows of this?"

"The three of us," Auraq replied. "There are others that know something of it. But who they are, how many, or how much they know is unclear."

Chenigal gave him a quizzical look.

"Someone wants me dead," Kane said flatly.

Chenigal sat at attention, his back straight and chin held high. "Is that so? Interesting. You have no idea who?"

"None," Auraq said. A small lie, but technically Auraq only had the name of the organization hired to eliminate Kane. The subtle shift in Chenigal's expression told Auraq that he knew he was holding something back, but the mage didn't challenge it.

"Can you get rid of it?" Kane asked.

Chenigal stood from the table. "I need to fully understand what it is before I can determine that." From a desk, he retrieved a wide, bound book, inkwell, and quill, then returned to the table.

"Chopping off my arm not an option?"

Chenigal looked at Kane in surprise, his eyebrows forming a high arch.

Kane's expression was hard as he glared back at him. His arm was still extended across the table. The runes were no longer surging with light, but they still seemed inflamed and angry. "I want it gone. It is responsible for too many deaths already."

Chenigal sat down again, opened the book, and flipped through the pages. It was filled with sheet after sheet of notes scrolled in a delicate but handsome script and illustrations of stunning quality. He flipped through until he found a blank page.

"Try and remain still," he said as he slipped half-moon-shaped spectacles on the end of his nose. He dipped the quill pen into the well, then began to form the basic shapes of the runes on Kane's arms. "Your friend is free to sit if he desires," he said to Kane "This will take some time."

Auraq expected some response from Kane. Something. Either a denouncement that they were not friends, or perhaps finally a look his way—but neither came. Kane kept his full attention on the mage. So Auraq remained standing. He watched Chenigal work, expertly forming the shapes and bringing the nuances of the mark to life. He penned notes along the side in a language Auraq did not know.

"How does your friend fit into this?" the mage asked after a time.

"My guard dog, apparently."

"A good one too, I presume." The comment made Kane look up with surprise. "Well," Chenigal added. "You are still alive, are you not?"

He finished the drawing, added a few more notes to the side, and dropped the quill into the well. He blew over the ink to help it dry, but kept the book open as he slid it aside. Pulling the spectacles from his nose, he leaned back with his elbow on the arm of the chair and considered Kane with a tightly pressed mouth.

"You came here because you believe this to be an augural mark," he said to Auraq. It was not a question, but a statement made with utmost confidence of accuracy. "A message from the Gods."

Auraq kept his face passive. "I do not know to enough to presume. Which is why we came here."

"I'm surprised you didn't seek out a shepherd for confirmation."

Auraq didn't respond. He preferred to avoid the accusing eye of the prelacy of late.

"Well," continued Chenigal, "it's good that you didn't. A shepherd would have seen what they wanted to see and claimed it a miracle. But I can say with confidence it is not a divine message."

Auraq wasn't sure if he was disappointed or relieved. "You're certain?"

"Quite. It is lacking some distinctive markers that I would expect to see." He gave Auraq a narrow look. "That is not to say this isn't a remarkable find."

"If not a mark of augury, what is it, then?"

"It may still have come from the realm of shadow."

Kane straightened, pulling his arm back. "From the dead?"

Chenigal seized Kane's wrist again to keep the arm firmly on the table. He picked up the quill and used it to point to the inflamed symbols. "This rune in particular...." Chenigal trailed off and shook his head as if perplexed by it.

Auraq stepped closer to the table.

"See how it connects with the next," Chenigal said. "That is closely related to a rune I've encountered regarding history. Or perhaps a chronicle of sorts. But this symbol here, it is clearly a rune of the mind. And this... this here resembles the archaic imagery for the eye, which I take to mean 'vision' in this context."

Auraq leaned in closer as if he too would comprehend what was in the mark. "What does it all mean?"

"I can say with some confidence that this is someone's memory."

"A memory?" Kane echoed.

"Yes. But that is not all. It is the memory that has crossed over from the shadow realm. The memory of someone who is no longer of this world."

He let go of the wrist as Kane slowly fell against the back of the chair. Kane's complexion had grown even more pallid.

"Whose memory?" Auraq asked. "And what is it a memory of?"

"Both excellent questions," Chenigal replied. "Ones I cannot begin to answer until I've had more time to study it fully."

"Is it from someone I know?"

Something in way Kane spoke told Auraq he was thinking of his parents.

"Unlikely," Chenigal said. "The bracer you wore was somehow the link, the connection to the shadow realm. A conduit of sorts. That sort of magecraft would have had to have been established in advance. The barrier between life and the shadow is too strong for the dead to penetrate without some assistance." He let out a long sigh. "Pity we don't have that bracer to study as well. Anyway, when it came in contact with your skin, it opened the link and transferred the memory to you. A fascinating idea and an intriguing discovery."

"Yes. Lucky me," Kane said.

Chenigal stood from the table. He didn't seem to have picked up on Kane's dry tone as he closed the book and tucked it under his arm. "If I'm correct about this, and I'm fairly certain I am, someone went through a lot of trouble to see that this memory reaches the world of the living. Would indicate something important, yes? Would explain why some may want whatever is in it left unknown." He returned the book to the desk, then sat on the edge of the desktop and folded his arms. "This is no novice's work, I can tell you. I don't know of any mage today capable of accomplishing it. I would wager that you were not the target of this, the one supposed to bear the mark. My guess is the owner of the memory had a specific person in mind. You acquired it by unfortunate happenstance." He waved a hand in the air. "Ah, we are getting ahead of ourselves here. This is all conjecture. Academic. I'll have to establish first if it is, in fact, a memory at all."

"Will he need to stay here at the academy, then, for you to study it?"

Chenigal frowned. "I'm afraid that won't be possible. Only approved members of the academy are allowed to stay beyond dusk. It is why I made a copy of the mark. I will give it all my attention. Come back tomorrow and I will inform you of what I've discovered."

Kane stood from the table and slowly pulled his tunic sleeve back down over the mark. Chenigal gestured to the antechamber. Their audience with the mage was coming to an end.

"You were wise to keep knowledge of this quiet," Chenigal said when they arrived at the door.

Auraq reached for the latch then stopped, a question occurring to him. "Master Chenigal, how could others have learned of this mark?"

The mage pursed his lips. "Bracers tend to come in pairs, do they not? I imagine the other was discovered and its partner traced to him. There is magecraft that can be used to find specific items if they are known to exist."

"Thank you, Master Chenigal." Auraq bowed to him. "What do we owe you for your service today?"

"Oh right. I'm expected to charge you something." He shrugged. "Ten nobles."

Auraq was unable to hide his surprise. Ten nobles? That was a fraction of what he had expected to pay. He pulled out his purse and fingered out the coin, then handed it over feeling guilty. Auraq felt he was taking advantage of him.

"Relax," Chenigal told him, as if reading his thoughts. "You're not robbing me. I will, in fact, make out quite well when I eventually publish this discovery and reveal it to the rest of the academy. Until tomorrow, then."

Kane drifted back out to the corridor, but as Auraq turned to follow him and depart as well, Chenigal grabbed him by the arm. He bent close and spoke in a quiet voice, presumably so Kane would not hear. "There are no limits to what certain men will do to keep a dark secret from reaching the light of day. Keep him safe."

He released Auraq's arm and wandered back to his parlor and the large tome on his table.

Chapter 14

DUSK WAS settling over the city when the academy guardsman escorted Auraq and Kane out of the building. Once they were deposited at the desk, he turned about on his heel and marched back inside without a word. Auraq reclaimed his weapons. He returned the longsword to his belt and slipped the short sword's baldric over his shoulder and adjusted it into place, thankful to feel their reassuring weight pulling on him again. Then he started down the long stone steps. Kane followed a pace behind him. Neither of them spoke.

Auraq hadn't known what to expect, but the information Chenigal was able to discern from the mark was too much for him to take in. His mind was swimming. He knew little of what mages were capable of, but this seemed beyond the plausible. A message from the shadow realm? Sent to the living world through a rune mark?

They stepped off the last of the stone stairs and made their way across the plaza toward the street that would take them back to the Market District. Dusk had thickened rapidly and the air was noticeably chillier. Auraq pulled the edges of his cloak in tighter to better cover his shoulders. The lamplighters had already been through the area. The grand plaza was lit with a warm glow. Auraq wondered why the mages bothered with oil lanterns at all and didn't install the glowing orbs that lit the corridors of the Academy Building.

On instinct, he lifted his eyes to the tops of the buildings again. He scanned the crenulated lines of each, but the light from the street didn't reach that high, and twilight had consumed them. There was nothing he could see from below. He angled their trajectory away from the center of the plaza and had them walk closer to the buildings, where they would be more shadowed.

Kane broke the silence. "So, I assume you are disappointed?"

"Chenigal provided us with much information." *And at a low cost*, he thought. The mage could have easily emptied out his entire purse. "Why would I be?"

"You are still shackled to me. At least for one more day. Do not deny that you were hoping to dump me off onto the mages today."

Auraq's brow tightened into a knot. "In order to keep you safer, yes."

"That's your reason," Kane replied flatly.

Auraq bit back a reply. The danger for Kane was in the secret held in the mark. Once the secret was exposed, the need to eliminate Kane would also be eliminated. Should the mage succeed in unlocking the memory tomorrow, Kane would no longer need his protection.

"I thought you were keen on my leaving," he said without turning his head.

"That was before," Kane replied, then fell silent again.

Before? What had changed, Auraq wondered. Beyond the open plaza, the streets of the Academy District were quiet and vacant. But coming from somewhere beyond the gates, Auraq could hear the pulse of a drum and perhaps a horn or two, followed by abrupt surges of shouts and cheers. The sounds had the uncanny and disturbing resemblance to a battle being waged in the distance.

"I don't trust them," Kane said after a time.

"Who?"

"The mages."

Auraq chuckled. "And well you shouldn't. Most of them anyway." Chenigal seemed a rare exception.

Kane seemed close to saying more, but he fell quiet as they approached the Academy District's gate. The portcullis was already closed, and guards now stood at attention beneath it. They were dressed in similar livery to their guard escort in the academy. Interesting, Auraq thought, that the academy supplied their own guardsmen even here. More evidence that the Academy District was a city within the city. One of the guards waved them to the side and wordlessly steered them through a narrow passageway in the gatehouse.

Beyond the gate, Auraq quickly learned the source of the music he'd heard. The market square was in the throes of a festival. During the few hours they spent with the mage, colored flags had been strewn between buildings and bunting hung in merry swoops across balconies. Throngs had turned out to see the parade of acrobats that tumbled through the square. Cheers, laughter, and applause moved through the crowd in waves. Someone at the center of the action called out in a deep resonant voice.

Auraq slowed and considered turning about and taking a different route, circumventing the festival altogether, but more people were pouring into the square behind them. In moments, they were surrounded. The multitude of people that had turned out for the festival was astounding and spiked Auraq's unease. It would be easy enough for the two of them to blend into a crowd of this size, certainly, but if they were being tailed, Auraq would have a difficult time spotting it.

He glanced at Kane. Unaccustomed to such crowds, he was tensing up. He'd pulled into himself, tightening his arms against his torso as people pushed into his space, elbowing their way through and forcing themselves closer to the action. He was already being taken by the tide of bodies, drifting farther from Auraq. Losing him in the crowd would be catastrophic. Alone in this city, Kane would quickly fall prey to it. Auraq shoved someone aside who was attempting to squeeze between them, and then he reached out and scooped his hand around Kane's arm just above the elbow.

"Stay with me," he said, and led him deeper through the churning mass of bodies.

They cut through the square at a bias toward the nearest street that led out, and wove against a tide of new arrivals. The street was narrow and took a steep incline. It eventually intersected with a larger byway, and the number of people

116

thinned. Auraq released Kane's arm.

"We are going back to your father's?" Kane asked.

Auraq nodded. "Still the safest place for you tonight." He had struggled to think of alternatives, but until he knew more about the Order, his father's shop seemed to be the best hole for Kane to hide in.

"And you?"

"I would not be welcome under his roof." He saw the protest forming on Kane's lips. "I will be nearby," he added.

The thumping festival music and the cheers of the crowd faded as they drifted farther from the square. The festival had the added effect of bleeding the streets dry of all others—few roamed through these narrow byways. It seemed the entire city had joined the party, and the vacancy it created in the streets left Auraq with an odd, unsettled feeling in his gut.

He kept a steady pace, not wanting to be out in the empty streets too long. He wasn't sure what was worse—a crowded square where he couldn't keep his eye on everyone around him, where someone passing by could put a knife into Kane before he was even aware of it, or alone on a street where they could be ambushed, and there'd be no one around to hear it.

But no ambush came.

The shop was locked up tight. His father had left for home for the night, or perhaps had joined the festivities in the square. He would have clients there, and he always felt it was good business to have a pint or two with those who paid his way in life. Auraq dug out the key from behind a loose brick in the wall and unlocked the shop door.

Inside was dark but still warm. Auraq moved into the shop while Kane stood at the threshold holding open the door. Even after his years of absence, Auraq knew his way around well enough to navigate through it with confidence. He grabbed a tallow candle from the cupboard against the wall, not surprised his father still stored them there. The embers in the fireplace had enough glow yet for Auraq to light the candle, and with it, he lit the lanterns hanging from iron nails driven into the posts.

Kane stepped in once the place was lit and closed the door

behind him. "We've not eaten anything."

"He'll have food here somewhere. In the back, most likely. For clients. It bothers him if he doesn't have something to offer them."

Kane wandered deeper into the shop, looking around as if it was his first time there. He seemed more ill at ease now than he had earlier in the day. Something about being in Malgar's space without him around made Kane uncomfortable. Or perhaps it was because he was alone in the shop with Auraq. Kane leaned against the work counter, arms wound tightly against his chest.

Auraq made one more sweep through the shop, checking all the hiding places he had known as a youth. Then he moved toward the door. "Lock the door behind me."

"I'd rather not be left alone, Auraq."

"I'll be nearby."

Kane breathed out heavily. "That is not the same."

"I told you. My father—"

"Is not here." Kane spread his hands wide. "Malgar may take issue with your past, Auraq, but I told you, I don't care."

"You should." If the army finally did catch up with him and Kane were with him, there was a danger for him as well. He could face punishment for harboring a known fugitive. "And the less you know of it, the better."

Irritation flashed across Kane's features. "Gods! Stop treating me like some lost country mouse. Just be honest. You don't want to stay here because you're afraid."

Auraq almost barked out a laugh. He couldn't remember the last time he had been accused of that. "Afraid?"

"Yes. You are afraid I'll press you further about your past. About these crimes of yours. It's why you wanted to pawn me off onto the mages. I ask too many questions, and it makes you uncomfortable."

That last part that was certainly true.

Kane put his hands on top of his head. "You can be so… maddening at times. You pretend that nothing bothers you, that you feel nothing. But it's all there, just locked up tight in some little box. No one is ever allowed to see it."

"My past is no concern here."

"So again, I'm expected to trust you fully, but I'm not allowed to know anything about you. Is it because you think I'm too naïve to understand? You believe I can't handle hard truths about the world?" Kane raked his fingers through his hair and looked toward the ceiling. His arms lingered about in the air as if they did not know where to go next, so he folded them up again. "Well, perhaps I'm not the innocent you seem to think I am."

This time, Auraq could not help but laugh. "You come from a tiny corner of the map. What can you know of this world?" Auraq could see by the way Kane's face fell a bit and the way he shifted his eyes away that his words stung.

"I know what shame looks like," Kane replied coolly. "I know guilt. And I know what they can do to your insides when left to fester. I recognize these in you because I feel them myself. Every day."

Auraq felt a rush of heat on his cheeks. His hands tightened until fingernails bit into the meat of his palm. What can he know of his own grief and his shame? He wanted to turn on his heel and march out, putting a decisive end to the discussion, but instead he found himself responding with a sharper edge to his tone than he intended. "What crimes have you committed that can compare to mine? You once let a sheep get away and it was taken by a wolf?"

Kane's eyes shot up to meet Auraq's. "The fire that killed my family? Both my parents, my sister, and my baby brother? I set it."

Auraq was stunned into silence. He stared back at Kane, suddenly having nothing to say. Some unseen energy was robbed from the entire room, leaving him unable to respond.

"Yes, you heard that correctly. I set our home on fire." Kane held his eyes on Auraq with a hard glare, waiting for a challenge. After several moments, his expression softened. He turned his head away, and his body followed. "Not intentionally. But it was me nonetheless."

"How?" Auraq heard himself ask. He did not recognize his own voice.

"I dropped a lantern coming in from the privy. The oil splashed on a quilt Ma was making and it took." Kane lifted his eyes. "I could not believe how quickly. I panicked. I did not want to face my dad's belt for damaging the house, so I never yelled for help. I thought I could take care of it myself. I ran out to the well to get a bucket of water. By the time I got back, the flames had already spread throughout the house and I couldn't get back in. I couldn't get to them. I tried shouting. But they never came out."

Auraq felt he should say something, but he didn't know what, so he stayed quiet.

"So," Kane continued after a time. "Whatever it is that is in your past, I am hardly the one to lay a verdict upon you."

"That was an accident," Auraq said quietly. "And you were a child."

"And you think that lessens the burden of guilt that I bear every day?"

"Still. It is not the same." The argument was losing potency, he knew, but he wasn't willing to admit that just yet.

Kane sighed in frustration and turned away. Auraq could see his shoulders rise and fall with his breathing. Kane picked up one of Malgar's tools from the counter and turned it about in his hand to inspect it before he dropped it hard on the counter again. It landed with a sharp thud that seemed to shake the dense silence between them. Then Kane's shoulders squared up and he turned back around again. "Well… that settles it, I suppose."

"Settles what?"

"I thought perhaps…." Kane shook his head and left the thought unfinished. "But no, I will never really be a person to you, will I?"

"What are you talking about?"

"I'm a task, Auraq. An oath made to an old man. I'm a mission to complete so you can rest at night that you've done your *duty*."

Auraq stared back at him. His body stiffened as echoes

from his past burst cruelly into his mind. This was not the first time he'd heard this. This was not the first time he'd been reproached for taking his duty and obligation seriously.

"You have done more than what you agreed to, I think. Far more," Kane continued. "Old Tan's spirit will not haunt you, I promise. You have brought me safely here to this city, introduced me to the mages. Tomorrow I will ask them for their aid and shelter. Which means I will no longer be in need of your protection."

Auraq felt something flip in his stomach. Kane's tone was different. It was cooler than before. Tighter.

"I can find my own way tomorrow," Kane added. "I remember the route well enough."

"I don't think—"

"I cannot thank you enough, Auraq." Kane looked at him with a slight tilt of his head, a fresh serenity in his eyes. "I truly would not be here if it weren't for you. I only wish there was some way I could repay you someday." He gave a slow bob of his head. "But I can't imagine we shall meet again after tonight."

"The oath I made—"

"Fulfilled," Kane cut in, opening his arms wide. "Tenfold over."

Auraq stepped forward, extending out his hand as if he expected Kane to take it. "You know the danger. Why are you saying this?" He felt a distinct twist to his insides—the cause of which he did not understand.

"Because it's time. Because this is what you want. And I won't be a burden to you further."

"I want to see you safe."

"I will be," Kane said softly. "You needn't worry." When Auraq didn't move or make a sound, he added, "Really. You can go."

Auraq felt as if his legs had turned to stone. He turned his head to stare at a single gray brick in the wall and was oddly aware of his own breathing. This wasn't right. He knew he was not going to walk out of there, leave Kane alone, and assume he would be safe. He had made an oath—

But even as he thought the words, he recognized that it was now more than the oath he had made to Old Tan. Without even being aware of it, his involvement had evolved into something new. He could not, of course, live with himself if he learned later on that something had happened.

He didn't understand why, but something deep in his gut told him the truth of it. Unseen forces had brought Old Tan and Kane to his fire that night. Perhaps the Gods themselves had guided him to that spot for his camp and, in doing so, charged him with Kane's protection. Was this done so he could atone for his earlier sins?

He belonged there—with Kane. He knew this right down to the foundation of his core. He was destined to see this through.

As shocking as Kane's own story had been, he trusted Auraq enough to share it with him. Perhaps… just perhaps, he was supposed to trust Kane in return.

He had nothing to lose, really. Kane was now pushing him out the door—for a reason Auraq didn't entirely understand. And even more strangely, Kane had taken Auraq's declaration of being a murderer in stride, as if it were the most common of experiences. Kane's unwavering trust in him had not been affected in the least. So… what was stopping him?

Nothing. Nothing was stopping him.

The alarms ringing in his head, warning him of the dangers that could come, fell silent. His stomach still quivered with nervousness, but there was an odd feeling of peace too. He need only open his mouth and it would come. He took in a long breath and, for the first time, gave his account of the events that occurred four years ago.

"I was married once," he said.

Chapter 15

AURAQ COULD sense Kane's energy change, but he didn't dare look up. He kept his eyes fixed on the wood grain of the floor.

"Her name," he continued, "was Bellora. She was a good woman. Kind, gentle. By all accounts, I was a lucky man." He paused, and in the thick silence that followed, he half expected Kane to interject something. Anything. But he remained perfectly quiet and perfectly still.

"But, as it turns out, I was not a very good husband."

He paused again as the memories began to breach the wall he had constructed in his mind. Kane's prodding had weakened the resolve he had spent years building. Now, saying Bellora's name aloud and acknowledging she was once in his life provided the tiniest of cracks and the images flooded back to him unbidden in a dark and unhappy torrent. He took another long breath and shook his head. "I don't even know, really, where to start."

"Wherever you need to," Kane said softly.

There was something in his voice that Auraq couldn't quite discern. Sorrow, maybe, but it was something more. Was he regretting now that he'd pushed Auraq to open up this vein?

"I was a lieutenant at the time. Second in command in my division. I rose through the ranks quickly and was awarded an officer's position only a year after I joined the king's army. As an officer, I was provided a small cabin at our post and wives and such were permitted to live with us when our division was not considered to be active. Happy to be out of the city, for a while at least, Bellora lived with me then."

He felt his mouth pull down. He shook his head to ward off the wave of regret and self-recrimination that threatened to overwhelm him. He had not allowed it to affect him in so very long—just a scratch on the surface and all the pain was there again, forgotten for a time perhaps, but still unhealed. "Married life was… not what I expected. Had you considered taking a wife before any of this happened?"

"I am not one to marry, I think," Kane replied.

"I should have waited," Auraq said with a nod. "I see that now. I was… too focused on my career." He remembered all too well his state of mind at the time. There were duties—to his men, to his region… to his king. He had tried on occasion to explain the burden of his commission, the necessity of his full commitment. But looking back, he questioned how earnest he was to convince her. He had just expected her to understand.

"An officer's responsibilities are many, I imagine," Kane put in.

"Yes, but not so many that I cannot attend to my wife's needs now and again."

"Surely, she understood. A talented officer such as yourself has obligations, and your progress through the ranks benefitted her and her station as well."

Auraq nearly smiled at Kane's kind attempt to absolve him of his role in what happened. He tilted his head and considered how to craft the words. "Well… at the time, Bellora didn't really consider that. She was young and fiery and passionate in a way that I was not. In my absence, she sought out someone else to take care of the duties that I wasn't providing her."

A moment passed before Kane's eyes lit with sudden understanding. "Oh," he said.

"It was in the arms of my lord commander that she landed. My superior… and at the time, my friend."

"Quite the betrayal. From both of them."

Auraq chuckled. "I suppose. But I knew of the affair and didn't care, oddly enough. I felt relieved, to be honest. Relieved that I could now concentrate on my duties without distraction."

"Then…. Auraq, I'm confused. If you weren't angry…."

Auraq took a deep breath, his heart tightening as he realized what Kane was implying. He believed this was about wild jealousy. "No, it wasn't like that. Bellora apparently felt some measure of guilt at the affair. She was not a wicked woman. Only lonely. She broke off the affair with Lord Renthe. But it would seem he loved her too, only his love was more… volatile. As many lords are, he was unaccustomed to not getting what he wanted."

Auraq stopped. He closed his eyes, but his vision was filled with the gruesome scene. All the blood…. There was so much blood from such a small creature.

"It was he who slew her," Kane finished for him in a very small voice.

Auraq nodded. "I had left our cabin that morning to conduct an inspection. But I'd forgotten something… I don't remember what anymore. Doesn't matter." His voice had grown thin, he noticed. Old rage, buried deep, rose up and pressed beneath the surface of his control like a hot spring ready to erupt. "I found him standing over her, still holding the sword he used to run her through. She was not yet dead. She was on the floor of our home, bleeding out, sobbing. There was no hope to save her."

Silence flooded into the room like a galley taking on water. Auraq stared down at the floor, not seeing anything. He reached out and pressed his hand to the wall to steady himself. He took in several long breaths before he continued.

"Renthe was not even aware that I had come in, I think." It was strange, thinking back on it now. He could recall Renthe—his face, his stance over Bellora—with uncanny clarity. He could see in his mind's eye all the blood. But he could not picture her. "I had my sword through his neck before his head ever turned. He died instantly, unlike Bellora who struggled for nearly a half an hour longer. All I could do was hold her while she cried her apologies in the last moments of her life and slowly lost consciousness.

"Of course, I knew they would blame me for both murders. I killed my lord commander, a nobleborn, which alone was a capital offense. I would see the ax. I could accept that, but I knew I could not bear to stand trial and hear them accuse me of killing Bellora. So I fled."

He lifted his head and risked a look at Kane. He stared back at him, ashen. But Auraq could not read what was behind his eyes. Repulsion? Fear? Pity?

"The swords," Kane said.

"Yes," Auraq answered with a nod. "One killed my wife. One killed my friend."

"And you carry them as penance, then."

Auraq nodded again. "I may not have faced the executioner, but I am reminded each day of my crime."

From the corner of his vision, Auraq saw Kane tilt his head up and cross his arms. His expression changed. He furrowed his brow and pressed his lips together. Auraq could sense the sting of the condemnation to come.

"I'm sorry," Kane said, finally. "But what crime are we talking about?"

Auraq threw him a surprised look. Had he not been listening at all?

Kane shook his head as if trying to untangle the issue in his own mind. "I certainly understand your grief. It is a tragic tale. But I'm unclear what you need to feel repentant about."

Auraq stood with rigid stillness and watched Kane's face carefully. This was not the response he'd expected. Far from it. Kane had nodded along with the story, adding a comment from time to time, so Auraq assumed he'd understood. What part of it was unclear?

"Auraq," Kane began and then paused. One side of his face contracted slightly as if he experienced a sudden pain. "That man was not your friend."

Auraq was stunned into silence. Was this some kind of jest? Some heartless mockery on his part? He searched Kane's features for signs of… something other than dogged seriousness, but Kane's expression remained steadfast and earnest.

"A friend does not sleep with his friend's wife and then kill her," Kane added.

Every muscle of Auraq's torso constricted at once. Kane was at it again, forever questioning and prodding. Why was he complicating a matter that should remain simple and straightforward? Kane challenged him on everything—it was his singular talent. Auraq had not prepared himself that Kane might actually challenge him on *this*.

"Don't," he said in a deep growl.

Kane pushed onward, unheeded. "Your *friend*, at the least, took advantage of her vulnerability. At the worst—"

"Kane." His inflection rose in warning.

"—acted like a spoiled noble who took what he wanted and disposed of her—"

Auraq threw out a hand to stop him before he went any further. "Do not think to muddy this with your callow, backwater logic—"

"Callow?" Kane's head snapped back as if slapped. "I'm not worldly enough to understand? Betrayal is too complicated a concept for me?"

"I slew him, Kane!"

"A just end for the man who ran your wife through."

Auraq was mystified by Kane's response. His head spun with the outrageousness of this. "He was nobleborn!" His voice was rising still louder, nearing a shout. Why didn't Kane understand the severity of that?

"Yes, yes. I got all that. Military rules aside for a moment, he'd killed a defenseless woman because he did not get his way. This was not a man of quality, Auraq. He deserved what he got. Oh, and don't you dare say it wouldn't have happened if you'd been a better husband. Bollocks! She made her own choices in this."

Auraq's face heated up until red started to tighten in around his vision. "Do not think to cast blame—"

"Defend her if you like, but she did not need to choose your friend and the commanding officer."

His rage was pushing at the crest of the levee, threatening to burst through. He clenched his fingers so tightly his knuckles popped. "This is dangerous ground you tread on, Kane."

Kane seemed unfazed. "What would have happened to your career, I wonder, if the men discovered you were being cuckolded by the commander himself? What view would you hold in their esteem, then?"

"That doesn't matter."

"Tell me, what would have happened if you hadn't run him through that day? Would he have let you live?"

Auraq knew the answer to that, but he said nothing.

"My guess," Kane continued, "is no." His eyes possessed an intensity that Auraq had not seen before. "He would not risk his military career for you, I wager. Not risk his noble station and prestige with the black cloud of a scandal. He would have struck you down and blamed you for the murder of your wife. He would tell the tribunal that he stumbled upon your wicked deed when he came to investigate a scream he heard—"

"Enough!" Auraq said through his teeth.

"—and you attacked him. He had no choice but to slay you. He would say you were wild and out of control—"

"*Enough!*" He took a heavy step toward Kane and stood over him with his arm cocked and ready to swing. It took all his will not to strike Kane in the face. A part of him wanted desperately to do it—it would finally put an end to his incessant questioning, his ceaseless pushing. "You've made your point."

Kane stared up at him with a hard glare and did not back down. He had no fear in his eyes. "The guilt and the pain has clouded your perspective on this, and cast this impenetrable shadow on your soul. You've assumed all the blame and left none for them. I'm trying to figure out why. What part of this has filled you with such shame, Auraq? The murder? The defection? Your role as a husband?"

The question unexpectedly bore deep into him like the shaft of a spear, causing him to stagger a moment. The cloak of anger he'd wrapped around himself was suddenly gone, leaving him exposed and cold. He felt empty inside, like a wineskin wrung dry.

"All of it," he said, and he turned away. "I am not the man I believed I was, Kane. If I had been, they both would still breathe today. Their blood is on my hands, and I will never escape the truth of that. I have become something else now, I think. What, I'm not entirely certain. But it is a thing without honor. A thing disgraced." His hand drifted to the hilt of the longsword that took Bellora from him. "A thing that takes the life of those he loves then runs to protect himself."

"It's true, then" came a voice from the door. "You admit it."

Auraq looked up and saw his father standing in the open doorway, the latch still in his hand.

"You admit you killed her." Malgar stepped into his shop. He turned to Kane. "He tells you of it, but to his own father he is silent."

"It is not what you think, Malgar," Kane replied weakly.

"I hear of his dishonor from soldiers who came to my door. They were searching for him. They tore my shop apart thinking I would harbor him here. I learned of his crime from strangers seeking to put him in irons."

"Malgar—" Kane tried to interject.

"He cannot even face me and tell me himself. He blackens my own service to the king, sends me into the pit of dishonor along with him, and he cannot even tell me himself."

Auraq felt his heart rate rise, but he forced his breathing to remain under his control.

"He is a coward," Malgar growled. "A gutless mouse unwilling to face the fate he deserves. And to put such a lovely creature to the sword. What could she have possibly done to deserve that?" Auraq could hear the pain in his father's voice. He had loved Bellora too. "Each day I am forced to look citizens of this city in the eye, knowing that they are aware that my own son is a monster. I am ashamed, but I am forced to endure it."

"Then tell the world that your son is dead," Auraq told him softly.

"I have for years," Malgar replied.

Auraq nodded. "I shall make this infinitely easier on you, then. You have my word that I will not think to darken your door again." He pushed past his father toward the door.

"As if your word has any meaning," his father told him.

Auraq stormed out into the dark street.

"AURAQ, WAIT."

He heard footsteps run up behind him.

Auraq slowed to a stop. But he did not turn around to face him.

"He doesn't mean what he says, Auraq," Kane said.

But Auraq knew the truth of it. He knew his father well enough to know that he did mean it. Every word. And what stung the most was he was not wrong in what he said.

"Will you be back tomorrow?" Kane asked.

"That is up to you."

"Yes," Kane answered without hesitation. "I want you to come with me back to the mages. I need you to be there."

Auraq nodded. "Then meet me here. At dawn. I will be waiting."

For some time, he felt Kane's presence behind him. Auraq could tell he was thinking of more to say, and the silence hung between them like a thick curtain. Eventually, he heard Kane's boots on the cobbles as he walked back to Malgar's shop. The door closed softly, and Auraq was left in the middle of the street wondering why he had agreed to any of this.

Chapter 16

AN HOUR or so before dawn, Auraq climbed down from the roof of the neighboring shop.

The carpenter's workshop had the benefit of a storage attic, which put the roofline higher than the surrounding buildings. The roof also had a low parapet that faced the alley. As a youth, Auraq had learned how to scale a nearby trellis and climb up onto the carpenter's rooftop from an adjacent building—a secure hiding place to both keep an eye out for his father and wait out his temper. From the roof, Auraq had a clear vantage point of the whole cul-de-sac below and the door to his father's shop. The small alleyway had only one lit lantern, but with the aid of the moonlight, it was enough.

He hadn't slept well, or much. The brief exchange with his father spawned a dark temper that settled deep in his gut. The words saturated his mind like a toxin and kept him on the precipice of sleep for most of the night. Instead of fighting it, he resigned himself to stare out over the alley below, watching for any movement. As far as he could tell, no one had approached Malgar's shop during the night. And strangely, he hadn't seen his father leave either. There was only one cot, so it didn't seem likely he'd stay. He must have slipped out late in the night during one of the few times Auraq had nodded off.

When at long last the sky started to lighten, he climbed down from his perch and slunk off to the baker's shop around the corner and bought a small warm loaf, apple butter, and cheese. Circling back, he ran into a food vendor laboring to push his cart up the street. Auraq purchased a couple of sausages from him. He sat on the cobbles outside the candlemaker's shop and ate his breakfast without really tasting any of it.

There was a moment while he ate that he considered

standing up and walking off. He wanted to pick a street that led him away and leave. Leave the neighborhood. Leave the city. How would that feel, he wondered. Right now, everything felt somehow wrong. Out of balance. Like someone had reached a stick deep into his mind and stirred up something that had settled at the bottom, and now everything was murky and dark. He'd had clarity once. He hadn't liked what he saw then, but at least it made sense to him. He wanted that clarity back.

He stood up, brushed the crumbs from his chest, and returned then to his father's alley. He expected to see Kane outside the shop, looking anxious. A figure was there waiting for him.

It took Auraq's exhausted mind a moment to realize it was not Kane.

Malgar was leaning against the wall, his chin down and arms crossed over his chest. He glanced up and spotted Auraq as he came around the corner, and then he stumbled out into the street. He looked haggard, unkempt. As he crossed the alleyway toward Auraq, he seemed as if he'd aged years in the span of a single night.

Auraq's heart skipped. His first thought was that something must have happened to Kane. But the expression on his father's face told Auraq it was something else. He'd seen that look before.

He stopped and let his father come to him.

Malgar came to a staggering halt in front of him. He glared hard at Auraq with an expression that lingered somewhere between anger and pain. "You fucking bastard."

Auraq stood very still.

His father's hands were clenched, and he shook his head from side to side as he looked at his feet. "All these years. All these fucking years." He seemed reluctant to even look up.

Auraq instinctively glanced to his father's belt for a weapon. He seemed in the mood to want to use one.

"Is it true, then?" Malgar asked through tight teeth.

Auraq fought back a surge of anger, but still felt heat ignite through his entire face as the realization set in. Kane. Of course.

He had opened his mouth to his father last night. Auraq had trusted him with his story—and in a matter of hours, he had already betrayed him.

When Auraq didn't respond, Malgar pulled his shoulders back. He pressed his lips into a white line. "It is true, isn't it? Gods burn you to ash, it is true."

He stared hard at Auraq with a tight brow, surely expecting him to voice some kind of denial. But Auraq did not have the strength to fight it. He exhaled carefully, attempting to control his own pain rising fresh to the surface. He was certain his face told Malgar everything.

The silent pause that followed felt like poison in his gut.

"Why didn't you tell us?" Malgar snarled low in his throat. He made a lunge forward, punching Auraq in the shoulder with the heel of his hand, and his voice rose to a near shout. "Why didn't you fucking tell us?"

"There was no point?" Auraq responded. His voice was barely audible, even to himself.

His father reeled back as if Auraq had struck him. "No point? No *point*?" He lunged again, thrusting both his hands against Auraq's chest with surprising strength for a man his age. This time, Auraq was forced back a step. "I believed you were craven. That you were a monster. You… my only son, a fugitive. A *criminal*."

"I am a criminal, Pa."

"That is not what I meant," Malgar snapped back. He took an unsteady step backward and closed his eyes. "It… it killed me a little each day. It tore at my heart to even think your name."

Auraq felt his own heart twist, but he said nothing.

Malgar's eyes lifted with fire behind them. "How could you do this to me?"

"I did nothing—"

"You fucking let me believe you were not the man I raised you to be. You let me think you were a man without honor. You let me think I *failed*. Your mother died thinking…." He turned his head away. "Thinking the worst."

"Blood is on my hands, Pa." His voice was weaker than he

intended. Strangely, the words sounded flat to his ears, as if some part of him no longer believed that—and that fueled his anger. He would not allow himself to be tricked into not taking responsibility for his part in it.

"But not her blood," Malgar growled.

Yes. Her blood was there too. He would not allow himself to think otherwise.

"I abandoned my commission to escape punishment. Beyond that, the particulars do not matter."

Malgar pounded down the air with closed fists. "It does matter, dammit! All this time, I reviled you. Cursed your name, wished you were not my son. I burned anything I found that belonged to you." His expression changed then. The anger weakened like a lantern short of fuel, and Auraq caught sight of the deep pain and betrayal that lay beneath it. "Now I find out the truth of it. From a stranger, no less. I learn that you are not the devil I believed you to be."

Auraq stood utterly still.

"All these years… all these years I could have been there for you. You took that from me."

A force from deep within compelled Auraq to respond. There was much he wanted to say, had imaged saying over the years, but now—at that moment—he dared not form the words. So he choked them all back down again and said nothing.

The door to the workshop opened again, and Kane stepped out, looking uncertain. His eyes shifted from one to the other before he approached the two of them slowly, cautiously.

Malgar made a quick swipe of his cheek with the heel of his hand. "I could never understand how you could…." He seemed to lose all strength. His shoulders sank, and he let the words trail off, unfinished.

Auraq's insides ached. He had never seen his father affected so. He'd always been the symbol of stoic strength in Auraq's life. This was not a side of his father he wanted to witness.

He turned a cold gaze to Kane. "We have to leave."

Malgar's eyes lit as if he'd just come out of a dream.

"Leave?" He took a step closer and held out his palm. "No. Wait." He seemed to gather himself and twist himself into some calmer version. "Wait. Come into the shop."

The sudden shift was jarring. All the anger from moments before had evaporated, and now he almost seemed on the verge of panic. Auraq could tell his father was now regretting the words he'd said. But the words didn't matter. None of it did.

He turned to leave.

Malgar grabbed his arm. "Auraq. I should have trusted you, not listened to the gossip—"

Auraq shook his head and lifted his father's hand from his bicep. "It would have changed nothing."

He started down the cobbles toward the street below.

"Dammit, fucking speak to me!"

He stopped—almost against his own will. His father's booming voice always seemed to have some insuperable power over him. A heartbeat passed. Then two. "I cannot," he said. Then he forced his legs into motion again and abandoned the small collection of workshops, leaving his father standing in the middle of the narrow alley.

KANE RAN to catch up. For a time, he simply walked beside Auraq, struggling to match his hard pace, yet he said nothing. Auraq could not bring himself to look at him. He handed off the small gunnysack of the remaining bread, apple butter, and cheese without turning his head. At least, Auraq figured, eating would keep him quiet for a while.

They traveled yet again back through the streets of the city. The Merchant District was slow to recover from the festival the night before. The long market square looked as if a riot had occurred. Bunting and flags had been torn down, food carts were overturned or smashed, and the pool surrounding the central fountain was filled with so much floating debris, the water was no longer visible. Auraq thought there might have even been a body floating in it, but he didn't get close enough to check for certain. The dregs of the city had filtered out from their holes to scavenge through the remains while city porters tried without much success to attend to the mess. At this hour, traffic should have been starting to fill up the streets, but too many were likely nursing hangovers. The district would not rebound until the afternoon.

"You're angry with me," Kane said.

Auraq didn't respond. Angry didn't begin to describe it.

"I'm sorry. He'd only heard the last bit of what you said. I… couldn't let him believe that about you."

"It was not your story to tell."

"But he believed it was you who had run her through."

Auraq stopped and met Kane's eyes. "Yes, precisely."

Kane stared back at him dumbfounded. "Auraq, I don't understand. He's your father. Doesn't he deserve to know the truth?"

"The truth." Auraq shook his head at the word, and a low humorless chuckle escaped his throat. "You think I relish that he views me as a butcher?"

"Then why have you let him believe it?"

"To keep him out of it, Kane. You heard him. He would have tried to help me. He would view my sentence as unjust, and would have risked all to save me."

Kane clearly hadn't considered that. "You're protecting him?"

"It is easier this way." His mouth turned down. "Or was, rather."

Auraq resumed his march onward without comment, but Kane grabbed his arm. "Auraq, Malgar would rather die protecting his son than live on thinking he's a monster."

That, Auraq thought, was obvious.

After they traversed the ravaged and widely vacant market square at a bias, they cut up the street that led to the Academy District. As they approached the gates, Auraq stopped.

"Something's happened."

Chapter 17

THE PORTCULLIS at the Academy Gate was still down. By this time in the morning, it should already have been raised to allow supplies to make their way to the academy complex. When Auraq and Kane approached the pass-through along the side of the gate, a young guard stepped up and held out his hand to ward them off. He was not garbed in the academy livery. This was a city guardsman.

"State your business here," the guard said. The helm covered a good portion of the face, but Auraq could still tell he was young. The stiff back and uneasy way he carried himself branded him as inexperienced, but Auraq could tell he relished his newly acquired authority. A second guardsman, equally young, stood close by, watching the exchange.

Auraq gave him a level stare. "We are expected."

"The academy is closed until further notice." The line had the quality of a rote answer he'd been provided by superiors.

"The academy?" Auraq asked. "Or the entire district?"

The question seemed to throw him off a step. He hadn't anticipated a challenge. "All scheduled appointments have been suspended. You'll have to come back another time."

Auraq didn't have time for this. There could be only one reason to utilize new recruits like this to ward people off from the district. The rest of the city guardsmen were needed elsewhere.

"We have important intelligence to deliver," he said, stepping into the guard's space. "Captain Bennidar himself is awaiting it." Auraq could see the effect the name had on the lad in his eyes. Auraq waited for a new objection, but when none came, he guided the young guardsman out of the way with a sweep of his arm.

Once past the gate, Auraq could immediately sense the strange suspension of energy inside the district. People were clustered on street corners in tight circles, leaning in and talking in harsh whispers. Their faces showed fear and apprehension. As Auraq and Kane crossed the broad square and drew closer to the academy compound, Auraq noticed a significant increase in the presence of both the academy and city guard. Some were posted at regular intervals through the square, and others were questioning civilians. A few more were running off with urgent messages to report.

Chaos dominated the steps leading up to the main hall. Mages, dressed in their telltale silken robes, milled about wringing their hands and speaking to members of the guard. Most were visibly shaken; some were crying or comforting others who were. An elderly woman was trying to usher along a group of children who looked confused and frightened. Auraq had never seen so many mages gathered in one place before. He was surprised there were that many in the town at all.

Auraq felt a deep hollowness in the pit of his stomach.

"Auraq?" Kane asked quietly at his elbow. "What is going on?"

"We have to go," he said. "Now." He turned to head back across the wide plaza toward the gates, but Kane seemed rooted in place.

"Why? What's happened?"

Auraq grunted with impatience. He stood close to Kane and spoke only loud enough for him to hear. "Chenigal is dead, Kane." He hoped he was wrong.

Kane stepped back away from Auraq, eyes wide. "How can you know that?"

"Look around. There's been an attack here. The entire academy's been mobilized. City and academy guards—"

"That doesn't mean—"

"Kane, this is no coincidence. They found out about our visit with Chenigal. Somehow. We need to leave before someone recognizes us." Members of the Order would certainly be in the churning crowd looking for them. If they knew of the visit to Chenigal yesterday, they likely knew of their appointment today. Luckily, they'd set no specific time to meet him.

Kane's face had drained of color. "They're here? In Har Tesera."

Auraq could tell by his expression that he'd hoped they'd lost them for good. So had he, really. But he knew better.

"They attacked the mages? Gods burn us, Auraq, who are these people?"

Auraq realized he had never filled him in on what he learned. "A conversation for later. Let's go." He turned again to leave, but Kane grabbed his arm.

"You know something?" A flash of anger crossed Kane's eyes. "You know who's after me?"

Someone was moving toward them at a jog. Driven by instinct, Auraq reached for the hilt of the longsword—but his brain caught up a moment later as he recognized who approached.

The young mage arrived breathless and frantic. He was accompanied by two guards from the district.

"You're here," he said between gasps. "I saw your name on today's roster, but didn't know if you'd come."

It was the mage at the desk Auraq had scheduled the appointment with. "Hargan, what's happened?"

He shook his head. "Oh, it's terrible. Just terrible. But, you need to come with me. I'm supposed to bring you straight to my master if I located you."

His master. Auraq allowed himself a moment of hope. Whatever had happened, perhaps it didn't involve Chenigal after all.

Auraq made a quick audit of his very short list of options. He could refuse, and he and Kane could flee the district, and then the city while there was time. Before the Order realized they were there. But if the guards were instructed to bring them by any means necessary, that could instigate an altercation. He could handle the two of them easily enough, but that would bring about unwanted attention. Or they could agree and follow

Hargan. A conversation would take place somewhere less public—away from eyes that were potentially searching for them—and maybe they would learn more about what happened.

A part of him needed to know if Chenigal had survived the attack. If they left now, they'd never know.

"Lead on," he said.

Hargan nodded, then scampered up a pathway that diverged left of the great staircase rising up to the main academy building. The two guards waited for Auraq and Kane to move. "Quickly, quickly," Hargan called back.

Auraq glanced at Kane, offered a simple reassuring nod, and then followed after Hargan. Kane remained at his elbow. They jogged along the winding pathway up a hill. At its crest, the path led them beneath an ancient stone archway that may have once been part of a building that no longer existed. Auraq and Kane were thrust into a quiet and thinly occupied courtyard garden—a striking counterpoint to the whirling commotion down in the Academy Square. A wall of trees and thick shrubbery circled the perimeter, shrouding them from the surrounding city and creating an illusion of isolation. The path snaked through perfectly manicured beds of lush flowers.

A few guardsmen in academy livery marched about, looking official. Hargan veered toward a cluster of three mages who stood conferring under a tree laden with pink flowers.

The small group consisted of two men and one woman, each lanky and thin with age. Long white hair draped down the backs of their ornate silken robes. The men had great flowing beards, braided and strung with beads. Brightly colored scarves with elaborate stitching spilled from their shoulders and down their fronts—clearly auspices of authority. They broke off their conversation when Hargan dashed toward them.

"Master Lysere," he said. "The one on the ledger."

His master. Not Chenigal after all. Auraq's heart felt like stone and sank deeper into his chest.

The oldest of the mages regarded them with a suspicious eye as they approached. He leaned on a long staff of dark banewood for support. What little of his face that wasn't covered in beard was deeply furrowed around the eyes and across the brow. "You the one named Auraq?" The mage's tone was dripping with hot condescension and disdain.

Auraq's jaw tightened in irritation. "I am."

"The one who conferred with Chenigal yesterday? And this is the one who accompanied you? You are?"

"Kane, Master."

"What's this about?" Auraq cut in. He could hear the sharpness in his tone but was powerless to curtail it. He was ready to put this place behind them and get Kane somewhere safe—they didn't have time for a long, drawn-out interrogation by three haughty mages. He knew where this conversation was heading, of course. Their meeting with Chenigal yesterday had made them suspects. If he wasn't careful, he and Kane could end up in irons.

The man scowled at him. One did not talk to a mage like he was a simple shopkeeper. "What was your business with him yesterday?"

Auraq looked at each mage in turn. "Is it not your policy that anything discussed remains confidential?"

"Circumstances change, surrah," the woman said. She was tall and thin, with swirling silver locks spilling down the front of her shoulders. Her eyes were crisp blue, like a winter's sky. She turned her cool attention briefly to Hargan, and some silent exchange took place between them.

Hargan made a sudden and nervous bow to her. "Of course. Forgive me, Mistress. Auraq, this is Mistress Pyta. She is headmistress of the entire academy and first of our order here in Har Tesera."

Auraq had guessed as much. He could tell by the way she carried herself that she was the leader among them. She stood with a straight back and her chin up, and had the look of someone who suffered the presence of only an elite few. Auraq took a bold step forward and addressed the woman directly. "We'll not answer any more of your questions," he replied flatly. "Tell me what this is about."

Silence among the three mages hung in the air as they

stared back at him in shock. Auraq knew he had crossed a line and was marching into dangerous territory now. These mages were unimaginably powerful, and certainly unaccustomed to anything other than complete compliance. All it would take was a nod from Pyta to the guards and he would be dragged away and thrown into a dungeon.

The two other mages caught each other's gaze, their expressions sour. They were trying to decide how to handle his insolence.

"The academy suffered an attack last night," Mistress Pyta replied. She did not seem fazed by his lack of reverence. She spoke plainly, with little inflection to her tone, as if describing what she had for dinner. But Auraq could see the sorrow she tried to conceal behind her eyes. "In the attack, Master Chenigal was murdered. Brutally. In his own chamber." She narrowed her eyes, studying his reaction to the news.

Kane made a slow exhale behind him.

It didn't matter that Auraq already knew it in his heart. Hearing it spoken aloud felt like a physical blow. His insides tightened and quaked.

There could be no greater catastrophe for them. It left them no closer to finding out the truth about the mark on Kane's arm. And in the aftermath of this, any chance of getting further help from the academy now was close to zero. To get any answers, their only hope now was to travel to another city, find another mage guild and another mage willing to help. And more so…. Auraq had once again underestimated the reach of the Order of the Jackal. They had infiltrated the sanctum of mages and murdered one of their elite. Of all places, he had believed this one was at least relatively safe from them.

"That is sad news," Kane said gently.

Auraq could hear the disquiet in Kane's voice. He too understood the implication of Chenigal's murder.

"Indeed," Pyta replied. "Others too were slain. Apprentices, guards, servants. Twenty in all, but they appear to just have been in the wrong place at the wrong time. Master Chenigal was clearly the target of this assassination." She spoke in a tone that was a delicate accusation that all of that was somehow his fault. Which, Auraq figured, was in a sense more accurate than he cared to admit. Pyta closed her eyes and shook her head slowly. "An unprecedented massacre. Unlike anything the academy has ever seen."

"Are you certain Master Chenigal was the intended target?" Auraq himself had no doubt, but he wanted to hopefully shake loose how much they knew.

"Without question," Pyta said. "The assassins themselves made that clear enough."

Auraq wondered what form of indication was left behind—then decided he didn't want to know.

"I would like for you to account for your whereabouts, surrah. Can someone vouch that you indeed left the academy campus yesterday when your meeting was concluded?"

The mage at Auraq's right stole a glance at the swords at his waist. Did they expect to see a mage's blood dripping from the bottom of the sheath?

His skin prickled around his shoulders as they tightened up toward his ears. His hands clenched into balls at his sides.

"You are suggesting I had something to do with this?"

"Answer the question," Lysere scolded him as if Auraq were a child.

"And you will speak to her with the proper deference, surrah," the man to Auraq's right added. They were growing less tolerant of his uncivil tone.

"I am not of your order," Auraq replied. He felt himself pushing them into a reaction, as if daring them to arrest him. "Your existence alone does not warrant my veneration." Lack of sleep and gnawing unease about the Order's presence here was fraying his patience. They were losing valuable time. Despite the relative isolation of the garden, Auraq was not convinced that the Jackals were not lurking about nearby, searching for them. Now that he'd learned of Chenigal's fate, he was ready to quit the place.

"We were escorted out of the building by one of your own guards," Kane said. He was attempting to de-escalate the rising tension, Auraq knew. "You have our word." Always the peacemaker. Always trying to make things right.

Pyta caught the eye of one of the guards and tilted her head to the side. "Locate that guardsman," she said. He nodded and dashed off.

Their word was not enough, apparently. But there was a subtle change in Pyta's expression. Her gaze on them was less antagonistic. Less accusatory. A part of her had already accepted their story.

"When did your meeting conclude?" she asked once the guard had gone.

"After the academy was officially closed to the public," Kane answered. "I am not aware of the precise time."

Pyta's features betrayed a moment of deep sadness. "I cannot expect you to fully grasp the severity of the incident. Chenigal was held in the highest of esteem here at the academy. He may even have replaced me one day." Her eyes focused on Kane. Perhaps she recognized him as the real reason for their meeting with Chenigal. Perhaps she saw Kane as the more cooperative of the two of them. "I respect the confidentiality you shared with him. Under normal circumstances, I would not ask this of you. But we are desperate. Desperate for any intelligence that could lead to the ones who perpetrated this atrocity. I must insist that you tell us anything that you can. The smallest of details might lead to answers."

Auraq felt the pull of her words. Telling them about the mark on Kane's arm could potentially lead to her aid—but he was still hesitant to share too much. Auraq was growing more and more convinced that the attack was the work of someone inside the academy itself. How else could the Order have overcome the academy's formidable defenses? Any one of the three in front of him could even be directly involved.

And the longer they were there, the more likely it was the Order would learn of their presence.

He felt Kane's eyes on him. He was waiting for Auraq to decide what to do.

"Was anything taken from his study?" Auraq asked.

144

Pyta's eyes widened a fraction. "Curious question. Why would you think to ask that?"

"I would think it obvious. It would answer if this was solely an assassination. Or were they after something specific?" Auraq would've wagered all he had that the book with Chenigal's notes on the mark was nowhere to be found.

"That is something we are investigating, yes," Pyta answered. It was clear she would say no more on the subject.

The sounds of boots approaching made everyone turn. Guards marched toward them, led by none other than the captain of the North Gate himself, Bennidar. His face was tight with aggravation. It appeared he had had quite the morning already.

He bowed to the mages first—with far more respect and esteem than Auraq could have managed. "Masters," he greeted. "Mistress Pyta. Please excuse this intrusion. Can I be of assistance to you?"

The third mage rolled his eyes. "Hardly, I'd wager. We are questioning a person we deem of interest in this atrocity. Someone I would have thought you would have already tracked down and questioned. These are the two who met with Chenigal late yesterday. A suspicious occurrence in and of itself, if you ask me. Master Chenigal would not have receive—"

"That is why I've come, Masters. I assure you, this man does not merit your attention. He had no role in last night's attack."

"And exactly how can you be so certain of that, Captain?"

"He is known to us, Madam Pyta. And witnesses put him elsewhere at the time of its occurrence."

Auraq frowned. Witnesses?

The third mage lifted a skeptical eyebrow. "Hardly a dependable alibi. With mages involved in this, the possibility of an illusion would make any witness unreliable."

Mistress Pyta shot the mage a hard look. The man had clearly spoken out of turn. They were aware then that someone within their circle had betrayed them—information that the academy did not want publicly known.

"The fact is," Bendo continued, "this man does not possess

the skills necessary to infiltrate your defenses here. And the evidence is consistent with a larger force. This man is a loner. He does not work well with anyone."

Pyta stared down at Bendo with a glower of disdain. It was clear she did not care for him. "We are attempting to ascertain if he has information that he is withholding—"

"Forgive me," he interrupted with a bow of respect. "I assure you, this dullard has no knowledge of the grisly matter. But if it pleases you, I will take them from your custody and interrogate them both thoroughly myself. We have effective methods in obtaining information from suspects, and there is no need to for you to sully your own hands with this."

Auraq stiffened. Bendo was providing the exit he needed—but he worried the mages wouldn't let him leave so easily.

Mistress Pyta held her cool stare on him for a time, then pursed her lips and exhaled through her nose in quiet agreement. "Assuming I can trust the city guard to handle this properly. Bungle this matter, Captain, and I assure you there will be repercussions for your division."

Bendo replied with a calm demeanor and a slight smile that nearly seemed genuine. "Mistress Pyta, I promise you that it will be handled with the greatest import."

"Then keep him for now," she answered with a nod. "But I will want to question him later myself. Ensure that he's available when I require it."

"Of course, Mistress."

The mages all turned in unison and glided away.

Once they were out of earshot, Bendo huffed loudly. "Come on. We don't have much time."

Chapter 18

AFTER DISPATCHING the other guards with him on some pointless errand, Bendo moved at a clip down a narrow street leading away from the academy plaza, Auraq and Kane trailing close behind.

"Insufferable gasbags," he said over his shoulder.

"Deal with them often?" Auraq asked.

"More than I care to. Part of the job, I suppose. They use the North Gate more than the others. Lucky me, eh?"

Kane tugged on Auraq's arm. "Who is this?"

"Old friend," Auraq answered dryly under his breath. He was as surprised as any that Bendo had stuck his neck out to help them.

Bendo was still talking. "That lot is all ego and bluster. Sometimes you just got to massage their nut sack and let them wiggle their fingers around in your ass for a while. Eventually they feel respected enough to leave you in peace."

"Where are you taking us?" Kane called out to Bendo's back.

Bendo glanced behind him and seemed to notice Kane for the first time. His eyes raked over him as if evaluating him before he turned his gaze back to Auraq. "Got word Jackals are combing the entire district for you two."

"Jackals?"

Bendo's mouth scrunched on one side. "He doesn't know? Never told him?" He shook his head. "You never change, do you?"

"Tell me what?"

Auraq shot Bendo a hard glare. "They call themselves the Order of the Jackal. That is all I know."

A flash of uncertainty crossed Kane's eyes—a look that

said he was wondering if Auraq was holding back on him.

"Assassins," Bendo added. "Nasty ones. Bloody ruthless, they are. I'm getting you someplace safe for now. Then I'll work on a plan to get you out of the city."

Bendo was jumpy and strung tight—not his typical, cocksure self. Something had spooked him.

"How did you find us?"

"Pure luck. The Jackals painted the wall of the mage's chamber with their emblem. With his blood, mind you. After our conversation at the gate, I guessed it involved you somehow, so I started a sweep of the district. Down here." He ducked down a narrow alley behind a row of shops and flagged them along.

Bendo shouldered his way through a locked door and plunged into the back room of a cloth merchant, with Auraq and Kane close behind. A woman screeched and dropped a bolt of fabric on the floor.

Bendo barreled straight through the shop without slowing. Auraq stayed close to his heels while Kane made soothing sounds to assure the woman she wasn't in any danger.

"You're in it deep this time, friend," Bendo said. They exited out the front of the shop onto a narrow street thick with morning shoppers. Auraq didn't recognize the area at all, which meant they were still in the Academy District. "Amazed you're still standing and talking, to be honest. Not sure how much help I'm going to be. You'll probably just get me slaughtered right along with you." He chuckled, but it had no humor in it.

"Why're you here, then?" Bendo was never one to stick his neck out for anyone.

"Suppose I owe you one. You got me out of a pinch or two back in the day. But we have to move fast. Good thing Pyta found you so quick. Few would attempt to make a move around that powerful old bag."

Bendo slowed their pace some and merged with the lumbering crowd, attempting to blend in—then Bendo unexpectedly cut through another alleyway without warning. They zigzagged their way through the quarter until they came to the wall that surrounded the Academy District. Bendo pulled a thick ring of keys from his belt. He made a quick scan to see if anyone was watching, then ducked into a shadowed alcove. A heavy iron door was in the back. Bendo inserted the key into a keyhole and spun it about twice. After a hard click of the lock's release, it took Bendo three shoves before the door gave way and swung aside on stiff hinges. This door hadn't been used in a long while.

The three of them dashed through a dank corridor that landed them in the north end of the Merchant District. Auraq had to give Bendo credit; he certainly knew his way around the city.

After a quick scan, Auraq recognized the area—though it'd been years since he'd been through it. It was an older region of the city, rundown and largely abandoned—and more ramshackle than he remembered. Even nearing midday, the area was deserted and eerily quiet. The street, hardly wide enough for a cart to pass through, twisted and swerved like a mountain trail. The cobblestones had clearly gone years without seeing any repair, and many of the buildings seemed vacant and forsaken by their owners.

The street ended at a cramped plaza. A cart with a missing wheel was left abandoned next to a dry fountain pool. A larger building faced the plaza. It appeared to have once been something grand, but with much of its paint and plaster chipping off and its shutters rotting away, it appeared to have been converted into a makeshift warehouse. Two wide and considerably newer doors had been added to the front.

Bendo stole across the plaza for the warehouse, leaving Auraq wondering how he could have learned of the place. As Auraq and Kane followed, Bendo heaved on one of the handles of the wide doors. It rolled open with a squealing complaint on its overhead track. He pulled it open just enough to allow passage inside.

"How'd you find this?" Auraq asked.

"Ah, you know, patrol an area long enough, you're bound to uncover a few things."

"You're certain it's safe here?"

Bendo formed a weak smile. "Safer than out on the street,

I can tell you that."

With a theatrical wave of his hand, he signaled for Auraq and Kane to follow him on through. Auraq turned sideways to pass inside while questioning Bendo's overall plan. A big open warehouse didn't seem the best nook to hole up in.

Once everyone was inside, Bendo pulled the door shut again.

The gloom of decay hung over the place like a death shroud. Damp musk choked the air. The inside of the old building had been gutted and all that remained was its shell, leaving one wide-open space. Wood pillars had been added in the center to support the high roof. Pale sunlight streaked into the space from the windows on the street-side wall, igniting the swirling motes of dust that filled the air. The single glowing oil lantern that hung on a pillar offered a bit more light, but did little to push back the bleak dereliction.

The vast space was largely empty except for two pallets loaded with stacked crates—one at the far side of the warehouse, the other only a few steps from the door. Auraq strayed deeper into the room, allowing his eyes to adjust. He flipped back the lid of one of the crates. The inside was packed with straw. He reached beneath the layer and felt the long neck of a bottle. Frowning, he pulled it up, knowing what he was going to find before the rest of the bottle broke the surface.

No words identified the contents. There was just a crude image of a black rose painted on the glass.

He heard the click of the lock behind him. "There," said Bendo, tugging on the chain to make sure it held fast. "I think we'll be safe in here."

Auraq slowly replaced the bottle.

Black Rose. Contraband. A dangerous spirit that ended up killing most who drank it.

Frowning, he glanced over at the lit lantern hanging from the post.

With a quick tilt of his head, he gestured for Kane to move away from the door. Kane looked confused but complied without question. He moved along the wall, putting distance between himself and Bendo.

"So, tell me," Auraq asked. "How *exactly* did you learn about all the Jackals searching the Academy District for us?"

Bendo lifted his head like a startled rabbit. "What do you mean?"

"I find it strange. An organization as secretive and skilled as the Order allowed their activity to leak to a low-ranking Gate Captain."

Bendo's eyes flashed in irritation. "I still keep my ear to the ground. I have my sources."

"Who lit that lantern, Bendo? If no one knew we were coming here, why is it lit?"

Bendo swung his head to the lantern. His face fell and momentary panic flashed in his eyes. He tried to recover, feign a look of surprise and confusion, but it was too late, and he knew it. The ruse was exposed.

"You might as well have your friends come out now," Auraq said. One at a time, he put his hands on the hilts of his blades and slowly pulled them from their sheaths.

Bendo's expression shifted from innocence to contempt. "You're a fool, Auraq. You always were." The nervousness from before had evaporated and was now replaced with his characteristic puffed-up hubris. He'd led the wolf to the trap and believed the hard part was over.

The men hidden behind the crates slipped out into the pale light. Four in all. Dressed the same as the ones who had come for Old Tan and Kane at the campfire, complete with black fabric tied to hide their faces.

"Did they come to you?" Auraq asked. "Or did you run to them the second I left the North Gate?"

"Predictably simplistic," he replied with an eye roll. "As always. No imagination. I've always kept a happy relationship with the Order. Not a member per se, but they've been fruitful allies. How do you think someone like me rose up in the ranks this quickly?"

"Helping you establish your run on contraband as well, apparently." Black Rose was strictly banned by the king's edict.

Peddling came with a severe punishment, but for someone willing to take the risk, it was said to be a lucrative affair. And running the toxic spirit as a district captain would have obvious advantages.

"A little added income. As if I'm one to be satisfied with a guardsman's wages."

Auraq's jaw tightened. "Fancy yourself an up-and-coming player in the underground here? Looking to be invited in with the Shadow Elite?"

"All but assured," Bendo replied, his mouth widening in a self-satisfied grin.

"I think you can forget about any further advancement."

This time, Bendo let his head fall back as he laughed—a big genuine laugh of true mirth. "Same arrogant prig. My career path is assured, Auraq. Yours?" He shrugged. "This time tomorrow, I will be turning your body over to the king's magistrate and accepting the reward for your capture. And your friend here will be dead too. They get what they want, I get what I want. Everybody wins." Bendo removed his own blade from the scabbard on his belt. "Well, except you."

The Jackals moved closer. Auraq repositioned his grip on both hilts. "Kane," he said over his shoulder. "Keep back."

Kane positioned himself behind the crates.

Auraq understood their chances of getting out of this were slim. These were no ordinary street thugs or low-ranking greenhorns. The Jackals had worked out by now that Auraq was someone to be reckoned with, so they weren't going to take any chances this time. These were their seasoned assassins. They crossed the open space at a glide, separating to make it harder for Auraq to keep tabs on all of them at once. He had to act fast.

Bendo chuckled merrily as he stepped farther from Auraq, presumably to give the assassins the room they needed. He expected the Jackal assassins to be doing all the heavy lifting in this fight. Auraq knew he had one advantage here. Bendo was ignorant of the extent of his training. Other than the occasional tavern brawl, he had never seen Auraq in combat.

Auraq stepped back with one foot and shifted his weight

to it, making it look as if he was moving away from the assassins. He bent at the knee, leaned back—then sprang.

He launched his entire body forward, twisting his torso and raising his left elbow. By the time his other foot landed onto the dirt floor, he'd cut the distance between them in half. Bendo's eyes opened wide in surprise as his brain recognized the danger—but by now it was already too late. Auraq pushed off with his other foot and thrust the short sword.

Bendo tried to lunge back, but his reaction time was too slow. His sudden cry was cut short as the point of the blade caught him underneath the chin. Blood erupted into Auraq's face as he pushed the sword through.

Bendo stumbled back, eyes wide in shock and horror. As Auraq pulled the sword free, Bendo clawed at the hole in his throat as if he could somehow contain the bleeding with his hands. His jaw hung slack, and bubbles formed in the crimson flow as he tried to scream. His legs gave out, and he collapsed to the floor in a lifeless heap.

The assassins all simultaneously hitched.

That's right, fuckers, Auraq thought. *I'm not going to be so easy to take out.*

He swept his gaze over them, noting their stances. He hoped to glean insight as to the origin of their training or style, but it told him little except that each knew how to handle their weapon.

Two of them bore short swords and bucklers. One twirled about a quarterstaff that had small blades affixed to each end. The fourth carried a crossbow. This didn't bode well. A ranged weapon put him at a nearly impossible disadvantage. His only hope was to keep moving and thwart any attempt at tracking him and aiming.

"Stay behind the crates," he called to Kane behind him.

The delay caused by Bendo's quick end was only temporary. The crossbowman hung back while the other three inched closer in a wide semicircle, each taking turns at feigning an attack. They were gauging him as well—but Auraq kept his body loose and ready without giving anything away.

The assassin to his far right was the first to leap for him.

Auraq stepped back into his stance. The longsword was horizontal behind his neck, gently resting on his shoulder, while the short sword was out in front of him, chest level and pointing in the opposite direction. He waited and let the attacker cross the distance to him.

The first strike came as a quick diagonal slash—a straightforward assault intended to test him as much as engage him. Instead of meeting it, Auraq pivoted back and out of range of the swing. The cut swept past his center, and he used the longsword to guide it up and away. Then he thrust the short sword at the assassin's heart.

The assassin's reflexes were sharp. The shield arm spun up to intercept it. Auraq's sword struck the face of the buckler, sparking against the steel bulb at the center and leaving a deep groove in the wood. As the shield arm lifted to direct away his thrust, Auraq glimpsed beneath the buckler. The small shield, strapped to his wrist and forearm, concealed a black dirk in his grip. Like Auraq, the man was dual wielding.

A sneaky tactic. Auraq guessed the dagger was likely poisoned as well.

Movement from Auraq's left pulled his attention and he pivoted again. The second assassin charged in, quarterstaff spinning. The attacks came in quick bursts. The first came high toward his head—then a quick reverse and the low end of the staff was thrust upward toward his side. Auraq's blades met each, but an uppercut came at a sharper angle than he expected and the impact forced his wrist back. He ignored the sharp pain. The high end of the quarterstaff was whirling toward his head again. He lunged back out of range.

As he landed, he heard the snap of the crossbow's release. He rotated his torso to make himself a thinner target. The bolt whistled past and struck a crate behind him with a sharp crack.

He'd been lucky. The crossbowman would not make the same mistake again. Auraq had to keep at least one of the other attackers between him and that weapon at all times to prevent him from getting a clean shot.

The swordsman was a blur of motion to his right. He came at Auraq with a straight thrust. Auraq parried and was ready for the low stab of the dagger that followed, intended for his abdomen. His short sword deflected the small blade aside. The attacker's eyes narrowed with a flash of annoyance.

Auraq danced back again, his feet in constant motion. The attacks came in rapid succession after that—from his left, then his right, and back again. Both his swords flew in mad circles to keep up while they drove at him, searching for his weakness.

A shattering crash from across the room pulled his attention. He glanced in time to see the crossbowman ducking back, covering his face with his arm. A wooden crate near him was spattered with dark liquid and glass shards rained down around him. And a moment later, another bottle was sailing through the air.

Kane was lobbing bottles at him to distract him and keep him from tracking Auraq.

"Stay in cover!" Auraq shouted.

Over the clamor of the melee, his ears picked up the distinctive jingle of the chains at the door. For a fraction of a second, he thought perhaps Kane was trying to get out. Then the chains fell to the ground.

Only the Jackals knew they were here. Gods! They were already bringing in reinforcements.

They were doomed for sure.

The staff came in low and fast from his flank—a move intended to strike behind the knees and take him off his feet. The tiny distraction almost cost him. He pulled his leg back, twisted, and stabbed the longsword down into the dirt floor. The staff clapped against the flat of the blade with a loud crack, making the hilt sting in his hand. Auraq stomped down hard on the staff's end with his boot heel and drove it into the ground. The small blade snapped off.

He jabbed upward with the short sword.

With the staff end pinned to the ground, the attacker could only fling his torso back and pivot. The edge of Auraq's blade caught his shoulder at the collarbone, splitting the thick hide armor. The skin beneath was untouched—but the man's balance was thrown. He took a staggered step to keep his feet.

Auraq kicked sideways and struck him just above the knee. The man cried out and stumbled backward, fighting to stay up.

The swordsman to his right was lunging for him again.

Auraq forced the incoming blade downward, grounding its tip, and then countered with a low angled jab, hoping to get under the shield and skewer the man's forearm. But the swordsman was clearly practiced at defending against two weapons. With ease, he wheeled his arm up to deflect the attack and guided the sword harmlessly aside, and then he nimbly sprung back and fell into a defensive guard.

The second swordsman was now on the move too—but not to join the fray. He was stomping to Kane's hiding place behind the crates.

Auraq could not fight these opponents and defend Kane. He sprung back farther to gain himself a moment to breathe and to think. There was not much farther for him go—he was nearly at the wall.

Sunlight flooded into the warehouse as the door was pulled open.

The assassins in unison stalled their assault to glance at the doorway. Whoever was at the door, the Jackals weren't expecting them either. The warehouse owner, perhaps? The second swordsman knitted his brow, and he changed direction, heading toward the door instead. Kane was momentarily forgotten.

A force beyond reckoning blasted outward.

Fiery heat shoved Auraq backward, nearly taking him off his feet. The sound of it—like being inside of a thundercloud—shook the entire building and the ground beneath him. Debris flew past him like escaping birds, and something scraped hard against his cheek. As Auraq reeled back from the impact, black smoke billowed up and out, choking everything within the building.

It took his mind a few moments to grasp what had happened.

An explosion.

Auraq forced himself to recover, ignoring the ringing in his ears and the burning along the side of his face. He shook the dizziness from his head and took stock around him.

The heaviest smoke was lifting toward the high ceiling, but a thick haze still hung throughout the empty warehouse. Flaming piles of debris were everywhere. The crates at the far end of the warehouse were gone. Something had ignited the Black Rose.

The body of the crossbowman was on the ground, twisted and charred. The second swordsman too was on the ground—alive but writhing in pain. He was badly burned, and a long fragment of wood had pierced his shoulder and protruded out behind him.

Both Auraq and Kane were extremely lucky that the explosion hadn't set off the other stack of crates closest to them. They'd be dead too.

Auraq's remaining opponents had been closer to the blast and taken more of its impact. The one with the quarterstaff leaned on his weapon like a weakened old man. With a tight grimace, he pulled out a long shard of glass deeply imbedded in his thigh—a remnant of a shattered bottle, flung across the room like a projectile. The remaining swordsman staggered about like a drunkard. His face was blackened on one side around the eye, and half of his mask was scorched away, leaving only a few small straps to hold it on his face.

Two down. Two left. His odds were suddenly much better.

Auraq's equilibrium was off as he pressed himself into action. He took a few steps forward, but instead made a diagonal stumble to the right and almost toppled over when he tried to correct it. His muscles lagged in response. But he had to act. He had to gain the upper hand before they recovered from the blast.

The swordsman saw him coming and struggled to put himself in a defensive stance, but he too was sluggish. He brought his buckler up just in time as Auraq cut upward in a sloppy backswing. The swordsman made a desperate lunge backward beyond the reach of Auraq's second swing.

Auraq's blood was flowing again. He felt his strength and

control seeping back into his muscles. His limbs were responding again. He pushed in harder, driving him back. The Jackal swordsman, still struggling to regain his stability, depended too heavily on the shield while he tried to regain his stance and control. Auraq repeated the same attack—slashing in from the right and deflecting his weak parries with the left. Three times. Then four.

Then Auraq came in low, attacking from his left.

The blade's tip pierced the abdomen at an upward angle just above the beltline. The resistance of the heavy leather armor lasted only a heartbeat, then the blade cut through him with ease until Auraq felt the resistance again from the other side.

He yanked the blade out as the man fell back, rotating it to rip his insides even more. The swordsman stumbled and fell to one knee, then tried to stand up again—not yet grasping that he was already dead.

Too late, Auraq realized that in focusing on the swordsman, he had let his own defenses lag for too long. As he turned, the quarterstaff struck hard against the back of his head. It sent him stumbling, the room listing violently, spinning about. White spots flashed at the periphery of his vision. Instinct told him the next attack was coming. He threw up his short sword almost blindly and felt the staff crack against the flat of the blade. A lucky parry. He guided it aside as he shifted his weight to pivot and swing his left foot behind him.

But his opponent was not yet ready to concede the advantage.

The staff came round again. A flash at the edge of his vision. It caught him behind the knee while his left foot was still off the ground. A quick yank upward, and Auraq fell backward.

His back hit the ground. Hard. The air burst from his lungs, and blackness tightened in around his sight. He was a breath away from passing out. But he knew what was coming next and had to move. He threw his arm up and over, forcing himself into a roll. Just as his shoulder left the ground, the remaining blade at the end of the staff impaled the dirt where his neck had been.

He rolled back immediately, putting the full weight of his

torso against the staff before the attacker could retrieve it. His weight pulled the staff from his attacker's hands and it snapped to the ground.

Auraq was rewarded with a kick to the face.

Bright pain exploded through his jaw and nose, and the metallic taste of his own blood flooded his mouth. He felt something sharp poking the inside of his cheek. A broken tooth? It was the least of his worries at the moment. When Auraq looked up again, the attacker had replaced the staff with a dagger.

Just as he was ready to pounce on Auraq, a figure came up behind him. Kane. An explosion of glass and black liquid shrouded the assassin's head. A wave of the sweet toxic smell of the spirit burned inside Auraq's nostrils. The assassin staggered forward—then responded with unnatural reflexes. He whipped about and slashed at Kane. The tip of the blade caught him just below the eye.

Auraq thrust the short sword into the assassin's unprotected calf. The angle was awkward and he was nearly out of reach, but the blade penetrated. The man cried out and arched his back. He shifted his weight to the other leg—the one already injured from the glass bottle ejected from the explosion—and it buckled out from under him. The man collapsed onto his side.

Auraq tightened his grip on the longsword, rolled his torso, and swung hard. The blade came down in a clean chop onto the exposed neck of the assassin. Blood sprayed upward in a red geyser. He could tell the spine was severed by the vibration he felt. The man's body made one final leaping spasm as if the ground had pushed him upward, and then it was still.

Chapter 19

AURAQ EXHALED and flopped his shoulders back to the ground again. Panting, he stared up at the ceiling and waited for his whirling vision to clear.

Kane stumbled around the nearly decapitated body and dropped to his knees next to Auraq. Blood streaked down one whole side of Kane's face from the gash beneath his eye. The deep cut curved up and was split open like an ugly red grin.

"You all right?" Auraq asked Kane.

Kane emptied his lungs in one full burst. "Me?" he nearly shouted. "You dim-witted oaf, I thought you just died."

Auraq's face broke into a broad smile. It was awkward and ill-timed, he knew. The exuberance from a battle won drove it in part, and maybe delirium from the head injury added to it as well, but he thought it funny to hear Kane speak to him so colorfully.

"No, I'm good."

Clarity seeped back into his head. Albeit slowly. The room had slowed its spinning and tilting, and he no longer believed he was going to pass out or vomit. That could change the moment he stood up. The best thing for him probably was to stay on the ground and let himself recover.

"Help me up," he said.

Auraq and Kane locked arms, and Kane strained to pull his sizable bulk up off the ground. "Gods! You could help me some, you know," Kane said amidst a long grunt.

Auraq stood still a moment to assess his stability. His legs were a little wobbly underneath him and his head throbbed something terrible, but he was otherwise sturdy enough to remain vertical. He stretched his mouth open wide and moved his jaw around. Sore, but not broken. The kick could have done far more damage. He spit out the broken fragment of his tooth. It hit the dirt in a thick red blotch.

Now that they'd survived, it was time for some answers. He turned to the doorway.

Hargan stood at the threshold, his face looking slightly green. He was turned away from the carnage he'd helped wrought. One hand gripped the long, twisted staff Auraq had seen earlier, while the other gripped the doorframe for support. He held the staff away from him as if it were somehow tainted or infected.

Auraq limped over to the second swordsman sprawled out on the ground. "What are you doing here, Hargan?" Surprisingly, the assassin was still alive. Barely. He made short rasping breaths and his hand pawed at the dirt.

"Mistress Pyta sent me to follow you," Hargan replied.

Auraq frowned as he turned his back to the dying man. He briefly considered expediting the death, but at the moment he wasn't feeling particularly charitable. Let the last moments of his life be in agony. "Still suspicious of us, is she?"

"No," Hargan said quickly, looking up to face Auraq directly and nowhere else. "Quite the contrary. It was the captain's behavior that made her uneasy."

Auraq should have caught the significance of Bendo sending off the guards and was irritated with himself for missing it. He assumed Bendo was going to unofficially sneak him out of the city. He should have known better. "Seems a thin reason to pursue us." What did Pyta hope to accomplish?

"Mistress Pyta has an uncanny gift for spotting deceit." The way his voice lifted on the word "uncanny" told Auraq he spoke from experience. "She never cared all that much for Captain Bennidar. None of them did, really." Hargan must have caught sight of some of the gore, for he turned his head away with a quick snap. He puffed out his cheeks as if warding off a wave of sickness.

"Why send you?" Auraq asked. Clearly, he was too green for this. The lad did not have a future as a battle mage, certainly.

"There was no one else. And no time. I was only supposed

to follow you and report back. But you were in trouble. When I realized the captain had locked you in, I melted one of the links of the chain so I could see through the gap. A simple incantation. Metals belong to a—"

"You shouldn't be here," Auraq grumbled. He wiped the blades clean of blood on the torso of the dying man, who made a quiet whimper under the pressure of the blades. "It's too dangerous. There are likely others."

Hargan clearly hadn't considered that. He looked back over his shoulder at the street in sudden alarm as if more assassins were sneaking up behind him, then took a quick step into the warehouse. He stayed against the wall, averting his eyes from the bloodshed.

"What did you do that caused that explosion?" Kane asked. He had knelt down on one knee next to the body of the other swordsman. He shoved the body onto its back. His face scrunched in disgust, but Kane seemed to fight against his own squeamishness and began to rummage through the man's belongings.

"My master's staff," Hargan said. "He gave it to me in case I ran into trouble myself." Hargan shook his head. "He should have warned me. I… I only used it to send a small fire bolt at the crates. To distract them."

"It wasn't the staff," Auraq told him. He sheathed both weapons, and then slid his hand to the back of his own skull. He felt an egg-sized welt under his fingertips. The skin around that whole side of his head was tender to the touch, and his hair wet and tacky. The crack had broken the skin. "The crates were filled with Black Rose."

"The vile elixir?" Hargan looked up in surprise and immediately looked down at the ground again.

"Volatile stuff. We were fortunate. The whole place could've gone up in flames."

"I don't think she would have sent me had she known… any of this would happen."

Auraq agreed. He squatted down next to the swordsman to search his body. Life had finally left him, and he was still.

"Was Captain Bennidar involved in the death of Master Chenigal?" Hargan asked.

"Not directly, I don't think."

"But he led you here. He knew of this place. Knew those men were waiting to ambush you. Did this have something to do with smuggling? Was Master Chenigal involved in a smuggling ring?"

Auraq shook his head. "Easy, lad." Now that the shock was loosening its grip on him, the novice's mind was whirling out of control. "Head back to your master and Mistress Pyta," he told him. "Report to them what you saw. And don't embellish."

He had wondered how Bendo climbed the ranks so quickly. He should have guessed it was something illicit. Bendo never seemed the type to find respectability. He'd been romanced by one of the powerful criminal elements here in the city. They needed him as gate captain to grease the gears for running the goods in and out of the city.

Hargan nodded. "All right. But you need to speak with Mistress Pyta straightaway."

"Hargan, why would I—"

"She knows you are somehow connected to the events at the academy last night. She told me as much. She no longer believes you were behind it," he said with a quick palm out to ward off Auraq's impending protest. "Somehow you convinced her of that. But she knows you are keeping something from them." His eyes made a quick sweep of the place. "I'm inclined to agree with her."

Auraq saw no point in denying it, but he said nothing.

"She only wants to talk. But not at the academy. You need to meet her at her personal residence."

Auraq stopped patting down the dead man's thighs to look up at Hargan. That was certainly curious. "Her residence?" he repeated. He wasn't sure what surprised him more. That she lived apart from the academy and had her own residence, or that she wanted to meet with Auraq there. "Why there?"

Hargan looked around nervously as if someone might have snuck in to overhear. He took a few tentative steps closer but wasn't keen on getting too close to the body Auraq inspected. "She believes the academy has been infiltrated. The attack on Master Chenigal had help from someone *inside* the academy."

The Order of the Jackal had mages working for them certainly, but it was an unsettling notion that some were entrenched in the academy itself. It meant nowhere was safe, and there was no one he could really trust.

Could he trust Pyta, then? Or was this just another ruse to get him alone?

He almost swore at himself. Of course he could trust her. He was tired, and still light-headed from the quarterstaff blow. It all fogged up his thinking and made him paranoid. Why send Hargan at all if she knew Bendo was part of the plot to get Kane?

Auraq found more coin on the man's belt, which would be helpful—if they were going to be on the run again soon, they'd need it. But there wasn't much else. He was hoping for a little more information that would lead him to whoever was behind this. And why. Someone had hired the Order of the Jackal. He needed to find out who that was. It was their only hope of ending this—get to the one funding the price on Kane's head. The Jackals would not make the same mistake a third time. Auraq and Kane would not survive another ambush.

"Auraq?" Kane stood up from the body he'd searched, holding up a folded scrap of parchment. "Hidden pocket in the boot?"

Auraq took it and unfolded it. Strange symbols lined the sheet.

"What is it?" Hargan asked. Curiosity won over his skittishness, and he stepped closer.

"A cipher," he answered, unable to hide the disappointment in his voice. "Likely instructions for setting up the ambush. But without the key, it's useless." But he tucked into the pouch at his hip anyway. "Hargan, where is Mistress Pyta's estate?"

"The Mage District of course. I will take you there."

Auraq shook his head. "Take Kane. I will catch up with you later."

Kane broke off his search and bolted up to his feet. "Excuse me?"

Auraq extended a palm in an effort to calm him. "They will not expect their mission to have failed again." And by all rights it shouldn't have, he thought. "You have a window of time yet to get away cleanly." He gave Hargan a pointed look. "Don't dally. I will catch up with you as soon as I am able."

Kane stepped forward. "And where are you going?"

"Because of Bendo, the Order knows I'm involved, and Bendo knew my father. I have to go to him."

For a flash, Kane had that look that meant a protest was on the edge of his tongue, but he tightened his lips as if to not let it escape. "Bring him back with you," he said after a moment, a new determination in his tone. "He's no longer safe there."

As Auraq started for the door, Kane grabbed his arm. Auraq turned to meet his gaze and was hitched into Kane's dark eyes. Kane was anxious—that was clear enough, but there also was a new strength Auraq hadn't seen before. He looked as if he had more to say, but the words didn't come.

Auraq understood nonetheless. Kane wasn't worried about being left alone. He was concerned about him. It stirred something inside of Auraq—but he didn't have room in his mind at the moment to sift through it.

He squeezed Kane's shoulder reassuringly and offered a weak smile. "I'll be as quick as I can."

Kane nodded and released his hold on him.

Hargan outlined the location of the estate and how to recognize it. Auraq didn't know the area that well, but it seemed straightforward enough to find. Hargan stepped out of the way to allow Auraq to pass through the doorway. At the threshold, Auraq stopped and turned around. He tightened his brow and tapped Hargan's breastbone with a stiff index finger. "Keep him safe."

Hargan was still nodding furiously as Auraq rushed across the abandoned plaza and down the street.

He KEPT to the back alleys as he cut through the merchant district toward his father's shop. He needed to avoid not only any Jackal spies that might be about but also the city guard. As unlikely as it was, he didn't want any questions about Bendo. He had no idea what that cretin had told his men so it was best to avoid them—especially since once again he'd just murdered a commissioned guard in the king's service.

An investigation of the scene would probably tell a story that Bendo was ambushed when he stumbled upon the contraband, but it was unlikely that anyone would believe that Bendo himself took down four of the Jackals. People would have questions certainly. And some of Bendo's own guardsmen knew that Auraq was with him when he left the academy campus.

That could cause problems. No question, they had to get out of the city. And he had to come up with a better plan of what to do next.

The door to his father's shop was ajar when he arrived. He positioned himself with his back to the outside wall, listening. He leaned toward the opening and with a hand ready on the hilt of his longsword. His heart pounded in his ears. He was too late. The Order of the Jackal had already been here.

No sound came from inside his father's shop.

He used the toe of his boot to push the door open farther, and then bent his head into the opening. His heart twisted when he saw the amount of blood spattered about his father's workstation, walls, and floor. He drew his weapons and stepped into the shop. He kept his weight on the front of his feet, but still the floorboards creaked beneath him. At a crouch, he maneuvered around the small counter into the main workspace, his ears straining for any sound that might tip off that an ambush was imminent. Two bodies were on the floor beyond his father's workbench. Neither was his father.

So the old man had taken two of them out at least. They probably hadn't expected that he too was a former officer in the king's army and well trained at arms. He was Auraq's first instructor at how to handle a sword.

He skulked deeper into the workshop, expecting the

worst—but there were no more bodies. His father was nowhere to be found. He searched through the small back room and supply store, peering behind every hiding place and rocking each barrel to make sure it was empty. The broad doors that led to the loading dock behind the shop were closed and barred shut with a heavy beam.

Could he have somehow survived this?

As he returned back to the workshop, an eerie glow caught his eye. A glass orb no larger than Auraq's hand rested on the floor among the carnage. Auraq thought it strange he hadn't noticed it until now. It emitted a velvety blue light, and as Auraq stepped closer, it grew brighter. He lunged toward it, ready to smash it to bits before it unleashed some terrible hex upon him, but as he took two strides, a sudden flash drove him back again. He threw up his arm to shield his eyes, but still his vision danced with spots as he pulled his arm away again. When his sight recovered, Auraq saw that a man now stood over the glass sphere, glowing in the same bluish haze.

Auraq's training took command of his reflexes and he snapped into a defensive crouch.

The man turned as if he just noticed Auraq was in the room. He was clothed not in armor, but in court finery—a richly tailored burgundy surcoat and boots. He stood relaxed and unconcerned with one hand clasping an ornate cane, the other holding a crystal goblet of wine. Waves of blond hair tumbled onto his shoulders.

"Ah," he said. "So here you are. Astounding."

Auraq adjusted his grip on the swords.

"Gods! I don't know how you do it. Truly. You continually manage to vex me, Auraq Greystone of Har Tesera, son of Malgar."

Auraq felt his blood chill. "Do I know you?"

"Technically, no. But I have learned much of you of late. You can put your weapons away. Clearly, you've nothing to fear from me right now. I can do you no harm from here. And you can exact none on me. So, you might as well sheathe those and relax." There was a strange quality to his voice, as if he was speaking into a steel drum.

An illusion. A bizarre mage-crafted projection of some kind. He was communicating with someone who might be leagues away. The notion made Auraq's already throbbing head swim a bit. He had never dreamed such a feat was possible.

"Who are you?"

"I go by many names, but you may refer to me as Kanar the Ravager. I am what you might call the guide, the humble doyen, of my order."

There was nothing remotely humble about him, Auraq observed. "The Order of the Jackal."

Kanar made a flourished bow. "I'm flattered you have heard of us."

"I've killed enough of your members to learn something of you."

The corner of Kanar's mouth lifted slightly in mild amusement. "So you have. Bravo, indeed."

The man was entirely at ease and unfazed, like a bored cat toying with a mouse. He seemed to think he had Auraq by the tail and was just waiting for Auraq to realize the fight was already over. The chill that gripped Auraq deepened. What had been done with his father? "What do you want, Kanar the *Ravager*?" He added undue emphasis on the man's ludicrous and clearly self-appointed title.

"Only to talk. I request only a moment of your time, Auraq." Kanar's attention shifted to something unseen. His expression darkened, brow tightening. "Not now," he snapped to someone Auraq did not see. "Just handle it." Then the sudden flare of anger was gone as quickly as it arose, and Kanar once again held the look of control and congeniality.

A peek into his true nature. This affect Kanar wore, this visage that sang of both prepotency and patience in equal measure, was only a thin and fragile veneer. Beneath it ran a deep well of ruthlessness and malice.

Auraq forced his expression into something he hoped was calm control. "You have me here. So talk."

Kanar's smile broadened, but Auraq could now tell it was

a calculated expression. "You have kept us on our toes, Auraq, but that time is over. I don't know why you got involved in this business in the first place, but"—he shrugged casually—"here you are nonetheless. I am a fair and patient man, so I'm willing to, as they say, let bygones be bygones."

Auraq knew instinctively that he was neither of those things.

"You've probably already concluded that we have your esteemed father in our care."

Auraq felt simultaneous relief that his father was still alive and a rising fury. It was as he feared, and he knew what was coming next. His neck and ears burned with sudden heat.

"He gave us quite the struggle," Kanar continued. "I can see from where you get your rare talents. But alas—" His face split with a sinister grin as he lifted his palms up in a shrug. "—he is in good health, all things considered. I will require your cooperation if he is to remain so."

Auraq gripped both hilts with white-knuckle intensity. "What is it you want?" he asked. He was stalling for time. His mind strained for a solution but the deep throbbing in his head muddled his thinking. He could think of no way to escape what was to come.

Kanar's merry expression soured. "Do not insult me any further, Auraq," he replied with a roll of his eyes. "My patience is long, but it is not without limits. Hand him over to us if you want your father to live."

Auraq felt his insides wrench into a knot. So it had come to this. Betray Kane, betray the oath he'd made to Old Tan, or lose his father. All the years he'd spent trying to protect Malgar from the consequences of his crimes—only to doom him while attempting something honorable. The notion of betraying Kane to this man felt like a punch to his gut. But could he stick to his oath at the cost of his own father?

Regardless of his decision, someone would die tonight because of him.

He turned his back to the smug look Kanar leveled at him. He couldn't stomach it any longer. The leader of the Jackals had already decided he'd won and was just waiting for Auraq to acknowledge it. Auraq tossed the swords on his father's workbench, which landed with a loud clatter, and he gripped the wooden edge to prevent his hands from shaking. His head dropped between his shoulders. *Think!* he chastised himself. There had to be another option. He simply would not sacrifice either Kane or his father. His insides tore at him as if he'd swallowed tiny blades.

"Stalling will not help you. Your time is up," Kanar pressed.

But no solution came to him. He knew his father would understand that Auraq was duty bound to Kane—would even respect it—but he couldn't bring himself to make that choice. He lifted his head, gathering his willpower to turn around to face Kanar once again. He didn't have any idea what his decision would be, but he knew he had no choice but to make one.

But something caught his eye in the center of the workbench.

He tilted his head to the side as his mind pieced together what he saw. It took a moment for it to saturate through the layers of anger, frustration, and anxiety, and the constant throbbing at his temples and behind his eyes. But the meaning of it took shape… and a grin lifted the corners of his mouth. He had to fight back the urge to laugh.

That crafty bastard.

"I will have your answer," Kanar said in a growl. His thin patience was fraying.

"My answer?" he said as his hand drifted toward the hilt of his longsword. His fingers curled around the grip, and he turned around to face Kanar. "This is my answer. And our business is far from concluded."

In one smooth motion, he brought the blade up into the air. As he moved, Kanar's expression shifted. His eyes widened a fraction, the look of triumph and self-satisfaction fading into surprise and confusion. Auraq sprung forward and brought the blade down onto the glass sphere on the floor beneath Kanar.

The sphere shattered and wisps of blue flashed through the

workshop like birds of pure light released from a cage. And Kanar's image was gone.

Auraq turned back to the workbench. Placed precisely in its center was the metal ring from a barrel. Inside the ring was one of his father's tools—an awl. His father was particularly fussy about his tools. He did not ever leave them sitting about the workshop when not in use, and the placement of it there could not be happenstance. The tip of the awl pointed directly to a single wooden cube positioned just outside the circle.

To anyone else this would not hold any importance. But Auraq recognized it as a message for him the moment his eyes caught it. The barrel ring was meant to represent the walls of the city. The wood piece—his father's hunting cabin in the woods outside the city. His secret retreat. No one else knew of the cabin but Auraq.

His father was alive and waiting for him there.

Chapter 20

AURAQ KNEW he didn't have much time to act. Kanar's agents were already en route to the workshop—certainly some were already nearby, either awaiting orders or watching for him so they could trail him to Kane's location. But Auraq wasn't about to be so accommodating.

The strange blue orb certainly answered a few questions. It explained how Kanar was able to mobilize and coordinate his assassins so quickly. Surely, he had a number of those devices about and he was already getting out the word that Auraq had seen through the ploy.

He tried to breathe calm back into his body. The threat had never been real. He couldn't imagine he'd ever betray Kane— the idea of abandoning a sworn oath was anathema to him, and his father was never in danger.

His father was safe.

Every muscle of his body seemed drenched with relief, which oddly made his headache pulse even worse. Little dots floated about at the edge of his vision. He wanted to sit down, take a minute to gather himself, but he didn't have a moment to spare. He moved around the pieces of his father's message to make sure—however unlikely—someone else didn't decode it. Perhaps there was some type of magecraft for that too.

He had the advantage of knowing the streets better than most, having spent the days of his youth haunting them, either seeking out mischief or hiding from authorities when he found it. He intended to use that advantage. He pulled his father's ladder from pegs in the wall and carried it into the back storeroom; the same room that held his father's cot, the one Kane had likely spent the night on. He was careful not to let the ends of the ladder drag on the floor or leave any other telltale signs.

He positioned the ladder underneath the hatch his father had installed in the ceiling. It was small and nondescript, practically invisible to anyone who didn't know it was there.

Atop the ladder, he used the heel of his hand to punch up at the four corners of the hatch to knock it loose. It popped open, and he slid it aside.

One more task before he escaped.

He climbed back down and headed to the back of the shop. With a grunt, he lifted out the heavy horizontal beam that barred the rear doors and dropped it to the floor. He then gently pushed on one of the doors until it was slightly ajar—hinting that this was his route of escape and the agents watching the shop had somehow missed it.

He made one last quick scan of the shop. Satisfied, he zipped up the ladder again and pulled himself up through the hole. Then he hauled the ladder up too, returned the hatch over the hole, and placed the heavy ladder over the top of it. Even if they found the hatch, they'd have a hard time getting up through it.

The attic was thick with hot, musty air that made it hard to breathe. The roof over him was higher at one end and had a single slant from one sidewall to the other. Auraq hugged the highest wall, but still had to crouch and keep his head low. Afternoon light streamed in like white arrows from places where the roof had small holes, igniting the dancing motes of dust that swam about the air.

Years ago, Auraq had made modifications of his own to the rooftop attic. He'd fashioned a similar hatch in the roof itself—a way for him to sneak into the shop at night and pilfer his father's hidden stash of wine, or pinch a coin or two that Auraq was convinced Malgar wouldn't miss. The thought occurred to him that in the years of Auraq's absence, his father could have discovered the second hatch and boarded it up. That would put an effective end to this plan pretty quickly. At the far corner of the attic, he punched up at the roof and a square section swung clear, exposing the bright afternoon sky. Relieved, he hoisted himself up onto the roof.

After a quick moment to take stock, he slunk off at a low crouch to the next roof, and then to the next. His muscles seemed to remember the movements from so many years ago as he skirted the places he knew to be visible from the street and skipped over the gaps between some of the buildings. He shimmied over the clay tiled roof of a temple and found a quiet place behind a low parapet that was blind to the street and also hidden from anyone else who might be lurking about on the rooftops. He leaned against the wall and pulled his cloak up over his head to shield his eyes from the sun.

Now he could take a much-needed rest.

Members of the Jackals had probably arrived at the barrel shop and were tearing the place apart for signs of how he escaped without their notice. He only needed to wait until night and he could slip away under the cover of darkness. He closed his eyes and was asleep almost instantly.

THE MAGE'S hand dropped into his lap and he leaned back.

"Better?"

Auraq pressed the side of his head with his fingertips, gingerly exploring the area. It was still faintly sensitive to the touch but certainly improved. He nodded.

It was a strange sensation to have a mage weave his power through his head. He could feel a discomforting tingling deep inside, like thousands of needles pricking at the underside of his skull, and his vision blurred and warped as the mage moved his wiggling fingers closer to his eyes.

The two of them sat facing each other in a small, nondescript room that was apparently part office and part storage. They were somewhere deep in Pyta's estate—Auraq hadn't paid much attention to his surroundings when he was swept off by the servants to meet with Master Ozden, Mistress Pyta's personal healer. His headache had worsened, and it was about all he could focus on when he arrived. For an hour he sat naked on a short stool with his hands on his knees while the mage poked and prodded at him as if he were a horse on the

174

auction block.

"You are rather lucky," Ozden said. "That injury could have caused some permanent damage to your brain that even I wouldn't have been able to repair. Left untreated, it would have affected you over time. Coordination, mood, memory. But I believe I mended the worst of it. You may perhaps have a mild headache for a while. I can work on it a bit more if you'd like."

"I'm fine." Auraq didn't like the idea of the mage twiddling around in there any more than he had to. If he was out of danger, he'd suffer through any discomfort and heal the rest of the way naturally. "Thank you," he added, not wanting to sound ungrateful. The treatment he just received was something that would have cost him more gold than he'd see in a lifetime.

Ozden pressed at Auraq's cheek with two fingers. "All right. The bone here appears firm. Sorry I couldn't save the tooth."

"Not worried about it."

"These lacerations will heal just fine. No scarring if you leave them be. I took the liberty of warding the injury from any festering, but by chance if it should still occur, I suggest a poultice of laserwort. Should remedy it."

A gentle knock at the door preceded it swinging open. A servant, dressed in simple black robes, stepped into the room. Dressed as he was, Auraq might have assumed he was a novice of the academy assigned to care for the headmistress, but he was older. He bowed to Master Ozden but ignored Auraq entirely. "The Mistress will see the guest if you are finished here, Master."

"We are." Ozden nodded to Auraq, indicating he could get dressed again. "Inform her he will be there shortly."

Auraq rose and grabbed his tunic from the top of the crate. "I want to see Kane first." When both looked at him with raised brows, he felt compelled to provide a reason. "He'll want to know I'm safe."

"I can dispatch the message—"

"No. I'll go myself." He pulled the tunic on over his head and slipped his arms through the sleeves. The movement made the muscles along his side cramp and complain, reminding him how hard he'd landed on his back during the fight.

"Very well," the servant replied coolly. "But it is not wise to keep the Mistress waiting."

"I'll not be long."

Providing the healing was enough to establish that the head of the academy was someone he could trust. At least for now. He had no desire to irritate her or test her patience—especially since she might be able to provide him with some valuable information as well—but he wasn't going to leap at her command either.

The servant waited with hands clasped at his waist for Auraq to finish dressing, and then he led him through the estate's maze of corridors. The journey ended on the second floor in a wood-paneled corridor. The servant gestured with a wave of his hand at a closed door.

Auraq knocked gently. If Kane was asleep, he didn't want to wake him. But when no response came, he decided he should check on him anyway and ensure he was safe. He thumbed the latch, which depressed with a hard click, and he swung the door inward.

Mistress Pyta had not shirked on her hospitality. The chamber was spacious and well furnished—a room suitable for much more discerning guests than themselves. A small oil lantern on a table by the window cast a faint but warm hue throughout the chamber and across the grand bed against the opposite wall. A figure was buried underneath the bedcovers.

Kane appeared safe and comfortable, and the room secure. Auraq had hoped perhaps he would have remained awake for his return, but since he had gone to bed, Auraq would slip out and see him in the morning. He was about to pull the door closed again when the shape groaned and moved.

An arm lifted from under the covers and flung them off. Kane pushed himself up and sat on the edge of the bed, his back to the door.

Auraq remained still, not wanting to startle or unnerve him.

Kane rolled his shoulders and stood. He was nude. The lantern softly lit the muscles of his back and the curve of his buttocks. He rubbed his eye with the heel of his hand before he stumbled sleepily over to the corner of the room. Auraq heard the ring of metal as Kane relieved himself in the chamber pot.

Auraq watched him, feeling strange, but unable to pull his eyes away.

During their travels together, he'd not seen Kane without clothing. It wasn't something he thought about really, but looking back, perhaps that was unusual. While back in the king's army, he'd seen plenty of his comrades naked while at the baths or around the barracks and thought nothing of it then. Like anyone would, he appreciated their fitness and strength, the result of training and hard work. But now… this was different. Seeing Kane standing there nude, at this moment, tugged at him in a way he could not have predicted. He found himself captivated by the shape of Kane's body.

His eyes traced down the length of his form, following the curves and lines of his shoulders, back, and legs. Kane was stronger than he'd imagined him. The muscles of his shoulders and arms were thick and defined. Auraq's attention lingered around Kane's two well-formed cheeks. He wondered at the unblemished quality of his skin, glowing in the light like clean parchment.

Again, he felt something inside him stir awake.

It was buried deep, but present.

The stream against the side of the chamber pot weakened to a stop. Kane shook himself and started to turn.

Auraq's heart leaped. He made a quick step out of the open doorway and into the hall. The last thing he needed was for Kane to catch him watching. He waited, giving Kane time to climb back into bed. When he heard the squeak of the bed, Auraq knocked on the door.

"Yes?" came a faint, uneasy reply.

Auraq pushed the door open farther and stepped into the room, hoping there wouldn't be any questions as to why the door to the bedchamber was already open.

Kane's head fell back and his shoulders went limp a moment. "Thank the Gods!" He moved to pull the bedcovers off himself, but then stiffened and covered himself up again. "Shit! The servants took my clothes."

Auraq chuckled. "I'll come to you." He tried to walk casually into the room, but he felt stiff and artificial. He sat down at the foot of the bed.

Kane shuffled up to a sitting position, holding the bedcovers to his waist with one hand. His chest heaved with his breathing. Kane's torso was shaped as well as his back side, and mostly smooth except for circles of hair around each nipple and a thin path that followed the length of his sternum. "What took you so long?"

Auraq forced himself to look about the room and not at Kane's bare torso. "I needed to make sure I wasn't followed. Quite the bedchamber they've provided, *m'lord*."

Kane didn't appear to hear the comment. His lips pressed together into a thin line. He snorted out his nostrils like a bull. "Is your father safe?"

Auraq nodded. He was reluctant to tell him more.

"And you convinced him to come back with you?"

"That's complicated. I'll explain later."

Kane's eyes narrowed.

Auraq held out his palm. "He's safe."

Auraq could tell Kane wasn't sure he believed that, but he seemed to relax some. "Have you spoken with Mistress Pyta yet?"

"I came straight here." Auraq wasn't sure why he avoided telling him about the time he'd spent with the mage.

Kane's legs slid under the bedcovers, which made Auraq distinctly aware of Kane's nudity beneath them. He had no idea why—he felt awkward, unsettled, and for some reason felt he was invading Kane's personal space by sitting on the bed. He stood up.

"She met with me briefly before I was swept away," Kane said, leaning back against the bed's dramatic headboard. "We spoke but nothing about what happened. Just courteous introductions. I don't think they see me as very important."

"Probably a good thing." The less attention on him, the better. But he wasn't convinced that Pyta was so naïve as all that. If she'd established Auraq's involvement so definitively, she would have connected Kane to the events just as easily.

Kane shrugged. "They've been very nice to me, I must say. They fed me. Drew me a bath." He waved his hand at the room. "Gave me this absurd bedchamber. There's wine over there on that table. Good wine."

"I better not."

Kane's expression turned more serious. He dropped his voice to nearly a whisper. "So what do you think? Can we trust her?"

After a moment, Auraq nodded. "I believe so." *For now*, he added silently.

It was the rest of her staff he wasn't ready to fully trust yet.

"I get a very different feeling around her than with Chenigal," Kane said. "You ask me, she seems less concerned with our interests… or more concerned with her own."

Auraq smiled weakly. "I'm certain you're right."

Kane shook his head. "Then will she help us? Well… more than just hiding us for the night?"

"I intend to find out." The grand mistress of the academy was playing at something. Auraq just didn't know what yet. This clandestine meeting at her estate instead of at the academy had his interest piqued. He needed to find out what she knew about the people who attacked Chenigal, and if she could tell him anything about the mark.

"I'll go with you. I just need for someone to bring my clothes back. Or borrow one of their black robes."

"No, it's all right. I'll fill you in later. Get some sleep. It may be a while before we have comforts like this again."

Kane chuckled. "If ever. Now that I know you're back, maybe I'll actually get some real sleep. I've been tossing about for hours."

Auraq smiled warmly back at him and then turned to leave. He crossed the room and put his hand on the latch of the door.

"Auraq?"

Hand still resting on the latch, he looked back over his shoulder.

"Am I the first person you ever told about what really happened?" Kane asked.

Auraq remained quiet a moment. "Yes," he said finally.

"Why me? Why was I the first?"

Auraq's jaw tightened as he considered the question. "Maybe there isn't a reason. It just happened that way."

In the dim light of the room, he saw the corner of Kane's mouth lift in a smile as if Auraq had said something amusing. "There is always a reason for such things. And I have my own suspicions. But I suppose that is a conversation for another night."

Auraq looked at him, puzzled. But Kane's expression shifted to something more serious, and he changed the subject.

"What is the plan for tomorrow?"

Auraq was relieved the other topic had dropped so quickly and the focus was now on something he could answer. He knew what he needed to do next. He just wasn't entirely sure how it was going to happen yet. With everything that had occurred that day—an attack on the academy, a gate captain murdered, the Order of the Jackal out in full force looking for them—the city would be in chaos tomorrow. "First thing, we get you out of this fucking city."

Chapter 21

THE ELDERLY servant swung the massive door open and stood to the side with a straight back and arms stiff at his sides. He clapped his gold-tipped cane on the marble floor twice. "Auraq Greystone of Har Tesera," he announced in a booming voice that filled both the hall and chamber beyond.

The introduction felt rather histrionic, more like something he might have experienced at court, not in the personal estate of a mage in Har Tesera. Sure, Pyta was head of her order here, running the mage guild and the academy, but that seemed hardly deserving of this particular level of pomp.

Auraq took the cue and stepped across the threshold into Pyta's private study, which was likely larger in volume than most rich merchants' entire homes. A goodly portion of the wall space was taken up with grand wooden bookcases that rose to the ceiling like giant sentinels. Wheeled ladders were leaned against the stacks to provide access to the uppermost shelves. All available shelf space was occupied, and more books still were stacked in piles at the bases of the bookcases and on various tables around the chamber. Auraq wouldn't have imagined that so many books existed in the entire kingdom.

Great woven rugs covered much of the terra-cotta floor, and clutches of furnishings filled the vast space that would suit any manner of purpose. Meeting, dining, studying. A wide fireplace dominated the far end of the chamber. It was capped in an immense stone mantle carved in the likeness of a dragon. The tail swooped down one side to reach across the tiled hearth, while the reptilian head reached down the other, its mouth open to the depths of the firebox as if the blaze within was caused by the beast's own fiery breath. A robed figure stood at the fireplace, silhouetted by the fire inside.

The servant slipped out silently and closed the door behind him.

Mistress Pyta turned from the fireplace with a look of mild irritation as Auraq stepped farther into the chamber. "Well now," she said, her tone cool, yet still thick with admonition. One hand held a poker, the other a goblet. She shook a few fiery embers from the poker's tip and with a blasé turn of her hand, she let it drop into the metal hopper on the hearth. It landed with a jarring clang that echoed about the chamber like a dinner bell.

"Quite the hour to present yourself. You certainly have taken your time, surrah."

Auraq forced his irritation to remain in check. "I had other matters to attend to first."

"Your companion has been here for hours."

"I stopped to see him. Thank you for providing your protection here at your estate."

Pyta made a small pregnant huff. She was no longer dressed in one of the ubiquitous black robes seen around the academy, but a silver one made of fine silk. On her thin frame, it spilled straight down from her shoulders like the long veil of a waterfall and pooled around her feet. Her hair had been braided for bed, and the gray rope swooped down the front of her breast. Absently, she dragged her hand down the length of it before she took a seat in a cushioned high-back chair. She set the goblet down on a side table without looking and gestured that Auraq should do the same in the chair opposite her.

Auraq closed the distance between them, but instead of sitting, he stood next to the chair and rested an elbow on the back. The chair looked too comfortable. Fatigue was beginning to take its toll on his ability to focus, and he still felt the tingling effects of the mage's workings in his head. He worried he might offend her further by nodding off.

"I don't wish to sound discourteous"—he watched her expression closely as his fingernails scraped across the fine upholstery of the chair—"or ungrateful for your invitation. But can I assume we are safe here?"

Pyta raised a brow at his directness. "By 'we,' I assume you mean your companion."

Auraq was somewhat taken aback, but he forced any sign of it off his face. He could not help but wonder how much she already knew. "Specifically, yes. But you have equal cause to be concerned, frankly."

Pyta held her gaze on him as she considered him closely, her lips slightly pursed. "We are quite safe. More so here than anywhere else."

Her confidence needled him a little, especially considering everything that had occurred just that morning. Yesterday, a murder at the academy under the nose of hundreds of mages would have been unthinkable.

"I've taken every precaution," she said. "My guards are on alert and glyphs have been woven at all entrances. As we speak, a ward is being crafted around his bedchamber that will alert me if anyone approaches it."

"By people you trust?"

Her head moved back, seemingly taken aback by the implication. "Explicitly. But, if it would put you at ease, I will inspect the work myself before I retire."

Auraq nodded. "I appreciate that, Mistress." The use of her title was a small thing, but he still recognized the effect it had in her eyes. His simple act of acknowledging her position had done much to ease her own raised hackles.

"You seem to have no difficulty in trusting me," she said.

"None." There was no need for him to get into a long explanation about it. She accepted the response with a satisfied nod of her own.

"Well and good, then. Let us skip past the pleasantries and move on to the business that brought you here." Her eyes lifted briefly to the side. "Please sit. You are making this awkward."

Auraq lowered himself into the chair. The cushion beneath him was thick and he sank deeply into it. His bulk filled the chair like trying to stuff too much flour into a sack.

"Wine?" she said once Auraq had leaned back into the chair.

Auraq declined with a lift of his hand.

Pyta studied him further for a time, as if trying to unravel some mystery surrounding him, and seemed to gather her thoughts about how to proceed. "Let's agree that perhaps things began on the wrong foot between us. It is clear to me we were both trying to process the events that unfolded this morning and may not have been at our best."

A fair assessment. "Agreed."

"For my own part, it has not been the best day," Fatigue and sadness surfaced in her features. Her fingers teased the end of her braid as her eyes unfocused for a moment. "My academy has been infiltrated by murderous thugs—something that has not been known to occur in a millennium at least—and a dear friend has been butchered in his own study. Doors down from my own. Considering this, I pray that you don't take too much umbrage at my initial suspicion of you."

Her tone was civil, even genuine to a point. But Auraq could almost taste the subtle and oily attempt to disarm him and drive the conversation in her direction. He guessed that she couldn't care any less about his personal view of her.

"Especially," Pyta added, "when one considers your own history. One can hardly blame me, yes?"

So… she'd done her research. Auraq kept his face neutral as she narrowed her eyes a fraction, clearly waiting for a reaction from him. It was a subtle nudge, letting him know that she could involve the city guard and have him arrested at any time. It was obvious she wasn't concerned in pursuing that—or she would have done so already—but she wanted him to know she was in control and expected his cooperation.

"Can we agree to speak freely with each other?" she asked.

As always, Auraq was hesitant to divulge too much, but the head of the mages' guild and the academy would be an invaluable ally he couldn't ignore.

"I would prefer it."

Pyta smiled wryly. "How refreshing." Her expression seemed to soften as she fiddled with the end of her braid "Your companion is quite loyal to you, by the way. Were you aware of that? He would not talk to me without you present."

For some foggy reason, that made Auraq want to smile too, but he resisted the urge. "He's had good reason to not trust anyone."

She gave a slow, thoughtful nod at that. "Well, his loyalty to you is well-placed, I think." It was spoken plainly, without any sense of flattery, yet Auraq still felt guarded against it. "So tell me, Auraq, why did my mages die last night?"

Auraq hesitated. "I have your assurance that what I say here will remain in your confidence?"

"I make no promises."

Auraq liked that answer more than an unqualified yes. It felt more genuine, which furthered his trust in her.

"Chenigal was investigating a mark that had appeared on Kane's arm."

A single eyebrow lifted. "A mark, you say."

"Yes. Of an unnatural sort."

"Indeed." Pyta's expression darkened. "And what is the nature of this mark?"

"That's what we came to the academy to find out. It is a series of runes that run the length of his forearm. They are part of the skin, not unlike a tattoo, but endowed with power. Chenigal studied them closely and concluded that they were somehow a link to memory. Delivered into Kane's flesh from across the shadow realm." He outlined the events Kane had described as to how the mark had first appeared.

Pyta reached for the goblet and took a long draught from it. She leaned back in her chair as she wiped a droplet of red from the corner of her mouth with her thumb. "So, the runic power was carried on the inside layer of the bracer?" For a moment, she seemed to forget that Auraq was there. Her tone held a sense of reverence.

"When Kane placed it on his own forearm—"

"Yes, it triggered it. The runes were infused into his flesh, creating the link through the veil that separates the living world and shadow realm. Astounding. I had no idea such a thing was possible."

"Chenigal was equally intrigued," Auraq said.

"No doubt. What else did he tell you?"

Auraq outlined what little they had learned from him.

One hand held the goblet by her shoulder while the second hand drummed the arm of the chair. She held her expression static, but Auraq could tell her mind was reeling. "The real question, then, is who does the memory belong to?"

Auraq shook his head. "Chenigal had not yet determined that. I suspect he learned the identity last night and that was why he was murdered."

"Or someone feared that he would learn of it." Some of the exhilaration had drained from her voice. She replaced the goblet again and leaned in. "So others know of this mark too, clearly. And they are powerful enough—and audacious enough—to orchestrate an attack on my academy. What have you learned about those behind this?"

"They are an organization that calls themselves the Order of the Jackal."

Pyta tried to hold her expression neutral, but it was clear she'd heard of the organization before. "And how do you know that?"

Auraq reached into the pouch on his belt and pulled out the scrap of cloth. He held it up a moment for her to see. She nodded, accepting the answer, and he returned it to the pouch.

"What do you know of them?" he asked.

She frowned and turned her eyes away. "Precious little, I'm afraid. I am aware of them by reputation alone. And based on that reputation, I know that you are very fortunate to be sitting here having this conversation with me."

Auraq did not disagree.

"So why would the Order be concerned about this mark?" she asked. She didn't seem to be speaking to Auraq at all, but more to herself.

"That we have yet to uncover." He paused, weighing what he should say next, and how much. It was tender ground he was starting to tread on. "But I believe it somehow involves mages."

Pyta did not appear as surprised by the announcement as

Auraq would have expected her to be. She rose from the chair and glided to the fireplace. "And why would you believe that?"

"Who else but mages could infiltrate your well-guarded campus so efficiently?"

"Compelling argument. Hardly conclusive."

"Before we arrived here in Har Tesera, we were attacked by wolvren."

Pyta looked over her shoulder at Auraq. "Wolvren?" She chuckled, but it held no humor. Auraq knew she understood the implication. Wolvren could only be controlled through a mage. "You are mistaken surely. It was likely only a wolf you saw. They grow large in the mountains to the south."

"With respect," Auraq replied, "I know when I've seen a wolf. Mistress, you know as well as I do that you likely have a traitor in your ranks. Why else choose this location for our discussion? Someone inside your own academy was involved in last night's massacre."

"Suspected. Not confirmed." She retrieved the poker from the hopper again and adjusted the logs on the fire. "I personally vet my mages with the utmost care, you know. It's an unsettling feeling to learn that one close to me may have been able to so effectively deceive me." With a long sigh, she replaced the poker and strolled back to her seat. "We mustn't let arrogance and pride triumph over reason, of course, but… let's not forget that a few bruised grapes don't spoil the wine."

In other words, this was an isolated incident, not a larger widespread conspiracy among her order. Whether she actually believed that or not, Auraq couldn't tell. He still had his doubts, but the folding of her arms told him she was closing off from him. He wasn't going to get any further with her if he pressed the matter. He changed tactics.

"I was told the Jackals were a religious order first." He kept it to himself that the detail had come from Bendo. There was no telling how much of what that backstabbing cretin had told him was credible. "But it is said that they could be hired out for the right price. The question is whether this is their own agenda, or did someone outside the organization pay the coin."

"I presume there is no way to know that," she said. Auraq could see that her mind was focused again, her expression controlled. "I have no knowledge of their beliefs or what may motivate them. The memory locked in this mark of his could be some heretical offense that the Order does not want made public. Or perhaps it could be information about the Order itself, revealing their secrets. If they have been hired by someone, it is widely rumored that they do not come cheap, and there are few who could actually afford them."

"Then let's narrow down that list. Who could?"

Pyta thought a moment with her mouth scrunched to the side. "Some merchants. The very, very wealthy ones. But that would be only a handful. Various nobility certainly. We could exclude the lower tiers of nobles, I'd say, but there are a number of others with the income and influence to afford it."

"So this could be politically motivated? Evidence of a scandal that someone wants buried for good?"

"Certainly."

"What about mages? Would they have the available coin?"

Pyta's eyes narrowed and her mouth pressed into a firm line.

Auraq held out his hands. "It is a fair question to ask, Mistress." He was surprised when she answered.

"Individually, no. But a guild from one of the larger cities might have the resources. But what secret would they want hidden from the world?"

Something about the way she answered him gave Auraq pause. Much of the world was suspicious and distrustful of mages in general. It would not take much to push the tide of public opinion from tolerance to open hostility. "Mages are a mystery to me, Mistress. But no group is immune to secrets and scandal." He shrugged. "There is an easy way to solve this question. You could complete the work Chenigal began."

Pyta's pale lips puckered into a frown. "I'm afraid that will not be possible."

Auraq raised his brow. That was not the response he expected. "May I ask why?"

188

"The type of magecraft required to accomplish such a thing is… not my area of expertise. The investment in time alone…." She shook her head. "It is not remotely feasible that I commit the time it would require. I have the academy to manage. As to other mages? I am disinclined to involve them. You admitted yourself that anyone who knows of the mark is at risk. And seeing what the Jackals are capable of, I am not likely to subject any of my top mages to your companion. I would not ask them to assume the risk."

Auraq fought to hide his disappointment. He could not help but wonder if this was some form of dodge, that she suspected something about the mark and wanted no part in it. "You can offer us no help, then?"

"I can offer you my counsel. I believe you should head to the capital. Covertly, of course, and with all haste. I believe there you will have more luck finding both the help and protection you will require. Considering the power and skill that would have been needed to create this link to the shadow realm, I suspect it originated there anyway. I can provide you with a few contacts. But I caution you to tread carefully and be constantly on your guard."

She stood once more, lifted the goblet again to her mouth, and finished its contents. "It has grown quite late and I must retire, I'm afraid. I am needed at the academy tomorrow at first light. I am sorry that I can provide you with no further assistance."

Auraq pushed himself from the chair onto his feet. He offered a respectful bow. "You are providing us with a safe haven tonight. That is something."

She smiled weakly at him as she turned to leave, but then stopped, lifting a finger into the air. "Check in with Teno Whitehall in the morning. He is my personal assistant here at the manor. Any of the servants will be able to locate him for you. I believe I can provide you with one more small service."

Chapter 22

THE CRATE had been built for transporting textiles—large rolls of tapestries and floor rugs. A shipment of rugs had arrived at Mistress Pyta's manor estate earlier in the week from Har Mooryl, a duchy to the northwest known for the quality of their weaves and dyes. The crate was kept in order to lug off the old rugs to be repaired and then sold at market, but Teno Whitehall decided that morning to hold off on that errand for the day and commission the crate for a different purpose.

Auraq hated the idea from the beginning.

He was not fond of tight places. And minutes after the horse had pulled the cart from the stable, he regretted that he ever agreed to it at all.

The crate was long enough, even for someone of Auraq's height, and were it just him inside, it would have been plenty big enough. But with both of them confined inside, lying side by side facing each other, it was congested and hot. Even with his heavy leather jerkin removed, Auraq's tunic was soaked through before they left the stable yard. He felt contorted and bent into an unforgiving shape. To give Kane more room, he'd angled his torso, leaning somewhat half on his shoulder, half on his back. As soon as the cart was in motion, he felt every cobble and every hole in the street as a hard jolt to his body.

He tried to shift his position to something remotely comfortable, but he was wedged in with no room to maneuver. "Don't know why I agreed to this," he grumbled.

Kane answered with a surly grunt. It was dark and dusty inside, but enough of the morning sun streamed in through the cracks between planks that Auraq could see he was equally uncomfortable. "No one asked me. I was open to other ideas."

This felt cowardly. Like he was somehow cheating.

The truth was Auraq knew it was their best option for getting beyond the city walls, but he hated it all the same. If it were just him, he might have risked a direct approach and tried leaving by the gates. But he had Kane to consider.

And it wasn't just the Order of the Jackals they needed to worry about now. There was a solid chance the city guard would be after them as well. The Jackals would have likely tipped off the city guard that a noble-killing defector was on the loose in the city. They could have even implicated him in the killing of Bendo, adding to his capital crime.

The cart's wheel hit a particularly deep hole that made the whole cart lurch, and the sudden jolt made both of them grunt as if punched.

"Not much of a rescue if every one of our bones is broken by the time we get out of the city," Kane said.

"These are the good roads," Auraq replied.

"Quiet back there," a voice came from the front.

Teno himself was driving the cart and they were accompanied by four guards from the mage district. They wore Mistress Pyta's personal emblem on their sleeves. Teno insisted that few would have the balls to challenge them or insist on inspecting the crate.

Auraq wasn't so sure. Military types tended to be territorial. The city guard would likely resent the mages bringing in their own swords to protect them—a tacit message that they were unable to handle the job. Or couldn't be trusted. Or both. Interactions between them might be laced with an underlying hostility. He wondered if having the escort in mage livery was more a detriment. They could insist on inspecting the cart on principle, just to fuck with their rivals.

"We are out of the Mistress's compound and on the street," Teno added. "Nearly to the Market District and heading to the North Gate."

They were silent for a time, both afraid to talk for fear of being overheard. But they could hear the bustle of the street outside as the driver carried them toward the city gate.

"What do we do if this doesn't work?" Kane asked in a

whisper.

Auraq tried to shrug, but in his current position, he couldn't really pull it off. "Just be ready if it doesn't," he answered flatly.

"And do what exactly?"

Auraq didn't have an answer.

Kane gave him a level look. "Maybe I should learn how to defend myself. You could teach me how to use the sword."

On the surface, the idea didn't seem a bad one—with all the danger they faced, Kane should have at least some of the basic skills needed to protect himself. But something about visualizing Kane with a weapon bothered him. Auraq had done enough killing for the two of them. He didn't want Kane to ever have to face the reality of what that was like.

"An idea that won't help us any today."

Teno's boot heel kicked twice at the back of his bench seat. A clear signal to quiet down.

"Guards ahead," Teno said in a low voice.

Moments later, the cart slowed and Auraq could hear a muffled conversation. He couldn't really distinguish any distinct words—they must have been some strides away from the cart. He waited with his breath locked in his chest, expecting to hear a change in tone or the ringing of steel. But the conversation was brief, and the cart started rolling again.

"All clear," Teno said.

The cart turned a corner and put the crate into direct sunlight. In seconds, the temperature was spiking inside even more and Auraq was finding it harder to breathe. Sweat dripped from his face and formed a dark stain on the bottom of the crate. Across from him, Kane's cheeks and neck were flushed crimson.

"Can't that beast pull this cart any faster?" Kane said.

The cart lumbered along, rocking and creaking around them. It was impossible to gauge the speed or how much distance they'd traveled. Sounds of the city ebbed and flowed around them. At times, the cart was surrounded by what seemed like throngs of people. Auraq could make out distinct conversations as people walked close to the cart, going about their morning routine. A man pounded his fist against the side of the cart and screamed at Teno. "That was my foot, you wine-soaked clod." Merchants barked out their wares. Chickens squawked. The repetitive chime of a blacksmith's hammer sang out in perfect rhythm. Auraq tried to think where a blacksmith was on their route, hoping it might give him some clue as to where they were.

"Can't stand much more," Kane said with a quick exhale. His breath was the blast from a furnace against Auraq's face.

"No choice."

Kane's eyes flashed with annoyance. Auraq knew that he'd come to some decision, and for a moment, he thought Kane was going to push off the lid of the crate and climb out. Auraq was ready to grab him and hold him down if he did. But instead, Kane started unfastening the buckles on his jerkin.

"What are you doing?"

He'd been given new travel clothes by Pyta's estate—the staff deeming his old ones unfit for any further wear and disposing of them. The fresh tunic was now saturated, and the sweat had begun to soak into the fabric of the jerkin. "Should have thought to not wear it in here anyway."

Kane started to squirm about next to Auraq. Little by little, he negotiated his shoulders, then his arms, out of the armholes of the jerkin. He knocked against the sides of the crate and elbowed Auraq at least a half-a-dozen times. The wet fabric twisted and locked his arm underneath and behind him at one point—which made him flail about even more.

"What the fuck is going on in there?" Teno asked in a harsh whisper.

Auraq tugged on the edge of the jerkin until Kane's arm was liberated again.

Kane slumped back against the side of the crate. The sweat-soaked tunic clung to the contours of his torso. "That was hardly worth it."

"I could have told you that."

Teno heeled the bench seat again. "Coming up on the gate."

Auraq and Kane fell silent as the cart wheeled on for a time. Then they slowed to a stop again.

"There's a queue," Teno said.

Auraq could hear the concern in his voice. *Inspections?* he wondered. Were they checking all merchandise leaving the city? Auraq wondered if they somehow anticipated a clandestine attempt at getting out of the city. Or were they tipped off?

The cart moved a short distance, then squeaked to a stop again. Then moved, and stopped. Mercifully, the cart rolled back into shadow. It provided some relief, but hardly enough. Auraq was beginning to feel light-headed.

If they had attempted this during midday, they would have cooked to death for sure.

The cart moved again.

"Far enough," someone shouted.

Auraq heard footsteps crunch on the road all around the cart.

"State your business" came the same brusque voice. "What's this, then?"

"Rugs," Teno replied. "From the estate of the esteemed Mistress Pyta, prime magus and headmistress of the academy."

"Rugs? Where you taking them?"

"Back to the merchant who sold them to her, who is awaiting us in the outer city. They are the wrong color."

A silence followed. "You need a detail of four guards to accompany rugs?"

Auraq could almost imagine the face Teno made. "Have you any idea the value of a well-made weave, *surrah*?" Teno said. Auraq could tell he emphasized the title to remind the guard that Teno was above him in station. "What is all this about?"

"Duke Salisar's orders. With the events that occurred yesterday, he wants a detailed log of all coming in and out of the city. We will need to inspect your cart before we let you proceed."

Teno sighed. "Events that occurred at the academy, I'll remind you. Events that deeply affected the Mistress herself. Are you going to insult her further by accusing her of transporting

194

contraband of some sort?"

"No one is accusing—"

One of the academy guards spoke up. "Need I remind you that you have no jurisdiction in academy matters?"

"Transporting rugs is an 'academy matter'?"

"Are you, surrah, worthy of judging what is and what is not a concern to the academy?" Teno put in.

"If you have nothing to hide—"

"This is a matter of trust and honor," the academy guard replied. He spoke firmly, with authority—but without aggression, carefully and skillfully edging his toe up to the line without crossing it. "Gate guardsmen searching the merchandise of the headmistress in front of a host of witnesses would undermine her authority and admiration in this city. It would be a show of distrust on the part of the duke. I cannot allow that, surrah."

A silence followed.

"We would accept a writ from the Duke himself, authorizing the search," Teno added. "Nothing less. Shall I dispatch a messenger?"

Auraq held his breath. If they called Teno's bluff and sent for a messenger, Auraq and Kane would be dead from heat exhaustion by the time authorization came.

Again, silence. Auraq could feel the guards trying to figure out a way around Teno's deceptively reasonable, yet unrealistic, ultimatum. Teno had outmaneuvered them. They could attempt to inspect the cart by force, but that would end in a bloody fight. Something no one wanted. Causing bloodshed with the academy's guards would put them at the losing end with their superiors if nothing was found. That was too big a gamble.

"Move along."

The cart started moving.

"We are clear of the gate," Teno said after a time. "A bit longer to get beyond the outer city and we can let you out."

Kane exhaled in relief.

"None too soon," Auraq replied.

The road outside the city walls was indeed worse. The cart

pitched and bounced over deep ruts like a dinghy on a rough sea. The two of them were banged about inside. Kane's elbow cracked Auraq in the temple. Auraq braced his arms against the sides to steady himself.

"Still wish I'd been there for the conversation with Mistress Pyta," Kane said.

"I told you. You didn't miss much."

Kane lowered his voice, presumably so Teno wouldn't hear. "Why wouldn't she help us?"

"She said she didn't want to put any more of her mages at risk."

Kane studied him a moment. "But you don't believe her."

Auraq bit his lip, tempted to keep his thoughts to himself. "No. She's hiding something."

Kane fell quiet, pensively gnawing at the inside of his cheek. He was worried and anxious. Last night's treatment of a good meal and full night of sleep in a safe bed had revived him some, returning a little color to his face and light back into his eyes, but it couldn't erase all the strain on him and the trauma from the day before.

"I honestly didn't think I'd see you again," Kane said.

Auraq looked at him with a knitted brow. "What are you talking about?"

"Last night. I had convinced myself that you wouldn't make it back. I… I don't know what I would've done."

"That's one thing you don't need to ever worry about," Auraq said flatly. "I'm not that easy to be rid of." His tone was cavalier. Offhand. But somehow—perhaps it was the way Kane knuckled the meat of his palm, or the way he pulled his lower lip into his mouth—somehow Auraq sensed that Kane needed something more reassuring. He gave him a level look. "I will always make it back. That's a promise."

The cart lumbered along at a steady pace now. The sounds of urban activity faded to dull muffled background noise. They could hear the steady clop-clop of the hooves on the road, and the squeak of the cart's wheels. The guards marching along on either side began to talk among themselves in low voices.

One of the wheels hit an especially deep rut in the road.

One side of the cart plunged in a sudden and violent jolt. Auraq felt himself pitch and drop. He put out his hands to brace himself. His hands landed on Kane's chest just before his full weight fell on top of him. Their cheeks brushed as Auraq's chin ended somewhere along the curve of Kane's neck and shoulder.

Kane let out a whoosh of air as he was crushed beneath Auraq's bulk, but a moment later he was laughing. His chest bounced underneath Auraq's hands. Heat radiated off of Kane's chest against his palms.

The cart righted itself again and Auraq felt his face flush as he pushed himself up. His hands hitched on Kane's sweat-slick tunic, and slid it farther up his torso until Kane's nipples pressed against the heel of his hands. They were face to face—their noses almost touching. Auraq looked up and his eyes locked onto Kane's. For a heartbeat, or maybe three, he was frozen there, unable to pull himself away.

"Sorry," Auraq grumbled as he pushed himself back and fell against the side of the crate—then realized his hands were still pressed against Kane's chest, his fingers practically cupping the curve of his pectorals. He yanked them back and hugged them against himself as if they were somehow dangerous.

Kane's laughter tapered off.

A part of Auraq's brain recognized that it was the first time he'd heard Kane laugh so freely. And it was a welcome sound, one Auraq knew he enjoyed hearing. But he was too frazzled and uncomfortable at the moment to appreciate it. He averted his eyes to the lid of the crate.

He felt Kane's eyes on him still. Auraq noticed their legs were touching too—his knee to Kane's thigh. He wondered if he could move his leg casually to break the connection. The contact between the two of them felt like an invasion. An odd overwhelming sensation of guilt and shame gripped him—he shouldn't be touching Kane. The crate felt even more confined than before.

Kane shifted again, his body moving closer.

Then Kane was kissing him.

A hand glided up the side of his face, and fingers curled around the back of his neck—and Kane's mouth was against his. Soft lips pressed against him, lightly pinching his own upper lip between them.

Shock gripped him. His entire body stiffened like a corpse. His legs kicked out, locking the knees. His back arched. His eyes widened to full circles while his lips remained solid and lifeless, afraid to respond.

In that single moment in time, his mind was flooded with so many things, he had no idea how to untangle them. Emotions tugged him in all directions like he was being drawn and quartered. Fear whipped through him first—though he wasn't entirely sure what he was afraid of. Then layers of surprise came at him in waves as tiny realizations spawned in his head. They all whirled about in a maelstrom of new revelations. Kane's attraction to him was never something he foresaw. Never considered. But then—stranger still—awareness rose up to the surface of his consciousness that Kane's lips felt warm and soft against his own, and the touch of Kane's fingers made his face alight with energy.

And most shocking of all, his cock responded with a surge of hot and sudden arousal. It swelled in an instant and bulged painfully against the lacings at the front of his trousers. His entire groin was inflamed with unexpected desire—understanding something his brain still struggled to comprehend. Waves of fresh yearning tingled down his legs and up through his tightened abdomen.

All this transpired in the span of only a few heartbeats. The shock faded and his mind caught up with his heart.

It wasn't until Kane pulled away again that he realized he should have kissed him back.

Kane turned away, his cheeks burning. "Gods, I'm sorry," he whispered, the pain of rejection and humiliation rasping his voice. "I thought…."

"No," Auraq replied quickly. Too quickly. "No, it's all right."

But it came out all wrong. Too stiff. Even to his ear, it

sounded aloof and patronizing. Like he was trying to comfort him for doing something wrong or embarrassing. Not at all how he wanted it to sound. He immediately regretted it and wanted to pull the words back into his mouth and try again. Gods! He hadn't expected this to happen. How could he have?

Should he have?

Should he have seen this moment coming?

The sensation of Kane's lips pressed against his lingered on his own like the taste of sweet wine. His mouth tingled and his entire body shuddered.

The spark of something he felt the night before ignited. It had been there all along, he realized… tucked quietly in a corner. Like walking past something every day of your life and never noticing it before. But it was there… and now he couldn't help but see it.

Kane pushed his body farther away, plastering his back against the side of the crate. He closed his eyes. "What a fool I am."

Auraq ached to tell him he wasn't a fool. He felt something too—he just didn't know what yet. But he couldn't say it. His tongue had swollen and clogged his throat, choking him. He couldn't swallow. He could barely breathe. And every heartbeat that pounded on without him saying anything widened the crevasse between them.

If he couldn't talk, he could at least kiss him back. His head spun in dizzy circles. Desire pushed him, yet fear restrained him—a fear of crossing over into some unknown territory. Gods! This was not him. He'd faced a horde of barbarians in battle, he'd been chased down by wolvren, and all the while he kept his head. But now… never had he experienced such apprehension and fear. Why did this simple thing make his heart pound so wildly?

He felt the moment slipping from him. He had to act. As if preparing to jump into a cold lake, he pulled in a breath to ready himself.

A hard knock came on the crate from above making Auraq lurch, his heart nearly bursting.

"We're here" came Teno's muffled voice from outside.

Auraq hadn't even noticed they had come to stop. Before Auraq could grab him and pull him in, Kane punched open the top of the crate. As blinding sun crashed in around Auraq and cool air rushed in to bite his skin, Kane was already on his feet and leaping out.

THE DELIVERY cart had pulled off the road into high grass and rested alongside a copse of young trees. They were well outside the outer city. The walls were about a mile off. Not as far as he wanted to be, but he was out of the city and that was what mattered. He rose up and stepped out of the crate, painfully aware of the hard cock pressing against his leg. He retrieved his pack from inside an empty barrel, his swords from under a duck weave tarp, and dropped off the back of the cart.

Teno and the guards watched him and waited.

"Thank you," Auraq said. His voice was quieter than he intended. And laced with an awkward sadness. "Please tell your mistress that her aid in this is appreciated. I doubt we would have made it out without your help today."

Teno nodded. "Safe journey to you both." He shook the reins and the cart lurched into the motion again. One of the guards nodded to him as the four of them took their positions on either side of the cart and they all headed back to the city.

Kane stood off by the trees, arms laced against his chest, staring at his feet.

Auraq joined him. He thought about addressing what had happened, but the look on Kane's face dissuaded him from making any attempt at clearing the air. The moment was lost.

"What now?" Kane asked.

Auraq took stock of where they were. "A bit of a walk from here. Through these woods." He gestured with his chin, but Kane wasn't even looking in his direction.

"Lead away," Kane told him.

Chapter 23

THE SMALL cabin was nestled in a thick cluster of pines at the top of a rise. From the streambed below, it was nearly invisible. Despite having been here dozens of times in his youth, Auraq would have missed it himself, if not for the stone marker his father had placed along the bank.

He spotted fresh boot prints in a patch of soft mud—and the knots loosened in his back and his shoulders. Until that moment, he wasn't even aware of how tense he'd been about this. Of course, he trusted in his father—trusted that he had escaped the city unharmed—but he'd underestimated the reach and tenacity of the Jackals before. The uncertainty had quietly gnawed at him more than he'd admitted to himself.

The prints were a welcome sign. He climbed up and over the steep bank, using branches and roots to haul himself up.

Kane watched him from the bottom of the narrow gully, balancing on rocks in the middle of the stream. "Where are you going?" he asked.

Auraq could still hear the sharpness in Kane's tone that was more than just impatience or fatigue. He had hardly spoken in the hours since they delved into the forest, but when he did, his voice had an edge. It wasn't anger, but something else near it. Auraq hoped it would have faded by now, but instead it seemed, if anything, to settle in deeper.

He lowered to a squat and held out his hand. "Just up this hill."

Kane gave the hand a look of suspicion. Pressing his lips together, he took Auraq's hand and allowed Auraq to pull him up.

Auraq led him along a thin trail. Strategically placed flagstones created a rustic and narrow staircase up the steep incline. Much of the path had become overgrown. Auraq pushed through a wall of needled branches and held them aside so Kane could follow.

The cabin seemed even smaller than Auraq remembered it.

The surrounding foliage had encroached on the simple log structure like a soft green shroud. Wild ivy draped much of the outside, smoothing out the rolling curves of the logs, and hardly any of the fieldstone foundation was visible anymore. Auraq remembered being sent along the streambed to collect those stones as a child, hauling them back one by one. The small, four-paned windows cut into the walls were largely useless. Any light that would make it through the heavy curtain of overhanging boughs would be further hindered by the film of gray that lined the inside. The slate shingles Auraq had helped install were covered in a lush blanket of moss. Adding to the overall camouflage, the plank door was painted a deep woodland green.

"How did you even know this was here?" Kane asked, his brow knitted.

"I helped build it," Auraq replied as he triggered the latch on the door with his thumb and pushed inward. Swollen by summer humidity, the door resisted as it always had, before it opened with a pop. He ducked under the low frame and allowed Kane to pass into the cabin before closing the door behind him.

The single room was lit by a few candles and a dwindling fire in the hearth. Auraq's father was seated at a small workbench in the corner, scraping away at a piece of wood with a small whittler's knife. He jolted at the sound of the door, dropping his carving and snatching a larger knife from the tabletop next to him. When he saw Auraq, his entire body slumped forward and the knife dropped from his hand.

"Thank the Gods," he said, looking up at the ceiling.

They crossed the room and met in the middle and, without a word, embraced heartily. Auraq's throat constricted as his father's thick arms enveloped him and his hands closed into fists around the fabric of his tunic. It had been many a year since his father had hugged him so.

Neither spoke. They stood there gripping each other as if

compiling all the years of lost contact in that one moment. "I'd convinced myself they found you," his father said finally into his shoulder. "Or that you would not see my message."

Auraq released his hold on his father and pulled back. "Nearly true for both."

Malgar's complexion was pale and his face gaunt. It accentuated the deep lines at the corners of his eyes. Malgar patted Auraq's right shoulder three times and looked away as if suddenly embarrassed. He spotted Kane still standing by the door and a smile split his face. "Glad to see you're safe as well, lad."

"I have your son to thank for that," Kane answered gently. Seeing Malgar again seemed to soften his dour mood. "I understand you had a bit of a run-in yourself with our new friends."

Malgar waved it off. "Idiots. Who the fuck did they think taught this reprobate how to use a sword in the first place?"

Kane chuckled. "You made short work of them, I understand."

"Without breaking a sweat. I didn't even have to set down my mug of ale," Malgar said with a widening grin. "Come." He signaled them over to a small table. "You're hungry, no doubt. I threw together a stew. Just in case."

As Auraq and Kane took seats, Malgar pulled out two wooden bowls from a cabinet, ladled the steaming mixture into them, and dropped them onto the table. "Nothing fancy, but it'll fill you up. Don't wait on me. I've already eaten."

The rich aroma wafted up into Auraq's face and set off his stomach into a sudden and angry twist. He hadn't realized how hungry he was. The two of them dug in. Aside from the grunts of approval to Malgar, they hardly said a word as they shoved in spoonful after spoonful. But the silence between them felt sullen—each mouthful of food used as an excuse to not talk. Auraq stole quick glances up at Kane while he ate, but Kane never once looked up from his bowl.

When they were scraping the bottoms of their bowls, finishing up their second helping, Malgar wandered back to his cabinet and scrambled through its contents. Grumbling, he moved various jars and boxes aside to reach around in the back. "Ah," he said with a grin and pulled out a dusty ceramic bottle. "Knew this was back here somewhere. Some good ol' gut burn for cold nights and special occasions. I'd say this qualifies."

He pulled out the cork stopper and filled three wooden cups with the contents. He then gestured to the space in front of the fire. Kane and Auraq moved their chairs closer to the hearth. The cups were distributed, and Malgar took a seat in his own chair.

Auraq felt like he was in some strange dream. This was the father he remembered from his youth—the one he had not known for many years. The animosity wedged between them for so long was simply gone, as if it had never existed. Auraq knew his father well enough to realize that he would not speak of it, but would now pick up the threads of their relationship where they had left off, back when Auraq first packed up and left for his post in the Lendera province.

Auraq took a sip from the cup and winced. The warmth traveled in a slow tide from his throat on down. As a youth, he would sneak quick nips from the bottle when he thought his father wasn't looking. It was as terrible as he remembered it. Kane's entire face puckered and contorted each time he swallowed it down.

Malgar smacked his lips in appreciation.

"You served in the king's army too?" Kane asked.

Malgar nodded. "Eight full years. At the time, felt like a thousand." He had a momentary distant look, and a small smile lit the corners of his mouth as some memory returned to him. "Now, feels like it was only a few months. Rose to officer, like Auraq here, though not as quickly, I'll admit. Reached as high as I could for a commoner. Then… well"—he shrugged, almost apologetically—"with nowhere else for me to go, there didn't seem much point in remaining, so I took my king's pension with a thank you and left."

His father was oversimplifying the story. It was around that same time he had met Auraq's mother, so there was more happening than just the lack of career advancement. But he let his father tell the events the way he wanted.

"Used the coin to buy that shop," Auraq interjected, spinning the amber liquid around in the cup. He preferred a mug of ale, personally. Or even wine—something Sederian. His father's swill was eating out his stomach from the inside.

"Were you stationed at the border?" Kane asked.

Malgar nodded. "Lendera Province, same as him. Patrol mainly, protecting the region from the rat hordes." An old army term for the Volfic raiding parties. He paused to take a swig from his cup, then shook his head. "Insurgents would spring up from the villages from time to time as well. Sympathizers, idealistic youth with too much time on their hands. We'd have to move in and put an end to it."

It always surprised Auraq how similar their experiences were, even two decades apart. Years after taking possession of the Lendera Province, little had changed. The region was still a hotbed of rebellion and conflict. The only difference was his father had little regard for Volfic barbarians. But Auraq's mother came from the region as well. She always claimed she was Kachian, but it was very possible some barbarian blood was in her, which would put some in Auraq's own veins too—a notion his father conveniently ignored.

Some memory seemed to pull Malgar's eyes away from the moment for a time, but then his face scrunched as if he was annoyed, and he shrugged. "Most of my time was spent with my thumb up my ass, really. Some areas saw more action, but for the most part, raids were few. The most exciting part of a patrol was watching a fresh turd steam on a cold morning."

Auraq couldn't help but chuckle. His father was right about that. "But when there were raids…," he heard himself say in a low voice.

"Aye," Malgar replied with a slow bob of his head. "But when there were…." Again, his thoughts appeared to take him away for a time. "Glad to learn that my training from those days hasn't abandoned me after all these years," he added and tilted the cup all the way back, draining the last of the contents.

"Agreed," Auraq chimed in.

His mind slipped back into his own memories as a pensive silence descended around them. Kane moved around in his chair and looked uncomfortable. With a small clearing of his throat, he changed the subject. "How long has this cabin been here?"

"My own grandfather built one on this spot an age ago," Malgar replied. "Grandma was a bit of ripe pepper, if you get my meaning, so he would trek out here to escape her wrath. When it passed to me, it was in a bad state. So I rebuilt it. With his help," he added with a smile. Auraq knew how much help he provided. At the time, he was barely able to swing a hammer. "Used it mostly as a hunting cabin when I've a mood for it. Less and less, lately. I keep the place tucked under my hat though— don't need squatters thinking they've a free roof."

Malgar filled his cup again, this time slower with a reflective look in his eyes. It was a look Auraq recognized. The mood was shifting. "So it's high time, I think, for the two of you to catch me up." His eyes shifted upward beneath a knitted brow to stare hard at Kane.

Kane seemed interested in the contents of his mug for a time. "Not a good idea. You don't want to be involved in this."

"Well, that particular horse is already halfway down the road, lad."

Kane scratched behind his ear, frowning.

"Let's say you let me decide how involved I want to be," Malgar added in a stiff tone Auraq knew well.

Few could stand against his father when he took that tone. It did not surprise Auraq when Kane nodded.

Kane kept the story simple, giving Malgar the bones of it. Malgar listened without expression or interruption. When the story turned to involve the mages, Auraq expected him to announce he'd heard enough. His father had little fondness for the mages of the world and their strange and unnatural craft. He'd always been suspicious of them, wary of their motives. They were far too secretive and acted far too superior. It was likely the root of Auraq's own feelings on the matter.

But Malgar let Kane speak without interruption. Once

Kane was finished, his father stared at him a long while with a furrowed brow and tight lips, until Auraq grew concerned. His father could be a hard man, and though generally stoic, drink could put him quick to anger. Auraq worried that his father might chase Kane right out of the cabin.

"You going to show me?" he said at long last.

Kane hesitated, unconsciously pulling his arm closer to his body. Auraq could see conflict darken his features. The last man he'd shown it to ended up brutally murdered within a well-guarded mage's academy.

"Show him," Auraq said.

Kane still seemed reluctant, holding his forearm against his chest. But he eventually lowered his arm and pulled back the sleeve of his tunic. His forearm was wrapped in a linen bandage.

Auraq frowned. This was the first that he'd noticed that Kane had the arm wrapped. Even in the dim light of the cabin, he could see dark spots had seeped through the linen to the surface.

Kane kept his eyes down as he slowly unraveled the bandage from his arm.

Then Auraq understood.

Kane hadn't been afraid to show the mark to his father after all—he'd been afraid for Auraq to see it. When the mark was finally revealed, his teeth clenched.

The fluid lines of the runes were raised up and inflamed like a branding. They pulsed angrily. The skin was split at edges of the mark, peeling back as the writing pushed its way to the surface. The wounds were crusted with black, and seeping with blood and ooze. Tendrils of flame reached around his forearm and traveled up beyond the elbow.

Malgar set down his cup and leaned in. "Gods burn us all," he breathed.

Auraq lifted slowly to his feet. "Kane...."

Kane wouldn't look at him. "You've had enough to worry about." A section of the bandage clung to the open wound. Kane hissed through his teeth as he tugged the linen free.

"Leave it," Auraq told him. He swung the chair closer,

lowered onto it, and gently took Kane's wrist for a closer look.

The wound was severe. The splits in the skin ran deep, exposing raw flesh beneath. If Kane had at least said something at the mage's estate, Pyta's healer could have done something. Now, they were days away from the nearest city.

He looked over his shoulder at his father. Malgar held his eyes with a hard stare of concern. Auraq had seen enough injury during his time in the army to know what that look meant. If those wounds festered, Kane would at the least lose his arm, but would more likely lose his life.

His stomach wrenched.

"How long has it been this bad?" he asked.

Kane shrugged. "It started worsening after we met with Chenigal. Whatever he did, it seemed to trigger something."

Two nights. It was advancing quickly.

Auraq squinted in the low light of the cabin and leaned in. He turned Kane's wrist in his hand to change the angle of the forearm. He searched for the early signs of the festering. "We need to get it clean before we bandage it back up again."

"I have linens," Malgar announced, lifting from his chair. "We can strip them for fresh bandages."

"I'm fine," Kane complained, trying to pull his arm free, but Auraq held it firm.

"You won't be if we don't take care of this," Auraq told him flatly.

Malgar dug out the cloth from a wooden chest at the foot of his bed, then plunged it into a water barrel. He wrung it out and handed it to Auraq. "I have some dried lady's mantle, I think," he said as he moved toward a line of jars on a shelf. "And some blue yarrow too. We should put a poultice under the dressings."

Auraq nodded in agreement. He wadded the wet cloth in his hand and made gentle dabs along the line of wounds. The muscles in Kane's jaw clenched, but he didn't complain or make a sound.

Then the edge of Auraq's finger brushed Kane's skin. He only grazed the line of the rune.

A barrage of images commandeered his vision. It must have been mere seconds only, but Auraq felt as if time around him had stopped. The world vanished and he was catapulted elsewhere, someplace dank and foul. Pain flared through his muscles and skin like a fire. He was bound—hands shackled behind his back, the metal cutting into wrists that had been rubbed raw. Others were around him, he realized, large looming shapes that shoved him coarsely and cursed him—

His body flailed. He lurched to his feet, knocking the chair back, and he broke contact with Kane's skin—and the images were gone. He was himself again, in the quiet of his father's cabin in the forest.

His heart pounding wildly, he staggered back.

"Auraq." His father was at his side in an instant, grabbing his arm to steady him. "What happened?"

But Auraq could not form the words. It required all his focus to bring his breathing under control.

Kane glanced over as he pulled the bloodstained bandages back over the runes. "You've seen it too." It was not a question. "By the look on your face, I can tell."

Auraq found he could at least nod.

Kane exhaled and swept his hand up his brow to push back his hair. His eyes were darkened and filled with torment.

"Seen what?" Malgar asked.

The shock of the experience was waning, but his knees quivered weakly. The incident had shaken him more than he wanted to admit. He righted the chair back onto its legs and lowered himself down. "You... you've experienced this before?"

Malgar stepped back, confused. "Auraq, what are you talking about?"

Kane lifted his head and he made a weak shrug. "They are sporadic. Brief. But they do seem to be occurring more frequently now." He lifted his arm to display the rune. "As this worsens."

"Visions?" Malgar asked. "You are experiencing visions?"

"It's more than a vision," Auraq replied, shaking his head.

The sensation clung to him like hot oil. "I was there. I felt it all. I could even smell the rancor of the place."

Kane nodded. "You were in the dungeon then."

"Yes, a dungeon. I was being led somewhere… by several men. I was shackled and… and I had been beaten. No." He closed his eyes as he searched the memory. As brief as it was, the details were carved into his mind. "No, I had been whipped. My back felt like it was on fire."

Again, Kane raised and lowered his chin in a slow bob. "There is more to it. You would have been taken out into very bright sunshine that hurts your eyes and blinds you. Many people are around, shouting and throwing rocks…."

Auraq's father seemed troubled. His face contorted, and he lowered himself on the edge of the chair. "You feel this is *his* memory… the one who placed his mark on you? This is what he experienced in life?"

"I believe so, yes."

"Then the encrypted memory is being revealed to you," Auraq said. Perhaps that meant they didn't need a mage to unlock the secrets of the mark after all.

Kane winced. "In part only, I think. There is more that I am not shown. It's as if pieces of it are leaking out." His gaze dropped to the loosely wrapped arm in his lap. "Like blood seeping through a bandage. I seem to only glimpse the most powerful moments he experienced. I just don't know what any of them mean, or why they're significant."

"I would think it obvious," Malgar said.

Kane's head shot up in surprise.

"You're experiencing the final moments of the man before his execution."

Chapter 24

MALGAR PUT a stop to any further conversation until Kane's wounds were addressed. While Auraq resumed cleaning the forearm, careful to not come in direct contact with the skin again, Malgar prepared the poultice in a wooden bowl. He smeared the aromatic paste in a thick layer over Kane's forearm with the back of the spoon, then rewrapped the arm in the fresh linen bandages.

Kane grimaced. "Stings."

Malgar nodded. "Means the essence in those herbs is doing the work it's meant to do. Tuck that end under." He swung his gaze to Auraq. "It'll have to be reapplied every day if we hope to stave off festering."

Auraq could tell from his father's tone that he didn't hold out much hope of even that being enough.

The effect of the herbs was quick. Kane's eyes were soon drooping and his chin sank in sudden jerks as he nodded off. Malgar helped him out of the chair and across the room. Kane was deposited into the cabin's solitary cot. His protests were short-lived. He was asleep and gently snoring before Malgar returned to his chair.

"So, what is your plan now, son?" Malgar asked, retrieving his cup from the floor. He tilted the bottle to it again, giving the cup an even more generous pour than earlier.

"Not sure. I'd hoped the mages would have been more help."

His father made a grunt.

"Chenigal was willing, but…." Auraq left the thought unfinished.

"Self-serving bastards. They saw no coin in it for them was the problem."

Auraq didn't agree—the healing he'd received from

Ozden would have cost him a small fortune, certainly. Pyta never asked him for even a single noble. But there was no point in challenging him about it. "Pyta suggested the capital. Said we'd find someone willing to help him. She gave me a list of names." He shrugged. "I suppose we head there."

Malgar swirled the liquid around in his cup. "This is dark business. Assassins. Strange magecraft. Messages from the dead. I don't like that you're caught up in it."

Auraq resisted the urge to remind him that only a day ago he wouldn't have cared what activity he was involved in. "I made a promise, Pa." The full answer was too complicated. That was at least something his father could understand. He put honor and duty before all else. "I'm going to see it through."

Malgar made a grunt and took a drink. His own way of accepting the answer. "Talk to me more of what you saw in this vision."

"Ask Kane. I didn't experience all that much."

"I'd wager you noticed more than you think." He shot a glance at Kane on the cot. "And he's out for the night. Indulge me."

In truth, the event had disturbed him more than he wanted to admit. He didn't care to relive any of it. But he took a deep breath as he reflected back and allowed the images to come forward in his mind's eye again.

"You're right, I think. He was to be executed. Kane's description of being led out of the dungeon into an angry crowd fits that too." He frowned, not knowing how to word what was next. "But it was more than just that. I felt his despair. He knew he was doomed. He was trying to come to terms with that."

"You felt his emotions?"

Auraq nodded. "And the state of his mind at that time. This was no horse thief, Pa. Something about him told me he was a man of great importance."

Malgar's eyes narrowed. "Nobleborn?"

"Maybe. Probably. I'm not certain." He didn't know what it felt like to be a noble.

He shook his head. Having someone else's experiences

intermeshed with his own thoughts was disconcerting. It wasn't like waking from a dream, where the details evaporate away. The sensory memory lingered with unsettling clarity. His instinct was to push the sensation away, but his father's questions kept them at the forefront. "I got the sense he felt betrayed. Alone. No one was there for him. At that time, he had no friends."

Malgar leaned back and absently pressed his knuckles to his lips. "The mark appeared on Kane's arm after he put on a bracer, or a gauntlet, yes?"

"That's right."

"And that doesn't seem strange to you?"

Auraq leaned in, elbows on knees. "What are you getting at?" He knew this look from his father. Something about the vision was like meat stuck in Malgar's tooth—and he was going to fuss with it until he figured it out.

Malgar made a slow swing of his head. "This mark is without a doubt something exceptional."

"Both Chenigal and Pyta said as much, yes."

"Which means it was crafted by a very powerful mage."

"Of course." Where was this going?

"Let's make a few assumptions, then," Malgar said, leaning back and tenting his fingers at his chin. "Nothing too outlandish or implausible. I don't know much about the business of being a mage, but I've been around few. As have you, I assume. So, we can speculate."

Auraq nodded.

"The first assumption we can make is why he trapped these memories in the mark in the first place. You said he felt betrayed and alone. Whatever it was that he was executed for, he believed he was innocent of the crime. Therefore, we can assume these memories were put there to prove his innocence."

Auraq folded his arms. "Stands to reason. But why not reveal the memories before he was executed?"

"Who knows? Perhaps he tried and was unable to. A mage this skilled would have been greatly feared, so he was likely kept in isolation. Perhaps he could not get close to anyone in time."

Auraq bit his upper lip. Seemed possible, but there were still too many unknowns. They had no way to determine with any certainty why the memories weren't revealed until now.

"Second assumption, then. An incantation this powerful probably took time to craft, yes? So, the object used to trigger the spell and transfer the mark to someone else had to be in his possession for a time. Presumably, he would also have wanted it to remain secret too, until the incantation was completed. Therefore, can we assume that the object used was something that belonged to him?"

Auraq's eyes narrowed. "Perhaps." This seemed a bigger leap than the first assumption.

"Let's assume that it was. For the sake of argument. Why, then, was he in possession of the bracer?"

Auraq's eyebrows lifted. He finally understood what his father was prodding at.

Mages didn't wear armor.

Or rather… *most* didn't.

"Ah," Malgar said with a grin lifting one side of his mouth. "I see now you understand."

"He was a battlemage."

Malgar nodded. "I suspect that he was. That uncanny ability to wear armor *and* still access power makes them exceedingly rare creatures."

Auraq knew, like most, that a mage's robes were not a choice, but a necessity. When a mage wore armor, it somehow obstructed their connection to their source of power. Some believed it was metal too close to the skin that interfered. Others claimed the weight of the armor or its fit against the body affected their concentration. No one knew for certain—perhaps not even the mages.

And no one knew why it was different for battlemages.

"There is only one battlemage known to me. And"—Malgar leaned forward and rested an elbow on one knee—"he was executed for treason twenty years ago."

Auraq sat up straighter in his chair. "Lord Norreg."

Malgar nodded.

"You think that vision…." Chills gripped his neck. Now more than ever, he wanted that imagery scrubbed from his mind completely. "I just experienced the final hour of the man who assassinated a king?"

"The man *accused* of killing a king," Malgar replied with an index finger in the air.

"There's a question?"

"Some claimed, at the time, there was a rush to judgment." Malgar tilted back his cup again, draining it one more time. "Who can say?"

Auraq fiddled with the beard on his chin, thinking. He never heard about that.

When the massacre occurred, he was too young to fully grasp what had happened—but an atrocity such as that wasn't something the kingdom recovered from quickly. The repercussions of that night were still felt kingdom-wide.

But no one really knew what had happened. No one outside of the king's palace, anyway.

Rumors were plenty, and every tavern patron across the realm had an opinion and would freely share his theory to any and all who would listen. But two things were agreed upon by all: the entire bloodline would have been lost if not for the gallant efforts of the Black Guard, who fought to save the king's youngest son, and the culprit behind it was the sinister Lord Norreg.

"Surely, there was evidence implicating him."

"One would think. The finger was pointed his way rather quickly. I remember the notice of his arrest was posted in the square only days after the assassination. Norreg and the king were once friends, I understand, but they'd had a falling out only a few days before. At least that's the story that people tell. Norreg apparently betrayed the king by speaking out publicly against him."

"About what?"

Malgar shrugged. "I never paid that much attention to the happenings in the capital, to be honest. It sounded as if Norreg had some radical views that people didn't like. It had something to do with the mages, if I remember. Anyway, it made him an easy suspect."

Mages again.

"Then his execution could have been politically motivated," Auraq said. As an officer in the king's army, he'd heard enough talk from the noble commanders to get a sense of the skullduggery that took place in Dar Arendia.

"The palace would not have wanted this to be a long, drawn-out affair. The people were already on the verge of rioting over it. A quick resolution was in everyone's interest, I would think. Impossible to say what really happened, but...." He swiveled his head around to glimpse the sleeping figure on the cot. "This raises the question of whether the wrong man lost his head."

"Perhaps Norreg is simply trying to implicate his coconspirators."

"Does that fit with what you experienced in your vision?"

Auraq frowned. It didn't. The man he became for those few moments felt great sorrow. Betrayal. Not the anger or bitterness a man would feel toward the accomplices who had gotten away. "If we are dealing with those actually behind that massacre"—his eyes flicked to Kane briefly, and the sight of him sleeping so peacefully pained him—"it would explain why someone wants him dead."

Malgar nodded. "Someone very powerful does not want the truth about that attack known. It also could explain why that mage was hesitant to offer help."

Auraq pressed his lips together, thinking. If Norreg was angry with the king over a mage issue, other mages would be as well. "Pyta was reluctant to admit to me that mages were involved. She may have been protecting someone."

"Or simply afraid of where this might lead. If some larger confederacy exists inside the mage guild and they are responsible for something as... unpardonable as a regicide, aiding you might compromise her own position in the guild. Or worse. They clearly have no qualms about killing off one of their own. She has much to lose. So she sent you off to the capital with a hearty good luck."

The heft of their conversation seemed to catch up to both of them then, and they fell quiet. Auraq's mind tried to wrestle with the enormity of it all—and failing, he found his mood sinking into a darker place. He was a simple man, suited for a soldier's life but not much else. He was not built for such grand heroics as this.

His head turned to Kane again, as if pulled by invisible strings. How was he to break any of this to him? With the amount already on his shoulders—the wounds on his arm, the assault of visions, the constant threat of death—how would he cope with this new information? Perhaps it was better if he didn't know of it yet.

The memory of their kiss infiltrated his thoughts. He closed his eyes, and the feel of Kane's warm lips pressed against his washed over him again. What a fool he was. If only he'd seen it coming. If only he'd reacted the way he truly wanted to, and not allowed himself to be usurped by a fear that made no sense. Now, there was a sour divide between them. Kane seemed detached from him—whatever had drawn them together was unraveling, and he felt powerless to stop it. Auraq's body physically ached at the thought that he'd missed his chance, that he would never experience those lips again. It felt like a knot constricting around his heart.

No, he decided then. He couldn't go on with this awkwardness—this deep chasm widening between them. Tomorrow, once they were on the road together, he would address it with Kane. He'd find the right moment and tell him that he felt it too.

His heart rate increased at the thought, and his insides turned to a gummy porridge. Whether it was from anticipation or nervousness, he couldn't tell. Perhaps both. He wondered if he'd sleep tonight.

Perhaps he needed to force down more of his father's potent firebrew.

"Your plan is still Arendia, then?" his father asked, breaking the silence.

Auraq nodded.

"You will need to be cautious, son. The army presence there is high. It will be harder for you to avoid notice. You could be recognized."

Auraq knew this was his father being overly concerned. The capital was a big city. "I'll be all right."

"You cannot help Kane if you get yourself arrested."

"Don't worry about it, Pa."

"Where will you go? Any ideas?"

"None," Auraq answered flatly. "I have the list provided by Pyta. As good a place to start as any."

"Or not," Malgar said, more loudly than he probably intended. The drink was starting to affect him, it seemed. He threw a quick look to Kane, who was still snoring softly, then lowered his voice. "I worry about you pursuing a name given to you by a mage. Knowing what we know, I would be wary of trusting any of them."

A valid point. "I have to start somewhere. I don't have any contacts in the capital." At least he didn't anymore.

"Well, I think I can help with that," his father said. "My former commander from my days in Lendera was from Har Rodell, but he lived most of the year in Dar Arendia. Lord Farris. A well-connected noble of a good family. He would be able to provide you sound counsel, I think. He can be a temperamental sort, but…. We got on well back then. I'm certain he'd help."

"Can we trust him?"

"More than you can any name on that list, I'll wager. And he's well versed in the politics at court."

Auraq nodded. He preferred the idea of meeting with someone who could be vouched for.

"How will this Lord Farris know us?" he asked. "We will not be admitted on my word alone. Will you send word to him? Pen a note?"

Malgar stood from his chair. "Easily done." He reached under his bed, careful not to waken Kane, and slid out a leather travel bag. "I'm not leaving anything to chance. I'm going with you."

Chapter 25

THEY LEFT the cabin shortly past dawn.

After breaking their fast on some dry cheese, wild cherries, and oat cakes that Malgar fried on a griddle, they took turns washing up a little with water heated over the fire. While Malgar inspected Kane's bandages, Auraq foraged around the cabin for any useful supplies his father had on hand. The cabin was locked up tight, their prints brushed away as best as they were able, and with full packs on their shoulders, they started their march north through the woods.

It was a dreary and damp sort of morning, the kind of weather that promised to linger stubbornly and refuse to improve. A swirling mist moved through the trees like an army of specters. Moisture collected on the leaves and branches, and as they pushed through the underbrush, their clothes were soon soaked through, as if they traveled through a downpour.

The cold gray suited Auraq's mood. He hadn't slept well. He woke up often enough to feel like he hadn't slept at all, and when he did sleep, he was plagued by troubling dreams he could no longer remember, but that left him feeling sullen and on edge. With his plan of having time alone with Kane frustrated by his father's company, he withdrew into himself and did not speak much.

Kane, on the other hand, seemed rested and relieved to have Malgar's company. He spent most of his time marching along at Malgar's side, talking quietly with him, while Auraq followed behind, alone with his thoughts in self-imposed isolation. Occasionally, he'd glance back to see if Auraq was still there, but nothing more. He didn't show any signs of wanting much to do with Auraq at all.

Auraq had selfishly tried to dissuade his father from

joining them on the journey, but the level of danger only seemed to convince Malgar further that he needed to tag along. He didn't want his father exposed to the dangers, of course—but if he were honest with himself, it was better to have another skilled swordsman along. Despite his age, his father had proven himself still capable in a fight. Plus, Auraq could not deny that an added set of trained eyes and ears wouldn't hurt their cause. But as long as his father was right there, how could he have his talk with Kane? The longer he waited, the less likely it was that he could repair the damage between them.

Malgar seemed happy to lead the way, taking charge of their little party with a natural authority, marching along with his old commander's hat on like he was leading a charge into battle. Auraq was just as content to let him. They traversed the thick wood—it was slow going, but Auraq agreed that staying clear of the main road was a good idea. The terrain steadily grew hillier. It rose and fell in undulating waves, sometimes with steep declines that made traversing them perilous—especially with ground beneath their heels made slick from the persistent wet of the day. Small streams cut through the low points between hills. Taking some unseen cue, Malgar veered and followed the direction of one of the streams. Auraq did not know what his father's plan was, but it was clear he had one. Auraq didn't ask.

Malgar was in the middle of some tale about his time stationed in Lendera when he stopped short. Something had caught his eye. He lowered to a squat along the muddy bed of the stream and inspected the ground.

He flagged Auraq closer.

Auraq dropped to one knee beside him. A single print in the mud. One he'd seen before.

"Bear?" his father asked. He moved a few trampled leaves aside to get a better view of it.

"No," Kane said before Auraq could respond. He stood behind Malgar and Auraq looking down over their shoulders. When Auraq glanced up at him, he expected to see dread on Kane's face. Instead he saw something harder—anger perhaps. "Not a bear."

Malgar's gaze swung from Kane to Auraq, his brow raised in a furry arch.

"We've run into these before. Wolvren." Auraq rose up and scanned the surrounding ground for more prints. He found more behind them. The beast was traveling southward, upstream—the opposite direction.

"Wolvren?" Malgar repeated and looked down at the print with new unease. "Wolvren?" he said again, only louder. He stood and backed away from the print as if it was a danger.

"Still sure you want to join us?" Auraq said dryly.

"And you've encountered them before?"

"On our journey to Har Tesera."

Malgar yanked off his hat and raked his fingers through his sweat-soaked hair. "Gods, Auraq. These rat fuckers aren't playing at games here, are they? Wolvren?"

"We managed to avoid them last time," Kane said.

Barely, Auraq thought.

"Clearly," Malgar said, shaking his head. "You're here talking to me, aren't you? Let's hope we remain as lucky. You might have mentioned this to me earlier."

Auraq wished he had. If he thought it would have dissuaded him from coming along, it would have been the first thing out of his mouth. His eyes drifted to the track again and his insides tightened. This meant the Order either learned they were out of the city or weren't taking any chances. "The beast came through before dawn. They are not tracking us. Just searching."

"How many do they have control of?"

"At least two. Though, we think there were more of them," Kane said.

Malgar grunted.

"They don't have our scent," Auraq said.

"Yet." Malgar pulled his hat back on his head. "Stay in the water as much as you can, and keep your ears open. You'll hear one before you see it. But by then, it'll probably be too late." Malgar started marching downstream again, this time avoiding the banks and splashing through the ankle-deep water. Auraq and Kane followed, but no one was in the mood to talk anymore.

THEY FOLLOWED the stream as it snaked its way through the terrain. An unsettling stillness hung in the air like the inside of a crypt. No sounds emerged from the wood surrounding them save the wind in the leaves and the steady murmur of the stream at their feet—no birds, no chattering of insects, no scurry of creatures through the underbrush.

And no more signs of the wolvren.

But Auraq knew they were still out there. The forest was holding its breath in fear. He prayed that their path through the deep ravine would keep them out of direct sight and the wind would not carry their scent into the air.

The small stream converged with a second, forming a larger single stream that flowed more than bounced. More rivulets tumbled out of the foliage from sharp angles to join in. The rushing waterway swelled, the force of it intensifying against their ankles, as the terrain around them calmed into more gentle rolls. Thorny brush hugged the banks and grabbed at their sleeves and packs.

They kept boots in the water for as long as they dared, but when the watercourse tumbled down a series of rocky landings that looked like a giant's staircase and then spilled into a wider river, they were forced to climb down alongside it.

They'd arrived at the King's River. The waterway that flowed directly to the capital.

Steep banks confined the river in its course, which made the waters too deep and too strong to wade through, even along the edge. Forced to continue on dry land, Auraq and Malgar slashed through thick bracken with their weapons, careful not to make too much noise. It was slow going and exhausting work. Despite the day's chill, they each were soon sweating from the effort—which only served to encourage the swarms of flies that circled their heads, biting at the back of their necks. Malgar took to waving about his hat in sudden uncontrolled fits.

Kane trailed behind them. Auraq could tell the journey was wearing on him. He was less sure of his footing, stumbled more, and his breathing seemed labored. Auraq told himself it could still be the sapping effect of the poultice, but no, he knew the truth of it. The wounds were worsening. The medication might slow the progression but until the mark was addressed, the wounds would not heal.

Auraq suggested they rest, but Kane refused. He insisted they keep moving.

Biting his lip, Auraq nodded and pressed onward. If they could only have retrieved Spirit from Ruck's stables somehow, Kane could have reserved his strength by riding. They would have covered more ground too. As it stood, Auraq could only hope Spirit would be well cared for until he could return to Har Tesera someday to reclaim her.

In time, the thicket untangled and gradually gave way to areas of grassland. Auraq was relieved for Kane's sake—traversing the land would be easier on him. And at long last, the dense clouds began to break apart and dissolve away, and their first glimpses of blue shone through. Warm sunlight reached the land.

Malgar pointed farther ahead.

Auraq shielded his eyes from the fresh sunlight reflecting off the water's surface. Up ahead were two bodies of water—the river of sparkling blue and a sweeping oxbow lake of green west of it. On the land bridge between the two was a wooden building—a simple utilitarian structure, old but sturdily built, and a large dock that reached out into the river.

A way station. A stop for supply barges heading downriver toward the capital—a place for crew to rest, procure supplies for their journey, or pick up new cargo. And a place for travelers to negotiate passage.

This had been Malgar's plan all along. The crafty old badger had figured out how to get them to the capital quickly and quietly—and with little chance of being tracked.

Malgar led the way toward the building, circling around to the side facing the river. A seasoned tradesman, and used to such establishments, Malgar showed no hesitation and stepped in through the large double doorway with familiar ease.

The inside was one single chamber and a chaos of stacked barrels and crates with no discernible organization. Kane sat down heavily on the nearest crate from the opening and slumped forward with elbows on his knees.

A man sat at a table in the corner toward the back, filling out ledger pages in a wide book and humming to himself. Small in stature, he was almost lost behind the piles of ledgers on his table. Wild tufts of white hair spilled out from under his ruby-colored flat cap that hung down over his ears like goat ears. He wore a ragged old leather jerkin with no tunic, which exposed his thin arms and bony chest—which were weathered and tanned nearly the same color as his vest. His head popped up at the sound of Malgar's footfalls on the floorboards. On reflex, he snatched the handle of the knife on the table next to him.

"I keep no gold here," he spat out, "if you be bandits looking for an easy take. Grab an apple or two if you be hungry, but don't think to cause me trouble."

Auraq had no doubt the man could use that knife. Alone out here in the wilderness, he'd seen his share of danger to be sure. He wouldn't have reached this age if he couldn't defend himself.

Malgar held out his palms to the man, and his face lit with a smile. "Your worm-eaten apples, Paugen? Rather eat my shoe."

Paugen leaned in and squinted. "Ugh," he said with something between disappointment and disgust. He tossed the big knife down on the table. "As I live and breathe. Malgar the Menace."

Malgar's hand went to his chest. "You wound me with such titles, Paugen."

"Save me the act. I've a good mind to wound you true." He made a meaningful tilt of his head toward the knife before he turned back to his ledger.

"Still sore are you? Still think I cheated?"

"Not a question of if, you sorry old buzzard," Paugen grumbled. "Just can't figure out how you done it, is all." He dipped his quill into the well and scribbled something onto the page. "Why you all the way out here? I've no need of your barrels."

"Have none to sell. Here for a different purpose. Looking for passage."

That caught Paugen's attention. He stopped midstroke, tilted his head and lifted one fuzzy white eyebrow. For a moment, he seemed to try and process what this new information could mean. He seemed to only just notice the other two standing behind Malgar.

"You? You leaving your shop to head north?"

Malgar's chin lowered a fraction. "Aye. Heading on downstream. That's all you need to know."

"Who'd you cheat this time? Must be someone powerful if you need to run off and hide."

Malgar didn't say anything.

Paugen didn't seem to notice Malgar's silence. "Not a lot between here and Dar Arendia. If you're thinking of visiting the capital, good luck to ya. It's goin' to chew you up and spit your grisly old carcass back onto the street." He lowered his head back over the ledger. "Pay good coin to watch that."

Malgar's tone remained level, though Auraq could tell his father was growing aggravated. He folded his arms and spoke in a flat tone. "Any more barges scheduled in today?"

Paugen lifted one shoulder in a halfhearted shrug. "One more likely. Can't say when. Hope soon so I can head back."

That at least was good news.

Paugen was back to his work, scratching away at his ledger and grunting to himself. The three of them were already forgotten.

"How do we know they'll stop?" Kane asked.

"They almost always do, but to be sure...." Malgar grabbed a pole that was leaning against the wall by the open doorway. It had a long red banner dangling from the end. He carried it out to the river, marched to the end of the dock, and slipped it into a holder attached to the farthest pylon. The flag hung out at an angle over the water.

Returning to the small warehouse, Malgar dusted his hands

proudly as if he'd completed a difficult task. "That should do it."
He grabbed apples from an open bushel and tossed some off to
both Auraq and Kane, and then he climbed up on a crate and
sunk his teeth into his apple with a juicy crack. "Now we wait."

AURAQ TOSSED the stripped apple core outside into the tall
grass.

The small way station warehouse had fallen into a quiet,
timeless lull. Paugen still sat at his table, scribbling into his
ledger and softly grunting to himself. Malgar had reclined back
against another crate. Arms crossed and eyes closed, he seemed
ready to nod off. Kane had drifted outside the warehouse. He sat
against the building on the south side, taking in the sun that had
finally escaped the clouds.

River sounds were the only things to reach Auraq's ears.

Now was his moment, of course.

With Malgar resting inside, he could take this opportunity
to talk to Kane. Part of him was reluctant to disturb him. After
the day's exertion, Kane could use the rest. Part of him knew he
was stalling. Once they'd taken passage on a barge, Kane would
have plenty of time to rest and save his strength.

Auraq's stomach was tight again with that same
unidentifiable apprehension. But he needed to make things feel
right again. He would face this strange fear that ate at his gut as
if he faced one of the barbarian horde. He pushed himself into
action and rounded the building, trying to think of how to put
together the words he wanted to say.

Kane sat with his head and back to the wall and elbows on
his knees. His eyes were closed, his face drinking in the sunlight.
Auraq tried to swallow but found his throat had formed a lump
and didn't allow it. He thought Kane was asleep, but as Auraq
approached, Kane opened his eyes and lifted his head. Squinting,
he shielded his eyes.

"Came to check on you," Auraq said.

"No need. I'm all right." His voice held a coolness Auraq
had not heard before. He seemed awkward then, and he looked

down at the ground between his knees.

"How's the arm?"

Kane made a weak shrug. "Medicine seems to be working. It doesn't hurt."

"Visions?" Auraq wasn't even sure why he asked that. It wasn't anything he cared to hear more about—especially after the conversation he'd had with his father the night before. Just thinking about it made the hand that had touched the mark tingle anew. But he was clumsy with this sort of thing.

"Some," Kane said.

And then silence.

It hung there between them for far too long and grew more painful with each heartbeat. His mind cycled through things he could say to keep him talking, but nothing right seemed to come to him.

He had to break through it, put an end to it. Somehow. He had no way to gently ease into the topic. So, Auraq decided to jump.

"Look, Kane," he began, and realized he had no air in his lungs to continue. He'd forgotten to breathe and his tongue felt thick. He took in a long breath. "I want to talk to you about yesterday."

Kane's eyes closed. His cheeks flushed and jaw muscles tightened. "Auraq, I appreciate what you are trying to do, but I'd rather not speak of it."

"I wanted to say—"

"I know what you plan to say, and you are… kind to try. Please. I would prefer that we just pretend it never happened."

"That's not—"

But he was interrupted yet again.

The clang of a bell echoed out across the water. Two tolls, a pause, then two more. A few moments later it repeated the sequence. Before Auraq could finish his thought, Kane was on his feet. He rushed around Auraq and jogged toward the dock.

To THE south, upstream, the river followed a long, lazy swoop with a steep embankment on the inside of the curve. A great willow grew right out of the embankment and dangled its wispy branches into the water like a green maiden rinsing soap from her hair.

The barge was coming into view from around the bend—a long, flat vessel, more raft than boat. It sat low in the water, burdened by the stacks of crates crowding most of the deck. The small cabin to the rear looked as if it was being crowded right off the back of it. Deck hands scrambled about, preparing the ropes and guiding it closer to the bank with poles. When the way station dock was fully in its line of sight, the bell ringer began his sequence of tolls once again.

It lumbered closer, skillfully maneuvering toward the dock.

Malgar strolled out from the warehouse, a wide satisfied grin across his face. "Perfect," he said, clapping Auraq on the shoulder. "We'll be in Dar Arendia before you know it."

Auraq's heart was too heavy to find a way smile back at him. His chance to set things right with Kane had failed. Again. Kane's reaction had caught him off guard. Perhaps if he'd only pushed harder….

On the barge, there was no telling how long it would be before he had another chance. It may already be too late. Kane didn't even want to speak with him.

But he had to try. Once aboard, he would make the opportunity. He would pull Kane aside and make him listen.

Malgar elbowed him in the side. "Still wish I'd stayed behind?"

It was a good plan, Auraq knew. Their travel time would be more than halved, and tracing them would be next to impossible. The Order would have a time of it figuring out where they were now. And considering the state of Kane's arm, the faster they arrived in the capital, the better.

A noise snapped Auraq's attention from the approaching barge. As he turned to look at the dense thicket south of them, he caught movement at the edge of his vision.

His heart dropped the length of his torso.

He pulled both his weapons from their scabbards. At the sound of ringing steel, Kane and Malgar both turned to him in surprise.

"Kane, get to the end of the dock. Board that vessel the instant you can. Pa, I hope you're rested after that nap. We're in trouble."

He spun about just as the dark shapes emerged from the thicket in a low crouch.

Chapter 26

THE TWO wolvren slunk out of the brush, hissing and snarling. They had spotted their prey and crept into the open with their bellies low to the ground, ready to lunge. The daylight did nothing to diminish how monstrous they were. Grizzled black fur that looked like iron nails. Yellow eyes and yellow teeth. They were something from a nightmare.

Auraq adjusted his grip on both swords. He eased backward toward the river as the wolvren drew closer, keeping himself between the beasts and the dock. He heard Kane's boots as he ran along the decking.

"Pa, go on the dock. Protect Kane."

He knew it was pointless. His father had that determined look in his eye that Auraq knew well. Malgar had his own sword in his hand and had somehow managed to locate a lit torch, which he held in his other.

"My place is next to my son," he growled.

One of the beasts watched the two of them with drooling intensity, its ears flat against its head. The other clearly eyed the dock.

Auraq heard shouting behind him—the crew aboard the barge had spotted the wolvren as well.

On some unknown cue, the beasts slunk sideways and drifted apart from each other. They moved slowly and fluidly with the elegant grace of a dancer. It might have been beautiful if not for their fierce grins.

Sudden movement to Auraq's right drew everyone's attention—including the beasts'. A horse sprung out from behind the way station at a full gallop. Paugen, straddling its unsaddled back, hollered and struck the horse's flank with a rod. The fool hoped to escape before the carnage began. He'd thrown on a bit collar, but not a saddle. Paugen must have had the horse tied in the field beyond the building.

The closest wolvren responded with staggering speed. The horse was moving at a full gallop—but the beast was still faster. It cut the distance between them with just a few colossal leaps and intercepted it. The horse saw the threat careening toward it and panicked. It reared up with a wild cry, and Paugen tumbled off its back. The wolvren seemed for a blink of time to debate which of the two to attack. The horse was the bigger prize, but Paugen was closer and in a heap on the ground.

It chose Paugen.

The old man screamed and attempted to rise to his feet, but the wolvren was already upon him. One massive paw stamped and pinned him back to the ground. The beast took Paugen's head and torso into its powerful jaws. It tugged and flung its head up and to the side. Blood sprayed in all directions. The cries of terror were mercifully short before parts of his body were ejected about the field.

The horse bucked and kicked, and in a blind panic, tore off into the brush and to safety.

The second beast bounded for Auraq.

One moment it was fifteen paces away—the next it was directly in front of him and moving fast. Auraq had no choice but to retreat. He sprung to the side and twisted his body forward. His shoulder hit the ground in a roll. He felt more than saw the wolvren pass over him. With his knees tucked in, he rolled back to his feet, his right arm already in motion. He slashed downward at the beast's flank as it barreled past. The edge caught the thick hide and sliced it open. Not as deep as he'd intended, but it was certain to sting. Auraq tried with his left sword arm too, but the creature had already responded and vaulted its bulk beyond his reach. With a spring, it turned itself about and was facing him again.

It hissed at Auraq, clearly unhappy, and its eyes narrowed to mere yellow slits, watching him with murderous intensity. Having encountered prey that could fight back—something of a novelty for the creature, Auraq imagined—it moved with an edge of caution now.

The men on the barge were shouting, but Auraq couldn't comprehend the words. The second beast, black gore glazing the length of its muzzle, was on the move and bounding toward Malgar. His father was exceptional with a blade, but he simply wouldn't have the required reaction speed anymore.

Auraq had to take one of them out quickly.

But he knew the truth of it; there would be no quick end to an unnatural creature like this. Killing one would grant anyone bragging rights for a lifetime. Killing two was more than he could ever hope to accomplish.

Auraq kept a steady distance between him and the beast. It feigned an attack, shifting its bulk forward, but then it pulled back and hissed. The fucker was playing with him.

In their spiraling dance together, his father came into view. He was doing much the same—moving sideways leg over leg, gauging the creature's movements.

The beast tired of waiting. It made a lunge for Auraq, a kind of pounce to test his reaction time. Auraq sprung back beyond the reach of its powerful swing, but tried not to appear too nimble, too quick on his feet. He needed it confident. He needed it to take chances.

It lunged again, more aggressively this time. With a deep-throated bark, it sprang with dizzying speed and swung at him three times—left, right, left. Auraq was ready for it, but this time he couldn't hold back. He danced farther away as fast as his legs would take him, and still the third swing very nearly caught him.

The wolvren snapped at the air in frustration. It was done playing.

It bounded sideways, then thrust itself forward with its powerful back legs. An unexpected maneuver. Auraq didn't have the time to retreat as before. He ducked and rolled forward, but the beast anticipated the move and reacted. When Auraq was back on his feet, the wolvren had turned to face him and was already midswing. Auraq used the full strength of his arm to deflect the swing over his head with the longsword.

But the beast was nearly on top of him now, leaving no

room to maneuver. It flung its head at him, snapping down with its powerful jaws. Auraq sprang backward, both arms up in the air and back, arching his spine. The jaws slammed shut a hand width from his arm. It swung its head again, this time crashing it against Auraq's torso. He was knocked back, landing hard on his back. Air rushed from his lungs in a single grunted *whoosh*.

The wolvren lifted one side of its muzzle to expose its teeth in a sinister and chilling smile. It reared back, ready to pounce on Auraq and finish him.

A whistle cut the air, and then Auraq heard a dull thud. Something struck the beast in the neck at the collarbone. It yelped in surprise and for a split moment, its attention was redirected to the river.

A crossbow bolt—lodged into its thick hide. The coarse black fur glistened wet in the afternoon sun. The men on the barge were firing at the beasts.

The distraction gave Auraq just enough time to roll and leap back to his feet.

He made a quick glance to see if Kane was on the barge yet. But no, the vessel wasn't any closer to this side of the bank or the dock. The polemen had guided the barge outward, keeping it in the middle of the river.

It wasn't going to stop.

Malgar was holding his own against the second wolvren, but only with the help of the men on the barge. They stood in a line along the gunwale, shouting and firing a continuous volley at the beast. Its sides were riddled with arrows and bolts. Not enough to kill it, Auraq knew, but it kept the beast off balance while Malgar fought to keep between the creature and the dock.

Kane was shouting something at him. He couldn't understand the words.

"Jump!" Auraq shouted back at him. With a running start, Kane could leap off the dock and make it safely onto the vessel's deck.

But Kane didn't move.

"Get on that fucking barge!" Auraq screamed at him.

He had taken his attention from the beast for too long. It

was bounding for him again. It tried the same tactic as before, only this time leaping first to the right. A limited arsenal, apparently. It sprang with both limbs outstretched. It sought to knock Auraq to the ground and pin him. Auraq pivoted and crouched, and the wolvren landed in the space Auraq had occupied a mere heartbeat before. Auraq now stood at the beast's shoulder. But it was twisting its head around, jaws gaping.

Auraq dragged the edge of one sword along the neck down the shoulder bone. The blade cut deep through hide, but there was no spray—he missed the large artery in the neck. With his left arm, he thrust upward and sank the short sword underneath the shoulder. Then he leaped away.

Neither blow was fatal. He hoped at least it would slow the beast down.

The move put him in line of sight again with his father. Malgar was struggling. He still managed to keep the beast at bay, but only barely. Auraq could tell his strength was flagging. Though skilled, and strong for his age, his arm was more accustomed to a hammer than the swing of a heavy blade. An arrow protruded from the wolvren's eye. A lucky strike that hindered the beast—but still it pressed hard. Malgar kept to the beast's blind side now, forcing it to spin to keep him in view. Even so, Malgar managed to only keep outside of its swinging claws by an alarmingly small margin.

The barge was in line with dock now but was picking up speed again in the main current of the river.

"Jump!" Auraq cried out again. Still, Kane did not move.

Now seriously wounded, the wolvren's fury was palpable. Its eyes were but narrow slits and a constant growl gurgled from its throat. It clawed at the ground, then pounced with renewed fervor, swung, and then pounced again. Auraq lunged backward, desperate to stay beyond its reach.

This time, he wasn't quite fast enough.

A claw caught him high on his right shoulder, slicing open his flesh. The razor point slipped under his leather jerkin at the armhole and hitched. Auraq's body was suddenly in motion, his head snapping backward, and he was off the ground. The wolvren flung Auraq through the air like a doll.

He tumbled for what seemed far too long, then hit the ground with an explosion of pain. He toppled ass over head several times before he came to an inelegant stop. Head swimming and disoriented, with no idea where the wolvren now was, he stumbled to his feet.

Then he felt the full impact of the beast as it rammed into him.

Auraq was slammed back to the ground. The back of his head grazed a fieldstone. His head spun—his thoughts disintegrated into fuzzy chaos. The bright afternoon sunlight nearly faded to nothingness as blackness closed in around his vision. He flung his head back and forth so as not to lose consciousness, and the well of darkness threatening to overwhelm him retreated.

But the wolvren was upon him.

Auraq tried to roll out of the way, but the beast stomped its mammoth paw on his right arm, pinning him. He cried out in pain as a claw cut into his bicep. His hand reacted with an involuntary spasm that flung his fingers open and the longsword leaped from his grip. The beast leaned in close and pulled back its muzzle to show all of its teeth. Hot, putrid breath blasted against his face again and again. Blood and drool dripped off the lower jaw and onto Auraq's face and neck.

The long, teeth-filled muzzle stretched open. The head reared back, preparing to bite off Auraq's head and torso. He had seen how this ended for Paugen. He wasn't about to let it happen to him.

Auraq pulled as much air into his lungs as he could—then thrust upward with the short sword clenched tight in his left hand. He put in all the strength he had left behind it. The blade punctured the soft tissue under wolvren's lower jaw, cut straight through, and pierced the upper part of its muzzle. Rivulets of blood gushed down Auraq's arm, and the beast tried to pull back, but Auraq pushed harder and drove the blade even deeper.

The wolvren heaved backward, releasing Auraq from the

hold. But as the beast tumbled, Auraq lost his grip on the sword. Panicked, the wolvren thrashed about the field, flinging its head in a mad frenzy in order to dislodge the blade.

Auraq staggered to his feet. His stomach threatened to empty and his legs were uncertain beneath him like a newly born colt. Weakly, he stumbled to retrieve his longsword, and with his head reeling, launched himself in the direction of the beast.

The wolvren saw him approach and tried to ward him back with a swipe, but the attempt was a frail one. Even in his own unsteady state, Auraq avoided it. From blood loss and exhaustion, the creature's legs gave out. Auraq moved in and thrust the longsword behind the head, underneath the line of the skull. The blade sank into the brain. It spasmed only once and was still.

Auraq slid out the gore-covered blade and spun toward the river. The barge had moved too far out into the river. Too far for Kane to jump now.

The remaining beast shifted its attention from Auraq to the dead wolvren, and back to Malgar. It backed away, hissing— then barreled forward. It was heading toward the dock in a final desperate attempt to get to Kane. Malgar tried to block its path, but the wolvren was undaunted. It bolted into him, sending him tumbling backward down the embankment and into the water.

In seconds, the wolvren was on the dock.

"Kane!" Auraq roared. Forgetting his injuries, he launched into a sprint. "Into the water!"

Kane backed away to the very edge and gripped the final pylon. He stared at the mammoth beast pounding down the dock. Boards snapped under the weight of it as it galloped toward him.

He looked up at Auraq for a heartbeat, then turned and kicked himself off the end of the pier just as the beast leaped for him. He hit the water with an ungraceful splash.

The beast skidded to a stop at the edge of the dock, hissing and spitting.

For several moments, Kane was nowhere to be seen. The waves from the impact propagated outward to eventually diminish and then were lost to the natural undulations of the river. But no Kane. Auraq felt his heart wedge into his throat.

He never considered the idea that Kane couldn't swim.

Then Kane broke the surface again, limbs flailing. He was far out into the river now, his body seized by the stronger current. He tumbled and turned, at the mercy of the river. Auraq watched him struggle, watched his attempts to pull his arms through the water and pull himself toward the barge, but he was too weak, fighting just to stay above the surface.

The crewmembers were all shouting, some at Kane, but others were barking orders. The men scrabbled about the deck like ants swarming atop a rotting apple. Men arrived at the barge's side with coils of rope. It was heaved into the water. Again and again. But each throw landed beyond Kane's reach.

The wolvren was not yet ready to give up its prey. It raced halfway down the dock again before it sprang off at an angle toward the shoreline. It soared over the water and landed on the embankment, then followed Kane and the barge along the shoreline at a lope. The distance of the jump was astonishing—and alarming. If the barge ambled close enough to this bank, the wolvren could possibly leap the distance.

Auraq stayed with it as best as he was able. He forced his legs into a full sprint, but limping and dizzy from his own injuries, he was not able to keep up with the beast. He glanced back—his father was nowhere in sight either.

The beast launched over a pile of firewood. Auraq was still several seconds behind it. As he approached, he spotted an ax, the blade stuck into the top of a log. Auraq snagged it by the handle as he ran past. He lifted the ax high over his head and thrust his arm forward, flinging it desperately at the beast. His entire body pitched forward. Taken off balance by the throw, he lost his footing, stumbled, and landed face-first in the dirt.

He lifted his head just in time to see the ax tumble one more time through the air before the head embedded itself right into the back of the wolvren's skull. The beast made a yelp like a kicked dog and dropped.

Auraq forced himself from the ground and kicked himself into a painful jog once more.

He glanced out across the river and saw one of the crewmen had finally managed to get the rope close enough for Kane to grab it. Kane wrapped the end around his wrist and clung to it with both hands. He was dragged in.

When Auraq caught up to the beast, it grunted and wheezed as it crawled along the embankment. Its eyes were fixed on the barge, which drifted farther away, widening the distance between them. Auraq ran the sword's edge along the underside of its neck in one quick slice. Warm ooze spilled out in a rush. He stepped back, panting, and waited. The wolvren still dragged itself forward as it bled out on the grass. It collapsed to the ground; its chest heaved and fell two more times, and then it moved no more.

Auraq looked up just in time to see Kane pulled onto the vessel by three of the crew. His body limp. Lifeless. They laid his body onto the deck.

Auraq could see no more of what happened. The barge lumbered into a turn and disappeared around a bend in the river.

AURAQ DOUBLED back at a limp to the way station and dock. As he drew closer, he could hear his father calling out to him.

"Pa?"

"Down here" came the return call.

Auraq skidded down the steep embankment and hobbled to where the dock's pylons met the water. Ten paces out and under the dock, Malgar clung to one of the pylons.

"You all right?"

"Aye," Malgar replied dryly. "Current's damn strong here, and there's an undertow I'd wager too. Not sure I'd have the strength to make it to the shore."

Auraq nodded. "Hold tight."

The water level was too low for him to reach up to the dock. He scurried up the embankment again and headed to the way station. He quickly found a skein of rope on a hook. Unfurling the length of it as he returned to the dock, he lowered the end into the water where his father waited, then fished him out.

Malgar grabbed Auraq by the chin and inspected him. "You took a beating," he chuckled. "I've barely a scratch."

"You had help."

"Aye, that I did. And thank the Gods for that too, or I'd be feeding the fish in the river. Kane get on the barge?"

Auraq nodded.

"Good. He's likely safer there than we are here."

Auraq wished he shared his confidence.

"Let's get you patched up," his father said.

"We have to go after them."

"By running alongside the bank?" He grunted out a sour laugh. "You can barely walk. And if we don't take care of those wounds, you'll be worse off than Kane soon enough, consumed by fever. What good will you be to him then?"

Malgar was right, of course, but it didn't make him feel better. His insides were twisted up like a wet sailor's knot. His mind cycled through every bad scenario: What if the crew didn't take care of him? Or the barge was overtaken by members of the Order? Perhaps there was even a Jackal on the barge already. There were too many things that could go wrong—and he was not there.

This was his fault. He should have done something to prevent it. There had to have been something he could have done.

His thumb massaged the palm of the opposite hand. The hand felt strange, he realized. He looked down at it, turned his wrist to see both sides, and flexed his fingers. There was no visible injury, but it didn't feel right.

Malgar bade Auraq to sit while he ferreted out supplies. He returned with a half-empty bottle of hard spirits and a bolt of linen, which Malgar proceeded to strip apart into bandages. Malgar cleaned out all of the deeper wounds with the strong liquor, ignoring Auraq's hissing and flinching when he poured the liquid directly on the opened flesh, making the wounds burn and sting like they were attacked by a swarm of angry wasps.

Once satisfied with the dressings, Malgar ordered Auraq

to keep still for a while and not fuck up his good work; then he returned to the building to rummage through more crates. Auraq drifted to the river and sat on the edge of the dock.

He let out a long breath and watched the rush of water beneath his feet. This was a waste of time. Every moment they delayed, Kane was farther downstream. Farther away from him.

But what could they do?

His father was right about one thing—for the time being at least, Kane was likely safer traveling on the barge. But Kane carried no coin in his purse. Auraq held it all. How would he cover the cost of the voyage to the capital? Would the crew dump him off at the next way station, or worse, just abandon him anywhere along the river? And Auraq had no way to know. How would he ever find him again?

And Gods! What if he actually made it to Dar Arendia? That city was no place for someone like Kane to try to tackle alone. Especially in the state he was in.

His jaw clenched as he pulled in his legs and brought his feet underneath him again. Sitting here was accomplishing nothing. It was time to move.

Since he'd stopped moving for a time, his body had tightened up. As he rose to his feet, every muscle he owned complained, and the back of his head throbbed. The wounds ached and burned beneath the bandages as his arms swung. Marching back to the way station, he absently massaged his palm, which still tingled with an odd sensation.

His father called out from inside the building. Auraq sped up to a jog and entered. From the far corner, Malgar flagged him over.

Leaning against the wall behind a pile of barrels was an old dugout. The wood was a dull gray and it had some deep fissures along the side, but Auraq couldn't tell if they affected its integrity. Several paddles were laid out on the inside.

"May not even stay afloat with both of us in it," Malgar said.

"Only one way to find out," Auraq replied. His heart raced with anticipation, but he kept his voice level. He couldn't believe their luck.

Malgar puffed out air from his cheeks. "Not going to be easy getting it out of there. You're not going to be much help."

"I can do it," Auraq said. Nothing was going to stop him from getting that dugout into the river.

Malgar stopped. His brow furrowed as he looked at Auraq with his head turned askew. "What's going on with that now?"

"What do you mean?"

"Why do you keep doing that?"

"Doing what?"

"That." Malgar pointed to his Auraq's hand. "Rubbing your palm like that."

Auraq looked down at his hands. He hadn't even been aware he was doing it again. "Not sure. It feels odd."

"Odd how?"

"Hard to describe. Sort of like it's gone to sleep but…." He paused to examine his hand again. The skin was pink now but only because of Auraq's thumb steadily worrying it. "But also like something is tugging on it… from inside."

Malgar stepped closer. He grabbed Auraq's wrist and pulled the hand closer to his face to examine it. His brow scrunched into deep lines. "Tugging on it?"

"I didn't injure it, I'm sure. But I feel like some invisible twine is constantly pulling on my hand from within. And always in the same direction too. No matter how I hold my hand or how I stand. Getting stronger too."

Malgar's brow lifted. "Same direction," he echoed.

Auraq nodded. "Yeah."

"And what direction is that?"

Auraq pointed. Downriver. The same direction the barge had gone.

Malgar shook his head. "Son, that's the same damn hand that touched the mark on Kane's arm. Remember?"

Auraq looked up. His father was right.

He didn't understand how, but the mark on Kane's arm was pulling on him. And as the distance between them grew, so did the sensation. The tingling was progressing into a throbbing ache.

"Come on," he said. "Let's dig that damn thing out of there and go after Kane."

Chapter 27

THEY WERE drawing steadily closer—Auraq could feel it in his palm—but they hadn't yet caught sight of the barge.

In the cramped dugout, the two of them pressed on throughout the night. They took turns guiding the craft through the dark water while the other curled up on the bottom and attempted to grab an hour or two of sleep—which neither really did. Moonlight seeped through the high diaphanous layer of clouds and shimmered across the surface of the water like rolling quicksilver. It provided just enough light to keep them from running aground on the shallower margins of the river, or passing through any of the tangled brush that drooped over the banks. The black and featureless landscape glided past, seemingly unchanging. The only sounds that emerged from the night were the deep croaks of bullfrogs and the soft splash of the oar as it broke the surface of the water.

Heavier clouds tiptoed in during the hours before dawn. Daybreak was delayed, and when the area around them finally did begin to lighten, everything was restricted to a dull pallor of gray. Soon after, expanding circles appeared on the surface of the river as a gentle pelting of rain began to fall.

Auraq tugged at his father's cloak and covered him better. Malgar stirred a little, grumbling, then fell quiet again. Auraq whipped the hood of his own cloak up onto his head with one hand and resumed paddling the craft along.

It wasn't long before the cold seeped through the cloak and into his bones. His joints ached, and his clothes felt like a layer of ice against his skin. His fingers had lost most of their feeling. He could barely sense the oar in his grip.

But his mind was hardly aware of it.

His thoughts were only of Kane. The strange tugging

sensation in his hand was a constant reminder of how he'd allowed them to be separated. How Kane was alone and unprotected. A parade of catastrophes that might have befallen him marched through his mind, one after another. He tried to tell himself he was letting his imagination commandeer his reason, but the images would not be deterred, and he caught himself slipping into their dark recesses again and again. So, he clung to the truth that he could still feel Kane in his hand. The tingling sensation was still there—which meant Kane was too.

He would not stop until they caught up to the barge.

Drawing closer to Kane made the effect weaken, and since dawn he had felt it noticeably fade. He worried that perhaps the cold had numbed his hand, causing him to lose his connection to the mark. Or worse. Auraq could not shake the fear that it could also mean Kane was dying.

Signs of civilization returned to the landscape gradually. Structures appeared along the banks of the river. Small ones at first—some ramshackle cottages and lean-tos that straddled the narrow zone between the river and the forest. Most looked abandoned. Others should have been. More buildings emerged, pushing back the wild. Then more still. Soon, they were crowding each other for space along the bank, like spectators along the street pushing their way in for a better glimpse of the pageant marching by. A boardwalk followed the margin of the river, and personal docks reached out over the water. The largest paddlewheel Auraq had ever seen sat in the river, turning and turning with a long, slow grace.

They had reached the outer rim of Dar Arendia, the so-called ring towns. The capital was surrounded by smaller cities that nuzzled up against her borders like piglets suckling off the teats of a sow.

The rain tapered off at last. The sky softened to something more white than gray, and the first fractures in the clouds appeared, showing off the crisp blue beyond them.

The dugout passed under a three-arched stone bridge that spanned the river's width, and then the river took a long lazy curve eastward.

A larger building came into view on the right, a hulking structure that seemed to partially sit right inside the river itself. The lower story that met the river was built of stone, and the stories above were constructed of long, sturdy planks. The building was at least three stories high. A great network of docks hugged the building like a great collar. The area seemed quiet. Several vessels were moored to a dock, but one in particular caught Auraq's attention straightaway—the barge that had rescued Kane from the water.

AURAQ ROUSED his father behind him. With renewed energy, he paddled the dugout toward the complex. As he guided their craft closer, Auraq could hear shouts coming from high inside the building and from around the docks. Their approach had been noted, and Auraq could see a sudden flurry of movement. A group of men jogged out from a wide opening in the building and ran along the length of a dock to intercept them. They were sturdy men, and visibly armed.

"What's happening?" Auraq asked.

"We're an unscheduled vessel. A warehouse like this isn't keen on people just showing up to their wharf space. We're going to be told to scamper off."

"What does it matter?"

"Unscheduled arrivals can mean trouble. Bandits sometimes raid warehouses like this for supplies."

They hardly looked like bandits, Auraq thought.

He paddled up to the closest dock space and held on to a pylon as his father scurried up the ladder onto the decking. Auraq handed up their packs quickly, then pulled himself up too. A burly dockhand, with a small crowd of equally large men in tow, marched up to them as Auraq's boots hit the wooden planks of the dock.

"You've got business here?" the brute growled. The three other dockhands flared out behind him to form a meaty wall. Auraq and his father were not going any farther down the dock.

"Not officially," Malgar said, stepping forward before

Auraq had a chance to respond. He assumed his buttery merchant's tone. "And our dealings here will be brief. We invite no trouble."

"You are not on my list."

"No," Malgar replied with a businessman's smile. "This was an unscheduled voyage."

The large dockhand leaned in and tapped his fat finger against Malgar's sternum. "No docking without the proper papers and without paying the fees."

"Docking fees? For a vessel like that?" Auraq put in hotly. "Does it look like we're shipping cargo?"

The dockhand turned his hard gaze to Auraq, his nose flaring slightly. "Rules is rules, mate. I don't write them."

Auraq's hands clenched and unclenched. They didn't have time for this. The desperation to know that Kane was safe felt like it could tear him apart. He was ready to shove past them and head toward the barge with or without their consent. With barely an effort, he could have half of them in the river before they could attempt to stop him.

Malgar reached back and put an inconspicuous hand on Auraq's forearm. A gentle reminder for Auraq to calm down and let him do the talking here.

"We're just returning this craft to its rightful owners, is all," Malgar put in, keeping his tone steady and unchallenging. He gestured across the network of docks. A small group was winding their way along the decking. They were coming from the barge. "See? They are coming for it now."

The brute glanced at the approaching men. "You're with them?" he asked with a tone of incredulity.

Malgar nodded, smiling.

"Don't think to play me as daft, you. You're no scow rats."

"Paying passengers," Malgar said as one of the crewmembers jogged up from behind. He gestured to him with a wave of his hand. "Tell them."

Everyone turned to the crewman at once. From his muscle tone, he was certainly younger than Auraq but had skin that was brown and worn like an old boot. He wore a sleeveless brown

246

tunic that was open at the neck and cut short at the waist, and he had a dirty cloth-winged cap set upon his head. He looked to each man with his jaw hanging loose in stunned silence, making him look like a fish pulled from the river.

"Tell them, man!" Malgar prodded again. "Tell them how we paid for passage on your fine vessel."

"Uh," said the crewman. "Uh, yeah. That's right."

Malgar nodded and started to circle around the brute.

"Not so fast, you." The brute put out his palm. "If you paid for passage, why aren't you on that barge now?"

"We got separated. Long story."

The leader of the dockhands scowled. "Sounds all peculiar to me. I don't like it. There's been strange talk lately, and I'm not keen on taking chances."

"Strange talk?" Auraq asked, unable to stop himself.

"Yeah. Talk of killings. Some say it's a beast roaming the woods upriver."

The younger crewman threw up his hands. "You don't know the half of it, mate!"

The dockhand's forehead furrowed and his eyes narrowed.

Auraq nearly shoved the crewman into the river to quiet him. The dockmen were already suspicious of them. Tales of wolvren attacking them would get them shooed away for certain. Or worse—get them detained for questioning.

Malgar loudly jingled the purse at his waist. The sound of coin had the desired effect—the brute's head whipped back around as if yanked by strings.

"We will gladly cover the additional docking costs for this vessel," Malgar said. "Whatever you deem as fair."

The brute frowned with a scowl—but Malgar had his full attention. His eyes shifted several times to the purse hanging from Malgar's belt.

It was the opening Auraq needed. For the moment, the brute was transfixed. Without waiting for invitation, Auraq grabbed the crewman by the arm and led him through the small crowd of dockhands before any of them thought to stop him.

An old crewman from the barge intercepted Auraq on his

way. "You best not have brought some disease onboard."

"Why?" Auraq asked. "What happened?"

"Your companion. Best come quick. He's still below deck."

THEY FOLLOWED the network of docks to where the barge was moored. The old crewman gave Auraq a once over from boots to head as if unsure he was real. "Didn't think I'd be seeing you again."

Auraq grunted. "You are not alone."

The other crewmen were already at work removing cargo from the deck of the vessel, passing up and down a narrow plank that connected the gangway to the deck. The plank bowed precariously as each man crossed over to the dock with a crate loaded onto his back, held in place by thick leather straps. One by one, the crates were loaded onto a pallet.

"Name's Erpo. You killed off both those vile things?"

"With your help," Auraq said.

The old man waved him off. "Couldn't just watch and let you all get ripped apart, now could we? Gods burn me, never seen anythin' like 'em. Beasts like that shouldn't exist, you ask me. Poor ol' Paugen, though. Grisly scene that was."

Malgar jogged up and joined them. He gave Auraq a subtle nod to let him know the other matter had been resolved. With plenty of coin, apparently. Auraq stole a glance back at the group. The brute was laughing cheerfully with the other dockhands. He gave one a rough shove that nearly sent him over the edge and into the river. They were all most likely headed to the tavern to enjoy their unexpected windfall.

A gap in the traffic going on and off the barge provided Auraq and Malgar the opportunity to tread across the narrow plank and step onto the deck. The wood was still slick from the earlier rain. The barge captain was waiting for them with crossed arms.

"That lad of yours ain't going to get my men sick, is he?" He was a gruff man with a sizable midsection. He wore an old pocketed vest that may have fit at one time, but now there was no hope that any buttons would meet with their prospective holes again. Apparently, his crew did all the heavy lifting.

"Recovering from an injury," Auraq replied. He flexed his fingers. They were close to Kane—he could feel it in his hand. The sensation was different now. It felt warm inside, and oddly soothed. "Where is he?"

"Below deck, that a way." As Auraq started to move, the captain grabbed his forearm. "Now, we did ya a kindness, sur. Keep that in your mind now. Didn't have to offer the lad passage, but me men here were feeling generous."

"Go," Malgar told Auraq as he gave the captain's shoulder a cheery clap. "We'll settle up here."

A short, narrow staircase led to the underbelly of the barge. The ceiling was low. Auraq could not stand to his full height. Beyond a maze of crates and equipment, he found Kane in a small cabin. He lay on a cot, his back against the wall. As soon as Auraq arrived in the open doorway, Kane lurched up.

"Oh, thank the Gods!" he exclaimed with a massive sigh. His head fell back and hit the wall behind him.

"You all right?" Auraq asked, fighting to keep his voice calm.

"Certainly better now." Kane turned and swung his legs off the cot. He moved slowly and glanced up to catch Auraq's look of concern. "That swim took a lot out of me. I'm just having some trouble regaining my strength."

Auraq moved in and helped him off the cot. Kane's legs were unsteady as he rose to his feet. Auraq slid his arm behind Kane's back and moved his shoulder under Kane's arm to support him. Kane's body felt good against his.

"I can manage on my own I think," Kane said.

Auraq ignored him. "Let's get you out of here."

"I was trying to decide what to do. I felt I should wait here, but it was clear the barge captain really wanted me off his boat. They seem to think I'm a plague carrier or something. And I didn't know if they were pushing off soon or not, or how far we are from Dar Arendia...." He shook his head. "How did you find me so fast?"

"That might take a bit of explaining," Auraq replied.

Kane's dark mood from earlier seemed to have dissipated, and the awkwardness between them—for the moment at least—was gone. He was genuinely happy to see Auraq.

They wove through the underbelly of the barge, and Auraq helped Kane negotiate the stairs. Malgar was waiting on the deck. The captain and his crew were nowhere to be seen.

"Ah, you're in one piece, then," said Malgar, arms outstretched. "Excellent. Well, shall we be off, then?" He gestured to the gangway leading to the dock.

"You and the captain came to an amiable agreement?" Auraq asked.

"We are now the fastest of friends."

Auraq raised his brow at him.

Malgar shrugged. "Figured I'd purchase a little loyalty in case anyone came around asking questions. I took the liberty of procuring a carriage too. We are about an hour or two out from the city wall."

Chapter 28

AURAQ WAS the last to return to Lord Farris's small waiting chamber.

Kane and Malgar sat up straighter in their chairs as he lumbered in. Kane stared back, wide-eyed and loose-jawed. Malgar blinked twice before a laugh bubbled up to the surface. He fought to suppress it, and failing that, attempted to disguise it by adding a cough.

Auraq scowled. "Don't start."

He hadn't realized the lengths involved to be granted an audience with a nobleman. One didn't just walk in from the street, apparently. There was a standard, a level of acceptable presentation—lest the nobleman be offended by the grit and odors of the world outside their gate.

His entire body had been scrubbed down with a stiff-bristled brush until his skin was raw and flushed. The attendants spared him no dignity as they reached under the water and scoured the areas that were typically left for himself to clean. His head and beard were lathered with perfumed soaps, trimmed, and combed through to ensure they were free of nits. They made him soak his hand for nearly an hour before they would even attempt to scrape out the dried blood and dirt that was wedged deep under his nails.

All of which was a colossal waste of time. Kane was weakening by the hour. Posh grooming for the sole purpose of not offending an aristocrat was the least of his concerns.

They dressed him in the only garments they could find in their wardrobe that would fit the girth of his shoulders and chest, or that would make it up over his thick legs and ass—a ruffled chemise, and a soft green doublet with gold sun-symbol buttons, and gray trousers tied at the knees with yellow ribbon. The trousers still didn't fit well and pinched the tender skin between his legs. His boots had a high heel that made him clump along awkwardly like a drunken goat.

He felt ridiculous. He felt like a peacock.

Both Kane and Malgar were dressed far more sensibly—clean tunics with a fine, sleeved jerkin.

"Were you somehow welcomed into the gentry in our absence?" his father jibed.

Auraq grimaced as he tugged at the outfit. "All they could find that would fit me, it seems."

He was instructed to leave his weapons back with his garments. Besides the dress requirements, one did not stand before nobility armed. It was always disconcerting for him to not feel the comforting weight of the weapons on him. His hand kept drifting to his waist to rest on the cross guard, or to his chest to grip the strap of the baldric. Each time he was surprised to find nothing there.

"You'd make a fetching nobleman, I think," Kane said.

Auraq turned and caught his eye. Kane looked even more pallid than he did a few hours ago, before they had been separated, and Auraq's concern for him chewed away at his insides again. Some fraction of Auraq's thoughts must have reached his expression, for Kane turned his eyes away, looking suddenly uncomfortable.

Malgar had changed the soaked bandages and added more of the poultice to the wound while in the carriage, which had Kane asleep for the whole journey into the city proper. But his time in the river seemed to have sapped him of his strength, and he was slow to recover.

Auraq grunted and took a seat.

"Well, he has the scowling countenance for it, certainly," Malgar replied dryly.

Everyone's attention was drawn to the doorway by the conspicuous clop of hard heels on the wood floor. Lord Farris's personal valet strolled into the room with the intention of being noticed. He was dressed simply in a long, belted robe, but with fastidious attention to every detail. He waited a moment to ensure that the eyes in the room were on him. "I would refrain," he said as he came to a halt in the middle of the chamber, "from any more comments like that if you still expect cooperation from His Lordship, who has so generously agreed to meet with you."

Malgar's expression sobered into something sheepish. "Of course. My humblest apologies," he said with a bow. "It was a jest only, and no way represents my feelings for His Lordship."

The valet turned his narrow-eyed attention to Auraq. He leaned back a fraction, rested his hands on his hips, and scrutinized Auraq from boot to head while making soft noises that may or may not have been actual words. "Acceptable," he grumbled aloud at last. "Follow me."

The valet did not wait to see if they obeyed. The three of them fell in behind him as he marched with a superbly straight back through a series of wood-paneled corridors. The manor estate of Lord Farris of Har Rodell was an expansive structure and even more grandiose than the estate of Mistress Pyta—something Auraq would not have believed possible. They passed room after room of staggering opulence. Surrounded by such inconceivable wealth, Auraq felt like a trespasser, that no amount of scrubbing could cleanse him of his baser nature.

What is the king's palace like? he wondered.

He refused to react to it. Being born into a noble family and inheriting an estate didn't warrant adoration. Kane, on the other hand, was awestruck. He looked about like a boy at a street festival.

They turned down a wide portrait-lined corridor. Generations of Har Rodell's noblemen stared down at them from their gold-leafed, ornamented frames with haughty expressions of disapproval and contempt. At the far end, the corridor ended at a pair of richly carved doors, flanked by guardsmen. These were not military, but ceremonial stand-ins positioned there for decoration only. Auraq quickly saw that their armor and weapons were not remotely suitable for any combat. He doubted either man had ever actually trained with the poleaxes they held perfectly vertical at their sides.

The valet stopped and spun on his heels to face them.

"Wait here until announced," he said. "Take exactly seven steps into the room, perform a proper bow—I assume you know how to perform one—and greet him as 'Your Lordship' only. No pleasantries. Do not address His Lordship until he has explicitly acknowledged you first. Clear? Splendid."

The valet spun about again and pushed open the doors to Lord Farris's chamber.

Kane swayed a little next to Auraq, and shifted his foot quickly to keep his balance. Auraq grabbed behind his elbow to steady him.

"Are you up for this?" Auraq asked. "Perhaps—"

"No," Kane replied sharply. He pulled his elbow away until Auraq let go. "I'll not sit out of another conversation that's about me."

Auraq nodded.

"Master Malgar of Har Tesera," the valet announced. "Accompanied by Auraq, son of Master Malgar, and Journeyman Kanteron of Har Purdea."

The three entered the chamber and did exactly as they were instructed—bowed deeply and greeted the nobleman by his title. Lord Farris didn't seem to be paying any attention. He was seated at a broad desk by the window, bent over a parchment document, scribbling with intensity. Having done his duty, the valet backed out and closed the door.

Lord Farris was every bit what Auraq would have expected. His importance filled the chamber like a perfume. Auraq estimated him to be well in his sixties. His rugged features seemed to hint back to his old military service, while deep lines around his eyes gave him an aristocratic quality as well. He had, as all nobles seem to have, a full head of hair—silver and thick. Baldness seemed a rarity. Auraq wondered if there was some mage spell that helped noblemen avoid the unsavory traits of their bloodline and keep their hair.

Farris finished with his scribbling while the three waited stiffly. At last, he tossed his quill into the well with finality and leaned back. "Malgar," he said in a tone a father would use toward a recalcitrant son. His elbow propped on the arm of his chair, he looked over at the three of them with his head rested on his fist. "Please tell me you did not broadcast your arrival here to anyone beforehand."

Malgar stepped forward. "No, My Lord. As far as I know, no one is aware of our presence here."

"Thank the Gods for that, at least." he pushed back his chair from the desk, stood up, and straightened his bronze-colored surcoat. He was larger than expected—perhaps equaling Auraq's own height. And still fit for a man of his years. His shoulders were broad and his chest full, but he had more girth around the beltline than he likely had in his younger days. He carried his large frame with undeniable self-assurance, as if it was a thing of power. Auraq could feel the strength of his character radiate out from him. His success as a commander in the king's army was no surprise. "This would be a glad reunion if not...." Farris paused and glanced Auraq's way.

Auraq knew where this was going. "If not for me," he put into the silence that followed.

Farris's head snapped toward him as if he'd been rudely insulted. Auraq had broken protocol—he'd spoken before being spoken to. "You are aware of my crimes, it would seem."

Farris frowned. "It is not every day a noble commander is murdered by his own second." He stood unmoving for a time and studied Auraq as if he were some strange creature to crawl out of the night. "A black stain on a proud family and a distinguished career." He took steps toward Auraq and spoke in a low voice. "As a courtesy to your father, honoring the loyal lieutenant he was to me, I have not called for the king's guard to have you arrested."

Auraq bowed his head. "Thank you, Your Lordship."

The hard glare broke, and Farris returned his attention to Malgar. "But... lo' we are reconciled, it would appear."

"There was more to the story than I realized, My Lord."

"Indeed? He was somehow able to convince you of his innocence?"

"Not entirely. He—"

But Farris held up his hand. "Wait." Malgar stopped

speaking instantly. "I think, actually, I'd rather hear it from him." He spun again to face Auraq. "I am not in the habit of harboring fugitives, but it's clear that something of some import compelled your father to bring you here. Let's see if your tale has the power to sway me." He lifted a finger. "If your version of events can persuade, I will hear what it is that brought you to my doorstep, risking arrest."

Auraq's cheeks flushed, and he fought the urge to turn on his heel and march out of the chamber. Farris's tone grated against his tolerance. He had come here on the insistence of his father, but had no desire to allow this man to stand in judgment of him. No one weighed his crimes harsher than himself. Farris's absolution was of no interest or value to him.

He flexed his hands a few times and drew in a long breath.

"Your Lordship," he began. "If my presence offends you, I will leave your house."

"Murder offends me. What makes you think I will allow you to leave?"

"The guards stationed outside this chamber are untrained and ill-armed. They would be unable to prevent me from leaving if I chose to." He spoke flatly, without emotion, as if he was stating the most obvious of facts. He held his level gaze on Farris, who lifted a single eyebrow. Auraq could tell the nobleman knew this was no idle boast. "But," Auraq continued, "if you feel compelled to have me arrested, then I will surrender to you freely—"

"Auraq," Kane barked at him.

"—as long as you, out of the love you once bore for my father, agree to hear him out about why we've come."

Farris's eyes shifted to Malgar for the time it took him to blink, then returned to Auraq. He made no effort to hide his surprise. "Knowing it would mean certain death?"

"Yes, Your Lordship."

Malgar took an unconscious step forward. He had lost all color in his features.

Lord Farris frowned. "Bold," he said, and half sat on the corner of his desk and folded his arms. "An honorable proposal, to be sure. One I would not have expected from a known defector who fled to save his own neck."

The words stung. Auraq clenched his jaw and did not respond.

"You have gained my attention, Auraq Greystone, son of Malgar. I respectfully decline your offer of surrender. I would hear more from you about what happened."

"I do not wish—"

"Your wishes do not concern me. You are correct in that the guards stationed outside my chamber would not be able to stop you. But I could."

Auraq knew that this too was no idle boast. He believed him.

"So," Farris continued. "Proceed. Am I about to hear some denial that you didn't actually kill Lord Renthe?"

Despite his will to remain in control, his voice failed him at first. "No, Your Lordship," he managed to say.

It was clearly not the response Farris expected.

The two were silent for a time as they considered each other. When Auraq eventually spoke, he did not recognize his own voice. It sounded very small. "I held Lord Renthe in high esteem and believed him to be my friend. But I admit that it was I who killed him."

"And what is it that drove you to this?"

"Lord Renthe slew my wife."

"Ah," Lord Farris said, his eyes lighting up with recollection. "I'd forgotten that detail. It was a double murder that you were accused of committing."

It grated Auraq that the death of his wife was less significant than that of the noble, that her life barely warranted remembering. "She had broken off their affair, so he killed her."

Farris's lips tightened in a sharp line. Something about his expression changed. "You came upon the murder yourself?"

"I did."

"Were you aware, before, that you were being cuckolded?"

"I suspected, Your Lordship."

Lord Farris stood very still, his eyes locked onto Auraq's.

257

"Fool," he said and stood from the edge of the desk. He grabbed the pewter goblet on his desk and brought it to his lips.

Auraq's body tensed, his arms tightening against his sides. He closed his eyes and fought the surge of rage rising up from his core.

"Renthe was a callous bastard. Even as a lad." Farris set the goblet down on the wooden desk with a hard thump. It took Auraq a moment to realize that Lord Farris had not called him the fool, after all, but Renthe. "Your wife was not the first to fall for his charms. It was… a game to him. One he rarely lost." His voice lowered to a deep resonance barely above a whisper, but it still filled the chamber. "And… everyone had seen hints of that temper. I never thought he would go as far as that."

"Then you understand, My Lord," Malgar said. "The murder was all but justified."

"Justified?" Farris lifted his head and barked out a quick laugh, but it held no humor. "The murder of a noble officer by a commoner is a capital crime, regardless of how *justified* he felt he was. I'll not contest that Renthe may have had it coming. I always wondered if that unctuous snake would someday meet his end by a jealous husband. But whether he deserved it or not does not matter." He turned his gaze to Auraq and pointed a thick forefinger his direction. "In the eyes of the king's law, you are guilty."

He turned about and dropped his bulk into one of the chairs by the wide hearth. "But I will not be the one to set your head upon the block."

Malgar closed his eyes and let out his breath. "My Lord, your compassion is without measure."

Farris ignored the compliment and continued to eye Auraq. "So you are safe for the moment. I'm curious, though. You took quite a gamble coming here. You could not have known with any certainty that I would aid you."

"No, Your Lordship. But I trusted in my father."

One corner of Farris's mouth lifted a fraction. "This city is filled with any number of those who wouldn't care two shits about your past if the coin was right. Why risk coming here?

Were I to wager, it has something to do with the quiet one there." He tilted his head to indicate where Kane stood.

Auraq looked over his shoulder at Kane. Beads of sweat were collected on his brow, and his body swayed in small circles. He looked as if he might collapse at any moment. Auraq fought with himself to not run to his aid.

"Your Lordship," he said, "if I may test your patience further, may I ask that he sit in your presence?"

Farris's expression sobered. "Is he ill?"

"In a manner of speaking."

"By all means, sit him down. Should I call for a healer?"

"I'm fine, Your Lordship," Kane protested as Malgar moved to his side and guided him to the nearest chair.

"What is the matter with him?" Farris asked.

"I think it best we show you," Auraq said.

Farris stood and approached. Kane carefully loosened the drawstring around his wrist and pulled the tunic sleeve up his arm. Then he carefully unraveled the bandage to expose the raw flesh of his forearm. Kane held out his arm so Farris could see the mark. The runes glowed like embers, as if his insides were made of fire. Angry tendrils traveled up and around his arms.

Farris stood very still. His face did not change for several moments. "What is this?"

Kane looked too weakened to tell the story, so Auraq told Lord Farris how Kane came to bear the mark on his arm and what they had learned from Chenigal. He told them of the Order of the Jackal and how they were hunting Kane down. During the telling, Farris gradually drifted back to his chair by the hearth and lowered into it.

"You're saying something's incriminating or dangerous in that memory, then," Farris said, leaning forward, an elbow on his knee.

"We believe so," Auraq replied. Farris had accepted the story without question, but then, the glowing runes on Kane's arm gave him little room to doubt it.

"Any idea what?"

"Your Lordship," Malgar began in a soft and hesitant

voice. "This may be difficult for you to accept. It is linked to a controversial and—"

"Out with it," Farris growled.

"We suspect that the memory is that of Lord Norreg," Auraq told him.

Farris's eyebrows lifted. "The king slayer?" His voice was low and dangerous. "The Demon of Loth Lorma?"

He lifted from his chair again in a sudden lurch. He stood there in stunned silence, his wide-eyed gaze shifting from one to the next. "What are you implying?"

Auraq and Malgar exchanged glances, knowing that they were treading on perilous ground. But before either could speak, Farris answered his question for himself.

"You're about to suggest to me that you think he's innocent."

"A possibility only," Auraq replied. "We have no confirmation of what memory is locked in the runes."

Farris's cheeks and neck flushed crimson. "Fuck. Have you any idea the chaos this would cause? Just the mere insinuation of his innocence… the entire kingdom would be affected." He dragged his fingers through his thick silver hair and held his hand at the base of his neck. "Does anyone else know of this?"

Auraq studied Farris's face. There was a moment Auraq believed that Farris considered that perhaps Kane *would* be better off dead, and the secret he carried remain hidden forever.

"The headmistress of the mage academy in Har Tesera," Auraq said quickly. "Perhaps more, by now." He doubted that Pyta would spread that information around, but he had to make sure Farris considered it.

"There would be an uproar if this information became public. It means that the true architects of the massacre are still out there. It means that the king could still be in danger if they decide to attempt it again."

Not to mention, Auraq thought, *that a powerful man, loyal to the throne, was executed needlessly.* "This is why we came to you. We risked all to seek out your counsel."

Farris walked over to a sideboard and refilled his goblet with dark liquid from a decanter. He shook his head and had the look of someone trying to shift through a cascade of thoughts that were coming at him too quickly. He took a long draught from his goblet. "I will tell you that there are damn few you can trust with this. People will not want to hear any talk that Norreg was blameless. And I certainly wouldn't go to any more mages for aid."

"I told him much the same thing," Malgar said.

Which complicated matters if they hoped to unlock the memories from runes. "Why was Lord Norreg implicated in the first place?" Auraq asked.

"He'd had a row with the king only the day before. Servants claimed they heard Norreg threaten the king, saying he would do whatever he had to do to stop him from moving forward with the mage edict."

"The mage edict?" Auraq asked.

"A new law designed to put strict limits on their power. King Haden had grown frustrated with the mages over the years. Guilds around the kingdom seemed to act as if they were outside his authority. The king believed they had grown too powerful and too influential, and he was intent on bringing them to heel. The mage edict was a bold attack on them. Outlawing certain invocations entirely, putting a heavy tax on others. Mages would have been required to enter their names in an official register maintained at the palace in order to be authorized to practice their craft. Severe penalties were included for those who did not abide by the new regulation. Naturally, the mages were outraged."

No surprise. Auraq could imagine how Pyta would have responded to such restraints. "And Lord Norreg? Sounds like he sided with the mages."

"He did, which caused a terrible rift between the two. Norreg was nobleborn, but he was also a mage. The first battlemage in over a hundred years. King Haden did not understand how Norreg could stand with the mages on this and not the nobility. Norreg made matters worse by publicly chastising the king and calling him out as a tyrant. It's what caused the final row between them."

"And it was that quarrel that led to his arrest?" Kane asked. He had more color now that he was seated. He leaned forward, elbows on his knees. "Seems a flimsy basis for sending a man to his death."

"There was other evidence, I'm told, but I was not privy to it." Farris looked down at the contents of the goblet in his hand and his lips pursed. "The council in charge of the inquiry claimed there was no doubt of his involvement. No one believed he acted alone, but he was named the architect of the plan. He was arrested within a day."

"They needed a head on a spike to put on display," Auraq said.

Farris's expression darkened. "The kingdom was being torn apart. A murdered king, the only survivor of the dynasty a boy too young to rule, the kingdom still entrenched in a long and bloody war with the Volfic tribes. Nothing was certain. There were fears that the regime would crumble apart. Everyone felt it had to be put to rest quickly to keep the public's fears in check."

Malgar took a step forward. He was looking a little pale. "So, the rumors...."

"That he was innocent? Some believed so, yes. Before the mage edict, Norreg was considered an honorable man and devoted to the king. He still had a few friends who spoke for him."

Auraq wondered if Norreg knew that. He remembered how the man felt in his vision. He died believing he was utterly alone.

"But," Farris continued with his mouth pursed. "I suppose we were all drunk on seeing justice done, then. We were all perhaps too willing to trust in the council's ruling without question."

Auraq could see the conflict building in Lord Farris's face. The nobleman had never questioned what he was told—that Norreg was guilty of the crime. But doubt had now wormed its way into his mind.

Farris leaned against the front of his desk, the heels of his hands resting along the edge of it. A single fingernail repeatedly clicked the underside edge as he thought. "We are getting ahead of ourselves, I think. There is just too much uncertain yet. You admit you're not even fully confident that the mark was caused by Norreg at all. Or if the memory would prove his innocence. Or if mages were even involved in the massacre." He drew in a long breath. "We need to know what is in that memory."

Auraq's spine straightened. "Then we have your aid, Your Lordship?"

Farris shot Auraq a look of astonishment. "Gods, man! I'm not letting any of you out of my sight. For all I know, this might all be horseshit, but I won't sit idly by if there is even the slightest chance that my king is still in danger."

"My Lord, how do we unlock the runes?" Malgar asked. "You said yourself we should trust no one. Any mage capable of it might have actually been involved in the massacre or may try to protect someone who was. They could sabotage the runes and destroy the memory."

"There are certainly mages around whose loyalty to the crown is beyond doubt."

"Finding them would take time, Your Lordship," Auraq added. "And we have little of it, I fear." He did not want to state it directly, but Kane's declining health was forefront in his mind. Proving Norreg's innocence was certainly important, but Kane was still his greater concern.

"I understand. And I don't wish to take any unnecessary risks. We go to the one person who would know."

A lump of dread fell deep into Auraq's gut. He did not like where this was heading. "Lord Farris, what exactly are you suggesting?"

"I think we have only one option available to us. We have to try to speak to King Harus directly."

Chapter 29

AURAQ TUGGED at the bottom line of the green doublet for the hundredth time. No matter how he adjusted it, he could not get comfortable. The longer he wore it, the worse it felt, pinching him in odd places and hanging loose in others. He was simply not suited for life at court.

"Stop fussing," his father grumbled.

Auraq grunted deep in his throat and let his hands drop to his sides, where his swords were noticeably absent from his waist. He felt naked without them, but he'd been forced to leave them back at Farris's manor.

Lord Farris glanced up from the leather-bound book resting in his lap. He was seated in one of the antechamber's upholstered chairs, one elbow leaning on the chair's arm, one leg crossed over his knee. He seemed perfectly at ease as if he waited about in his own study.

For the rest of them, however, it was a day of firsts. Their first time in a fine carriage drawn by four horses. Their first time in the king's palace and with access none of them would have ever imagined. Their first audience with a member of the royal family.

"Nerves are expected, Malgar," Farris said.

"Is vomiting expected?" Kane asked. "Because I may vomit."

He was seated in a chair opposite the nobleman, but slumped forward with his elbows on his knees, his head drooping.

Auraq frowned down at him. Kane's face was gaunt and the color of sun-bleached bone. He'd walked in of his own power but now seemed depleted of strength. His right hand quivered like that of an elderly man. Anxiety would account for some of it, but Auraq knew it was the mark taking a greater toll on him.

The sickness in him was deepening.

Farris had offered to call for a healer, but there were concerns about news of the mark leaking out. One only needed to glance at it to know that it was something of extraordinary power. The angry glow from the runes was beginning to shine through the layers of bandages. So they did what they could. Malgar had cleaned and redressed it before they turned in for the night.

"How much longer?" Auraq asked.

"No guarantee he will even agree to see us today," Farris replied. He'd sent a messenger to the palace immediately after their discussion the day before, requesting an audience with Lord Rhynhert, King Harus's uncle. After the massacre of his older brother and his family, Rhynhert had acted as regent during the years of the young king's minority. Farris hinted at some association he had with the man, saying it was their best avenue of reaching the king quickly, but wouldn't say more.

A messenger returned in the morning announcing that Rhynhert would find time in his schedule to grant them an audience. But they would need to wait at the palace until the opening presented itself.

"We may even be told to attempt an audience tomorrow."

Kane lifted his head. "Tomorrow?" His eyes were a web of red lines. Purple crescents darkened their puffy underside.

Auraq's heart went hollow. Kane might not even be fit to make the trip in a day. "Even though you expressed urgency?" His deteriorating health caused a persistent knot in Auraq's gut. They had to get help for him soon, or there may be no helping him at all. They were running out of time.

"All who seek an audience feel their circumstances are dire. Those already on His Highness's docket have been waiting for no less than a fortnight."

No one was ever directly admitted to the king, Farris had told them. Any grievances or concerns from the citizenry had to make their way through the palace hierarchy. Farris's hazy connection with Lord Rhynhert allowed them to bypass the lengthy chain.

"That said"—Farris tugged on his ear—"I hold out hope that my name still bears some leverage around here. Lord Rhynhert knows I would not waste his time with some frivolous concern."

Auraq sighed. To distract himself, he turned to the enormous tapestry hung the length of the stone wall. The tapestry was old, the colored threads largely faded, but the image of a great battle was still visible. He felt he should recognize the scene somehow, but couldn't place the battle or the location. The image annoyed him. The artist who wove it clearly didn't understand the logistics of battle or even how someone should hold a sword.

He rolled his shoulder up and down. It felt stiff, constricted. The wound from the wolvren claw was starting to ache and itch. His hand dropped to his waist to rest on the cross guard, only to be reminded, yet again, his swords were still back at Lord Farris's manor.

Malgar wandered to the round table in the center of the chamber for the tenth time. It was laden with fruits, baked sweet treats, and a decanter of wine. He scanned the contents, then drifted back to his seat. The food remained untouched. No one had an appetite.

The sound of a latch snagged everyone's attention. The double doors opened enough to admit a man dressed in a deep olivine-colored jerkin and sleeves. He stepped to the center of the antechamber, rapped his long cane on the tile floor twice, and took a moment to ensure all eyes were on him.

Everyone in the chamber had stiffened into breathless statues.

The man bore a serious expression that seemed permanently affixed. He spoke to the room without allowing his eyes to settle on any one of them. "The requested audience with His Highness Lord Rhynhert has been granted to Lord Farris and his party."

Malgar rose slowly to his feet, then helped Kane up with a

hand under his arm. He caught Auraq's eye, one brow elevated. "Here we go," he mouthed.

Auraq tugged on the doublet again, his heart rate spiking. He should be relieved—they were one step closer to finding help for Kane. Instead, he felt the gravity of what was to come.

"I am Master Urondo, seneschal to the house of His Highness, Lord Rhynhert. You are to follow me." Without waiting for a response, Urondo turned on his heel and departed the chamber through the open doorway.

The four of them exchanged quick glances. Auraq fell in line behind the others as they paraded out of the chamber, led of course by Lord Farris.

A short walk through a series of corridors led them up a short staircase and beneath a grand arched opening. Following in Urondo's wake, they entered the grand hall from the far end. Kane craned his neck around in all directions, his mouth slightly ajar, as he tried to take in the rows of statuary and the elaborate fresco that adorned the sweeping arched ceiling all at once. He seemed, for the moment at least, to forget how sick he was.

Auraq's eyes were on the people.

Courtiers, merchants, military, nobleborn. They littered the margins of the long chamber, dressed in peacock regalia and standing in self-important poses, chattering among themselves in small clusters. Auraq made mental note of the ones who glanced their way as they walked past. Anyone here could be from the Order. If they infiltrated the mage academy in Har Tesera, he'd be naïve to think that Jackals hadn't somehow infiltrated the palace as well.

Farris slowed until Auraq caught up to him and was at his side. The nobleman leaned in and spoke low near his ear. "Are you certain you want to be here? You can remain in the antechamber."

"No, Your Lordship," Auraq said.

"I cannot shield you if you are recognized, Auraq. You will be on your own."

"I understand." He would not leave Kane's side until he was certain he was safe.

At the far end, on a raised dais, was a small crowd that surrounded an older man seated on a cushioned bench. Lord Rhynhert, former regent, and uncle to King Harus V. Behind him, on an even higher platform, was the throne of the king itself.

Something about the man filled the hall. His presence was inescapable, power and confidence radiating off of him like a bonfire. Auraq found he could not pull his eyes away from him. Despite his age, Lord Rhynhert still cut a towering figure. His angular face was strong and severe, the deep lines cutting around his mouth seeming to only accentuate his self-assurance. Thick silver hair framed his face and came to rest on his shoulders like snowfall.

Auraq forced his breathing into a steady rhythm. Only a few years back, this was the most powerful man in the kingdom, and the enormity of that threatened to overawe him—but he would not allow it. He had to remain both alert and unintimidated.

He leaned close to Farris's ear. "How certain are you that we can put our trust here?"

"Lord Rhynhert is beyond suspicion, Auraq," Farris told him firmly. "He was offered the crown when his brother was slain, but chose to function as regent until Harus grew to his majority. If it was the crown he wanted, he could have simply taken it."

Auraq nodded, satisfied with the answer.

Rhynhert addressed what looked like a small group of wealthy merchants. Auraq gauged by their apparel that they hailed from one of the islands duchies of the White Sea. They bobbed their heads and bowed earnestly each time Lord Rhynhert spoke.

The rest of the people on the dais with him were his attendants—various courtiers, noblemen, and a few military officers of high rank. On Rhynhert's right side, a man was seated at a small desk, scribbling in a leather-bound journal with his ink-stained hands. A statuesque woman stood to his left, a hand resting gently on his shoulder.

"Lady Nenura," Malgar whispered into his ear.

She was dressed in an elaborate gown and headpiece, all made from a brocaded fabric of burgundy and gold. She spoke casually to one of the other dignitaries next to her, but her hand never left the regent's shoulder.

Auraq had heard of her, of course. She was often the talk among the people of the Lendera Provence.

Master Urondo tapped his cane twice on the floor, directing them to stop and wait.

Auraq felt dangerously exposed. All it would take was for one of the military commanders or one of the noblemen who served in the king's army to recognize him, or to have seen and remembered his likeness on a notice in a guard station. It would all be over then.

He closed his eyes. No. If the Gods were at all just, they would not let that happen. He had to believe that.

He could feel Kane's presence close to him—feel his labored breathing as if his own lungs were struggling to bring in air. Auraq's desperate need to see Kane safely in the care of the palace had become a burning in his veins, a furnace in his gut. They were so close now.

It was all that mattered.

And once the palace saved him… well, if it was the will of the Gods that Auraq was discovered, then so be it. His duty and purpose would be fulfilled.

Perhaps, he thought, it was best he never said anything to Kane about his true feelings after all. It was better this way. If something were to happen now, it would be harder on him certainly. And in truth, Auraq knew he wasn't such a great husband the first time. Why did he think this time would be any different?

The island merchants left the dais and walked down the center of the chamber toward the exit, quietly speaking among themselves and looking pleased. Urondo rapped the cane on the floor once again.

This was it.

They were led up the center of the hall to the foot of the

dais. Kane walked in front of Auraq and seemed more stable on his feet for the moment—most likely the exhilaration of meeting Rhynhert was affording him new strength. Urondo stepped to the right and gestured for the rest of them to proceed.

At the dais, they all bowed properly to Lord Rhynhert as Urondo listed off each name in turn from memory. "Your Highness, I present to you Lord Farris of Har Rodell, Malgar Greystone of Har Tesera, Kanteron Elrus of Har Purdea, and Agus Denn from the academy at Har Tesera."

"Lord Farris," Rhynhert greeted cheerily. "A pleasant surprise."

"I'm pleased you think so," Farris replied with a warm smile.

Rhynhert glanced at the other three with a curious expression. "A far-flung company you associate yourself with, Farris." His gaze centered directly on Auraq. "From the academy, eh? You don't strike me as a mage."

Auraq's mouth went dry. It was hard for him to find his voice. "Guardsmen captain, Your Highness. For the Academy District, not the city."

The alias was Malgar's idea. Mages were habitually secretive, making the fabrication difficult for anyone to verify.

Rhynhert accepted it without expression and simply returned his attention to Farris. "What brings you here, man? I admit I was surprised to see that you had made a formal petition to speak with me in person instead of sending a missive. Something I should be concerned about?"

"I believe so, Your Highness." He turned to the other three. "I have come to speak with you on behalf of these gentlemen."

Lord Rhynhert lifted his brow as he took in Kane with interest. "Involved in some commoner's dispute, Farris? Doesn't sound like you."

"It's much more than that, Your Highness. This is an unusual circumstance that may have dire implications. I ask you to consider what they have to say with all seriousness."

Lady Nenura turned from the nobleman she was speaking with quietly and took a step closer to the edge of the dais. Her chin was lifted in interest. "Lord Farris, My Lord husband considers all who come to stand before him with utmost solemnity." Her voice held a tinge of chastisement. "As to the nature of the concern, all who stand in that spot make claims of direness and ruin. I trust you are not wasting My Lord husband's time with some inflated concern."

Auraq could hear a tinge of a Lenderian accent still interwoven in her speech. Rhynhert's wife had once belonged to a Volfic tribe. She was the daughter of a chieftain, arranged to marry Lord Rhynhert to calm the tensions between Davenia and the Volfic people. But King Haden hadn't understood the tribal nature of the barbarian nomads. None of the other tribes recognized the arrangement, and no peace treaty was ever reached.

"I assure you most earnestly, My Lady, I am not." Farris took in a breath and made a quick scan of the hall and the others standing about the dais before he returned his attention to Rhynhert. "In fact, I feel this is a conversation best done with some privacy."

Nenura smiled down at him, but the look was cool. "I think that is a decision best left to Lord Rhynhert. State your concern and if His Highness deems that it continue further in his chambers, then he will be the one to suggest it."

Farris bowed. "Of course, My Lady. Forgive me."

Auraq noted during this exchange that Lord Rhynhert's attention was not on Farris, but had shifted to take in him and his father instead. It was a strange thing to feel the notice of someone so powerful.

"So, what is the concern or complaint of these men you brought before me?" Rhynhert asked.

"The concern is not for themselves, Your Highness. It is for the good of the realm that they have come."

"Altruists," Lady Nenura said with a cutting twinkle in her tone. "That is a fresh treat for this chamber."

A chuckle rippled through the small crowd on the dais.

Farris's voice rose to be heard clearly over the trivializing noise. "They have endured great hardship in an effort to bring you information, Your Highness. Information I hope will reach the king's ears. I am certain His Grace will want to hear it."

While everyone around the regent still carried the remnants of a haughty smile, Lord Rhynhert narrowed his gaze on Farris. "Let's not presume what may or may not interest the king, Farris."

"These men appear to be uninjured and in fine health," someone behind Lord Rhynhert called out. "What nature of hardships could these gentlemen have endured?"

Auraq felt the crowd was waiting for something further to chuckle about. This was theater to them. Country bumpkins stumbling in with petty complaints for them to laugh at. His blood was starting to simmer with a slow heat of indignation. Any intimidation he'd experienced earlier had evaporated as his dark view of the nobleborn concentrated into a thick syrup. He was prepared to remove the doublet and chemise and show them the gash on his shoulder if there was further doubt of their hardships.

"An intriguing point," Rhynhert said.

"Hired assassins, Your Highness," Farris replied. "Several attempts have been made on their lives."

It was not what the crowd expected to hear. Chatter among the crowd ceased. It seemed that assassins were something the palace took more seriously.

Auraq's gaze centered quickly onto each face, one at a time, searching for any indication that announcement was not a surprise.

Rhynhert leaned in, his interest now piqued. "Indeed? And you're certain that this isn't just some cuckolded husband intent on eliminating a rival? They aren't part of some regional quarrel that has deteriorated into hot bloodlust?"

"No, Your Highness. Quite the opposite. These men are of humble origins."

"The roads can be dangerous for the ingenuous traveler," Lady Nenura said. "Perhaps they were only set upon by bandits wanting their purse. How can you possibly be certain they were in fact *assassins*?" She spat the word out with a derisive sneer.

272

Farris turned to Auraq and nodded to him.

Auraq unlatched the pouch at his belt and pulled out both the scrap of linen and the coded message. He handed them over to Farris, who in turn stepped forward and handed them to Lord Rhynhert.

Rhynhert unfolded the linen. He froze a moment, blinking at it. His lips tightened as his eyes shot up to take in Farris—then moved to lock onto Auraq, who felt a chill as the man's glare passed over him.

"How did you come by this?"

"I took it off the body of the man I killed, Your Highness."

Rhynhert's eyes betrayed his surprise. He handed the linen over to his wife. "You killed one these men?"

"Several actually," Kane added.

Nenura's chin sprang up the instant she saw the emblem as if she'd been poked from behind with a stick. "Is this some form of jest?"

"No, My Lady," Farris said.

"You expect us to believe that these...." She paused, clearly changing her mind what word she intended to say first. "These men are pursued by the Jackals? And that they survived?"

Rhynhert reached over and took the scrap of linen back from her to inspect it again.

"Clearly," Lady Nenura continued, "this is a trick of some kind. It most certainly is a forgery."

One of the courtiers standing over Rhynhert's left shoulder leaned in to peer at it with wide eyes. "Yet how would these simple commoners know the symbol well enough to manufacture it so precisely? It appears authentic to me."

"Very well, then," Rhynhert said, placing his elbow on his knee. "You have my attention. If we are to presume that the Order of the Jackal is after these men, someone must want them silenced. This news must be indeed significant."

Auraq sensed that Rhynhert was still not taking Farris's claim entirely seriously. He had not yet grasped the gravity of it.

Farris hesitated. "I beg Your Highness to consider the

possibility of us speaking in—"

"Speak, man! I am losing my patience. What possible intelligence could these lowly citizens have discovered that is so valuable that it would warrant the attention of the Jackals?"

Farris drew in a long slow breath. Auraq could tell he was still reluctant to speak openly of it here, with so many ears now attuned to the conversation.

Auraq looked over to catch Kane's eye, but Kane was looking at the floor. On the exposed skin beneath his ear, Auraq could see a fiery red trail snaking up to his hairline.

"They have learned, Your Highness, that an innocent man may have faced execution some years ago."

"Is that so? Have they evidence to present?"

"That is complicated to answer, Your Highness. We believe there is evidence, yes."

"All right," Rhynhert said, shaking his head. "And does this innocent man have a name?"

"He does."

Rhynhert sighed heavily. "I grow tired of this game, Farris. Out with it! Who is the man that you speak of?"

"Lord Norreg, Your Highness."

Blood drained from Rhynhert's face, and a moment later, he sprang to his feet. "My chambers. Now!"

Chapter 30

RHYNHERT'S FACE was splotched with crimson as he dropped into the chair behind a long desk. The surface of it was covered in piles of parchment documents and ledgers. He brushed aside the pile in front of him with a sweep of his arm and leaned forward.

"Divine fires take you, Farris. What fucking possessed you to dump this pile of shit on me during my watch?"

Most of Lord Rhynhert's entourage had been denied entry into his private chamber. Only his wife and five of his most trusted advisors, including his scribe, were permitted to join him. They lined the walls behind his desk looking anxious. Farris, Auraq, Kane, and Malgar stood in a row on the other side of it like criminals awaiting a verdict. Lady Nenura took her place behind Rhynhert at his right side.

Farris did not respond immediately. Auraq wondered if he was fighting the temptation to remind Rhynhert that he had requested the private discussion in the first place. "I believed the magnitude of this warranted your attention, Your Highness."

"Horseshit. The kingdom is finally healing from that ugly mess. Stirring up this old muck will accomplish nothing."

"But, Your Highness, if there is truth to this—"

Rhynhert slammed a fist onto the desk. "Fuck the truth!" His eyes bore into Farris for several heartbeats before he turned his hot gaze away. He pulled in a long calming breath, and when he spoke again his voice was softer. "It doesn't matter anymore."

"Sometimes truths are better left buried, Lord Farris," Lady Nenura added. "For the greater good."

Farris was quiet a moment. "Yesterday, I thought as you did. I very nearly turned them away. But then I thought, what if the ones behind the massacre attempt it again? It seems evident their intent was to put an end to your family's bloodline. If Norreg was innocent, Your Highness, the king is still in danger."

Rhynhert leaned back in his chair. He considered Farris's words with tight lips. "How credible is this claim?"

"I would not be here if I believed it otherwise."

"How did *they* come across this evidence, then?"

Auraq's neck and face flushed with heat. Rhynhert was having trouble believing that such lowly dregs as them could have stumbled upon anything so important.

Farris glanced at Auraq and Kane. "That will take some explaining. We will need to show you, Your Highness."

Rhynhert arched his brow. "All right, then. Show me."

Lady Nenura slid her hand over her husband's shoulder. "I do not recommend you pursue this, My Lord." She spoke softly, traces of unease in her voice. "No good can come of it."

Rhynhert gave her hand a light squeeze. "We shall see where it leads. For now."

Auraq studied the regent's face. Something was behind his eyes that Auraq couldn't quite read. There was a stoic remoteness to him—a cold detachment. Was he going forward with this only to see if there was a way to squash or discredit the information somehow? But wouldn't he want to know who actually was behind his own brother's murder?

Farris nodded to Kane, who stepped forward and pulled up his sleeve. Malgar carefully began to unwind the bandages, but eyes were already widening with interest even before they were off. The red glow was visible through the fabric, the shapes of the runes discernible. Malgar stepped back, bandages clumped in a ball in his hands, and Kane held out his arm.

Rhynhert's features lost their color. "What, for the love of all that is divine, is *that*?"

"These runes are infused into his flesh, Your Highness. It is undoubtedly the work of a powerful mage. It has been determined that the runes are a message sent from the shadow realm."

An audible gasp erupted from the small crowd of onlookers around Lord Rhynhert. The entire room was

276

transfixed onto Kane's arm.

Rhynhert's expression was rigid and difficult to read. He looked over his left shoulder at a man clutching a large tome against his chest as if someone was going to take it away from him. He wore the high rounded cap of a scholar.

"Is such a thing even possible?" Rhynhert asked.

The man seemed to shrink into himself, anxious that he was addressed directly. "Theoretically, yes," he managed to choke out. "The old scrolls have alluded to it, though I know of no specific incidence of someone accomplishing it."

"Nonsense," Nenura scoffed. "It has long been established that the veil between the world of the living and the shadow realm is impenetrable."

The scholar made a nervous cough and bowed to her. "With respect, My Lady, if that were so, how then do the souls of our loved ones reach the realm?" He attempted a smile, but it only managed to distort his face into an awkward and painful grimace.

"This seems a wild and unlikely claim to me," Nenura said to her husband.

"Who proposed this theory?" Rhynhert asked, his eyes sweeping the four of them.

Auraq watched as Farris's eyes shifted to Kane briefly before responding. This was a delicate dance, and Auraq could feel how easily it could turn south. Farris was calculating the best way to nudge things in the right direction. "May they answer for themselves, Your Highness?"

Rhynhert nodded.

Farris nodded to Kane.

"A high mage at the academy in Har Tesera named Master Chenigal," Kane told them. Auraq could see his tight fists and the sweat forming on his brow—but he spoke clearly. "He investigated the mark closely for several hours. He was murdered by the Order of the Jackal, however, before we were able to learn more."

Another of Lord Rhynhert's advisors stepped forward—a high-ranking military commander. He leaned in and spoke by

Rhynhert's ear. "This fits with reports I've been handed recently, Your Highness. Some days ago the academy in Har Tesera was attacked and mages were slain."

Rhynhert's eyes bore into Kane as if he was somehow to blame. "And what does this message convey?"

"That is not fully understood, Your Highness," Farris said. "The message is in the form of a memory that remains locked inside the runes."

"A memory?" Nenura repeated incredulously.

Lord Rhynhert leaned in, elbow on his knee. "If you are unable to know what is in the memory, how can you claim that this—" He gestured to Kane's arm. "—came from Norreg?"

"Kane is able to glimpse fragments of the memory in the form of visions. It is from what he has described to us that led us to this conclusion."

Rhynhert frowned, then shook his head. "Visions," he grumbled under his breath.

"Fickle things to attempt to construe," Lady Nenura said softly, and her husband nodded.

"I do not disagree, My Lady," Farris said. "Which is why I believe there is only one way to know for sure."

"Even if we unlock these supposed memories," the commander interjected, "who is to say we can trust them? They could be fabrications, as far as we know."

Auraq watched Rhynhert's expression carefully. He looked unconvinced. Auraq could tell he was thinking that this might be better swept under the rug and forgotten about. They were losing him—their connection to Norreg was too weak.

"He was there," Kane said.

All eyes turned to him at once. Kane pointed at the advisor holding the tome against his chest.

The advisor stiffened, tightening his grip on the tome, his eyes bulging in surprise.

Lord Rhynhert's head slowly turned to see where Kane pointed, then swung back around and narrowed his gaze at Kane. "He was where?"

"Outside the cell of the man in my vision. The day he was

executed. He was much younger, but I recognize him. His name is Marellus, Your Highness."

The advisor jolted and had the look of sudden panic in his eyes. It was all the confirmation Auraq needed that Kane was right.

Lady Nenura considered Kane carefully before turning back to her husband. "He could have heard the name from the audience chamber."

"He spoke to him through a small window in the cell door," Kane added.

Rhynhert spun to face Marellus. "Is this true?"

Marellus was frozen for a moment, unable to pull his eyes away from Kane—then remembered who had spoken to him. "It… it is, Your Highness. I—"

But Rhynhert cut him off by raising his palm. He turned back to Kane. "And then what?"

Kane hesitated, as if suddenly unsure. He looked to Auraq. His eyes were deeply red around the margins.

Auraq nodded back to him.

"They had words, Your Highness. The man in my vision tried to convince him he was innocent. Marellus was… enraged. He wasn't listening to what the man told him. He screamed at him that his soul would never find peace for what he'd done. That he deserved a thousand deaths. Then—" Kane paused and looked down at his feet. "—then Marellus spit into his face through the cell door."

Marellus had lost all color. The thick tome slipped lower and lower in his grip. He recovered just in time to stop it from dropping to the floor.

"Marellus?" Rhynhert asked.

"All true," he replied in a very quiet voice. He looked like he might be sick. "All of it. I had asked the guard if I could speak with him alone. No one else was there to hear it."

The room was silent and still. No one moved or breathed. Auraq could feel the dark realization hit them all. Not only did the memory in Kane's mark belong to Lord Norreg, but they were now forced to consider the cold implication of that—

Norreg was probably not behind the massacre at all.

They'd killed an innocent man.

Rhynhert had pulled into himself and stared at his hands with solemn intensity.

"Your Highness," the commander spoke, breaking the thick silence. "This information can be contained and remain in control of the palace."

"It must," said one of the other advisors as he toddled closer to Rhynhert, combing his unkempt beard with his thick fingers. His substantial girth strained the gold buttons of his brocade surcoat. "If this memory reveals the true architects of the massacre, they can be dealt with swiftly and silently. They won't even know that they are found out and their days are done until it is too late."

"And the public need not ever know," the commander added.

Auraq felt his jaw clench. They would all allow the world to continue to believe that Norreg was the butcher.

Rhynhert cupped his chin and ran his forefinger up and down along the bearded jawline. "Can we trust these three to hold their tongue?"

Nenura smiled down at him, but there was a tenderness in her eyes. "These are but lowborn creatures, Husband. Who would believe they know something of the death of the former king?"

"The Order of the Jackal clearly knows of the significance of the mark," Marellus said. He had recovered some of the color in his cheeks. "They may have already have alerted the culprits involved."

Rhynhert nodded. "Then we act quickly. And it's safe to assume the Order is not likely to roll over now. We have to keep this man safe until the memory is unlocked from the runes."

"I suggest we put the strength of your own guardsmen behind that, husband," Lady Nenura said. "They will protect him."

"Agreed," Rhynhert said. "We'll need a mage too who knows what to do with those runes."

Out of the corner of Auraq's vision, he saw a guardsman enter the chamber discreetly from a side door. No one surrounding Lord Rhynhert appeared to take note, but he approached the military commander and spoke quietly in his ear and handed a rolled parchment over.

"Your Highness," Farris said. "There are some questions as to whether there was a larger conspiracy within the mage guild. May I recommend caution when selecting a mage to unlock these memories faithfully from the mark?"

Rhynhert frowned. "I'd not considered that. Norreg was not the only mage who opposed my brother's edict. Far from it."

"A sympathizer could sabotage the effort, or even leak the information," the commander said as he unfurled the parchment that had been handed to him. He looked down and studied it a moment with a deep furrow in his brow.

"A leak could reflect badly on the throne. It could be interpreted as a scheme to hide the truth," the plump advisor added. "Perhaps the king—"

"No," growled Lord Rhynhert. "No, I'm not yet ready to involve the king in this. I want to learn more first."

"There are mages we know to be honorable and loyal to the crown, my love," Lady Nenura said to him.

Auraq risked another glance at the commander. The man's eyes bore down directly at him. For a moment their gazes locked. Auraq needed no more confirmation as to what was on the note he'd been handed. His heart pounded in his ears.

Not yet, he pleaded silently.

Rhynhert looked up at his wife a moment, then swung his hard gaze back to Kane. "Are you prepared to have this examined again?"

"I am, Your Highness," Kane replied.

"Very well. Let's proceed with it, then."

No one seemed particularly happy with the announcement.

Lady Nenura touched her husband's shoulder. "I might recommend Master Earati. He's even here at the palace today."

Rhynhert nodded. "Precisely who I thought to handle this."

"I will take him to your guardsmen immediately," she said.

"And stress to them that his safety is of utmost importance. Then I'll summon Master Earati."

Rhynhert reached up and squeezed his wife's fingers. "Yes."

She glided around the table. At the door, she smiled to Kane and waited for him to join her.

Kane turned to Auraq. His flesh was pale and his hairline glossy with sweat, but his jaw was firm. "Your Highness, I wish to request that Au—." He stopped short and caught himself. "That Agus Denn join me."

"No need for that," Lady Nenura said. "Come."

"He has kept me from harm all this time," Kane pressed.

From the corner of his eye, Auraq could see the military commander stiffen, ready to respond. The note was crumpled in his hand. He was waiting for his moment to interject.

Auraq would not be permitted to leave the chamber.

With a lump in his throat, Auraq shook his head. "No. You'll be well protected here, Kane. Go with them."

Kane's eyes shifted to Auraq's, widened with surprise.

Auraq pulled in a long breath. He steeled his resolve and ignored the pain wrenching around his heart. He would not allow Kane to witness what was coming next. "I… I will join you as soon as I can," he forced himself to say. "I promise."

Kane's eyes were filled with confusion and disbelief. Auraq fought to keep his face neutral, but his insides felt like they were being shredded.

"You're safe now," he said again, "and my task is done."

"Your task," Kane repeated.

"The oath I made to Old Tan. It is satisfied. Go."

The muscles in Kane's jaw tightened and a chain of emotions flashed across his features. Auraq could still see Kane carried the hope that there would be something between them someday. It was a heartbreakingly simple thing to quash.

Kane's lips parted as if he was about to speak, but instead, he made a small nod and turned away. He crossed the chamber and joined Lady Nenura at her side. He took one last glance toward Auraq, and without another word, they exited the chamber together.

Auraq took in a deep, long breath and tried to stop his heart from breaking apart. This was last time he would ever see Kane again, he knew. He'd never told him how he felt, and now he would never have the chance.

But Kane was safe. That was what mattered.

Rhynhert put his hands on the arms of the chair preparing to stand. "Let's return then to the hall."

"Your Highness, a moment please."

As Auraq predicted, the commander stepped forward to address Rhynhert, who looked up at him with a mixture of annoyance and surprise.

"Forgive me, Your Highness, but I've another matter of importance that I need to address with you. Regarding one of these men."

Rhynhert returned his weight to the seat again, taking his hands from the chair arm. He shifted his attention briefly to the three of them with a look of confusion, then returned his gaze to the officer. "Is there a problem?"

The officer nodded. "There is, Your Highness."

Auraq was not about to wait for the dramatic unveiling. He took several steps forward to stand directly before Lord Rhynhert.

"He speaks of me, Your Highness."

His father was at his side in an instant. "Commander, this is a common mistake. It has happened before. Agus bears an unlikely resemblance for—"

Auraq put a hand on his arm.

Malgar turned to him, pain in his eyes. "Don't do this," he whispered.

"It is already too late."

Rhynhert looked to his officer, confusion knitting his brow. "What is happening?"

"Your Highness, I am Auraq Greystone of Har Tesera, former second to Lord Renthe. I am wanted for his murder."

Rhynhert's eyes widened with surprise. "You?"

Auraq nodded.

"A double murder in fact," the noble commander added. "Lord Renthe and this man's wife. He then deserted the army to escape his sentence and has been a fugitive for the last several years. He is suspected to have been involved in a number of other incidents as well."

This was the first Auraq had heard of other charges.

Anger flared in Rhynhert's eyes. He swung his hard gaze to Farris. "Were you aware of this?"

"He was not," Auraq answered before Farris could. "I came to him under the false name I gave you. He had no knowledge of my identity."

Rhynhert bore his narrow gaze at Farris. "This true?"

Farris hesitated for only a moment—almost too long to make any response believable. Auraq could see the conflict in his eyes, but he nodded. "It is, Your Highness. I did not know anything of this until this moment."

Auraq exhaled slowly. He would not have wanted Farris reprimanded or punished after he did so much to get Kane the help he needed.

"And what have you to say to these accusations against you?" Rhynhert asked him.

"I know nothing of these other charges, Your Highness. And I did not murder my wife. But the allegations against me regarding Lord Renthe are true."

"You admit this freely?" Rhynhert seemed genuinely surprised.

"I do."

The chamber had fallen into a deep quiet. Rhynhert frowned as if perplexed by this turn. "And you walked in here, knowing the risk to yourself? Rather bold. Either you are exceedingly arrogant or wildly foolhardy. Are you not aware that the penalty for that crime is death?"

Auraq took in a long, slow breath. "I am."

A strange peace washed over him then. It felt like standing in warm sunlight. He was ready for what was to come, he realized. Whatever happened to him now was of no real consequence. Kane was safe. He'd be protected here at the palace and liberated of the mark that was slowly killing him. Since the beginning, that was all that ever mattered.

Kane was safe.

Regardless of his crimes, Auraq was satisfied that at least he had accomplished that. It may not have absolved him of his sins, but it was something. The scale had been brought more into balance. Now his life would not be measured solely by the ill deeds of his past.

Malgar was breathing heavily behind him. More than ever, Auraq wished his father had not come—he did not want him witnessing what was surely to come. At least Kane was already out of the chamber and would remain ignorant of it. The familiar tingling in his hand increased as Kane moved farther away from him. It was something oddly comforting now. It reminded Auraq of the good he'd done. Would he feel something too when the memory was unlocked?

"Your Highness." Farris took a step forward, his face looking pained. "This man has risked everything to bring the bearer of the mark to us unharmed, and in doing so may have benefited the state—"

"That has yet to be determined, Farris."

"Of course, Your Highness. But his intentions were for the good of the kingdom. For the safety and well-being of the king himself. He sacrificed much, and at great personal risk. In light of that, I'd be willing to purchase a King's Pardon for the man—"

"You know the law as well as I do. The pardon does not extend to those who wantonly murder a member of a noble house." Rhynhert shook his head slowly. "He is ineligible."

With a nod from Lord Rhynhert, the guards stationed at the door stepped forward. They flanked Auraq. "Come along," one of them said.

He was happy at least not to be shackled in front of his father. That was a humiliation he was not sure he could bear. Lord Farris approached him and grabbed his arm.

"This isn't over," he said. "I will appeal to the king personally on your behalf."

"Thank you," Auraq replied. But he didn't hold out much hope that the outcome would change.

One guard put a gloved hand under his bicep and nudged him into motion. As he was marched toward the door of the chamber, he kept his eyes forward and his back straight. He had no wish to see any pain in his father's eyes, nor for his father to see him lose the remnants of his dignity by struggling. That would only serve to make this harder than it was. He wondered if it would have been better had he not reconciled with his father after all. It would have been easier for both of them, he thought, if Malgar still viewed him as a monster.

It was almost a relief when they were out of the chamber and in the corridor. The guards directed him along, not roughly but firmly. They remained close, one hand gripping the back of each arm. Even though Auraq stood a head taller than either of them, they seemed alert but unconcerned—perhaps dressed as he was, or without a weapon at his side, Auraq did not appear much of a threat. Auraq marched along obediently.

Everything around him was in a strange fog. His mind was whirling, trying to catch up. The moment he'd feared would come had arrived with such spectacular and dizzying abruptness—but now that it was here and he was being taken away to face his crimes, he was not afraid.

He looked mostly at his feet. But as they rounded a corner, he happened to glance up and see the end of the corridor. There he saw Lady Nenura. She was speaking with someone—and at first Auraq was surprised to find that Kane was not with her. Had he already been passed on to the regent's personal guards?

Then his eyes shifted to the man with her. A well-dressed man—perhaps not a nobleman, but wealthy certainly—smiled and spoke freely with the woman as if they were old friends reacquainting in the corridor.

A spark of recognition fired in his brain. Where had he seen the man before?

Then it hit him with an agonizing jolt. He had spoken to him only once. In his father's workshop.

Kanar the Ravager.

Lady Nenura hadn't taken Kane to her husband's personal guardsmen, or to the mages. She had delivered him directly into the hands of the Order of the Jackal.

Chapter 31

AURAQ'S INSIDES went cold with dread. His immediate instinct was to act, but he used the full strength of his will to fight the impulse down. Something reckless would get him killed or subdued before he reached Kane. He couldn't allow that to happen.

If it wasn't already too late. Kane could already be dead....

No. The sensation in his hand was still alive and throbbing.

He waited until the guards guided him around the corner of the corridor. Lady Nenura and Kanar were out of sight, and the corridor vacant. He pulled a full breath of air into his lungs and set his shoulders back—then released his muscles like the springing of trap. His left elbow shot upward. It struck the guard squarely in the side of the face. The guard's head flailed backward. Blood spewed from his shattered nose, splattering against the wall.

Before the other guard registered what was happening, Auraq jabbed to his face with the heel of his hand. The guard stumbled back, stunned. Auraq grabbed for the ponytail that came out from under the back of his helm. Looping it quick around his hand once, he yanked the head back, then thrust it forward again with the full force of his arm. The head smashed into the wall, denting the helm and chipping the stone. Auraq pulled it back and did it again. The impact made a thudded clank like a spoon hitting the side of an iron pot. The guard's knees buckled and he collapsed unconscious to the floor.

The first guard hunched forward, clutching at his bleeding face. Auraq slipped his arm around the man's neck from behind. He tightened his bicep against the man's throat—enough to block the air flow—but he was careful not to crush the man's windpipe. The man made small wheezing sounds and flailed about. He clawed at Auraq's arm and thrust his legs about to push himself free, but Auraq was too strong. The flailing lessened, then quit altogether. Auraq lowered the man to the ground. He checked quickly to make sure the man was still breathing.

Auraq closed his eyes and focused on the strange tugging in his hand. He could feel the direction of the pull, but in this sprawling palace there was likely no direct route. Kane wasn't far yet, but he was on the move and moving fast. Were they taking him somewhere to interrogate him first? Did they want to kill him somewhere remote? Auraq had no idea how much time he had.

He took the swords from the unconscious bodies and held one in each hand. They did not feel the same as his own, but he felt better having both hands occupied. He took off at a sprint.

His heart pounding, he wound his way through the network of corridors. He allowed the sensation in his hand to guide him. It tugged at him, leading the way. All too soon the guards would be discovered in the corridor—he had to gain ground before the alarm was raised.

Kane was somewhere beneath him, in the lower floors of the palace. He took the first stairwell he found, leaping down the steps two at a time. It only went down one floor—he needed to go deeper. People were in the corridor with him. Servants. They squawked and dove out of the way as he dashed past with weapons drawn. But he didn't slow. His breathing was coming in heavier bursts, but he refused to slow his frenetic pace. He would not allow himself to give in to the fatigue.

A deep, resonant knell erupted from somewhere and echoed throughout the corridor like thunder. The alarm. The guards had been discovered and his flight was now known. Despite the increased burning in his lungs, he pressed even harder.

Everyone would think he was attempting an escape. Capturing him would not be their aim. They would attempt to kill him.

Crossing an intersection of corridors, he heard a shout. A palace guardsman had spotted him from a distance. He pulled a horn from his belt and blew into it while launching into a run after Auraq. The man let out three bursts from the horn, then pulled out his weapon.

Auraq swore. He changed directions and stormed through the closest door.

The door swung into a small meeting room. Bookshelves lined the walls, and a long table and chairs occupied the center. It was empty—thank the Gods. He slammed the heavy door shut, then ducked behind it. The door burst back open, and the guard blundered in at full speed. Auraq launched and tackled him from behind. Arms flailing, the guard went down and landed face-first on the floor.

Auraq dropped a knee to the center of his back. The guardsman let out a pained grunt when he felt Auraq's full weight.

Auraq slid his fingers under the front of the man's leather helm and pulled it off his head. With the sword's pommel, he struck him hard against the temple. The guard's eyes rolled back, and he was out.

After a quick look into the corridor to make sure the way was clear, he tore off again at a dash.

Deeper into the palace he plunged, descending stairs blindly at a mad rush—following the persistent pull in his hand that guided him like stars guide a ship. More people dodged out of his way, but they were a blur to him. The sensation was weakening—he was gaining on them.

He heard a commotion behind him—shouting and the pounding of boots on tile. More guards had taken up pursuit. Without looking behind, he could sense their numbers converging on him. He had to move faster or somehow lose them.

He rounded a corner. An arrow splintered against the wall just as he turned.

Archers. They'd have a better chance at bringing him down than anything else. He had to keep moving and stay out of any open areas that gave them a straight shot.

He ducked into a dimly lit servant's passage and was all but blinded from the sudden darkness, but he pushed on. Startled servants squawked in surprise, dropping anything in their hands and leaping against the wall as Auraq barreled through. His pursuers were on his heels, closing the distance between them and shouting at him to halt.

Another stairwell appeared at Auraq's left.

He was delving into the bowels of the palace now, into the foundation of the original keep that had stood here eons before. The corridors were narrow, the walls built of roughly cut stones. At intervals, sconces hung down from the ceiling. They were lit with tallow candles that filled the passage with rank smoke that stung his eyes and burned his throat. The flames flickered weakly as he darted past.

He made a quick turn, then another. The shouting behind him was fading—he'd lost them for the moment. Auraq had bought some time, but he was far from safe. As more guards joined in the search, they'd break up and comb the passageways.

The pull within his hand was weakening still—he was getting close, but he was having a harder time interpreting the direction. He made quick turns down the dark passages with the hope they would lead him toward Kane. A miscalculation in the direction would not only delay his reaching Kane, but doubling back could lead him right into the path of the searching guards.

Where were they taking him?

His lungs burned, and the sharp pain under his ribcage felt like he'd been stabbed. His calves cramped into knots. Yet he wouldn't allow himself to slow. He pushed on. Sounds of pursuit were still behind him, along with shouts as guardsmen scolded the frightened servants to get clear.

Wherever they were taking Kane, Auraq prayed the Order's plan was to interrogate him first—perhaps to find out what others might know. If their intent was to kill him outright, in all likelihood, he'd not reach him in time. But it raised the question of how much danger Farris and his father were in now too.

He rounded another corner to come face to face with two men clad entirely in black leather armor, their faces covered. These were not palace guardsmen. These were men of the Order. He was close now.

They started, and it took them a heartbeat too long to respond and pull up their swords. Auraq was already moving in fast. He launched at the one on the right, knocking aside the blade as the Jackal attempted to bring it up. With momentum behind him, he careened into the man and struck him under the chin with his forearm. The man's head snapped back, and he was thrown off his feet, hitting the passage wall.

He spun and thrust at the second man. The sword he'd taken felt sluggish and unbalanced. He'd aimed the point toward the unprotected line beneath the lower edge of the leather breastplate, but the man twisted and the edge caught the side at the hip bone instead. It opened up a deep gash. Not fatal—but it likely would keep him out of the fight. The Jackal cried out in shock and pain, and fell back against the wall.

As the first man struggled to regain his feet, Auraq side-kicked him in the sternum, knocking him back to the floor.

Clutching his bleeding side, shoulder to the wall, the second Jackal cried out an alarm.

"Attack! Atta—!"

Auraq put an end to the cry by thrusting the point of the blade through the man's throat. Blood erupted from the man's mouth with a sickly gurgle. Eyes wide in shock and horror, he slid down the wall.

The damage was done. Auraq lost any hope of surprise.

They'd likely not take any chances now. Kane would be killed straightaway.

He burst into motion, sprinting down the narrow corridor as fast as his legs would take him.

The corridor ended with rough stairs descending even deeper beneath the royal palace. Auraq knew where he was heading from the smell rising up to assault him—the sewers. He burst onto a platform inside a long tunnel lit by a single lantern on the floor. The ceiling was a continual arch of red brick from one side to the other. Running down the center of the tunnel was a deep trench filled with dark water quietly flowing past.

Kane sat in a chair in the center of the platform, gagged and with his arms tied behind him. A man in black stood over him with a knife at his throat, ready to slice. He gave Auraq a sinister grin, a look that said, "You're too late."

Auraq was still moving fast, but there was no way he'd be able to reach the man in time.

He rotated the sword in his hand, gripping it almost like a spear, with two fingers on one side of the cross guard and his thumb on the other. He cocked his arm back over his shoulder.

It was a desperate gamble. The sword was common, with mediocre balance at best.

But there was no other option.

Still moving forward, he put as much weight and force behind the release as he could manage. The blade left his hand and spiraled through the air.

The man began to move the knife along Kane's throat.

Auraq staggered forward from momentum but he kept his eye on the sword, following its path. It sailed true as if guided by the hand of a God, whistling as it cut the air.

The man looked up at the sound, and his eyes widened as he saw the sword coming directly for him. At the last possible second, he pulled his hand from Kane's throat and leaped away inelegantly. The blade whirled past, missing him—but it had accomplished its purpose. The knife was free from Kane's throat.

Auraq, still at a full sprint, was upon him a moment later. He plunged the second sword through the assassin's unprotected gut, then rammed his entire body into him. The man gasped in pain and was carried along by Auraq's momentum, driven backward. At the edge of the sewer trench, Auraq came to an abrupt stop. The man slid off the sword and stumbled back off the ledge. Clutching at the wound in his belly, he dropped into the dark water below. In an instant, it swallowed him up, cutting off his final scream.

Ignoring his own fatigue, Auraq stumbled over to Kane.

He was barely conscious, his head tilting to the side. Auraq couldn't tell if he'd been drugged or if the mark was taking its final toll on him. Auraq gently turned Kane's head to the side to expose the neck. There was a gash under the jawline near the ear. It bled, but it wasn't deep. Nothing vital had been severed.

Kane lifted his head. "Auraq," he said with a weak smile. "You're here."

"I'm here," Auraq replied. He moved around to the back of the chair and sliced the bindings around Kane's wrists. Kane's body slumped forward, but Auraq caught him before he fell to the floor.

"They did something to me, Auraq. They did something to make me answer their questions. But I fought it. I wouldn't talk to them."

Auraq scooped his arm underneath Kane's arm and slid it behind his back, then pulled Kane gently to his feet. "I have to get you out of here." Kane was limp against him, unable to support himself. His skin felt cold.

The Jackal's intentions were clear—find out what Kane knew, then dump his body into the sewers. No need to transport Kane out of the palace or hide the body. But Kane's strong will and Auraq's quick action had thwarted their attempt to get the information fast enough.

They were not out of danger. Auraq was a fugitive, and palace guards were still canvassing the place for him. He would willingly turn himself over to the guardsmen if he believed that Kane would remain safe this time, but the palace had been infiltrated at the highest level and there was no one they could trust. Anyone they encountered could put Kane right back into the Jackal's hands. Auraq had only one choice—get Kane out of the palace. He would figure out how to help him. Somehow, he would find a way to remove the mark once they were safely away. Auraq no longer cared what information was stored in the memory. Keeping Kane alive was all that mattered.

Heading back up the stairs into the foundations of the palace was probably not an option. With Kane's current state, guardsmen or members of the Jackals would have no trouble overtaking them. His only viable choice was deeper into the sewers. The polluted water had to escape somewhere. Perhaps they could too.

He lifted the solitary lantern from the floor, and with Kane against his hip, he walked deeper into the tunnel. Up ahead he could see the platform narrow to the width of a stride, but it was enough. He prayed the ledge didn't disappear entirely.

Behind him, he heard a click, followed by a quick whistle. Something punched him in his lower right side with staggering force—then sudden, terrific pain.

His back arched in response. He lost his grip on Kane, who slid down his torso and onto the ground in a heap. Auraq's leg gave out—he fell down to one knee. Burning pain radiated out from his side in all directions. He tried to pull in a deep breath, but instead, his breaths came in ragged bursts and only made the pain flare out more intensely.

He looked down his front and saw the point of a crossbow bolt protruding from the right side of his abdomen. Without armor to protect him, the bolt had cut through him cleanly. Blood was already spreading through the fine doublet. He looked over his shoulder toward the stairs.

Kanar the Ravager, leader of the Order of the Jackal, stood in the opening with an easy grin. He chuckled softly and tossed the crossbow aside. "My, my" was all he said as he stepped down off the stairs, pulling a dagger from his belt.

Chapter 32

AURAQ KEPT himself from collapsing with an elbow on one knee, as if he were being knighted by the king. He tried again to pull in more breath, but the sharp pain in his side cut him short.

"Terribly sad, really," Kanar said behind him. "To have made it all this way only to die here. I thought tipping them off about you would be enough to get you out of my hair once and for all, but I suppose I should have known, considering the headaches you've already caused."

"Happy to disappoint you," Auraq answered through his teeth. He let the sword drop from his hand, and it hit the stone with a harsh clang that reverberated throughout the tunnel. He reached around and found the protruding tip of the crossbow bolt, gently pinching the shaft between his forefinger and thumb. Yet even that slight touch caused the bolt shaft to move, and shocks of pain burst out from the wound.

He pulled in air a little at a time and held it there. Then he tugged on the bolt. A bit at first, then harder. It resisted, the flesh around it gripping it as if he was trying to pull out one of his own ribs. He tried not to cry out, but a grunt escaped his throat. With a sudden jolt, it slipped out about a length of a finger. Pain like white fire forced him to let go and exhale. His vision darkened and swirled, consciousness threatening to leave him.

He let his head drop forward and he closed his eyes as his breaths came in quick succession.

"Well, my brave little mercenary, the outcome will be no different."

Auraq could hear his boots on the stone behind him as he stepped closer.

"You've certainly couldn't have made this part any easier

for me, really," Kanar continued. "Showing up here now, saving me the trouble of having you murdered in your cell. Though how you found this place so quickly is curious, I'll grant you. But that doesn't really matter, does it? Now, I get to kill you myself to make certain the job is done… and done properly this time. The added bonus is I will unquestionably enjoy it. And I can conveniently dispose of both of your bodies right here."

Auraq again locked breath inside his lungs and tugged at the bolt—this time with an even harder yank. His vision blurred in sudden tears, his teeth clenched, and his head swam dizzily. But the gore-covered bolt slid clear, the hard fletching at the end opening the wound up further. A fresh warm trail spilled down his side.

He would bleed out, he knew. Regardless of what happened now, he would die. There was no saving him. But he would stop Kanar and save Kane before he took his final breath. He repositioned the bolt in his hand.

Old Tan said that the Gods had forgiven him of his crime. Strange that he would remember them now. He hoped that was true. He hoped the Gods would accept his spirit and reclaim him.

Kanar was right behind him—Auraq could feel his presence over him. "Furthermore, you can die knowing that your meddling cost the lives of both your father and that insufferable snob Farris. I doubt they know anything, but can't leave anything to chance, can I?" The Jackal leader took Auraq by the hair and pulled back his head to expose his neck. "And now this little secret you stumbled upon gets buried along with you."

Auraq didn't resist, didn't fight, despite the rage that coursed through his body. The pain was forgotten.

No, it would end here today. He fought to keep perfectly still, though his body wanted to shake apart. It seemed like eternity, but from his peripheral vision he saw the point of Kanar's dagger come around over his left shoulder.

Auraq's hand shot up and grabbed Kanar's wrist. With all the force his anger could generate, he yanked the entire arm down, pulling Kanar down with him. Surprised, Kanar let out a sudden breath that blasted into Auraq's ear.

Auraq thrust up with his other hand gripping the crossbow bolt.

Kanar tried to avoid the attack by twisting and yanking his torso back. The bolt should have pierced his neck but instead struck his shoulder. The wet shaft slipped in Auraq's grip, preventing it from penetrating too deep into the flesh.

But it was enough. Auraq could tell the bolt's tip broke the skin and sank into the meat of his shoulder. Kanar cried out in sudden pain but reacted quickly. He was well trained. Instead of pulling back, he launched over Auraq's shoulder into a roll. The move turned Kanar's wrist about in Auraq's hand and broke the grip. Kanar came out of the roll in a crouch just outside of Auraq's reach. He ripped the bolt out of his shoulder and tossed it away with disdain into the dark river of sewage, then grinned back at Auraq.

"Still some fight in you, I see, my brave little soldier."

Auraq didn't answer. He picked up the sword again and rose to his feet. He focused everything on controlling the effort, keeping the motion smooth to appear stronger than he felt. But as he came to his full height, his head spun, threatening to unbalance him.

Kanar started to circle left, crossing one leg over the other in a sideways crawl. He moved with an unsettling snakelike grace. Auraq gleaned his stratagem immediately—he was attempting to gain the more secure position on the platform, putting Auraq between him and the drop-off. Kanar would try to drive Auraq backward and force him over the edge.

Auraq mirrored his movements, easing farther from the edge, all the while keeping his eyes fixed on Kanar's. He studied the Jackal leader's movements—he'd moved the dagger to his right hand, and the left hung awkwardly. The bolt to the shoulder had affected him more than he was letting on.

"Come now," Kanar prodded, smirking. "Surely you see the futility in this."

Auraq came at him, closing the distance between them with a springing leap. He made a sweeping diagonal cut. The pain in his side from the bolt was still there but somehow distant, masked by rage and purpose. Yet the movement seemed to accelerate the bleeding. He could feel the rivulets coursing down his leg and pooling in his boot.

Kanar slid right and parried the attack with his dagger. He then countered with a thrust of his own. Auraq's reaction time was slower than he expected. The dagger very nearly skewered his midsection. He had pivoted back barely in time.

"Who are you? Really?" Auraq asked the question only to take a moment to breathe. His heart was pounding furiously. His head felt light.

Kanar's eyes narrowed and the corners of his mouth curled up. "If by that question you mean to ask how is it I've acquired such unprecedented access to the palace, the answer is not only simple but obvious. I am the faithful personal steward of Her Highness, Lady Nenura."

"Is that why she brought you into her service, then? She wanted access to your order?" The notion of such an alliance was frightening. The Order of the Jackal had infiltrated the hierarchy at the highest levels, and Lady Nenura had a team of assassins at her disposal. This made her more powerful and more dangerous than he could imagine.

Kanar lifted his chin and laughed. "And here I thought you had pieced it all together already. My dear little soldier, I'm afraid I misled you earlier. I'm not actually the leader of the Order." His smile lengthened as he leaned in. "*She* is."

Auraq tried to rein in his disbelief. Now, he had one more reason to survive. The king had to hear of the treachery and betrayal that existed right in his own wing of the palace.

He lunged at Kanar again, making two quick slashes and then finishing with a hard thrust. Kanar easily evaded the first two and knocked aside the third attack with the dagger. Even injured, Kanar moved with staggering speed and agility. But Auraq knew his own attack had been sloppy. It lacked the force and precision it should have. Anger fueled him and kept him on his feet, but the truth of it was he was losing dominion of his own body.

Kanar made a few feints as if to attack, but pulled back

each time. Clearly, he was testing Auraq's ability to react.

Time was running out for him.

This time, he attempted a backswing toward Kanar's wounded side, putting what strength and control he still had behind a single attack. But still, Kanar moved nimbly beyond its reach. And the effort had cost him valuable energy.

"Gods, man! Why are you doing this?"

Auraq glared at him. "I will stop you," he growled. His skin felt clammy and cold, as if a winter wind had rushed in through the tunnel.

"It's delightful that you even still think so. But, look at you. You can barely stand."

It was true, he realized. He was swaying drunkenly now, and his vision was beginning to darken along the edges. It seemed as if he was watching it all through a black tunnel.

"Engage me!" he shouted at Kanar.

"What a foolish idea that would be. Why would I do that when I can simply stand here and let you bleed out?"

The slow realization was dawning that Kanar was right. Determination alone was not enough. Despite how deeply he needed it to be, he was not physically capable of putting an end to Kanar. Even with his injured shoulder, Auraq was no match for him. Auraq would die unable to fulfill his oath to Kane.

But he would die trying.

Auraq looked up at Kanar and focused his vision. At first he wasn't sure of what he was seeing. Then he chuckled to himself, and that expanded to an open laugh. Kanar tilted his head in confusion. Auraq must have appeared delusional.

"I beg you, share," Kanar said. "I'd love to know what it is you find funny."

"It appears," Auraq said, "there's something you didn't consider."

"Indeed! Well, you have piqued my interest. I am dying to hear. What could I have possibly missed?"

Kane came in from behind him and drove a dagger into Kanar's back. "Me," he growled into his ear.

With the last of his strength, Auraq pushed himself into

action once more. Wielding the sword with both hands on the hilt, he shoved the end of the blade directly into the center of Kanar's chest.

Auraq looked down at his hands to make sure the deed was done. Somehow it didn't seem real, so he stared at the blade where it impaled Kanar for what seemed an eternity. Then he looked up and met Kanar's eyes, which were wide in disbelief.

Yes, it was done. He let go of the hilt and stumbled backward.

Then both Auraq and Kanar collapsed to the floor. For a time, he was staring at the ceiling. Then Kane was there, speaking to him, but the words were garbled as if he spoke from under water. He had the sensation of floating too—he could not feel the stone floor beneath him. Earlier, he recalled feeling cold, but now his entire body was bathed in a warmth he could not explain.

Gripping the front of Auraq's bloodstained doublet, Kane hoisted his torso off the floor. "I'll be damned if you're going to die on me too!"

Auraq sighed. He wanted to sleep. Staying conscious seemed like too much work. He gripped Kane's sleeve. "What are you doing? Get out of the palace."

"You need help. We have to find help or you'll die."

"You're not safe here. Go."

"I'm not leaving without you."

The walls were spinning and darkness was closing in around his vision. Auraq closed his eyes. "Listen to me. Don't trust anyone here."

In the distance, faint echoes ran through the corridors. Shouts. Men calling out to each other. Kane looked to the threshold that led up to the palace—he'd heard it too. Someone had stumbled upon the bodies of the two Jackals. The palace guards had found the direction Auraq had gone. They were coming.

"Go," he said again.

"Got to stop the bleeding so you can walk—"

"I'm not going anywhere." He tried to lie back down but

Kane forced him up again. His head fell forward as if he no longer had bones in his neck. "Kane." It came out as a whisper.

Kane shook him. "You are *not* dying."

Auraq grunted and lifted his head. "I'm sorry, Kane." He took in a few long breaths and looked up into Kane's warm face. His dark eyes were red and glistening with tears. Auraq was pleased Kane's face was the last thing he'd see in life. It would satisfy his soul as he passed from this world and entered into the shadow realm. He smiled up at Kane. "Lived longer than I've had any right to, really. Should have been dead a long time ago." He pulled in a breath. The stabbing pain in his side made him wince and cut the inhale short. "They will be here any moment. Kane, before they come. There's something I need to say. Something I need to tell you…."

But he was interrupted.

Chapter 33

A SHOUT from the corridor announced their arrival and was followed by the sound of boots on the stairs and the rattle of armor. Men surged on the platform and fanned out, crossbows leveled at the two of them.

As Auraq expected, they wore the king's livery. Palace guards.

A man dressed in the formal armor of a ranking officer stepped through the threshold last and threaded his way to the front. His narrow face was etched by both age and experience, a scar running diagonally across his gaunt features from his brow to his jaw. Thick black hair crowned his head, but his beard was gray at the chin. He walked with a stiff back and with purpose. Frowning, he assessed the scene. His nose wrinkling a little at Kanar's crumbled body.

"What the devil happened here?"

Kane climbed to his feet and put himself between Auraq and the officer. Every guard wielding a crossbow shifted their aim at him. Kane held out his hands to stop them. "Wait."

"Step aside," the officer said, his voice cool and deadly. "That man escaped custody. He is a wanted fugitive."

"That man there"—Kane pointed at Kanar—"tried to assassinate me. Auraq stopped him."

"Assassinate?" His eyes narrowed as he scrutinized Kane more closely. Auraq could tell he was attempting to discern any possible importance that would justify calling it an assassination. "My men will shoot you where you stand if you do not step aside. That man is to face judgment. Do not interfere."

Auraq tried to sit up straighter. "Kane, don't. Move aside.

It's all right." Pain once again flared in his side. The insides of legs were tingling with the sensation of a thousand needles.

"He saved my life. And he's going to die if he doesn't receive help."

"If that's his fate. Now step aside."

Kane pointed at Kanar's corpse. "That man was a member of the Order of the Jackal." His voice was rising, growing more desperate, and echoed throughout the domed chamber. "I was dragged down here so he could kill me."

"A Jackal?" The officer's expression remained cool and resolute, but his voice betrayed his surprise, and perhaps even amusement, at the accusation. "All right. Easy enough to verify." He caught the eye of one of the guards and snapped his fingers.

The guard hurried to comply but stopped short when he looked down at the man's face. He sprung back as if the dead man posed some unknown threat. "Lord Eress, this is Lady Nenura's steward, Lord Kanar."

"*What*?" Lord Eress's stony composure fractured. "You certain?"

The guard grabbed Kanar by the shoulder and pulled him onto his back, exposing his face.

Eress's cheeks reddened when he saw Kanar's face. His gaze swung back and forth between the body and Kane. Auraq watched the realization emerge on Eress's face that he had stumbled upon something much bigger than reclaiming a fugitive. His eyes eventually settled on Kane. "What the fuck is he doing down here?"

"I told you. He tried to kill me."

"Or he tried to apprehend this fugitive and paid the ultimate price."

"That doesn't explain why he's down here. Listen to me. He was going to slit my throat and dump my body in the sewers. He's a Jackal."

Eress's mouth tightened, his lips turning white. "Check," he told the guard.

The guard took a tentative step closer and then squatted

down next to Kanar's head. Turning the face away from him, he pushed the head forward with one hand and swept aside the hair covering the neck with the other. Cocking his head to the side, he bent in closer. His body stiffened, and he swung his gaze back to his commander, his mouth hung open.

No words were needed. Auraq knew what he'd found—a tattoo of the same image he'd found on the dead assassin's tunic. He felt a surge of anger run through him. What a fool he'd been. Of course, there had to be something. There had to be some way for the Jackals to prove their membership. And he'd never thought to look for one.

He shut his eyes. The room still tilted and swirled and made his stomach reel. Bile burned the back of his throat. He wanted to rise to his feet and protect Kane, but he had no strength. It was taking everything he had to not lie back down on the floor and give up.

Eress's poise was crumbling. Auraq imagined him trying to digest the magnitude of the discovery. The Order of the Jackal were ensconced in high offices of the king's palace. He was becoming aware of the dark severity of what that could mean. He stepped closer to Kane, his eyes narrow. "Suppose I believe you." His voice was a low growl. "Why would the Order want you dead?"

Before Kane could answer, another guard stepped forward. "Lord Eress, forgive me. I recognize this man. He had an audience with Lord Rhynhert earlier. Both of them were there. With Lord Farris."

"What about?"

"I don't know. But I was told he was ordered to meet with the palace mages."

"The mages?" Eress's features betrayed his personal thoughts about the mages. His attention snapped back to Kane. "Why?"

"Because of this?" Kane pulled back the sleeve of his tunic and exposed the mark.

Everyone took an involuntary step back. Even Auraq gasped.

The mark was alight with fire. Light stabbed out from the fissures in the skin. Swirling tendrils of red and purple circled the arm like a nest of translucent snakes.

"What in the name of all the Gods is that?" Eress breathed.

"I don't have time to explain."

Auraq tried to climb to his feet. He rose up part way but dizziness and weakness overcame him and he dropped back down again, panting. Some of the guards wielding crossbows regained their wits and pointed their weapons his way.

"Running out—" Auraq pulled in a breath. "—of time." It was harder to pull enough air into his lungs to speak. "Get him to the mages."

"Those *were* Lord Rhynhert's orders, sur," the guard next to him whispered.

Eress gave a tight nod. "All right. Quickly. We have no idea if that…thing on his arm is a danger to us all."

Men moved in to take Kane forcibly by the arms, but Kane stepped back and brandished his forearm in front of him like a shield.

"He comes too. Bring him or I stay."

The men froze and turned as one to their commander.

Eress considered Auraq a moment. "Fine. Bring him too. But I want him alive. If he has any answers about what is going on here, I want to hear them. He can face judgment after."

AURAQ WAS in and out of consciousness as they dragged his body through the palace. Occasionally he would hear Kane's voice speaking to him, and he would lift up his head. He'd open his eyes, but the world around him was a whirl of confusing images so he'd close his eyes again and let his head drop.

He woke as four guards grunted and groaned to lift his bulk onto a table. Someone else shoved items aside to make room for him. The items fell and struck the stone floor with a discordant clamor.

"Keep him alive," someone said. Eress.

A woman with fiery red hair and dressed in silken black

robes drifted over to him. Her hands swept over his body, probing at his flesh. She pulled out a knife.

Auraq flinched and tried to push away.

"Relax, you idiot!" she snapped. With ease, she pushed aside his flailing arm. She gripped the front of his blood-soaked doublet and sliced it open down the front. Pulling the fabric aside, she slipped her fingers directly into the open wound. Auraq threw back his head, and he sucked air in through his teeth. The familiar tingling of magecraft wove through his insides.

Gritting his teeth from the pain as she dug around in his insides with her fingers, he forced himself to remain conscious. He turned his head and searched the round chamber for Kane. The room was part workshop and part library. Tables and workbenches cluttered the center, while shelves encircled the perimeter. Every surface was buried with strange equipment, tomes, and jars. A spiral staircase led up to a balcony that overlooked the chamber.

Kane was laid out on another table on the other side of the chamber. A group of robed figures fluttered around him like a murder of crows raiding a corpse. Some carried open tomes in their hands. Others positioned candles around him, and bowls emitting swirling wisps of smoke. Everyone was speaking at once. A second circle of nervous guards surrounded the flurry of activity around the table.

Kane cried out in pain. Through the chaos, Auraq could see Kane arch his back while mages gripped his legs and shoulders to hold him down.

Auraq tried to sit up. The redheaded mage pushed him back down. He wasn't strong enough to resist her.

"Stay still."

"I have to go to him."

"Stay still! I was told to keep you alive, and I can't do that if you keep squirming about."

She did something to him that made his eyes lose focus. His mind disconnected from his body. He tried to force his body to move, but he seemed to forget how to make his muscles work.

"Gods, I'm amazed you have any blood left in you," she grumbled. Her eyes were closed, her head tilted, as if she was seeing with her fingertips inside him. "How are you still alive?"

The tingling energy whirled around his abdomen like it was filled with snakes.

The mages had tightened around the table. Auraq could no longer see Kane at all, but coils of red and purple light rose up from the center of the circle of mages, twisting like vines toward the domed ceiling.

"What's happening to him?"

"How should I know?" the redhead said. "I'm stuck here with you."

She pushed her fingers in deeper. He flinched, but only from reflex—he expected sharper pain. But the pain had already started to retreat, and his head began to clear.

The doors to the chamber flew open, and a new group of guardsmen rushed in.

Lord Eress turned from the activity on the table to face the newcomers. He straightened and made a formal bow. "Ah, Lady Nenura, glad you received my message."

Auraq's heart went hollow. No.

The redheaded mage's face contorted in surprise. She stopped, slipped her fingers out of his wound, and turned to face the door as well.

Auraq grunted as he forced his torso up and propped himself on his elbow.

Lady Nenura glided into the chamber, hands clasped in front of her. She was surrounded by four guards wearing the colors and livery of her husband, Lord Rhynhert.

"What is happening here?" she demanded.

Eress stepped closer to her. "The man known as Kane has been delivered to the mages, My Lady." He had recovered his stoic composure and spoke without emotion. "As Lord Rhynhert had requested. I thought you would want to know. As you can see they are with him now."

Anger burned from Nenura's eyes, but Auraq could tell she fought to conceal it by forcing a smile. "Excellent. My husband will be pleased." Her voice was tight and severe. She held her glare on Eress a moment, as if trying to read him, then looked to the crowd of mages around the table. "Have they learned anything yet?"

Kane cried out again. The sound echoed throughout the chamber and cut deep into Auraq's heart.

Eress glanced over his shoulder and waited for the cries to subside. "Appears not, My Lady. Only that whatever magecraft has been infused into his arm, entering this chamber seems to have triggered it."

Nenura breathed in slow and straightened her shoulders. Her hands were clasped in front of her, her knuckles white.

"Strangest thing, though," Eress continued. "The man was found deep under the palace in the sewers. With your steward, no less."

She tried to hold her face neutral, but her nostrils flared. "My steward?"

Eress's expression remained blank and cool, his voice impassive. "Yes, My Lady. I'm sorry to inform you he's been killed. We are investigating." With a slight tilt of his head, he studied her face as he spoke.

Nenura stiffened and her face paled.

Eress was playing a dangerous game. He was goading her and measuring her reaction. He was smart enough to suspect her involvement, but her status could cause real trouble for him if he pushed it too far. So, instead he made it impossible for her to openly interfere without exposing herself.

Auraq pushed himself into a sitting position, swinging his legs over the side of the table.

"What are you doing? I'm not finished." The redheaded mage whispered harshly at him. She moved to stop him, but he swept her aside with his arm.

In a bold act of disrespect, Eress turned his back to Nenura without another word and faced the mages around Kane.

Nenura, unable to hide her fury, clenched her fists at her sides and stared at the floor.

Kane screamed in agony once again. The whirling snakes

of light took on a greater intensity. They spun up from the table, rising into a dazzling cyclone. Auraq could feel prickling against his skin. Tiny bolts of lightning discharged at the domed ceiling. The circle of guards took another step back, while mages continued to swarm around Kane like bees around their queen.

The redheaded mage stared up at the display, Auraq forgotten.

Something was about to happen.

Auraq kept his eyes locked onto Nenura as he slid off the table. She looked more than angry. She looked desperate. Cornered. Auraq knew she would act. Eress's suspicions were enough to cause her some inconvenience in the palace, but Auraq assumed she was connected enough and savvy enough to ride it out. Kanar's attack on Kane would not be enough to connect her with the Order or implicate her in the assassination of the king. The proof, he knew, was locked inside the mark on Kane's arm—and at any moment it would be revealed. She had to do something or her guilt and duplicity would be laid bare.

She stared across the room—not at the table with Kane, not at the maelstrom of lights spinning overhead—but off to the side. Auraq followed the line of her sight. One mage stood apart from the others. He wasn't involved in the activity around Kane. He was looking back at Nenura.

She gave him a single curt nod. The mage nodded back.

Auraq pushed himself away from the table. He stumbled and his legs gave out under his own weight. He caught himself on the edge of another table. Vials rolled and tumbled to the stone floor, shattering, as pulled himself along.

The mage reached inside his robes. A moment later, his hand reappeared wielding a dagger with a black blade that all but disappeared against the silken robe. He held it low and close to his side and started to move closer to the crowd around Kane.

Auraq pushed off harder and stumbled further across the chamber. He shouldered his way past a guard staring up at the ceiling with his mouth hanging open.

The mage's face was hard and determined as he slipped past guards and drew closer to the group around the table.

Kane's screams were continuous now. The mages around him were focused on the maelstrom, chanting, their hands gesturing in the air in front of them—to what end, Auraq had no idea. They were completely unaware of one of their number working his way toward Kane.

Auraq pushed himself as hard as he was able. He drew from the last of his strength and made a stumbling gallop across the remaining distance. The mage turned and saw him coming, and he tried to slip deeper into the circle of mages. He lifted his hand, ready to thrust the dagger down into Kane as soon as he was close enough. He was less than a stride away.

Auraq leaped and crashed into the group of mages like a charging bull. Screams and shouts erupted around him as people fell back from the impact. Blindly, he grabbed robes in front of him, having no idea if he had the right mage or not. He collapsed to the floor, dragging the mage in his grip down with him. The mage landed on top of him, and he felt the dagger bite into his chest.

He was vaguely aware of a flash of brilliant white light. It enveloped him and passed through him, warm and soothing.

Then everything changed as the memory entered his mind.

HE STORMED out of the king's chamber, his blood boiling with anger. King Haden was being a fool. A stubborn, ridiculous fool. This edict would only prove to create a greater divide between the mages and the crown. It would create more enemies than solve problems.

He stomped out into the corridor outside the king's apartments and slammed the door behind him. The guardsmen started at his sudden appearance. They snapped to attention.

"Good evening, Lord Norreg."

He nodded, but something caught his eyes. He looked down at their hands. Each man palmed the top of a tankard and tried to conceal it behind his thigh.

"What is that?" he demanded.

The guards looked at him guiltily. "A gift from the Lady

Nenura," one said.

"She said she spoke to the king. He wouldn't mind if we enjoyed one," said the other. "It is near the end of our shift."

"She is quite wrong," he snapped. "Dispose of that this instant." Without waiting for a response, he stomped down the corridor. He would have a long talk with her. Again. Her disregard for palace protocol had interfered for the last time. That sort of lenient behavior might go over fine among her Volfic relatives, but here among the civilized world, it would not do. And members of the Black Guard, sworn to protect the king, should know better.

He would have a word or two with their commander as well.

He rounded the corner, heading to his own apartment. Down a side corridor, he spotted Lady Nenura. She was speaking with a man he did not know. He was tempted to march over and have the conversation right then but thought better of it. An altercation in the corridor was not proper. And his anger and frustration with the king would certainly spill into his conversation with her and escalate the matter.

No, it was better to wait. He would wait until he had his temper under control. Perhaps he would ask to speak to her and Lord Rhynhert at the same time. With Rhynhert's help, maybe they could get her to see reason.

As he turned away, Nenura handed something over to the man, something attached to a small gold chain. He headed for his chambers.

Hours later, the guilt still chewed at his insides. Once the heat of his anger had cooled, his mind looped through his conversation with the king over and over again. He'd spoken out of turn, he knew. Regardless of how frustrated he was with the king's position, he had no right to speak to him the way he had.

He had no choice but to go back and ask for his friend's forgiveness.

Of course, it could wait until morning, but he didn't want this hanging over his head all night. Despite the hour, it was best to take care of it right away.

He put aside his goblet of wine, rebuttoned his doublet, and headed back to the king's apartments.

As he rounded the corner, his stomach heaved with alarm. Something was wrong.

The guards outside the king's apartments were on the floor, and the door was ajar.

He lurched into a run, pulling the sword from its sheath. The guards were dead, their throats cut. Two empty tankards were on their sides next to them, lying in the pool of blood that covered the floor and reached down the corridor. He had no choice but to track through the blood to get to the doorway, and one heel skidded as he rushed through the threshold. As he scrambled inside, a glint of something caught his eye. The key to the chamber. It was still in the keyhole of the door. A gold chain dangled from the end.

Two steps in, he froze.

The inside of the apartments was carnage. Enough moonlight filtered in through the windows for him to see that bodies were everywhere. The carpets had turned entirely black, their patterns no longer distinguishable.

He was too late.

He staggered through the butchery. His limbs were numb. The sword's tip dragged on the floor behind him. He surveyed each face as he passed by. Members of the Black Guard were mixed with the assassins, black masks hiding their identity. He bent and, one by one, tore the masks from their faces, if only to expose them and their treachery to the Gods that looked down on this atrocity. One of the dead assassins looked familiar. His stomach tightened and bile reached up to burn the back of his throat as recognition came. He'd seen this man speaking to Nenura only hours before.

He found the king in his back chamber, on the floor behind his wide desk. The bodies of three other Black Guards were near him—they died fighting to protect him. The king had been run through, and his neck had been sliced to ensure he was dead. Not five strides from him lay his wife, the queen. Her throat had also been cut.

The sword fell from his hand, forgotten. He dropped to his knees, reached out and placed his hand on the bearded jaw of his king. The chill of death seeped into his fingertips, but he didn't care. His heart withered in anguish. He would never forgive himself that his final words to his friend had been in anger.

The sound of others entering into apartment reached his ears, but he couldn't bring himself to move. He remained on his knees, stroking the soft beard of the king. The others burst into the chamber and came up behind him. He felt the tip of a blade press against the back of his neck.

"Enjoying your handiwork, traitor?" someone growled.

AURAQ RETURNED to himself.

His eyes opened and pain rushed in like a levee break. Gasping, he rolled off the mage onto his back. The dagger protruded from his chest.

No, that wasn't good. The Gods had made their will clear enough. He was not supposed to live out this day.

The chamber was gripped by an absolute silence. The maelstrom of light was gone, Kane no longer screamed in agony, the mages had ceased their chants. The mark had unlocked the memory and now fallen still, leaving everyone reeling in its wake. Guards and mages alike looked around in stunned confusion.

Auraq knew they all had been propelled into the same vision. They were all witness to the evidence that implicated Nenura in the massacre of the king. Lord Norreg, in death, had defeated her, and there was no way for her to escape the truth of that.

One by one, as each individual pieced together what they had experienced, they turned to the doors of the chamber.

But Nenura was gone.

Auraq sighed and closed his eyes. It didn't matter.

He hoped that Kane was all right now, but there was no way to know, really. He would have liked to look at his face one more time. He wished he could have had the chance to tell him how he felt. But that was impossible now.

Gods, he was tired. So terribly tired. The feeling was everywhere—deep, deep in his muscles. All he desired was to give in to the warmth that reached out to him from the darkness. He thought about trying to stay awake. Fighting it off. For Kane. But no, he didn't want to fight anymore. He was done with all that. All he wanted was to let the warm darkness take him.

So he did.

Chapter 34

FOR A time, Auraq was only vaguely aware of the warmth on his face, but it was the first sensation to permeate his frail consciousness. Some deeper awareness thought it strange he should be feeling such a thing at all, and it was that curiosity that drew him further out of the realm of sleep. His eyes opened to slits, and the glaring sunlight stung like bees and forced them closed again. With a deep grunt, he attempted to roll over to put his back to the sunlight, but sharp pain ignited in his chest and his side. He sucked in through his teeth and put a hand to his flank, and felt the bandages encasing his midsection.

It was only then he realized that he was in a bed.

A large bed. A very comfortable bed.

"I was told to tell you, when you awaken, that it is a good idea you not move."

The voice came from the direction of his feet. It was deep and had the timbre of a war drum. Auraq eased his shoulder back down onto the bed and lifted his head. His eyes still hadn't adjusted to the morning sun pounding through the wide window, but he was able to make out a shape—a large shape—standing from a chair on the opposite side of the room and approaching the foot of the bed.

Auraq rubbed his eye with the heel of his hand, hoping to bring his vision into focus. When he pulled his hand away, the man stood with his hands wide on the footboard. Auraq took in the man's face and, for a moment, thought he looked familiar. He was about Auraq's age, perhaps a few years older—and surprisingly handsome. He had a neatly trimmed black beard and deeply set eyes that bore down on Auraq with staggering intensity. He had a wry smile that broadened as Auraq's sleep-muddled mind tried to decipher who he was.

But then he saw the star amulet resting on his chest and the great signet ring on his finger.

Auraq's breath hitched in his chest like he'd been punched. Ignoring the pain, he tried to push himself into a sitting position as he diverted his eyes to the wall and yanked the blanket up to his chin. His face flushed with embarrassment when he realized he was naked beneath the thin fabric of the bedcovers.

"Your Majesty," he managed to choke out.

"Easy now," King Harus V told him, thrusting out his palm. "My mages worked tirelessly to put you back together properly. Don't go ruining their good work."

Auraq's entire body shook.

King Harus took a chair and moved to the side of Auraq's bed. He straddled it backward and crossed his forearms on the chair's back. "It is just the two of us," he said. "So we can dispense with all the formality and such. Are you comfortable?"

"Yes, Your Majesty." He still could not bring himself to look directly at the king, as if he were brighter than the sun outside the window.

"Just yes will suffice. And your wounds? How are they healing?"

"I'm well," he lied. His entire side was throbbing, but he was hardly aware of it. "Your Ma—"

A lifted brow from the king stopped him short with a wince, and King Harus smiled.

"Good," Harus said. "You are a lucky man. I suppose, if you are going to be stabbed in the chest, a room full of mages is the best place for it. Even so, you had me worried for a time."

His mind whirled with the idea of it. The king was worried about him? What was going on? "How long was I unconscious?"

"Three days. The mages kept you under longer than necessary, but I grew impatient. I had them bring you out of it so we could speak."

Auraq shook his head in wonderment. "Forgive me, Your Majesty." He couldn't help himself. There was no way he was going to be able to address the king casually as if they were equals, like old comrades sitting together over a mead. His entire body resisted the idea like water repels oil. "But you want to speak with *me*?" The notion of that seemed ridiculous.

King Harus chuckled a moment before his expression turned more serious. "You are a bit of a mystery to me, Auraq Greystone of Har Tesera, son of Malgar."

There was something deeply disturbing about hearing the leader of millions of people speak Auraq's name as if he knew him personally. "I do not understand, Your Majesty."

"I am informed by my advisors that you are a wanted man. Murder of a noble superior in the military, and desertion. Serious charges that come with serious penalties."

Auraq felt his heart twist, but he said nothing. Why go through the trouble of saving him if he were just going to be charged again for his crimes?

King Harus stood from the chair and moved it away from the bedside. He folded his arms over his chest and studied Auraq in his bed. "Yet in spite of that danger, you strolled right into my palace, bold as brass. Why? To bring forth some intelligence regarding the murder of my father, mother, and siblings. Then you run through my palace, evading a number of my guards in the process, and put a stop to the villains that are hiding right here under my very nose. People trusted by the crown. Can you blame me my curiosity as to what type of man you are?"

"Your Majesty, I apologize for—"

"Apologize? Good man, I am here to thank you. Personally. You have done the crown, and the realm, a tremendous service. Because of you, a mystery that has plagued this house for more than two decades has been solved." He formed a pensive smile. "It gladdens my heart to learn that Norreg was never involved in this affair. Now he can be remembered as the loyal friend to my father and great servant to this kingdom that he always was. I was young at the time, but I remember him, actually. He was always kind. And treated me in a way that seemed… genuine. Not always the case when you're the heir to the throne." He lifted his chin and he waved his hand in the air as if shooing away the memory. "Anyway, you have the gratitude of an entire kingdom."

Perhaps not the entire kingdom, Auraq thought. Everyone

in Lord Rhynhert's chamber had been concerned that this would cause no small amount of upheaval. Auraq didn't disagree. Anyone on record who had called for Lord Norreg's head would be thrust into the scandal, perhaps even accused of being part of the plot. And Lord Rhynhert would not be pleased to discover his politically arranged wife was behind the massacre all along. That embarrassment alone would ruin him and likely dry up any influence he had in the kingdom.

"I doubt this will be welcome news for everyone," he said.

King Harus shrugged. "Oh, some will think to cause trouble. Stir up some of the old grouses. My councilors are wringing their hands raw over this. They've advised me to keep it all from the public, but too many were witness to the memory to even consider attempting that. It would leak out and cause more problems for me later. So we face it head on and weather through it." A sadness reached his eyes. "I only wish that I had seen the memory myself."

Auraq's stomach launched into this throat, and he jolted up in bed, ignoring the pain. "Kane. Is he safe?" He couldn't believe he hadn't thought of his well-being until that moment—but having the king standing at his bedside was a suitable excuse.

"Easy." King Harus put a hand on Auraq's shoulder and guided him back down. "Kane is fine. Better than you, in fact. I had to chase him out of here so we could have this conversation, with various promises that I would not upset you or overtax you. For most of the last several days, he has not left your bedside."

Auraq frowned. He hated the idea of Kane seeing him like this. Hated that he'd caused Kane so much worry. "The mark?"

"Gone. Just like that. As soon as the memory was unlocked, it disappeared from his arm. He is healing nicely."

Auraq fell back against the headboard and exhaled.

"Your Majesty, why did she do it?"

"I suppose she always remained a barbarian in her heart. Perhaps it was some type of retaliation for the war. But my guess is she wanted Uncle Rhynhert to be king. She probably believed she could then influence him to release the Lendera Province back to the Volfic people. My survival ended any chance of that occurring. Had the remaining Black Guard not fled with me out a window, perhaps her plan might have worked. But with me alive, Uncle Rhynhert refused to take the throne for himself, and as regent, could make no such change."

"Then the Order of the Jackal was behind the attack on your family all along?"

"Appears so."

Auraq nodded. The Order had spent the decades since protecting her and preventing her involvement from coming to light. It was why Kanar acted as their leader. "Kanar told me she was the leader of the Order." A thought occurred to him. Jackals were desert creatures, and the lands beyond the Lendera Province were widely desert. He felt foolish that he'd never made the connection until now. "The Jackals are barbarians themselves."

"Mostly, yes," King Harus told him, chuckling at Auraq's reaction. "While you were napping, we've learned more about them. Seems a hive of them were discovered down in the sewers waiting for a chance to escape. Some have been inspired to cooperate. When the Order failed to put an end to my bloodline, they went underground and reformed as the mercenary group we know today. They did some local recruitment, but the upper tiers of the organization remained Volfic. I believe they were waiting for the next opportunity to strike." His eyes narrowed. "They'll be waiting a long time."

"What's become of Lady Nenura?"

"You no longer need to use that honorific with her." Harus paused, his expression darkening. "She has eluded us for the time being. But we will find her."

Auraq wasn't so sure. She'd successfully run the Order out of the king's palace for twenty years. She was a cunning woman, and likely had her escape planned for years.

King Harus folded his arms again and looked down at Auraq with a knitted brow. "Enough of all that for now. I am actually here to have a discussion about *you*."

"Me, Your Majesty?"

"I spoke with Farris at length regarding your... listed

offenses."

Auraq's stomach flipped. This was not a conversation he wanted to have with the king.

"Seems there was some confusion about it," King Harus continued. "One murder, not two, and you had a fairly just reason for that one." He gave Auraq a side glance and lowered his voice. "Between you and me, I despised that ruttish, goat-faced maggot. Deserved what he got, if half of what Farris told me was true."

Auraq worried that perhaps Lord Farris had embellished the telling.

"Lord Renthe's family will not be happy with any of this. Not that I care much," Harus added, looking up to the ceiling. "But… they can be a dangerous lot if amply motivated. They may seek retribution against you themselves, so I would advise caution."

Auraq shook his head in confusion. "Your Majesty, forgive me. I'm not following."

"Did you injure your head as well, man? I've granted you a full pardon. My scribes have already penned the document and I've signed it. Your honor, and the honor of your family, has been fully restored."

Auraq stared blankly at the king, trying to decide if he'd heard it properly. "I was told it was not possible…."

"My rules," the king said. "I can break them if I choose."

Tears stung the corners of Auraq's eyes. "Your Majesty, I…I am at a loss for words. You are far too generous. I don't know how I can begin to repay you."

"You are having a difficult time absorbing that this is, in fact, my way of thanking *you*. But no matter. We will talk further once you are stronger and less wool-headed. Then perhaps you will be able to grasp the proposition or two that I have in mind." King Harus straightened his doublet with a tug at the sides. "I will leave you to your rest. I've been here longer than I promised already. Would hate to garner the wrath of that friend of yours by overstaying my welcome." He turned toward the door. "I will tell him he can return—"

"No!" Auraq blurted, then winced.

King Harus twisted back around with a single raised eyebrow and a tiny smile in the corner of one side of his mouth.

"Your Majesty," he added quickly. "Apologies. But, please, I will go to him."

"That is most ill-advised. You are not ready."

"I must." He did not want Kane to see him like this anymore. Weakened. Helpless. It gnawed at him inside that Kane had seen him so close to death. He moved to throw the bedcovers off him, but then remembered he was entirely nude beneath them and quickly pulled them back over himself again.

Harus laughed. "Ah, an easy way to force you to comply. But, I suppose you wouldn't let that stop you either. You seem the willful type." He opened the door open a fraction and put his head through the opening while still gripping the latch. "Fetch a tunic and breeches," Auraq heard him say to someone.

In moments, the king opened the door wider to admit an older woman in a white shift and bonnet, garments draped over her arm. She bowed to the king before she gently laid garments on the edge of the bed and made a hasty exit.

To Auraq's great chagrin, the King of Davenia, ruler to millions and the most powerful man on the continent, helped him pull on his tunic and breeches. Auraq's protests that he could manage well enough on his own, or that others might be brought in, were ignored. King Harus not only saw his naked body, but laid hands on it as he helped him pull the trousers on over his legs and buttocks. He at least preserved a modicum of his dignity by allowing Auraq to tuck his own genitals into the front of the trousers and tie the drawstring around his waist himself.

Harus helped Auraq stand from the edge of the bed and held his arm to steady him until Auraq found his balance. The floor felt cool on the soles of his feet.

"Are you certain of this?" the king asked.

"I am, Your Majesty." He swayed a bit, the room tilting as he stood on his own, but he held his hand on the bedpost until the sensation passed and the room settled.

King Harus swung the door wide. "Very well. Who am I to deny you? You will find him in the antechamber beyond the next."

Auraq glanced up at the king's face as he started to shuffle forward. King Harus had a strange look in his eye. A knowing look. A look that told Auraq that he understood this need he had.

"Thank you, Your Majesty," Auraq managed to say. "For everything."

He used the doorframe for support as he hobbled out of the chamber. His legs felt weak, as if they were not his own. The doorway outside the bedchamber was flanked by guardsmen wearing the king's livery—the lion and eagle crest upon a split field of burgundy and plum. Chainmail cowls were draped over their heads, and they clasped halberds in their gauntleted hands. They remained as motionless as statuary as Auraq shuffled past the threshold. The presence of the royal guard outside his bedchamber made the experience seem strangely dreamlike, as if none of this could possibly be real.

He ventured deeper into the next chamber. It was small and sparsely furnished. Finely carved wood panels covered each of the walls and the ceiling. He was dimly aware of others in the room with him, but his full concentration was centered on putting one step in front of the other.

A robed figure drifted toward him.

"Your Majesty?" A woman's voice. The figure was at his side taking his elbow. "What is happening?"

"Against my wishes, I assure you," said the king from the doorway.

The woman threw a scornful look to the king. "Is that so? What nature of man ignores a direct order from the king, I wonder?" Without waiting for any permission, she slipped her hand under Auraq's tunic and glided over the bandages around Auraq's midsection. His breath hitched in his chest at the chill of her touch. He felt a strange tingling under the skin wherever her palm moved over him.

"You will have to ask the queen about that, Lennora. She regularly ignores my wishes."

The power emanating from the woman's fingertips knitted its way around inside his flesh.

A door across the room opened and Auraq was aware of a blur of movement. Arms enveloped him with so much force, he nearly fell back. Lennora took a step back just in time or she would have been roughly knocked aside. Auraq couldn't help but chuckle. He lifted his own arms and hugged back.

"Hello, Pa."

Malgar tightened his grip on his son. "Thought I'd lost you. Again."

"Seems the Gods aren't done kicking me around yet."

Malgar laughed and loosened his grip around Auraq. He made a quick wipe of his eye with his sleeve. "Why are you out of bed?"

"An excellent question," the mage said decisively. She stood off to the side, glowering.

"I'm fine," Auraq said.

"So did you take the offer?"

Auraq's eyes narrowed. "What offer?"

"The commission," Malgar said.

"We didn't get that far in our conversation yet, Master Malgar," King Harus said.

"What are you talking about?" asked Auraq.

His father's grin widened—he glowed with pride. "He wants you to reestablish the Black Guard."

Auraq's knees weakened. His head swam in dizzy circles. The Black Guard? Did he hear that properly? He began to sway, and Malgar grabbed his arm to steady him. He turned to the king, certain this was some form of jest.

"Master Malgar, you have spoiled my dramatic reveal." King Harus scowled at Malgar, but his tone was warm and teasing.

Malgar paled. "My apologies, Your Majesty."

"Perhaps this is a discussion for another time," Lennora said firmly. She put a hand on the small of Auraq's back and gently started to guide him around. "Enough adventure for one day, sur. Let's get you back to bed."

"No. I need to see Kane." Auraq turned to his father. "Pa, where is he?"

The mage opened her mouth to protest, but Malgar held up his hand. "He's just in the next chamber, Mistress Lennora. I will take him."

"He has overtaxed himself too much already," Lennora said.

Malgar glanced up at Auraq, his smile warm. "This is important, Mistress," he said. Something in Malgar's eyes told Auraq that he understood. Auraq's heart swelled. "I promise to see him returned to his bed posthaste."

Lennora pressed her lips, then nodded begrudgingly.

Malgar helped Auraq along, supporting his weight as they shuffled through the door into the antechamber.

Across the room, Kane stood at the fireplace leaning against the back of a chair. With a chalice in his hand, he spoke quietly with Lord Farris, who occupied a chair opposite him. He glanced up as Malgar and Auraq entered, and for a heartbeat Kane clearly didn't understand what he was seeing. Then Kane's faced changed, like the moment a wick comes to life and shines. His eyes widened and his jaw fell slack. Color blossomed on his cheeks like a burn.

"Auraq?" he mouthed.

Auraq was helpless—seeing him, his face split into a childlike grin.

Kane stood rigid, staring back at him. He reached to set his chalice down on a side table, but the round base only partially caught the edge, and it toppled to the wood floor unnoticed.

Auraq broke free from his father's support and stumbled across the room. But halfway, his legs were no longer under his control. His legs gave out and he pitched forward. He landed on his knees. Kane sprang forward and tried to catch him but ended up on his knees too.

"Auraq, what are you doing? You are supposed to be in bed."

"I needed to see you."

"I would have come—"

"No. Not like that. Not in a sickbed. Like this."

"Auraq, you're going to injure yourself again."

"I have to talk to you. I have to tell you." His head was spinning now.

"Whatever you have to say can wait, Auraq. I'm not going anywhere."

"No. It can't wait," he snapped, and felt like a crazed fool. This was all coming out wrong. He could not let it come out wrong again. He closed his eyes and reined in his frustration and his nerves. "I waited before and… and it was almost too late. I'm not waiting, not anymore."

Kane got very still.

"I'm sorry. I've been a fool. I had my chance before, but I got scared. I don't even know what I was scared of. But it stopped me from saying it. And then… then I almost lost you forever. So, I'm not risking it again. I only hope I'm not too late."

Auraq could not read Kane's expression.

"I love you, Kane. Gods!" He looked up at the ceiling. "I can't believe that seemed so hard before. I love you." Tears stung his eyes, blurring his vision. He turned away, ashamed—but not sure what he was ashamed about. "I wouldn't blame you, you know. If you didn't love me back now. I've been a fool. I'd understand. Just tell me if I'm too late."

For a long time, an eternity, Kane was motionless in front of him. Auraq could hear his own heart pounding in his ears. His breathing came in short bursts. He waited for Kane's answer as if standing on a precipice. If Kane rejected him, he would be undone.

"You stupid oaf," Kane said.

He slipped his hand under Auraq's tunic, sliding his palm across the skin of Auraq's chest before circling around to his back. Auraq gasped, surprised. The touch of Kane's fingers made his skin tingle like the mage's power had. Kane's other hand cupped the back of Auraq's neck and pulled him in.

Their lips met.

This time, Auraq was helpless against the warm rush that

flooded through him in a torrent. He felt it everywhere at once. His eyes closed as he sank deeper into the kiss. Kane's lips were as warm and soft as he remembered, but this time, his body knew what to do. His arms enveloped Kane and pulled him in tighter. His lips parted and he drew in the air that came from Kane's own lungs. The smell of Kane filled his entire head and made his thoughts swim like he was in a fevered dream. The feel of Kane's body pressed against him felt like a hunger.

Auraq was dimly aware of footsteps retreating behind him and the door softly closing. They were alone.

"Took you long enough," Kane whispered, his lips never breaking contact with Auraq's.

The strength of the kiss pulsated through them—it would rival the power of any mage. And the flood of emotions nearly overwhelmed him. He tasted the salt of Kane's tears as they seeped into the corner of his mouth and felt the sting in his own eyes as well.

He knew how lucky he was. This kiss might never have happened—for so many reasons—but the Gods saw fit to let him have this moment. Perhaps Old Tan was right. Perhaps the Gods had forgiven him.

As long as he was granted life, he would never forget that he'd been given this gift. By all rights, he should not be this happy. By all rights, he should not be this blessed.

But he was.

He might never let this moment end.

Epilogue

THE TWO men that rode in under the gate's catwalk on black steeds brought the entire camp to a standstill. Everyone, either those standing guard on the wall or laboring about the camp, froze in place to stare at them. It was an eerie sort of stillness, as if time had decided to take a break from its unceasing march. The strangers pulled on the reins to bring the massive beasts to a halt in the center of the yard. Two soldiers recovered their wits and sprinted over to take hold of the bridles while the men lifted out of the saddles and dropped to the hard-packed ground.

Wella stood up from the small patch of grass where she was playing, her doll dropping from her hand, forgotten. She was no different—the two strangers had captivated her attention as well. The camp, which was deep into the Lendera Province and at least a day's travel from any settlements, did not receive many visitors. Certainly not ones like this.

The larger of the two was military, certainly. He wore black leather armor with steel rivets that caught the afternoon sun like ripples on a lake, and the lion and eagle crest was boldly displayed on his breastplate. A great sword hung from his waist. He stood with a very straight back and had a serious expression as his eyes scanned the camp. The second man, who was a head smaller than the other, wore no armor at all but was finely dressed in a blue doublet and cloak. He could have been nobleborn, but something about him made Wella doubt it.

The large one removed something that was tied to the back of the steed before the horses were led away to the troughs. It was long and wrapped in a heavy black tarp. Another soldier ran up and saluted them. They spoke briefly before the soldier darted off again, this time toward the military offices where Wella's father was currently working.

The two men headed deeper into the camp. She trailed them stealthily, keeping at a safe distance where she wouldn't be noticed. She traveled at a low crouch behind the row of barracks, peering around the corners of the buildings. They walked side by side along the center path, the package still tucked under the large man's arm. They spoke quietly to each other. The smaller one said something that made the larger man grin and then break into a laugh.

Soldiers passing by saluted them with fists to their chests.

As the two men walked up the steps to the camp offices, Wella's father, Lord Commander Paxon Tehl, stepped out of the building and met them on the porch. Wella didn't know what to expect, but her father did the most extraordinary thing. Her father saluted *them*.

The three spoke for only a few minutes. Wella was too far away to hear any of what was said, but she carefully watched how her father acted around them. It seemed a friendly conversation. He smiled and nodded a lot, but it was an odd sort of smile. His arms were restless too, as if they didn't know where they should be.

Her father pointed off in the distance, toward the line of trees beyond the walls of the camp.

The men nodded, clasped arms with her father, and took their leave of him. Wella ducked behind a water barrel as they walked back again through the center of the camp toward the gate. They didn't send for or retrieve their horses. They walked out of the camp on foot, the long black parcel still tucked under the big man's arm.

Curiosity compelled her to follow them farther. She tiptoed after them and slunk out of the gate too.

They were easy enough to follow. They were more interested in each other than what was around them. But Wella made sure she stayed well behind them so she wouldn't be heard. They kept to the winding path that led west. Wella knew what was back there and didn't like coming this way by herself, but she stayed with them.

The narrow path went up a hill, swerving through the trees.

At the crest of the hill, it broke into a clearing. The two seemed to know where they were going as they waded through the high yellow grass toward the back of the field near where the forest started up again. The large man and the smaller one split up as they searched about, pushing the grass aside to see the ground. The smaller man found something and waved the big man over.

Wella closed the distance at a crouch.

They stood over a mound of rocks arranged in a long rectangle. The field grasses were trespassing over and around it until it was almost entirely hidden it from view. At the foot of it was a marker. Wella didn't know her letters yet, but her father had told her that markers like these had names and messages written on them.

The big man lowered his parcel gently to the ground as if he was setting down an infant. He cut the twine that tied it closed and carefully pulled back the black canvas. Wella risked a better look over the grass by rising up a little higher.

The man picked up two swords.

Swords? That was not what she expected. One looked surprisingly similar to the sword Wella's father carried on his belt, and the other like the ones the men practiced with in the yard.

The big man knelt down onto one knee in front of the grave. One at a time, he took a sword by the hilt and sank the blade into the ground on either side of the name marker. He pushed them down so that none of the metal was visible anymore and the cross guards were touching the ground underneath.

And the two stayed there, quiet and unmoving.

Crouched in the grass behind them, Wella could feel the beating of her heart and wondered if she should leave. She felt as if she was intruding on something private, witnessing something she should not. The smaller man rested his hands on the larger man's shoulders, and for a long time neither moved. The forest surrounding them was quiet and peaceful, as if it did not want to interfere either.

After a long time, the large man finally stood up and faced the other man. He took the other man's hands into his, and for a time they only stared at each other. Then they did the strangest thing of all—they kissed.

They kissed for a *real* long time.

When at long last they pulled away from each other, they turned and started walking back across the field again, back to the trail that would lead them to the camp. Wella dropped her belly to the ground and hid herself low in the grass. They passed dangerously close to her. She could hear them talking to each other softly as they shuffled past her.

"She's at peace now, I think," the smaller one said. "And now you can be too."

The large man took the other man's hand into his. "Yes," he said. And they headed back down the hill.

More From Mason Thomas

Scoundrel by nature and master thief by trade, Mouse is the best there is. Sure, his methods may not make him many friends, but he works best alone anyway. And he has never failed a job.

But that could change.

When a stranger with a hefty bag of gold seduces him to take on a task, Mouse knows he'll regret it. The job? Free Lord Garron, the son of a powerful duke arrested on trumped up charges in a rival duchy. Mouse doesn't do rescue missions. He's no altruistic hero, and something about the job reeks. But he cannot turn his back on that much coin—enough to buy a king's pardon for the murder charge hanging over his head.

Getting Garron out of his tower prison is the easy part. Now, they must escape an army of guardsmen, a walled keep and a city on lockdown, and a ruthless mage using her power to track them. Making matters worse, Mouse is distracted by Garron's charm and unyielding integrity. Falling for a client can lead to mistakes. Falling for a nobleman can lead to disaster. But Mouse is unprepared for the dangers behind the plot to make Lord Garron disappear.

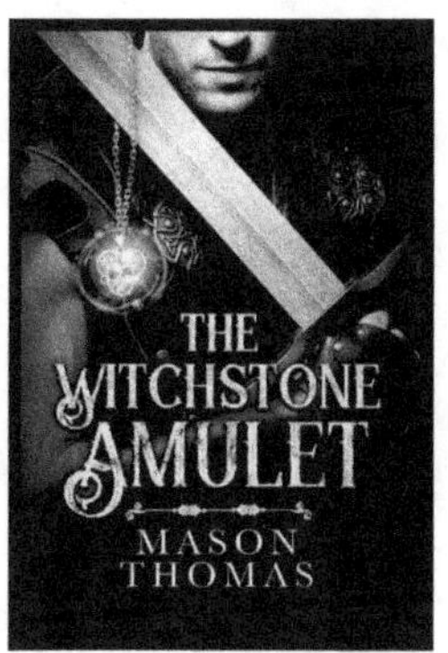

Protect it at all costs.

That's what rugby player Hunter Best's mother told him before she died. But when Hunter surprises an intruder in his Chicago apartment, he discovers her amulet missing. Hunter pursues the thief—all the way through a strange vortex. He wakes in a bizarre and violent world, a benighted realm on the threshold of civil war.

The queen has become a ruthless tyrant, punishing any who oppose her, and weakening the kingdom's defenses against the brutal Henerans. To survive, Hunter must depend on the man who robbed him, a handsome former spy named Dax, now a leader in the resistance and believes the queen is an imposter— a Heneran disguised by magic. She also happens to look identical to Hunter's mother.

There's no love lost between Hunter and Dax, and even if Hunter grudgingly agrees with the resistance, he just wants to reclaim what belongs to him and go home. But he might be the only one who can oppose the queen and end her reign of terror.

www.ingramcontent.com/pod-product-compliance
Lightning Source LLC
Chambersburg PA
CBHW071231300726
48975CB00002B/373